The Last
Integrationist

The Last Integrationist

By JAKE LAMAR

CROWN PUBLISHERS, INC.

NEW YORK

The author gratefully acknowledges permission to reprint from "My Life," by Billy Joel, copyright © 1978 by Impulsive Music. All rights reserved. Used by permission.

Published by Crown Publishers, Inc., 201 East 50th Street, New York, New York 10022. Member of the Crown Publishing Group.

Random House, Inc. New York, Toronto, London, Sydney, Auckland

CROWN is a trademark of Crown Publishers, Inc.

Manufactured in the United States of America

Design by Lauren Dong

Library of Congress Cataloging-in-Publication Data
Lamar, Jake.
    The last integrationist: a novel / by Jake Lamar.—1st ed.
    I. Title.
PS3562.A4316L37   1996
813'.54—dc20   95-30293
ISBN 0-517-59375-0

10 9 8 7 6 5 4 3 2 1

First Edition

For Robert Coles

"Sometimes I feel like a socio-genetic experiment."
—*THE DISPOSABLE HEROES OF HIPHOPRISY*

PART ONE

The Role Model

(1)

COULD KILL YOU ALL. A curious thought to run through the mind of a man being honored by five hundred admirers, but Melvin Hutchinson thought it nonetheless as he sat on the dais in the main banquet hall of the Millennium Club and looked down on all the white folks—the men dressed in black tie, the handful of women sprinkled throughout the crowd, looking glamorous in their black evening dresses—every single one of them there to pay their respects to him. *To him.* And it occurred to Melvin that if he could —instantly, bloodlessly, with a magical snap of the fingers, perhaps —he would kill them all. Snap them into oblivion. Because even though many of the most powerful people in America were sitting there in the audience, Melvin Hutchinson, on this early April evening, was superior to them all, every last one of them. And if he could, cleanly and without consequences, wipe them all out, he knew he would do it. With no regrets. And no mercy.

Then, scanning the crowd, Melvin's gaze fell on Clarence Eldridge, standing in his white jacket at the back of the banquet hall. No, Melvin thought, Clarence he would spare. Clarence was his man. Clarence Eldridge, keeper of the Eagle Room.

Melvin loved the Eagle Room. He loved its musky, enveloping armchairs, their cabernet-colored leather shiny under the amber glow of the delicate lamps that lit the parlor. He savored the room's sweet intermingling of aromas—cognac and leather, cigar and wood smoke. Melvin even loved the fearsome bald eagle that dominated

< 3 >

the intimate den: an enormous creature, frozen in menace, wings spread wide, tilted precariously on its perch, seemingly bearing down on you, talons barely touching a thick tangle of branch mounted to a lustrous oak-paneled wall, eyes fierce behind open beak. He loved the Eagle Room's late-nineteenth-century globe, with its auburn landmasses set against parchment-toned oceans, rivers, and seas. He loved the coziness of the dim, woody chamber that could hold comfortably only six or seven people, not including Clarence, the white-haired, white-jacketed butler whose chief responsibility, even before ensuring that glasses were filled and ashtrays emptied, was to see, through the subtlest of ministrations, that the shadowy alcove in the upper reaches of the Millennium Club maintained its calibrated atmosphere of power easefully held and judiciously executed. Melvin Hutchinson loved the Eagle Room because it was there that, twenty-five years earlier, he had officially become the first black member of the Millennium Club.

"We don't just want . . . a black member," Winthrop Robertson had explained as he and Melvin sat facing each other in their armchairs a quarter century ago, trying, Melvin realized, to pay him a compliment. "We want . . . the right . . . black member." Melvin had just made partner at Hull, Evans, Chamberlayne & Auerbach and was suddenly the right black to be courted by several of the more prestigious (in that day) men's clubs in New York, where he lived, and here in Washington, where he frequently did business. "We want . . . a man . . ." the Millennium Club chairman said, choosing his words precisely and taking his good time to do it, pronouncing each syllable with gravity, allowing capacious pauses between his words, ". . . who is . . ."

Yes, yes, Melvin thought, get to the point.

". . . worthy . . . and . . ."

Black, yes, go ahead, say it—

". . . black. . . ."

Why, Melvin wondered, did older white men like Winthrop Robertson, with his bronze skin and silver hair, always take so long to say anything, as if they were trying to make sure you would hang on to each word in recognition of the importance of what they had to state?

"Not worthy . . . because . . ."

"He is black." Melvin finished the sentence.

Winthrop Robertson blinked slowly, once—that was all. Then he continued his thought as if Melvin had not said anything: ". . . he is . . . black."

Melvin gave a single appreciative nod, deciding to be patient and keep his mouth shut until the chairman told him he was in. A few feet behind Robertson's chair, Clarence pretended to be preoccupied with tending the fire; but Melvin could tell from the faint tilt of his head, and the slightly exaggerated busyness with which he poked and prodded the logs in the Eagle Room's tiny fireplace, that the butler was eavesdropping. The first time he'd visited the Eagle Room, a month earlier, Melvin had noticed how Clarence couldn't stop casting furtive glances at him, the expression on the old servant's face somewhat puzzled but also, Melvin thought, a bit excited. As Melvin sat listening to Winthrop Robertson drone on, he sensed an anticipation in Clarence's posture; he could see the corner of the butler's mouth twitching slightly, as if the old man—old enough to be Melvin's father—could hardly suppress his smile.

"And so . . ." the Millennium Club chairman intoned, "allow me . . . Melvin . . . to be the first . . . to say . . . welcome."

The chairman and Melvin rose and shook hands. "Thank you so much, Mr. Robertson," Melvin said.

"Please . . . call me . . . Winty."

"Thank you, Winty."

"Have you met . . . Clarence?"

"We haven't really been introduced."

"Clarence Eldridge," Winthrop Robertson said, acknowledging the old black man for the first time, "meet . . . Melvin Hutchinson."

"*Mr.* Hutchinson." Clarence beamed, putting a joyous emphasis on the *Mr.* and giving Melvin a robust handshake.

"*Mr.* Eldridge," Melvin fairly sang.

The quiet camaraderie between Melvin and Clarence had been established. From that point on, they engaged in their own subtle call and response whenever Melvin entered the Eagle Room. "*Mr.* Hutchinson," Clarence would say, giving Melvin's name that jubilant spin. "*Mr.* Eldridge," Melvin would say, paying Clarence a courtesy that few other Millennium Clubbers ever paid the butler, addressing him by his last name. Melvin thought of their cheery salutations as an exchange of pride and mutual respect. Through their emphatic but joshing formality, Melvin liked to think, he and Clarence were expressing a brotherly communion. It was a special rapport that Clarence did not share with any of the other black members who had followed Melvin into the Millennium Club. After twenty-five years, there were now four of them.

And what of those other black members? Melvin thought as he sat on the dais in the main banquet hall. Would he rescue them from his instant, snap-of-the-fingers holocaust? Maybe. Maybe not. But as he saw Clarence standing at the back of the hall, a look of unutterable pride on his face, he knew that the butler was the one man in the room whose life was definitely worth saving. He felt a sudden urge to jump down from the dais, run to the back of the banquet hall, and slap Clarence a joyous high five. That would really shock the ofays! But Melvin reconsidered. Just staring at Clarence from this distance, this silent acknowledgment, was satisfying enough. Melvin still called Clarence "Mr. Eldridge." But for many years now, Clarence had addressed Melvin as "Your Honor." Because Melvin had served as a federal district judge. And tonight, at this Millennium Club roast honoring him, Melvin was the goddamned attorney general of the United States of America. The only government official present in the room that night who bore a rank higher than Melvin's was the vice president. And there was no way Melvin would spare that son of a bitch from his split-second mass extermination. *Yeah,* Melvin thought as he surveyed the audience, *I could kill y'all.*

➤   ➤   ➤

Among the members of the vast network of government officials, bureaucrats, lawyers, and journalists commonly referred to in the media as "Washington insiders," Melvin Hutchinson's first meeting with Vin Ewell had become legendary. It had happened in late August 1963. Melvin, then a law student at Columbia, was approaching the end of a summer stint with Herbert Montgomery, the great NAACP lawyer. Montgomery and Melvin were in Hazelton, South Carolina, to see that the local government complied with desegregation laws. The Hazelton school year was about to begin, the first in which black students would be enrolling at Hazelton High. Hazelton's mayor, a lean, chalky, crew-cutted thirty-year-old named Vincent Lee Ewell was extremely cooperative. Ewell considered himself a pragmatist. In a meeting with Montgomery and Melvin, Ewell said he knew integration was here to stay and he would do everything in his power to see that the change went smoothly. Later that afternoon, when Montgomery was not present, the young mayor pulled Melvin aside. "Y'all can do business with me," Ewell said in his turbid drawl. "You will find that I am a very reasonable man. But if it turns out y'all don't want to listen to reason and want to put li'l Negro schoolgirls in the line of fire, I *will* have my police fire."

To most insiders, this was an apocryphal tale. But Henry Beedle had heard the story recounted by *both* parties, and while perhaps it should have given him cause for anxiety, he found it piquantly satisfying that these two men would, more than thirty years after their first encounter, find themselves serving in the same administration: Vin Ewell as vice president, Melvin Hutchinson as attorney general. Only in America, Henry Beedle was tempted to say. But, really, such a confluence could only have occurred under the leadership of a man like President Troy McCracken. Or, perhaps, only under the aegis of the American party.

Though he was rarely given credit for it, Henry Beedle had been the first to suggest changing the names of the major political parties to the American and the National parties. He had not been motivated by any overwrought sense of patriotism. Nor was he attempting to revive—as some critics of the organization charged—the Know-Nothing American party of the nineteenth century. Beedle's inspiration was baseball—the American and the National leagues. The change, he believed, would capture what politics had really—and perhaps rightly—become for the majority of citizens: a sport. There were no substantive differences between the parties anymore—none more significant than, say, the designated hitter rule in baseball. So why pretend?

When Henry Beedle made his suggestion, in an op-ed piece in the *Washington Post*, he was not doing so out of cynicism. For someone who had spent his entire career in Washington, Beedle considered himself something of a sentimentalist. He had an unabashed faith in America. His mother's people had been among the first Connecticut settlers. He was fifth-generation Yale, fourth-generation Yale Law School. Though he would never say it, not even to a member of his —what was the correct term these days . . . social milieu?—Beedle felt as if the country somehow *belonged* to him. Not that he had sole ownership. Just that he had a greater stake in it than the descendants of people who had arrived later. He was, in a sense, a majority shareholder. It was Beedle's proprietary sense about America that led him to politics, first as a congressional aide, then as a political consultant, and now as deputy attorney general.

History. History was Beedle's ultimate concern. He knew it might be years, maybe even a century or two, before his role in American history would be properly appreciated. In his own day, he would have to toil in relative obscurity, an invisible hand guiding the politics of his era. Just as he was not given credit, in the here and now, for planting the seeds of the American party, few people recognized the quiet counsel he gave Troy McCracken in his quest to become the first major American party officeholder. Once Troy was elected governor of Colorado, Beedle was the only Washington insider to recognize the man's national potential. His colleagues at Hathaway Consultants—which traditionally backed Republican candidates— dismissed Troy as a flash in the pan. Then, Governor Troy McCracken—young, rich, charismatic—gave his famous speech at the New Constitutional Convention at Independence Hall in Philadelphia. Beedle was among the first to appear backstage to congratulate him. He was the first political consultant to sign on with Troy McCracken when he announced his candidacy for the presidency. And, after Troy had come back to trounce his main opponent, Senator Vin Ewell of South Carolina, in the primaries leading up to the American party presidential nomination, it was Henry Beedle who had gone to meet with Ewell and offered him the second spot on the ticket.

Vin Ewell, after he'd grown too ambitious for Hazelton's city hall, had become one of the most prominent members of the United States Senate. During his first two terms as a senator, Ewell was frequently mentioned as a possible presidential candidate. Neverthe-less, a good many insiders, Henry Beedle among them, regarded Vin as something of a joke. Beedle's favorite Vin Ewell story came from a reporter who had written a scathing article about the Great Prag-matist, chronicling Ewell's strong-arm tactics with other senators, the cruelty he displayed toward his staff, his penchant for patting the bottoms of female congressional aides, the shady fund-raising and under-the-table deals Ewell engaged in with powerful constituents. The senator from South Carolina had called the reporter the morning the article appeared in the paper. He didn't rant or rave, but he was thoroughly pissed off. Ewell challenged the reporter on a dozen points in his story. The reporter told him he could back up everything he'd written with multiple sources. After an hour of backing and forthing, Senator Ewell sighed heavily. At least, he noted, the article was the lead story in the "Lifestyle" section and featured a rather large and flattering photo of the politician (with his gaunt face and spiky white hair, Vin Ewell could use all the flattering photos he could get). "I reckon publicity's like pussy," Ewell told the journalist. "It's *never* bad."

Thwarted in his maneuvers for the Democratic nomination, Vin Ewell switched to the American party, calculating that the change would give him his best shot at getting elected President. Then along came this Troy McCracken, the new darling of the American party, yet another snot-nosed JFK wanna-be who would deny Ewell the opportunity he deserved, the chance he had *earned*. Ewell became consumed with hatred for the Colorado governor. While Ewell took an early lead in the American party primaries, he soon fell behind McCracken in delegates, endorsements, money, and momentum and wisely pulled out of the race before the bitter end. As emissary to the Ewell camp, Henry Beedle had had to engage in a little arm-twisting to get the senator to accept the position of Troy McCracken's running mate. Of course, no politician worth his salt *wants* the sec-ond spot on a national ticket; but, then again, how many have ever turned it down?

After the McCracken-Ewell ticket was swept into office, Henry Beedle, as a long-term member of Troy's inner circle, was involved in the selection process for all cabinet members. There was some debate over who should be named attorney general. But Beedle knew just the man.

>   >   >

Every modern public figure experiences two births: one natural, the other on television. For a politician, the television birth often takes place in the form of the press conference. You emerge from the relative darkness of a room offstage into the glare of harsh lights. Strange sounds assault you: shouts and yelps, the snapping and whirring of cameras, the insistent clacking of keys on laptops. Hostile questions come at you like slaps and needles. It amazed Henry Beedle that people didn't cry like babies during such initiations. Few politicians had ever had interesting first press conferences. Melvin Hutchinson's was unforgettable.

For a man—especially a black man—of his considerable stature in the legal community, Melvin Hutchinson had received surprisingly little media attention up to that point. After graduating with honors from Columbia Law School in 1964, Melvin joined his mentor Herbert Montgomery at the NAACP. Three years later, he took a job with the U.S. Attorney's Office in Manhattan. Melvin outworked all the ambitious young prosecutors—he showed a particular tenacity and zeal in prosecuting narcotics cases—and quickly rose to the number-three position in the office. He left the government to become the first black associate at the prestigious Wall Street firm of Hull, Evans, Chamberlayne & Auerbach and was eventually named Hull, Evans's first black partner. Henry Beedle first heard of Melvin Hutchinson when the latter received the rare honor of having his name formally added to that of the firm's. Soon thereafter, Beedle read in the *New York Times* that Hutchinson had been appointed to a federal district judgeship.

Beedle didn't see Melvin Hutchinson's name in the paper again until the judge presided over the trial of Cyrus "Puff Daddy" Rodgers, a West Indian immigrant and reputed "crack king" of New York. Rodgers was charged with personally executing one of his chief rivals in the drug trade, as well as his rival's wife and three young

< 10 >

children. After thirty minutes of deliberation, the jury found Rodgers guilty. New York had only recently reinstated the death penalty, and Judge Hutchinson seemed almost pleased as he sentenced Puff Daddy to the ultimate punishment. Stretching the bounds of judicial propriety, Melvin proclaimed from the bench that "drug-peddling parasites must be eliminated from the body of society." Beedle was struck by the judge's choice of words. It sounded like a speech by Troy McCracken.

Few of President-elect McCracken's advisers had even heard of Judge Hutchinson when Beedle suggested him for the attorney general's seat. Some of the more shallow and shortsighted members of Troy's inner circle argued that a "higher-profile" nominee was needed. Everyone agreed that the attorney general, whoever he might be, would have to serve as the administration's chief spokesman in the fight against crime. Some contended that a black crime-fighter might not be credible. Beedle argued that a black crime-fighter like Melvin Hutchinson would be far more effective than any white candidate any of them could come up with. Still, they just didn't get it. What they *did* grasp was the need for a black face or two in the McCracken cabinet—and, at that point, they had zero. It was the vice president–elect who came to Beedle's assistance. Vin Ewell remembered Melvin well from his days as mayor of Hazelton. He had followed Hutchinson's career and was abundantly impressed by the black man's ability to master the intricacies of civil rights, corporate, and criminal law. "He knows how to play the game," Ewell said with obvious admiration.

"Judge! Judge! Judge!" shrieked Wendy Hoffman, special correspondent for the Politics channel and one of the more abrasive members of the Washington press corps, at Melvin Hutchinson's first press conference. Hordes of reporters had traveled to Denver that holiday season, where Troy McCracken and his closest advisers were gathering to suggest and interview prospective cabinet members. Day after day, Troy would name a new nominee in the ballroom of the McCracken estate. The nominee would then meet the press. On the day of Melvin Hutchinson's nomination, Beedle was ensconced in the estate's library with Vin Ewell and other members of the inner circle. With the TV tuned to the POL channel, they watched the press conference that was taking place just two floors below them. Melvin stood at the podium, squinting under the blazing TV lights. The only concern Beedle and Ewell harbored about their man was how he would handle an early confrontation with the media. Melvin pointed to the reporter who was yelling the loudest.

"Judge Hutchinson!" Hoffman shrieked once more. "Some of your colleagues in the legal establishment have characterized you as a 'hanging judge.' Do you consider that label appropriate?"

Melvin paused, considered the question carefully. "I would say the term *hanging judge* is appropriate figuratively," Melvin said in an even tone, "but unfortunately not literally."

The crowd of reporters tittered. "A follow-up, Judge!" Wendy Hoffman barked. "A follow-up question, please! Could you elaborate on your last answer?"

"Certainly," Melvin replied. "I've believed for some time now that what America needs is not more prisons, but more executions. No one has convinced me that hanging is any less humane than electrocution or the gas chamber. Hanging is more cost-efficient than either of those methods and may be even more cost-efficient than lethal injections. You don't have to constantly dispose of expensive syringes. A well-built gallows can last an awfully long time, and a good, sturdy length of rope can even be used more than once, ultimately saving taxpayers millions of dollars."

Incredulous laughter rippled through the press contingent. Henry Beedle held his breath. After the laughter died down, Melvin Hutchinson, unsmiling, said, "I am entirely serious."

The reporters murmured excitedly. Beedle began to breathe again. He realized that Melvin had them precisely where he wanted them.

"Judge," a young reporter said, almost timidly, "what do you say to critics of the death penalty who consider it cruel and unusual punishment?"

"I didn't know there were any such critics left. Look, anyone who would take a human life— through murder, drug dealing, or excessive negligence—should, and must, I believe, pay with his or her own life." Melvin paused, then added, in a quiet, bone-dry voice, "I understand the value of a human life. I've lost a child. Anyone who has ever lost a child knows full well the value of a human life."

Never had Beedle seen a neophyte paralyze a roomful of journalists like this. For several moments, the only sound one could hear was the whirring of cameras. The reporters were silent. Vin Ewell turned and grinned at Beedle. "A star is born," he said.

Henry Beedle, as a reward for his long-haul service to the newly elected President, had hoped to get a top White House post. If not chief of staff, then perhaps special counsel or senior policy adviser to the President. Instead, he was appointed deputy attorney general. For several months, Beedle, though he concealed it well, was severely disappointed. Just because he had had the good sense to suggest Melvin Hutchinson for the attorney general's job didn't mean that he wanted to serve as his flunky. But Beedle accepted his assignment without complaint. This was what a loyal public servant was supposed to do. Little did he know that, in the McCracken administration, the Justice Department would emerge as the happening place to be.

➤ ➤ ➤

History. It was Henry Beedle's passion. And he came to believe that, someday, the early years of Troy McCracken's presidency would be remembered as one of American history's golden eras. He knew that his more cynical colleagues thought him corny when he said so, but during the first two years of the McCracken administration, there was a tremendous feeling of *togetherness* in the air. Beedle had not been around for the Great Depression or World War II, but he imagined that the feeling of unity Americans had in the early McCracken period—that sense of "We're all in this together; the times may be hard, but, by God, we'll win in the end!"—must have been the same sense Americans had had in the thirties and forties. During Troy's first months in office, all the reformist talk that grew out of the New Constitutional Convention led to a flurry of activist legislation. Tougher laws against obscenity and harmful expression were enacted. Army bases rendered defunct by the end of the Cold

War were converted into drug reeducation centers. The Federal Youth Corps was established, and it did wonders for national morale. It was inspiring to see young men and women in their khaki FYC uniforms, helping police patrol city parks, playgrounds, and schools, getting homeless people off the streets and into shelters or drug reeducation centers. Though the economy was still sluggish in those first two years or so, at least there was some real hope that things would turn around. The *spirit* of the times was magnificent. There were, to be sure, dissonant voices, naysayers, gloom- and doomsters. But they were all marginal types, far outside the mainstream. The dominant mood of camaraderie, so far as Henry Beedle could see, transcended the boundaries of race and class—at least for ordinary, decent citizens.

Melvin Hutchinson exemplified the times. The man exuded such dignity, such authority, such gravitas! People trusted him implicitly. When the attorney general visited your neighborhood on one of his frequent goodwill trips and told you he was going to sweep your streets clean of crime and drugs, you absolutely believed him. Melvin received the best press of anyone in the cabinet. By putting reporters in their place during his first press conference, he had won their slavish devotion. He had his detractors, naturally, people who wondered how a man who had begun his career fighting for black rights could go on to become a corporate lawyer and then a staunch advocate of the death penalty. How did a man who was once so *liberal* become so *conservative?* As far as Beedle was concerned, the very question revealed how out of touch Melvin's critics were. *Liberal, conservative, moderate*—the labels had ceased to have any meaning in the McCracken era. The attorney general understood that all decent Americans were engaged in a common battle: against crime, drugs, disease, recession, malaise. What was so incomprehensible about a man who had fought for civil rights yet was pro-business? What was so difficult to understand about a man who wanted justice for the victims of segregation *and* the victims of street crime?

Henry Beedle knew there were some blacks, retrograde fanatics and relics of the radical Left, who accused Melvin Hutchinson of being some sort of traitor to his race. But none of them ever escorted the attorney general—as Beedle had on many occasions—into the darkest heart of the ghetto. Those rabid anarchists never saw how Melvin was *revered* by the many decent, law-abiding members of the underclass. Beedle marveled as blacks would come swarming out of their tenements just to get a look at Melvin, to shake his hand, to tell him how grateful they were that he was looking out for them, protecting them. To Henry Beedle's mind, Melvin Hutchinson was no traitor to his people—he was their bloody champion!

But Melvin's other early booster on the McCracken team soon soured on the attorney general. Vin Ewell and Melvin Hutchinson had, after all, a history. And while Ewell's threat to use force during the summer of '63 may have been water under the bridge to the vice president, the attorney general was not quite so eager to let bygones be bygones. Publicly, Melvin and Ewell always spoke well of each other—they knew the protocol—but, observing the two in a relatively intimate setting, one could sense a palpable tension. Ewell might sidle up to Melvin at the Millennium Club or at a cocktail party and try to lay his patented good ole boy routine on him. Melvin would fairly recoil from the man. As Ewell prattled on in his chummy, profane way, Melvin would practically scowl at him, responding to his questions and punch lines with barely audible grunts or a shrug of the shoulders. When Melvin and his wife, Dorothy, attended a dinner where Mr. and Mrs. Ewell were present, they always left as early as etiquette allowed. Soon Washington's more astute hosts and hostesses knew better than to invite the Ewells and the Hutchinsons to the same affair.

Melvin's clear and present distaste for the vice president incensed Ewell. "That arrogant, ungrateful bastard," he was heard to mutter at the Millennium Club. By the vice president's calculus, the attorney general owed him a great deal. Not only had Ewell given Melvin the critical endorsement that led to his cabinet appointment but, as mayor of Hazelton, he had done Melvin a *favor* by cooperating with the integration effort. "I was the most goddamned progressive politician in the whole goddamned South!" Ewell once fumed as he and Beedle sat alone in the Eagle Room discussing Melvin. "I risked my whole goddamned career by not opposing civil rights! You would think that ungrateful, uppity—"

Beedle raised both eyebrows expectantly, waiting for Ewell to come out and say it: the *N* word.

The vice president stopped short, then smiled thinly. "You'd think the attorney general would appreciate that. Besides, even if he did hate me once before, who the hell in this town *stays* enemies? Shit, I'm sittin' here chattin' amiably with *you*, ya goddamned Yankee skunk."

Naturally, Vin Ewell would never have gotten so worked up about Melvin Hutchinson if he was not, in some way, threatened by him. After Troy McCracken, Melvin had emerged as the most beloved political figure in America. People liked the fact that Melvin was not really a politician (which, in the public mind, was someone who *runs* for office). Melvin was a crime-fighter. And even though the federal government was somewhat limited in what it could do to help local communities deal with their crime problem, Melvin was always out in front, assuring the public that Team McCracken was doing every-thing in its power to protect the citizenry.

As attorney general, Melvin Hutchinson *did* have jurisdiction over all the military bases that had been converted into drug reeducation centers, where first-time narcotics offenders and addicted vagrants were made to wear army fatigues, march, run obstacle courses, con-fess their shortcomings, and take classes on the dangers of drug abuse. Illiterate inmates were taught to read, and most others were given some rudimentary form of job training. The DRCs were hugely popular, and their success fueled Melvin's popularity. The attorney general's stern visage and no-nonsense manner only added to his appeal. The media never treated Melvin the way it treated *politi-cians,* digging into his private life, looking for flaws and peccadilloes. Reporters treated Melvin like a hero. It wasn't long before the press started buzzing about a tantalizing possibility: that Melvin Hutchin-son just might be the one—the first black man who could actually be elected President of the United States.

Such talk got under the skin of Vin Ewell. Even though Ewell had lost the presidential nomination to Troy McCracken, even though Troy was a vigorous, relatively young man who stood little chance of dying in office, and even though the immensely popular McCracken seemed destined to win reelection, Vin Ewell held out the hope that he might still someday become commander in chief. Never mind that he'd be in his seventies at the end of McCracken's second term. Vin Ewell thought he'd live forever—at least long enough to weasel his way into the Oval Office. "Hell," he once said to Beedle, "look at Reagan." As McCracken's vice president, Ewell figured it would only be fair that he should inherit the presidency.

Now along came this Melvin Hutchinson, who would try to take from Ewell everything he'd worked so hard to earn! Ewell grew to detest Melvin as he had once—and perhaps still—detested Troy McCracken. Privately, if one could call talking to reporters and politicians private, the vice president started mocking the attorney general's famous first press conference. "Hang 'Em High Hutch," Ewell dubbed Melvin. To Vin Ewell's chagrin, the moniker stuck and only enhanced Melvin's popularity and tough-on-crime reputation. The public *liked* referring to the attorney general as Hang 'Em High Hutch. There was a touch of Eastwood about the nickname. When Melvin spoke at anticrime rallies, someone was bound to cry out with triumphant glee: "Hang 'em high, Hutch! Hang 'em high!"

➤   ➤   ➤

And so, as confirmation of his prominence, the attorney general, one glorious spring evening, with the cherry blossoms in bloom, had the ultimate Washington insider's honor bestowed upon him: a roast at the Millennium Club. Just about every important member of the club was there—except the President, whose teenaged son, Justin, was playing for his high school basketball team in a night game (the President made a great show of attending many of the home games in which Justin played). One after another, Henry Beedle and other roasters stepped up to the podium and cracked good-natured—and carefully scripted—barbs about the attorney general. The whole affair was typically convivial—until the vice president spoke.

"We've all heard a great deal this evening about Melvin Hutchinson's *firsts*," Vin Ewell leered. "He was the first Neeeegro, as we used to call 'em, to become a partner at Hull, Evans. He was the first black man to rise to the number-three spot in the U.S. Attorney's Office for the Southern District. He was the first African-American —if that's what they wanna call themselves—"

There was squirming in the seats of Millennium Clubbers.

"—the first African-American to become attorney general of the United States. And the first to become a member of the Millennium Club."

Much nervous coughing and glancing about at this point. Clearly, the vice president was quite drunk. But what could anybody do about it?

"Well, I gotta tell y'all, my esteemed membahs a the club," Ewell continued, his accent seeming to grow thicker, more mean and rural, "there is one first y'all might not know about the attorney general. Last summer, on the Fourth of Joo-lie, my lovely wife, Muriel, and I had a cookout at the Ewell ranch. Well, we call it a ranch, but it's really a plantation—a *cotton* plantation."

Beedle looked at Melvin, who sat on the dais, right next to the podium. He appeared to be biting the insides of his cheeks. His eyes were growing more and more narrow. He looked as if he were about to implode.

"And I'll tell ya, when them *ribs* was ready to eat, Melvin Hutchinson was the *first* in line!"

The audience chuckled uncertainly.

"Well, anyway, I jes wanna present Hutch with this *token* of everyone's appreciation." Vin Ewell placed an indistinguishable object on the podium. "The Golden Noose Award," he intoned grandiosely.

The audience, not knowing what else to do, applauded politely, as if this was all very funny. Beedle got a good look at the award: an elaborately carved miniature wooden gallows with a gold-plated miniature noose attached. He glanced at Melvin. The attorney general actually seemed to be trembling with rage.

"We all know how fond y'are of a good hangin', Judge. So come on up 'ere and collect your prize!"

Hutch and Ewell brushed tuxedoed shoulders as the attorney general stepped up to the podium and the vice president returned to his seat on the dais. The anger Beedle had seen in Hutch's face only moments before seemed to disappear instantly. He waved the trophy above his head with mock pride, causing everyone to laugh, though more out of relief than any genuine amusement. With that one choice gesture, Hutch deflated all the tension in the banquet hall. He made a few courteous, if cursory, thank-yous to everyone who had roasted him. Then he fell silent for a long moment, looking intently at the Golden Noose Award.

"I hope I may be forgiven, my friends, if I bring a note of seriousness to tonight's festivities," Hutch said. "I received a letter just this morning from a Barbara Mae Jenkins of Amarillo, Texas. Mrs. Jenkins's husband, Earl, was killed in a car accident. A month later, Barbara Mae gave birth to their child, Earl Junior. Barbara Mae had a good job as a waitress at an all-night diner a few miles from her modest home. She liked working the four-to-midnight shift because it allowed her to spend most of the day with little Earl. Luckily, Barbara Mae knew a sixteen-year-old girl from the neighborhood who baby-sat for Earl. Well, when Barbara Mae returned home from the diner one night, she found the baby-sitter's nude body slumped in a corner of the kitchen. The sixteen-year-old girl had been raped, sodomized, and savagely beaten before having her throat slit from ear to ear. But Barbara Mae couldn't find Earl Junior. The police came and searched the county. They searched all night and still there was no sign of the little boy. Finally, around dawn, Barbara Mae happened to go to her refrigerator and open the freezer. Her baby was stuffed inside—frozen solid."

There was a collective gasp of horror in the banquet hall.

"Earl Junior had cigarette burns all over his tiny body. He'd been viciously tortured and sexually abused. By midday, the police had still not found the killer. When I got word of this unspeakable crime, I instructed the head of the FBI to make the capture of the killer a top priority. Within two days, the FBI had found Earl Junior's murderer, a drifter named Jeremiad Hardee. Well, this Hardee, this monster, this parasite, was recently convicted by a jury of his peers and sentenced to death."

The crowd began to applaud, but Hutch held up his hand to stop the clapping.

"In the letter I received from Barbara Mae Jenkins this morning, she told me that she knew nothing could ever bring back her son.

But she thanked me from the bottom of her heart for making the apprehension of Jeremiad Hardee a top priority for the Justice Department. She said it pained her to see anyone lose his life, but 'Thank the Lord,' she wrote, 'that we have the death penalty for people like Hardee and thank the Lord we have crime-fighters like you, Mr. Attorney General, to see that justice is served.' I can't tell you, my friends, how much that letter meant to me. I simply do not have the words. I get kidded a lot about my so-called obsession with crime. But I guess I don't see it as an obsession. I see it as a *mission*. And not only is it my duty to see that criminal parasites—especially those who would murder a child—are captured and eliminated . . . it is my pleasure!"

That brought the crowd to its feet. Many of the most powerful men and women in America were at the Millennium Club that night, and half of them—as they stood applauding wildly—had tears in their eyes. But Henry Beedle's baby blues were dry. He was already contemplating Melvin Hutchinson's run for the presidency. The attorney general stood at the podium, only the faintest trace of a smile on his lips, nodding his head slowly, majestically.

Only then did Beedle happen to spy the one person in the banquet hall who was not standing. Vin Ewell remained in his seat on the dais, a most grotesque look on his face. Was it Beedle's imagination, or did Ewell's skin seem to be turning purple? Beedle, evidently, was the only person noticing the vice president at all. As the crowd continued its feverish applause and Melvin Hutchinson stood at the podium, drinking in the adulation, Vin Ewell's face contorted hideously, his eyes bulging, then rolling back into his head. A long, viscous rope of saliva swung from his gaping mouth. It wasn't until Ewell collapsed to the floor that the ovation abruptly stopped and people realized the vice president was having a stroke.

Within a quarter hour, a White House helicopter landed on the roof of the Millennium Club. The vice president was choppered to Bethesda Naval Hospital, where he slipped into a deep coma.

(2)

EVERY MORNING WHEN EMMA Person left for work and every evening when she returned, there on her doorstep, awaiting her, greeting her to start the new day and welcoming her home at night, was a fresh turd. Though not always *a* turd—sometimes Emma would discover several firm little logs—and not always fresh: On a few mornings, the stench of the feces was so overpowering, slamming Emma in the face as she opened the door, that she wondered if the excrement had lain festering on her doorstep all night. Didn't Trudy smell it, too? The door to her de facto landlady's apartment was always open. Didn't the odor rise from the pile on the slippery tile floor of the vestibule, wafting up the staircase to the second floor of the two-family home Trudy Winkler owned, contaminating the air in her own apartment? Either Trudy didn't smell it or she didn't mind the smell (regarding it, perhaps, as yet another of her Doberman pinscher Scarlett's adorable qualities), or—and this, Emma suspected, was most likely—Seth's mother endured the smell because it was worth it to her, a tolerable trade-off for forcing Emma to encounter Scarlett's deposits; to inadvertently kick a hardened little pellet with the toe of her shoe; to slide in a puddle of watery diarrhea; or to place her foot squarely in a dense, earthy mound of the stuff. Or to be inclined to clean it up herself—something she never did—or call Trudy to complain about it—which she was disinclined to do, since she'd been living in her boyfriend's mother's house rent-free for six months—or sidestep it and wait for Trudy to scoop

< 21 >

the poop, something she usually did soon after Emma left in the morning or just after she'd return at the end of the day, allowing Scarlett to convey the message: You live in our house, you have to deal with our shit.

Emma had never been one for nostalgia—seeing it as a peculiarly morbid and self-defeating sentiment—but after six months of living with Seth (with Trudy and Scarlett, as it were, on top of them) in Blissfield, New York, she found herself yearning for a time past, the good old days, the years she and Seth had spent together in Vymar, Massachusetts. Emma had met Seth during her last semester at Vymar College. The day after graduation, she moved in with him. From that point on, Emma's life in Vymar was divided into satisfyingly tidy compartments: job (clerking at a bookstore); photography (her true vocation); love (Seth). Life had gotten much messier, much more undefined, in Blissfield. And the more chaotic her current situation became, the more Emma looked on her years with Seth in Vymar as the one extended period in her life when she had been genuinely, consistently happy.

But Seth, during that same period, had been miserable. He'd already abandoned three potential careers—in marketing, law, and stand-up comedy—and was trying to make it as a freelance journalist when he met Emma. Though he had not yet published any articles, he did have impressive-looking business cards embossed with his new self-definition: SETH WINKLER, FREELANCE JOURNALIST. His primary source of sustenance was the rapidly dwindling inheritance from his father. Even once his articles began to get published, Seth felt agitated and at sea in Vymar. He was over thirty and had not yet discovered what he truly wanted to do with his life. He felt an increasingly urgent need to establish himself, though he could never articulate what, precisely, establishing himself meant. But somehow he felt that all his friends were doing it, and that he was lagging far behind. Then, one day, a year and a half after he'd interviewed for the job, Seth received his summons to New York, the opportunity he'd discreetly, fervently coveted: employment as an assistant producer on America's most popular talk show, *Mavis!*

There wasn't enough time to look for an apartment in Manhattan —Mavis Temple had ordered Seth to report for work in one week—

and, with his starting salary on the show, Seth didn't think he'd be able to find a place to meet his tastes, anyway. So Seth considered his mother's offer too good to pass up. After Seth's younger brother, Eric, left for college, Trudy sold the old house in Blissfield, the home Seth and Eric had grown up in, and bought a two-family place on the other side of town. Her plan was to rent out the apartment on the first floor, not because she needed the money (Lester had left her plenty of that) but because, as a widow with both her children gone from home, Trudy was afraid of being lonely (she bought Scarlett for the same reason the same week she bought the new house). But Trudy, for one set of "personal differences" or another, had evicted three tenants in less than a year. As soon as Mavis Temple offered him a job, Seth's mother offered him an apartment.

"I don't think I could afford your rent, Mom," Seth said.

Trudy, on the other end of the phone, seemed to gasp at the thought. "You're my son," Trudy cooed. "You don't have to pay me a thing." She didn't mention Emma, and neither did Seth. But Seth had no intention of leaving his girlfriend behind in Vymar, and he told Emma that she, too, could live in Trudy Winkler's home free of charge. Warily, Emma decided to move with Seth to Blissfield—but not before extracting a promise that, as soon as they had the chance, they would acquire an apartment of their own in Manhattan or Brooklyn.

In all the years Emma had been involved with Seth, she'd met her lover's mother only once, a memorably awful encounter. Their second meeting occurred on the unseasonably muggy October evening when Emma and Seth took over the downstairs apartment. Trudy did not emerge from her own apartment to greet the couple when they arrived. While Seth ventured upstairs to see his mother, Emma stayed downstairs, helping the movers (paid for by the *Mavis!* show). Only after everything was unloaded did Emma climb the short flight of stairs and knock on Trudy's open door. "I'm in the bedroom," Trudy called out.

As Emma entered the bedroom, Scarlett, prodigiously muscular at thirteen months old, lunged toward her, jaws snapping at the air, leash, wrapped around a bedpost, extended taut. Scarlett's claws scratched Emma's forearms as she recoiled from the Doberman.

Scarlett was up on her hind legs now, front legs flailing in the air, neck muscles bulging as she choked on the leash, teeth flashing as she barked and snarled.

"Jesus!" Emma hissed.

"Some people are weird about dogs." Trudy yawned as she lay sprawled on her queen-size bed, glass of wine in hand, buried under several layers of blankets as the air conditioner whirred and Scarlett choked and growled malevolently, glancing from the television screen for a moment to give Emma a cursory appraisal before returning her attention to *Jeopardy!*

"Actually," Emma said, taking another cautious step backward, "I like dogs. I've never had one, but I generally like them. I guess I like . . . mellow dogs."

"Aw, she's just a baaay-beee," Trudy purred as she half-rose from her bevy of fluffy pillows, tugged on the leash, and pulled Scarlett onto the bed with her. She lay back and embraced Scarlett as the dog writhed on top of her, washing her face in long, languorous slurps. "Oooooh, good girl. *Some* people just don't like dogs," Trudy crooned into Scarlett's pointy ear.

➤   ➤   ➤

Emma made the effort. That was what she always told Seth, that she was *making the effort* to get along with his mother. But years of long-distance contempt had not made living under the same roof with Trudy Winkler easy. Emma established what she termed a "cold peace" with Seth's mother. If she arranged her schedule carefully, Emma could go days on end without seeing Trudy. Emma, on a typical weekday, left the house by 7:35 A.M. and commenced the long walk down the steep hill to Blissfield station to catch the 7:49 train into Manhattan. Emma would put in her eight hours at whatever temporary clerical job the employment agency assigned her to, then, after work, she'd shoot photos for the long-term project she'd begun in Vymar, or spend time in the darkroom that she rented for a few precious hours each week, having negotiated a darkroom time-share with several other young photographers; or she'd meet a friend for dinner, or visit her mother in Washington Heights. Trudy usually left the house a half hour after Emma; she worked twenty hours a week as a fund-raiser for the Blissfield chapter of the Jewish Heritage Foundation. Trudy typically returned home by two o'clock, at which time she opened a bottle of wine, popped a Seconal, turned on the TV, and cuddled up in bed with Scarlett. Seth, meanwhile, was working longer and longer hours on *Mavis!* Except for weekends, he and Emma rarely spent much time together. Emma understood. She knew Seth's job would be demanding. She only resented Seth's schedule on those nights when she had made no plans of her own and was forced to spend hours alone in the house with Trudy and Scarlett until Seth got home, usually around nine o'clock.

Emma found her situation in Trudy's home tense but tolerable— until the appearance of the turds on her doorstep, sporadically at first, then with a clockwork regularity.

"It's fucking revolting!" Emma fumed to Seth one night.

"I talked to Mom about it," Seth said as soothingly as he could. "You have to remember Scarlett's still young—"

"She's eighteen months old already. You're gonna tell me she's not housebroken yet? She was when we first moved in here! She didn't start shitting on our doorstep till a month ago."

"Mom says she has a digestive problem."

"Well, take her to the fucking vet and get it cured!"

Emma rarely lost her temper, but when she did it was frightening —a smoldering, seemingly bottomless contempt that made Seth think of the word he'd often heard black people use when describing an angry person: *evil.*

"Sweetheart," Seth said quietly, eager to lower the volume of their talk lest Trudy hear them.

"I'm moving out. Tomorrow. I'm gone. I've *made the effort,* Seth. For five months I've tried to get along with this woman. The longer I stay in this house, the more likely it is I'm gonna kill her!"

It was a long time before Seth could calm Emma down. He patiently explained to her that now was just not the time for a move. Things were just too hectic at the office. Besides, he expected to be promoted from assistant to associate producer any day now, and he was bound to get a hefty raise. In another month or two, they'd be able to look for a place in the city. Emma said she couldn't wait that long. She knew she couldn't afford an apartment of her own, but maybe she'd move in with her mother in Washington Heights. Seth had only to shoot Emma a skeptical look to convey the unfeasibility of that scenario: Trudy Winkler may have been a pain in the ass, but Alma Person was completely out of her mind.

Seth was beginning to resent Emma's resentment of his mother. Yes, Trudy had originally freaked out when she learned Seth was involved with a black woman. But hadn't she gone out of her way to make up for it? Certainly, allowing Emma to live in her home rent-free for five months already was a generous act of acceptance. Why couldn't Emma show a little more gratitude? Seth didn't say that, though. He just asked Emma to be patient.

Another month passed. Seth got his promotion, and his hefty raise. The turds continued to appear on Seth and Emma's doorstep. But still, they did not move out of Trudy Winkler's home. They were paralyzed. They both knew their relationship had deteriorated since they'd left Vymar for Blissfield. Emma and Seth saw less and less of each other, slept together less and less. Their conversations grew terse, almost businesslike.

Emma's breasts kept aching. . . .

Seth began to wonder what another move would signify, if it was worth it. He felt that he and Emma were either about to get engaged or about to break up. He didn't know which; didn't even know which he'd prefer.

Usually, they'd hurt for two or three days, then her period would occur. But they just kept hurting. . . .

Seth and Emma lived in static anticipation. They were both waiting for something, but they didn't know what—a sign, a quirk of fate, something that would force them into decisive action, perhaps even some sort of crisis.

And, lying in bed beside Seth, wide awake, breasts sore and bruised-feeling for the fifth straight day, Emma knew, intuitively but with an unshakable certainty, that it—the unknown thing they awaited—had arrived.

➤   ➤   ➤

Emma believed there were only two types of creative people: those who were crazy and those who were insane. The insane ones cut off their ears, stabbed their wives in the belly, sucked on double-barreled shotguns, waded into deep lakes, their pockets stuffed with rocks. The crazy ones were everybody else, all the artists who did their work with minimal damage inflicted upon themselves or their loved ones. Growing up, having decided at age twelve that she wanted to be a photographer, Emma had alternately feared and hoped that she might be insane. By her late twenties, though, she was quite content to be simply crazy.

It *was* crazy, was it not, that she sought out ordinary heterosexual couples, usually finding them rather easily through networks of contacts, invited herself into their homes, camera equipment in tow, proffering a bottle of wine and sometimes a plump blunt to relax her subjects, calmly chatting while she set up her lights and umbrellas in the bedroom or living room, engaging the couples in pleasant small talk as they drank and/or smoked, then gently coaxing them as they began to kiss and nuzzle each other, taking off their clothes, stroking and caressing each other, rolling about on the bed or couch or carpet while Emma roamed around the room, seeking intriguing angles, trying to be as unobtrusive as it was possible for a woman with a camera shooting a naked couple making love to be, sometimes asking them to hold a certain pose, her camera clicking, whirring, and occasionally flashing away: This was not something sane people did, was it?

Emma was always fascinated by how utterly normal her subjects seemed, how unself-conscious they were during the shoots. Maybe it was because they had signed a contract with Emma ensuring that she would not show their faces in any of the photos. Perhaps it was because the couples were usually quite drunk or stoned by the time Emma started shooting. Or maybe they were simply flattered. After all, they weren't getting paid to do this. The couples seemed titillated, exhilarated, by the shoots. These people with the most conventional, average bodies were being photographed in flagrante, as if they were movie stars or fashion models, the beautiful people.

Seth became alarmed when Emma finally told him what she had

been working on with such intense dedication for so many months. He warned her of the danger involved: How did she know that these people—these strangers!—might not rape her or kill her once she was in their homes? She didn't know anything about these couples before she walked into their apartments—providing them with booze and drugs!—and started watching while they had sex. What was to stop them from doing something unspeakable to her? Emma just laughed. How could she explain to Seth that the danger, the uncertainty, the possibility of menace, of physical harm, was part of the kick? Yet, in each of the five shoots, that frisson of danger faded almost as soon as she started chatting with the couples. These were not psychos, perverts, dangerous people. They were sane, almost bland even, perfectly pleasant folks. It was she who was the weirdo. She was the one who had become obsessed with the idea of photographing barely attractive people doing the do. It was she who felt the need to see what sex was like for others. Emma was thrilled by the intimacy, the mystery of it. She knew she was crazy. At least she wasn't insane.

If Seth had been upset hearing about Emma's series, he was appalled when he actually saw the work: murky black-and-white photos of headless bodies, contorted in angles and attitudes that seemed at once bizarre and squirmingly familiar; awkward-looking shots of fleshy, pimpled backs and behinds; a belly swelling into the frame; the dirty creases of a flabby neck glistening with sweat—or was that saliva? Most sickening of all was the fact that Seth had bought Emma, as presents over the years, most of the equipment she had used to produce these pictures.

"It's just pornography," Seth said as he sat at their dining room table, three months after they had moved to Blissfield, staring at the photos spread before him.

"It's antipornography," Emma said.

"Then it's erotica?"

"You're not supposed to get off on it, at least not that way. It's about contact."

"I don't know. I think it's just . . . I don't know, I just think it's too much."

"There's nothing perverse about it," Emma said, nary a trace of

< 28 >

defensiveness in her voice. "And that's what bothers you. No whips, no chains, no nipple rings, no knives poised under crotches. It's perfectly normal people having perfectly conventional sex."

"But, but . . . it's not appealing."

"You only say that because they're not beautiful. If they were beautiful, if they had chiseled physiques and you could see their gorgeous faces, it wouldn't seem so odd to you. But these are the bodies of people you know, your friends and colleagues."

"And you're sending this stuff out to galleries? In New York? SoHo!"

"Soon, yeah."

"Maybe you should just wait a while. Get your work shown in some small shows, make some contacts. Everything is connections, you know. I just can't believe a major New York gallery is going to pick your work out of the mass of unsolicited photos and decide to put you on their walls. Sure, it happens, but it's very, very rare. I just don't want you to set yourself up for a heartbreak. I know you're a very confident person, but you have to be realistic, too. I just don't want to see you get hurt."

"I can handle it."

Seth sighed in exasperation. "I mean, honey, look at this stuff. All it is is people fucking."

A slow, mischievous smile crept across Emma's face. "That's a great title."

"This isn't funny, you know."

"People Fucking. Catchy."

"This is very weird stuff here! Nobody is gonna show it. And even if they did, they'd probably end up in jail. I'm sure this would violate the new obscenity codes."

"Cool."

"That's what you want. You just want to shock people."

"All right, Seth, I knew you'd probably react this way. That's why I didn't tell you about it for so long. Let's just drop it now. Can we? Please."

"Sure, that's easy for you to say. You're not the one paying for it."

At that instant, Seth could see that something in Emma's eyes had switched off, a light had disappeared; or he could see it disappearing, swiftly fading away, like a rapidly closing iris at the end of a Warner Brothers cartoon, or when the only light in a small room is coming from the television and you press the power button on the remote control and the light quickly recedes but you can see that afterglow as it becomes enveloped in darkness: So he saw something, some light suddenly switched off behind Emma's eyes. And he knew it would never come back. He knew if you crossed a certain line with Emma, you were fucked. Permanently. He'd seen it happen with other people, like the way Emma had shut down with his mother. Zap. No return. He had just never imagined he would ever cross that line. He knew he'd been precipitously pushing the outside of the envelope, making more and more vaguely snide little comments to Emma in the three months since they'd left Vymar. Perhaps without realizing it, he'd wanted to see just how far he could go, the way a kid swims farther and farther out from shore, just seeing how far he can go before it feels dangerous. Never imagining he might drown. If Seth were that kid, at this moment, water would be filling his lungs. Seth knew that no matter what else changed in their relationship, no matter how much longer he and Emma would be together, he had lost a part of her, an access, that he would never get back.

"Okay," Emma said softly, in a voice that was pure ice.

➤   ➤   ➤

Nostalgia: This, Emma believed, was Simon's disease.

"You've got to love the life," Simon said, clutching the steering wheel of his tiny Honda hatchback, wringing the wheel anxiously as he sped up the West Side Highway, glancing once at Emma in the passenger seat, then craning his neck to cast a quick look at the pile of camera equipment that rattled in the back of the cramped little car as he and Emma raced to their Saturday-afternoon assignment, a wedding in Yonkers. "To be an artist, you've got to really love the whole shebang, the day in and day outness of it, waiting for the right ideas to present themselves to you, wandering around the city like I used to do, looking for the thing that grabs your imagination, makes you say, Yes, I *must* shoot this, having the patience to wait for the happy accident when you're doing the sort of elaborate setups I used to do when I was shooting in, say, Riverside Park and a pigeon waddles into the frame and that unplanned occurrence, that imperfection, makes the picture."

Simon, hair thinning and belly fattening at thirty-six, sounded more embittered than inspired as he warmed to his favorite drive-to-the-wedding topic: the exorbitant cost of conviction, the comfort of compromise. "You gotta love the hustle and the freedom, even though the price of freedom is poverty, or relative poverty, basically being broke all the time. But you can't mind the hardship, because the hardship is part of the life. You may not love the hardship, but because you love the life so much, the hours in the darkroom, hoping the photos will be as beautiful as what you saw that day, you put up with the hardship. 'Cause when you get it right, when the light you see before your eyes, when your own specific way of seeing gets captured in the photo—God, that feeling! Nothing else in life can equal that feeling. Not for me, anyway. And that feeling, more than money or fame or any of the bullshit that sham artists talk about when they talk about their aspirations, that feeling is at the core of the life; that feeling is what keeps you alive."

Though this was only her third assignment with Simon, Emma was already familiar with his monologue and knew where it was headed. And she wondered, Did Simon rehash this soliloquy as a way of justifying his choices to himself? To her? Or was he trying to get her to doubt her own choices? Or to make choices that were more like his choices? And if Simon regarded the life he'd left behind with such fervent nostalgia, what did his current existence amount to? Was it some sort of afterlife, a horrid, numbing death in life? All Emma knew was that she had to listen, and politely: Simon was paying her.

Emma had been living in Blissfield for four months and was beginning to feel that her life had somehow been hijacked, subsumed, by Seth's life. Emma felt that in order to repossess her life, she needed a plan. And though she did not yet have a plan, she sensed that whatever plan she eventually created would require money. But, since moving to Blissfield, she never seemed to have any. Where did the money go? It just went. Emma made more money from temp work in New York than she had at the bookstore in Vymar, yet she held on to less and less of it. The daily train ride into and out of Manhattan was expensive. Just going out for a drink with a friend could cost twice what it did in Vymar. Back in Vymar, she had paid cheap rent for the apartment she shared with Seth, and nothing at all for the darkroom time that she received courtesy of her old mentor in the college's visual arts department. Though she didn't pay rent at Trudy's, the rent she paid for a darkroom time-share in Manhattan ate up a large chunk of what she earned temping.

It was one of her darkroom corenters who hooked Emma up with Simon. Shooting weddings sounded easy enough. And since the work was always on weekends, Emma could spend even more time away from Blissfield. While the assignments with Simon required little skill, and even less talent, Emma felt a tingle of pride at the fact that, for the first time in her life, she was getting paid to be a photographer.

"You know I used to do this shit," Simon continued, "shooting these weddings, once in a while, as you are now, to support the life. The life was what was most important to me. But then, you know, you get a little success, a little money, decide to settle down and raise a family. Be a grown-up. And before you know it, it's not the life you're trying to support, but *lives,* the lives of your wife and your kids —or, in my case, your kid. And then, after a couple of years, you find the weddings are the only thing you shoot, 'cause that's where the money is, and you don't have time to do the other arty work anymore anyway, what with taking care of the kid and just trying to . . . to *maintain.* And when you do have time to do your own stuff, to shoot work that means something to you, you're usually just so fucking tired of shooting *period* that all you really want to do is veg out in front of the TV."

"Mmmmm," Emma hummed sympathetically. She was most annoyed by this part of Simon's lament, the way he always made it sound as if his wife and child had thwarted him from realizing his grand ambitions. Emma was beginning to suspect that maybe Simon had *wanted* to be thwarted, that maybe he knew in his gut that he couldn't hack "the life," that he lacked the faith or courage or ruthless discipline to put his talent to the test. So he'd given up, choosing the more conventional path, but having to believe (since it could not possibly have been a lack of faith or courage or ruthless discipline or

< 32 >

talent that thwarted him) that if only he hadn't had this albatross of domesticity around his neck, he coulda been a contender. If only he didn't have these responsibilities. If only he had more time. If only he didn't need to make those mortgage payments. If only and if only and if only . . .

"But I'll tell ya," Simon said, "I've got no regrets. Zero." He paused. "So . . . you sent your work out to a few galleries?"

"Uh-huh."

"Hear anything?"

"Not yet."

"Well, don't get your hopes up. Disappointment. That's another feature of the life. Constant, crushing disappointment. But you can't let it get to you. I know when I was living the life, I never let it get to me. I was hungry, man. A tiger. A hungry fucking tiger."

Emma nodded, said nothing.

"By the way," Simon said, "I'm looking for a full-time assistant. The wedding season really starts in another couple of months, and rather than just having someone to accompany me on shoots, I'm looking for somebody to help with the developing, with booking assignments, blah blah blah. Full-time. You interested?"

A wave of nausea swept over Emma. "Let me think about it a while," she said.

≻   ≻   ≻

Six weeks had passed since Emma sent her photographs to several galleries. She had received no news, good or bad. There was nothing to do but keep working.

Seth, with increasing frequency, would call Emma when she was working in the darkroom. He knew she could rent the space for only a few hours each week, that the time she spent in there was crucial, that she hated being disturbed. But Seth seemed to think that he alone could enjoy the privilege of distracting her. Emma felt obligated to answer the phone. It was, after all, a communal darkroom, and Emma felt it was important to take messages for the other photographers, who, evidently, did not mind receiving calls while they worked. Emma was wondering one evening if she should suggest to the other photographers that they all pitch in for a darkroom answering machine, when Seth called.

"So how's it going?"

"All right."

"I just wanted to let you know that I might not be home until nine or ten tonight."

"All right."

"I miss you."

"That's sweet, Seth, I miss you, too. I'll see you when you get home, baby."

"Oh, wait just a sec. You know, Matt Roth said to me again that he'd really like to hire you sometime, just on a freelance basis."

"That's great, Seth. Can we talk about it later? I have to work."

"I know you do. That's why I bring this up."

"I mean I have to develop these pictures of my own in this darkroom right now."

"I know what you mean. What I'm talking about is work you can get paid for. You know, Matt's been hiring your friend Bill Hannah to take a lot of these, like, incredibly easy shots of buildings and shit for *American Century*. It's really straightforward stuff and I'm sure Bill's making almost enough money to live on."

"Yeah, but he doesn't have time anymore to shoot anything else. I'd rather just make money doing my dumb temp work and shooting an occasional wedding. I don't want to shoot for magazines, Seth. I want to do my own stuff. You know this. So why don't you just get off it already?"

"Just letting you know that there's work out there if you want it. Well, I better let you go. Sorry to bother you, honey."

"That's all right."

"Okay. Well, I better—oh, hey, did you hear about Karen Osborne?"

"Who?"

"*You* knooooow, that really bitchy photographer, a year behind you at Vymar."

"Oh, yeah, purple glasses, purple hair."

"Yeah, well, she's got a show opening at the Duncan Gallery this summer."

"Really."

"I don't know what her stuff's like. Probably shitty. It's a group show. But very high-profile."

"Sure."

"She's suddenly the hot young photographer. That's what I hear, anyway. Weren't you friends with her?"

"Acquaintances. Seth, I gotta go. I only have another hour left in here. And, you know, I'm just not real interested in what everybody else is doing. You know that."

"I just thought you'd find it interesting—"

"Well, no, I don't. It just seems like you're always doing this, always telling me about the new hot, cool young photographer. I mean, shit, Seth, I'm not in some race with other photographers. I'm doing my own work at my own pace and I don't really care what other people are doing."

"Yeah, you really sound like you don't care, Emma," Seth said with an audible sneer.

"No, Seth, *you* care about these things and you just want to put pressure on me and try to make me feel like I'm falling behind in some race that doesn't even exist. That's *your* bullshit, honey, and I'm sick of you trying to dump it on me!"

"Jesus Christ, Emma, I'm only trying to keep you abreast of what's happening in your field. I know you tend to isolate yourself, and I'm just trying to keep you abreast of the latest trends."

"Well, I'm as abreast as I want to be. All right? I don't need to be any more abreast. Good-bye."

"Wait, wait, wait, sweetie, please, please. Would you just calm down? I don't want to hang up on this note. Please."

"Okay."

"Whew. Thank you. I just wish you could hear yourself. You make it sound like I don't want what's best for you. I mean, when it comes to your photography, I think—on the whole, anyway—that I've been very supportive. And I'm not just talking about money. I think the money should be a sign to you of how emotionally supportive I am. I have a lot of faith in you, Emmy."

It was happening again: Seth had wounded Emma and now she felt guilty, at fault for it. And though she could recognize what was happening, there was nothing she could do to expel her guilt. "All right, Seth. I guess I'm just a little oversensitive today."

"It's understandable."

"Thanks. I'm gonna go now. See you tonight."

"Ciao."

➤　　➤　　➤

Nothing inspired Seth quite so much as a good friend's misfortune. Any friend of Seth's knew that if she/he got fired from a job, Seth would be among the first to call with condolences. If a loved one died or a romance turned to ashes, you could always rely on Seth to indulge your anguish, to listen attentively to every detail of your heartbreak, to buy you a present, a book, perhaps, or a compact disc he knew you wanted. An illness, a car accident, a burglary: Any friend's victimization brought out a buoyancy in Seth, an optimism and good cheer that he tried to impart to his unfortunate chums. It was this quality that gave Seth the reputation, one he cherished, for being a friend you could count on.

One Sunday morning, sitting at his dining room table, drowsily flipping through the *New York Times,* Seth fretted over what a depressing and stressful week he had just endured. Mavis was riding him at the office, Trudy was giving him shit about Emma, Emma was giving him shit about dog shit. Then, he came across a review of a novel published by a college classmate. Though he hadn't seen Joe in years, he'd heard through other friends that Joe had been toiling on this book for a long time. Sitting across the table from Seth, sipping a cup of coffee, Emma watched her boyfriend's face undergo an uncanny transformation. His sleepy-eyed, sullen expression gave way to a look of unabashed, childlike glee. As his smile broadened and his face began to flush, Seth said, "You gotta hear this." The brief notice began with the statement that Joe had written "a dreary little novel." Seth giggled at the line and continued to chuckle as he read the escalating and unusually personal insults the critic heaped on Joe. As the review concluded with a recommendation that Joe give up writing altogether, Seth had to wipe a tear of laughter from his eye. "Brutal," he chortled, "just brutal."

"It's so gratuitous," Emma said. "Obviously, the critic has some personal ax to grind. It's just one person's opinion."

"Yeah, but a pretty influential opinion."

"Are you gonna read the book?"

"Not *now,* not after a notice like this," Seth said, stifling another giggle. "Maybe I'll give Joe a call."

As Emma looked on, Seth found Joe's number in his address book. "Answering machine," Seth said, the receiver wedged between his cheek and shoulder. "Howdy, stranger," Seth crooned into the phone, "long time no hear from. Seth Winkler here. Congratulations on your book! Read about it in the *Times* this morning. Those assholes. Anyway, don't let it get ya down, man. I mean just being acknowledged in the *Times* at all is a compliment. As for me, things are goin' good. I don't know if you've heard, but I'm a producer— well, assistant producer, soon to be associate producer, I hope, I hope, I hope—on the *Mavis!* show. It ain't *art"*—Seth put a sarcastic spin on the word—"but it do pay the bills. Who knows? Maybe it'll be good grist for a novel. Anyway, hang in there, good buddy. I'll call you again soon to hear all about how the book is doing."

That afternoon, David and Steve, Seth's best friends from Colgate, came over to watch a basketball game. The three old pals, who had all known Joe in college, laughed uproariously as Seth read the review aloud. "A dreary little novel," David said with a grin and a shudder. "Harsh, man. Harsh."

Emma, sitting alone in the bedroom, heard Seth recite the review yet again, to more appreciative howls from David and Steve. At first, Emma was mystified by their reaction. David, a lawyer, always talked about the novel he was working on. Steve, an advertising executive, professed to be an aspiring screenwriter. Seth had talked for years about writing a novel, but he was stumped as to how one went about it. He worried about finding "good grist" for a story. He then decided that the secret to a fiction writer's success was having "a real huckster agent." But Seth's novel remained unwritten. Recently, he had bought a computer program that provided various plots and incidents for potential screenplays. In his spare time, when he was not watching television, Seth would scan his screenwriting software, feeling that if he could just come up with the right formula, his script would "practically write itself." If all three of them wanted to write, Emma wondered, realizing suddenly, as the thought formed in her mind, that the question was its own answer, how could they gloat over the public trashing of a friend who'd actually had the tenacity to publish something?

Emma wanted to storm into the living room, unleashing a tirade: You spineless frauds! Wanting so badly to be different, distinctive, creative—yet wanting to be *normal,* just like everybody else. A mainstreamer—only better. Sticking with people you can consider right at your level, so you can mock all the people below you and all the people who might aspire to something you consider higher. Anyone who has the audacity to think of themselves as an artist—*Eeeeeew, how pretentious!* 'Cause y'all don't even have the nerve to try! So smug about your stupid-ass jobs even as you mock the work you do, laughing it off, sneering contemptuously at *everything!*

But Emma remained in the bedroom, reading the paper, finally putting on the headset of her Walkman and cranking up the volume on *A Love Supreme,* drowning out the laughter in the living room.

>   >   >

And yet, Seth *had* been kind, hadn't he? It wasn't simply nostalgia that made Emma think so, was it?

Few people had ever been as kind to Emma as Seth had been the weekend Alma Person tried to kill herself. They had been living together in Vymar for six months when Emma's aunt Dorothy called, late on a Friday evening, with the news. Seth held Emma as she wept and talked—trying to figure out what had pushed her mother over the edge, agonizing over what she could have done to prevent Alma from attempting suicide—and wept some more. Seth talked to Emma about his father's death from a heart attack several years earlier, trying to convey that, on a certain level, he could understand what she was going through, though never making a simplistic connection between the two incidents. After staying up almost the entire night, it was Seth who drove them from Vymar to New York while Emma slept uneasily in the passenger seat.

Seth stayed at Alma's apartment in Washington Heights while

< 38 >

Emma visited her mother at Columbia Presbyterian Hospital. Emma's insides tightened as she walked into the intensive care unit, past rows of people who had no business being alive: pale, withered heads with wisps of white hair, surrounded by white sheets and tubes.

Alma Person was sitting up in bed, an IV in her arm, a two-pronged tube stuffed up her nostrils. She looked a bit haggard and spoke slowly, quietly, but she was perfectly lucid as she explained to her daughter that she was here, alive, in this ICU because of a slight miscalculation, not any attempt to *almost* do it, no anguished "cry for help," but a critical glitch in a meticulously planned exit. Had there been but one more tablet of Elavil in the bottle, had Emma's aunt Dorothy not called that night, for no particular reason, and not become alarmed by the fact that Alma—who rarely left her apartment for more than an hour or so—wasn't answering the phone, Alma might not have (just barely) survived. Alma explained this to Emma in a detached tone, free of anger or self-pity, as if she was talking about someone else. She went to great pains to tell Emma that she was not even remotely responsible for her suicidal depression, that the last thing she should do was blame herself, or feel that there was anything she could have done to stop this from happening. Emma was somewhat relieved. But still, it was a hell of a feeling—an inconsolable desolation—to realize that she was not enough of a factor to make her mother wish to go on living.

Emma and Seth spent Saturday night in Alma's apartment. On Sunday, Emma visited her mother again, talked with Alma's doctors and psychiatrist, and, seeing that there was little else she could do for Alma—and eager to avoid seeing any of her aunts and uncles or, worst of all, her father and his second wife—decided she wanted to leave New York as quickly as possible. Seth understood, but he suggested that on their way back to Massachusetts, they stop in Blissfield and spend Sunday night with his mother and younger brother, Eric. Emma, too exhausted to argue, agreed.

Emma had hoped never to meet Seth's mother. All Emma knew, or cared to know, about Trudy Winkler was that she had flown into an hysterical tirade when she learned that her son was in love with an African-American. The fact that Trudy, two days later, apologized to Seth and told him she would accept any woman he loved meant nothing to Emma. Trudy Winkler was a racist, plain and simple, and no reconsideration would make up for her initial bigoted gut response. Emma would neither seek nor desire Trudy's approval.

When Seth and Emma arrived in Blissfield at dusk that Sunday evening—these were the pre-Scarlett days, before Eric left for college, before Trudy moved into the two-family home on the other side of town—Trudy was about as gracious as a person could be. She embraced Emma warmly as Seth introduced them. She asked how Alma was doing, with a seemingly genuine and deeply felt concern. Guiding the dinner table conversation, Trudy struck just the right balance between casual chitchat and respectful reticence, not inquiring further about Emma's family situation but not pretending that nothing had happened, either. Through the subtlest of looks and gestures, Trudy managed to convey a sympathy for Emma, and Emma, despite herself, felt grateful for Trudy's kindness. The past two days had, after all, been the worst of Emma's life.

After dinner, Seth showed Emma around the huge old house he had grown up in. Photos of Seth and Eric decorated every room; their bronzed baby shoes were prominently displayed on the living room mantel. Emma had not realized quite how wealthy Seth was: The Winkler property included tennis courts and a swimming pool. But Seth, as well as Trudy and the charmingly gawky Eric, seemed surpassingly casual about the opulence of their home. That night, as they snuggled in bed in one of the Winkler guest rooms, Seth said to Emma, "See, she's not so bad."

The next morning, while Seth was taking a shower, Emma sat at the kitchen table with Trudy and Eric, nibbling on a bagel and sipping a cup of coffee. "Ugh," Trudy groaned in annoyance as she read the *Blissfield Chronicle*. "Remember her?" she asked, handing Eric the newspaper.

"Not really," Eric said.

"What is it?" Emma asked.

"A woman named Ruth Westerberg," Trudy said, grabbing the paper from Eric and thrusting it at Emma. "Her son was in Eric's class at Hebrew school."

Emma quickly scanned the story. Mrs. Westerberg, the newspaper reported, had gassed herself in her garage.

"She succeeded at what your mother tried to do," Trudy said contemptuously.

Emma felt as if she had been kicked in the stomach, had had the wind knocked out of her. She looked up from the newspaper, feeling almost dazed. She had no idea how to respond to such an unexpected remark. The expression on Trudy Winkler's face was one of smug reproach. She seemed deeply *offended* that Mrs. Westerberg would commit suicide—and that Alma Person would have had the nerve to try such a thing, and then fail! It seemed an affront to Trudy's sensibility. And Emma wondered, Did Trudy think she was so immune to catastrophe; could she not believe that something inconceivably terrible might happen to her someday; that she might be driven to suicide —or drive someone else to it? Or maybe she did realize her vulnerability. And that made her all the angrier, all the more insulted. But what was the point of Trudy saying what she had said to Emma? Was she deliberately trying to hurt her? Or was she oblivious to the pain she could cause? Trudy was either breathtakingly insensitive or breathtakingly cruel.

Or perhaps she was just trying to keep Emma abreast of all the local suicides.

➤   ➤   ➤

"You've obviously got an eye," Shelley Sweet said, brushing a crimson strand of hair from her face and taking a sip of white wine as she stared at one of Emma's photos on her desk. "A unique eye. Really."

"Thank you," Emma said, wishing she could come up with some clever comment but feeling too intimidated to be clever.

Shelley Sweet looked up and smiled thinly. There was a vaguely wolfish aspect about her face—the narrow jaw and pointy chin, the slightly slanted eyes and sharp curve of her smile. "I guessed you were black, you know."

"Did you?" Emma said.

"One of the couples in your series is black and *three* are interracial. I don't mean to be presumptuous. But I *did* presume. So sue me." She smiled her thin, inscrutable smile, took another sip of wine.

Emma laughed nervously and took what she fretted was an ungainly gulp of her drink. "So I have an eye," she said, dabbing a drop of wine from the corner of her mouth.

"A *unique* eye. I just wonder if this is the right subject matter for you. The right subject matter for the Shelley Sweet Gallery. Do you have anything else you'd like to show me?"

"Nothing good. I mean, nothing I feel that excited about—at least not right now. Um, what's wrong with the pictures I've given you?"

"Nothing's *wrong* with them. In fact, three or four years ago, I probably would have displayed a couple of them. It's just that pornography, or erotica, whatever you want to call it—"

"I don't call it either. It's neither pornography nor erotica."

Shelley Sweet stared at Emma for a long moment, saying nothing but still smiling that enigmatic little smile. "Whatever," she said finally. "It's just not what's happening now."

"Are you worried about the new obscenity codes? A friend of mine thought that might be a concern."

"Well, there has been a strong backlash against the more, shall we say, explicit work of recent years. But I'm not worried about the police barging in or anything like that. At the same time, I don't want to alienate potential buyers. And, given the nature of your work, and the fact that you're just starting out in your career, I think we have to be a bit . . . well, why alienate buyers, you know what I mean? Ten years ago, you could afford to risk such a thing. Not in this market. This sort of work . . . it's just not that marketable right now. But what *is* very, extremely marketable is work with an ethnocentric edge to it. Work that reflects life on . . . the street."

"The street?"

"The street, the 'hood, whatever you want to call it. I mean, do you have any work, or are you interested in producing any work, that reflects your roots? Afrocentricity. The street. What it means to be a proud, struggling African-American woman. You know what I'm saying?"

"I'm afraid so."

" 'Cause lemme tell ya, girlfriend, straight up," Shelley Sweet said, lapsing into some odd lingo, a pseudojive, "that's the shit that'll break you in this market."

> > >

What was the strange appeal of using nothing, of eschewing latex sheath or sperm-slaughtering chemicals? Twenty-five or more days of the month, Emma was scrupulous about birth control. But often, just before, during, or just after her period, she and Seth would make love without precautions, using nothing, tempting fate, indulging in a sensuousness that seemed thrillingly pure—unfettered and elemental.

"So you hit a single," Seth said after Emma got home from her meeting with Shelley Sweet. "You can't expect to knock it out of the park your first time at bat. But, hey, you got on base. That's terrific, honey." His tone was loving, compassionate, encouraging. Seth's opinion of Emma's nude series had suddenly changed after Shelley Sweet called, asking for a meeting with Emma. "She's supposed to be pretty radical," Seth said excitedly after Emma got off the phone. "I bet she'll really go for provocative stuff like yours." Seth hurried home from the office on the night Emma met with Sweet so he could hear all about it as soon as she walked in the door. "Well," Seth shrugged after Emma recounted her conversation at the gallery, "time for plan B."

Emma recognized that Seth was trying to comfort her, but she wasn't feeling particularly disappointed. She felt that if one major gallery owner had been intrigued by her series then perhaps another would display it. What rattled Emma was the way Shelley Sweet had objectified her, looked to plug her into a preestablished niche. Still, after leaving the gallery that evening, Emma had felt more confident about her work than ever before. But she knew when Seth mentioned "plan B," he was suggesting not perseverance but surrender, implying that since Emma had sent out her work and not received the best possible response, she should quit the series, perhaps abandon personal work altogether and shoot pictures of buildings and celebrities for a glossy magazine like *American Century,* as if the lukewarm judgment of a single person would be enough to make Emma give up on an endeavor that she had never consciously chosen to take on in the first place.

< 43 >

"How 'bout I give you a massage?" Seth asked sweetly.

He *is* a kind man, Emma thought, lying on her stomach as Seth's hands gently kneaded her shoulders, isn't he? Why had she been so hard on him lately? Why must she apply the most unsavory motives to his every comment and action? It was Blissfield, living in Trudy's house: That was the problem. They needed to be on their own again, as they had lived in Vymar. The essence of their dilemma, Emma thought, was geographic. If they could just get their own place, she was certain their relationship could be good again. Maybe, Emma thought as Seth's fingers stroked her neck, she *would* work full-time with Simon, shooting weddings; maybe she *would* do a little freelancing for a magazine or two. There was no real reason why such work should destroy her creativity. Maybe Seth would get his promotion to associate producer soon, things would calm down on the *Mavis!* show, and then they could find a cozy little nest to feather in Manhattan or Brooklyn. And maybe even get married.

"You know I love you, don't you?" Seth said.

As they wrapped their naked bodies around each other, Emma thought fleetingly about putting in her diaphragm but, in the next instant, remembering that she'd only stopped bleeding that morning, decided to use nothing, recognizing, as the words formed in her mind, what a foolish rationale it was, but giving in to it nonetheless: I've never gotten pregnant *before.*

(3)

I T WASN'T EVERY MAN, or just any man, Melvin Hutchinson thought, who had a day named after him, a whole day set aside in his honor by the denizens of his hometown. Certainly, this was something rare. And though he was getting accustomed to being honored, though much of his life had become a series of speeches and tributes, of banquets and rallies where he was showered with awards and praise, even though he had become almost nonchalant about his status as something of a professional role model, he couldn't help but feel a certain gloating pride about this latest accolade: Melvin Hutchinson Day. So why not allow himself as he sat aboard *Justice One*—the luxurious plane paid for by wealthy admirers of the attorney general—heading for Norris, New Jersey, and the daylong festivities celebrating his life and work, a small private reward, a little gift from Melvin Hutchinson to Melvin Hutchinson, a splash of vodka in his glass of orange juice? So what if it was a bit early—eight in the morning? On a typical day, Melvin did not start drinking until ten. But today was special. Not only was it Melvin Hutchinson Day. This brilliant April morning offered another cause for jubilation: Vin Ewell lay dying.

"We're all praying for the vice president's recovery," Henry Beedle, sitting directly across from Melvin in a cozy little corner of *Justice One*—the "breakfast nook," Beedle had dubbed this section of the plane—said into the telephone he carried with him everywhere. "That is the line of the day," Beedle added in his arrogant drone, that tone of voice that always seemed to suggest he couldn't be more bored with these petty details of his job as deputy attorney general, when, in fact, these petty details were all that he lived for. "There will be no comment at all on a replacement for the vice president," Beedle continued. "No! Don't *say* 'No comment.' One more time: The line of the day is, 'We're all praying for the vice president's recovery.' There's no reason to elaborate."

Beedle glanced at Melvin and rolled his eyes extravagantly, as if to say, Can you believe what we have to put up with, that incompetent staff down in Washington that can't do a thing without us there to supervise them? Melvin responded with the slightest flicker of a smile and took another sip of his screwdriver. He liked Beedle—up to a point. He and Beedle both knew that when it came to the real nuts and bolts, the dreary minutiae of governance, that it was Beedle who actually ran the Justice Department. But it was Melvin who *presided.* Without Melvin, Beedle would be just another bureaucrat in just another dull Washington job, instead of being one of the most feared and envied operators in town. And Melvin realized he would be lost without Beedle, clueless about the machinery of the Justice Department. Theirs was a wary symbiosis. Melvin knew that Beedle thought he was smarter than Melvin, but he also knew that Beedle knew he'd damn well better never show it, that the status Henry Beedle so ardently cherished was entirely dependent upon his constant deference to Melvin Hutchinson. Beedle could be as imperious and cruel to his underlings as he pleased, but he must, at all times, kiss the ass of his boss, the attorney general of the United States.

This, Melvin believed, was the essential nature of Washington. Certainly, the general public liked to believe otherwise, liked to imagine that leaders at the highest levels of government were motivated, at best, by strongly held convictions or a selfless devotion to duty and country and, at worst, by venality or a lust for control. What people could never comprehend was that power was based on insecurity, that the most profound issues of the day were decided by relatively small groups of men—and occasionally a few women— whose loyalties and convictions were based on little more than who was *nice* to them—who complimented you, let you into their circle, showed you the proper respect in some completely insignificant meeting. Of course, there was room for principle. Once in a while, genuine ideas, serious plans, came into play. But power was about winning and losing, who was in and who was out; and wins and losses, inness and outness, were decided on the basis of the insecurities of various individuals whose insecurities could never be mollified, by men—and occasionally a few women—who needed constant reassurance, incessant reinforcement, daily reminders of their position, their status. If you didn't show certain people how important they were, they would fuck you. If certain people didn't show you how important you were—if they dared dis you—you had to make them pay.

Vicious? Yes. Silly? To be sure. But Washington was really no different from any New York law firm. And the calculus of power in any New York law firm was really not all that different from life on the street. Not that Melvin was an expert on the street. He'd grown up in a respectable home, father a mailman, mother a schoolteacher, church every Sunday, always enough food on the table, et cetera, et cetera—but still, he hailed from Norris, New Jersey, *black* Norris. And even in the forties and fifties, if you said the wrong shit to the wrong dude in Norris, it was *over*. Some of the stuff Melvin had seen in New York law firms, in the U.S. Department of Justice, in the White House—that whitest of all American houses—the way some of these ofays talked to one another! Damn. If you dared insult a brother in Norris the way these white folks talked down to one another, disrespected one another, you would *die* for that shit. You wouldn't be ignored by your (so-called) superiors, cut out of the loop, fired. You would die! You would be killed ! If you did the equivalent, the very equivalent, say, of insulting another man's memorandum, trashing his memo, he would *kill* you! And people would understand. Not that Melvin advocated such a thing. Not that he would ever *endorse* such behavior. He simply recognized it as the way of the world.

"An eye for an eye?" Harry Hutchinson, Melvin's daddy, used to say, mocking the Bible. "You want to take out my *eye?* My eye! You take out my eye and I'll cut your fucking head off! Don't tell me about no eye for an eye! Then the Good Book talk about this "Let he who cast the first stone" business. Cast the first stone? You gonna hit me with a *rock?* You hit me with a rock, motherfucker, I'll drop an apartment building on you. I will *crush* you!"

Not that Harry Hutchinson was a sacrilegious man, or a malicious one. He just recognized reality.

"No, no, no," Beedle droned impatiently. "We're going to be in Norris, New Jersey, all day. . . . Fort Brandriss? . . . It's on our itinerary, yes. A few miles outside Norris. . . . Yes, we'll be there. Didn't I just *say* that? . . . Well, that's *their* headache."

Melvin flagged Christian Emerson, his chief bodyguard, and ordered another screwdriver. He picked up the copy of the *New York Times* that lay on the table in front of him and stared at the picture on page one: Vin Ewell laid out on a stretcher; he, Melvin, standing vigilantly in the background as the vice president was lifted into a helicopter. He had grown to love seeing his face in the newspaper, on television. Public life had proved much easier, much more pleasant than Melvin had ever imagined it would be. But that had been the pattern through his whole career. Practicing law was easier than he'd envisioned, being a judge far simpler than he'd feared before he actually became one. Serving as attorney general came naturally to him. So why couldn't he, shouldn't he, get Vin Ewell's job? And if he could do Vin Ewell's job, well then . . .

"So, Judge," Henry Beedle said, finished with his phone call, "I'm afraid coverage of Melvin Hutchinson Day is going to be pretty scant. Everybody's obsessed with this Vin Ewell story." Melvin shrugged, trying to conceal his disappointment. "But," Beedle said, "the POL channel had already scheduled a segment on Fort Brandriss as a model DRC, so there'll be a camera crew out there during our visit."

"Fine, fine," Melvin muttered, taking a sip of his vodka and orange juice. He knew that Beedle knew how much he coveted every little bit of favorable media exposure, but they both made a point of not acknowledging this fact. "What's the word on Ewell?"

"Condition still critical." Beedle flashed his disgusting smile. The deputy attorney general had tiny teeth, the top row as small as the bottom and all of them tinted a rusty brown from twenty-odd years of daily pipe puffing. Beedle's little brown teeth always made Melvin think of small, vicious forest animals, mangy, rodentlike woodland creatures that gnawed on tree bark and weeds. "Be prepared for *lots* of speculation. I've got someone checking on this, but our current situation, so far as I can recall, is unprecedented."

"But it *is* the President's call?" Melvin asked. "Whom he picks or whether he picks someone to replace Ewell at all."

"Oh, yes. Which presents our Troy with an intriguing dilemma. When and under what circumstances does he name another vice president? Does Vin Ewell have to die before Troy can appoint another veep? Does Vin Ewell have a living will? If not, this situation could go on for some time. But if he does, when will Mrs. Ewell pull the plug? Now . . . let's say Muriel decides *not* to disconnect her husband. Can the President really afford to have a comatose running mate in the next election? But let's say Ewell emerges from the twilight zone. Might he not be a babbling cretin or rotting head of lettuce? Best of all, of course, would be if Ewell dies soon. But . . . if he lingers . . ."

Melvin nodded, took a long sip of his drink. "We're all praying for the vice president's recovery."

"Even if his job really isn't worth a bucket of warm spit," Beedle droned. Melvin shot his deputy a startled—and, although Beedle wasn't quite sure, it might have been almost an offended—look. Realizing that Melvin had probably not gotten the reference but being careful not to seem too much like a know-it-all, he quickly, gingerly said, "John Nance Garner."

"Yes," Melvin said with a single nod, still not revealing whether he recognized the quip or had any idea what Beedle was talking about at all. "How long till we touch down?"

Beedle glanced at his watch. "Another ten minutes or so."

"Good." Melvin downed the last of his screwdriver. "I have time for another drink."

➢   ➢   ➢

You *could* say that Harry Hutchinson had trained his son to be an alcoholic, though that was a word—suggestive, as it was, of degradation and disease—that Melvin hated. Popular as the term had become, folks needed to remember that, in the time when Melvin was coming of age, drinking throughout the day was not considered some terrible character flaw or dread illness. A drink, hard liquor even, was not an unusual lunchtime beverage in the fifties and sixties. But Melvin's taste for booze was cultivated even earlier, on a New Year's Eve, sometime in the forties. Melvin couldn't remember exactly what year it was, though he couldn't have been much older than five or six as he sat in the living room with Harry, his mother, Athena, his big sister, Alma. It was the first time he'd ever stayed up so late; they'd been listening to the radio—Guy Lombardo, was that whom they would have been listening to that night? Some big band. Melvin could remember hearing the countdown, kind of scratchy coming through the radio (though all his memories of listening to the radio had that scratchy, staticky sound). "Seven, six, five, four . . ." the voices on the radio chanted. Harry popped open the bottle, the cork bouncing off the ceiling. "Three, two, one . . ." The foamy yellowish liquid, like pale, carbonated urine, bubbled into the fluted glasses, part of Athena's cherished "heirlooms." "Happy New Year!" Harry boomed along with the voices on the radio. Alma squirmed in her chair, giggling uncontrollably while Melvin jumped up and down, screaming "Happy New Year! Happy New Year!" and Athena and Harry clinked glasses and sipped and Harry said, "Let's just let 'em have a little taste. Just a taste." And though Athena didn't approve— you could see that stern, iron look on her face, that expression of hers that Melvin remembered better than any other—Harry poured the kids some champagne.

Melvin remembered that first sip, feeling as if the bubbles had traveled up his nasal canal, tickling the inside of his head, making his face scrunch up. Alma drank a glass and her giggling grew even more compulsive. And Melvin drank a little more, then a little more.

"That's enough," Athena said to Harry.

"Aw, sweetie, just let him have another li'l taste," Harry said, pouring more champagne into Melvin's glass.

Harry and Athena danced around the living room as the sounds of the big band blared scratchily from the radio and Alma tried to show Melvin how to do the jitterbug, though Melvin doubted his sister had any more idea of what dance she was doing than he had. But, Lord, they had a good time. Sometimes, when he was alone in the bedroom he shared with Alma, Melvin would stand in the center of the room and spin around and around, then throw himself on his bed and close his eyes and feel the whole room floating, swimming through space. It was the same dizzying, floating, spinning, flying feeling he'd had dancing around the living room with Alma and his parents that New Year's Eve.

Finally, Athena had to drag Melvin off to bed as he kept yelling "HAP-pee New Year! HAP-pee New Year!" Certainly, it irked Athena to see her little boy in such a state. But she permitted it once a year. Melvin came to look forward to New Year's Eve as much as Christmas, for it was the one night a year when he could feel the exhilaration of drunkenness. Six, seven, eight, nine, ten, eleven years old—having the taste for liquor instilled in him in annual increments. And there was nothing sinister about it. Harry wasn't trying to perpetrate a crime, scar his son for life; he wasn't being "abusive." They were all just having fun.

Years later, Melvin could see how liquor was a daily salve for his daddy. Harry would trudge through the door in the early evening in his pearly blue-gray cap and uniform, back aching from carrying around that heavy mail sack all day, plop down in his rocking chair, pour himself a glass of beer, or bourbon, or scotch, or gin, and rock slowly back and forth, listening to Amos 'n' Andy or Jack Benny or Edgar Bergen and Charlie McCarthy, Walter Winchell, all those scratchy, disembodied voices that Melvin could barely recall. And though Athena, like Melvin and Alma, took a drink only once a year, she allowed Harry his daily salve—one of the few things she *ever* let him get away with. Melvin came to realize, the older he got, that Harry was a disappointment to Athena. But she didn't hate him for it. She treated him with kindness. With mercy.

>   >   >

"What are the three biggest nigger lies?" Harry Hutchinson, drunk and woozy, used to ask Melvin, barely pausing before offering his answer. "One: I don't want *no* Cadillac! Cadillac car? Take it away. I don't need that kinda luxury. No Cadillac for me! Two: White woman? Noooooo! Uh—*uh*. No white women for me! Take 'em away! Don't think about 'em, don't want 'em. No white women for

< 51 >

me! And three: Baby, jes lemme put the *head* in. I'll jes put the head in. Jes the head!" Harry Hutchinson would roar with laughter.

Lies. All lies. But we had to fight against the lies, didn't we? That is what Melvin believed. And yet, as he grew up, Melvin came to see that some lies, even nigger lies, were necessary. Melvin just didn't want to *live* a lie, didn't want his whole life to be one long, insidious lie. And it wasn't. He knew it wasn't. Melvin did not live a lie. He lived, rather, a life of half-truths.

> > >

Melvin Hutchinson Day swam pleasantly before its honoree. The marching band from Rutgers, Melvin's alma mater, blared away as the attorney general emerged from *Justice One* and descended the short flight of stairs, smiling and waving at the crowd, not quite as large as he'd hoped; in fact, a little on the skimpy side. But what the fuck.

As his motorcade cut a red light–running swath through central Norris, the attorney general, sitting in the back of his chauffeur-driven Lincoln with Henry Beedle, took an occasional swig from a pocket flask filled with Jack Daniel's—good ol' Uncle Jack—and stared through the tinted bulletproof window at Largent Street, the street on which Melvin had grown up but which was now occupied by drab, blocky apartment buildings—not projects, really, but architecturally close enough—instead of the neat little row houses and tidy, well-tended gardens Melvin had known as a boy. Melvin couldn't remember, as his car raced down Largent, past the stream of identical redbrick edifices, which block he'd lived on for the first eighteen years of his life, couldn't even recall the names of the cross streets. While Beedle jabbered into his telephone and the sirens of the motorcade screeched, Melvin felt a twinge of melancholy. How small and dirty his hometown seemed. Speeding through the downtown area, Melvin fairly cringed upon noticing the number of buildings—grand old structures, they had once been banks adorned with Greek columns, twenty-story-high towers modeled after the designs of Frank Lloyd Wright—that were now boarded up, completely shut down, abandoned.

< 52 >

On to city hall, where Melvin was presented with the key to Norris by Mayor Gary Dandridge, the son of one of Melvin's grade-school teachers, whom—Melvin suddenly remembered—he had actually met once, but that was back when Gary was still crawling around and shitting on himself. Melvin uttered a few gracious words before the thin crowd that floated ever so subtly in front of him. Then, on to breakfast with the Masons. Thank God they had mimosas and Bloody Marys to go along with the cold, spongy scrambled eggs, the scorched, gristly bacon and dry, tasteless toast. Melvin chatted with all the old men there— and all the men there were old—contemporaries of his father, some of them wizened and trembling, but most of them looking not very different from the way they'd looked forty years earlier. Except that now they all had white hair. It made Melvin think of high school plays where the youngsters sprinkled powder or whatever in their hair to portray old folks. All these men—Delroy and Bubba, Johnny B. and Brother Thomas, Willie C. and Eustace, Lonnie, Eddie, and Gizzard Joe—they all looked exactly the same, except for all this white shit that dusted their hair, this almost artificial-looking glaze, this snow that marked them as old men.

"Boy, I remember you when you was knee-high to a grasshopper!"

"Your mama always knew you would be *somebody*. Ya daddy, too. But your mama—she was the one that always *believed*."

"You memba me, boy—I mean, Yer Honor? I used ta play cards wid ya daddy. I know you don't memba me, but I sho memba you. You was one smart li'l nigga! Ya daddy shore would be proud ta see you today."

"We shore have missed your mama here in Norris. Athena was a fine, fine woman. Best woman ever come outta this town. And she done raised the best children."

"You done made all us proud. Turney genr'l of the You-nited States. A *black* man. You done made all a Norris proud. I jes wanna letcha know."

On to the First Baptist Church on Roosevelt Avenue. Except for the aged Masons, the preacher, and a few ushers, the congregation was made up entirely of women—ladies, really, finely dressed, meticulously coiffed ladies. Didn't black men go to church anymore? Melvin wondered, before telling himself that, well, it *was* a Friday, after all, and probably all the menfolk were at work, even though he knew that a lot of people had been given the day, or at least the morning, off, since it *was* Melvin Hutchinson Day, the day honoring Norris's finest son—you'd think some of those lazy black bastards might at least show up at church. But what the fuck. The preacher gave a long, fawning sermon-introduction that Melvin heard as if it came from a voice burbling underwater: "Melbin Hubinson nebbuh borgot air he came bum." When the congregation burst into applause, Melvin knew it was time for him to approach the pulpit and speak. He'd given this speech—or speeches not unlike it—many times before, and he spoke without notes.

"I'm inclined to tell you this morning, as some prominent politicians have, that my mother was a saint. But my mother was no saint." He paused, just for a moment, with the pro's sense of timing. "She was a goddess." The congregation's laughter burbled in Melvin's ears. "Athena was her Christian-pagan name. And she was a strong, proud exemplar of black womanhood." Melvin's eyes roamed over the congregation. He recognized many of the women's faces, but many more were unfamiliar to him. "A lot of you knew my mother," Melvin heard himself say, "and loved and admired her." Well, he thought after delivering the line, admired maybe. Athena Hutchinson was certainly admirable; a great teacher—no one could doubt it— the kind of stern, demanding disciplinarian students feared when in her class but spoke of with awe years later; a woman known for her dignified manner, her tireless work for the church, the local chapter of the NAACP, the Norris school board; most folks in town admired Athena, it was true, but she was definitely not a woman who inspired much love.

"I learned so many things from my mother," Melvin continued. "So many traditional values. Like respect for one's community."

"Get out of Norris," Athena had said to her son many times. "It's a dead-end town for you. You could be mayor here someday, if you wanted to be. But you'd just be a small-timer, a small-time colored politician in a little colored town. You have to go to New York."

"My mother," Melvin intoned from the pulpit of Norris's First Baptist Church, "taught me respect for the law."

Melvin could not have been much older than ten when Athena

laid a copy of the Declaration of Independence on the kitchen table before him and went down the list of signatures. "Fifty-six men signed this piece of paper. And half of them were lawyers. Get yourself a law degree. That's where the power lies in this society."

"She taught me," Melvin proclaimed, "the importance of family."

"Children are the *point* of life," Athena would say, thrusting a forefinger at Melvin. "The continuation of the line matters more than anything else. That's why God hates faggots. They don't procreate."

"She taught me that all men—and women—are created equal."

"We're superior people, Melvin," Athena said late on the night before her son left for college as they sat, just the two them, at the kitchen table, sipping glasses of warm milk. "We're different, you and I. And don't think I'm just saying we're superior to other colored people. We're superior to people *in general*. We're just *better*. And I don't care who knows it."

"She taught me that my race need not be a limitation. That I could be whatever I wanted to be, do whatever I wanted to do."

"There are going to be a lot of opportunities for colored folks from now on," Melvin's mother said on that chilly September night as they sat together, Athena refilling his glass with steaming, bubbly milk. "You're going to be exposed to a great variety of people in the years to come. And all I want to say is, you better never bring home a white girl."

"She taught me to be proud of my heritage, to be loyal to my black brothers and sisters, to do what I could, at all times, to uplift the race."

"A lot of trashy niggers will try to hold you back," Athena warned her son in their dimly lit kitchen just hours before he would catch the train to Rutgers. "A lot of your own kind will not want to see a colored man succeed. Now, you'll meet quite a few black folks who want to help you along, who will take pride in your accomplishments and who will be accomplished people themselves. But you will also encounter a lot of trashy niggers who will want nothing more than to destroy you. Those are the ones you have to look out for."

"But most of all," Melvin said to the fancily attired ladies who seemed to swim ever so subtly in the pews of the First Baptist Church, "my mother taught me humility."

> > >

Melvin did not disappoint Athena. At Rutgers, he found his niche among the other driven and serious Negroes in his class. And it wasn't the prettiest colored girl at Rutgers whom Melvin chose to date—it was the smartest. In a shadowy corner of Melvin's mind, he would always acknowledge, and realize that other men believed, that his woman was homely. But he had made his choice, a choice that he would find many ambitious but shrewd men made, marrying not for looks but for spine, for support, for intelligence. Dorothy Hale was as strong-willed, as humorlessly determined, and as invested in Melvin's success as Athena had been. Perhaps that was why the two women had never gotten along, could hardly bear to sit in the same room together despite a mutual, if tacit, admiration for one another. But whatever Athena's quibbles, Dorothy was precisely the sort of woman Melvin's mother had conditioned him to seek.

Even though he attended a northern university that was over-whelmingly white, even though he went on to an even whiter institu-tion—Columbia Law School—after college, it wasn't until the summer of 1963, just before his final year at Columbia, when he apprenticed with the legendary Herbert Montgomery and ventured, for the first time in his life, down south, checking up, as it were, on cracker politicians, telling them the law, that Melvin dealt, on a fairly regular basis, really conversed with, got to know the sort of white folks—or, more specifically, privileged northern white girls—that his mother had warned him about. These were activists, committed troops of the civil rights movement, products of Sarah Lawrence and Mount Holyoke, of Radcliffe and Smith, who had decided, out of some need they themselves could not adequately—to Melvin's mind —define—the desire "to do what's right" was their paradigmatic explanation—to risk life and limb to go door-to-door, shack to shack in poorest Alabama, Mississippi, Georgia, to register Negroes to vote. Though Melvin had to give them credit for their commitment, it still baffled him. *He* was down there not only out of a desire for justice but also an obvious self-interest, in so far as the best interests of his people were, since he was *one* of his people, his own best interests. No matter how much he appreciated the altruism of the white civil

< 56 >

rights workers, he couldn't help but feel a little skeptical about the bright-eyed idealists.

Another thing: They, these pale-faced innocents, seemingly had no sense of the danger they invited every day. That summer, Melvin lived each waking hour with a palpable fear, an excruciating knowledge that he could, at any moment, be killed, maimed, or, worst of all, castrated. Yet these white kids—*because* they were white kids— walked around without ostensible fear, ventured boldly into isolated rural areas, rode in buses, singing Pete Seeger and Woody Guthrie songs, Negro spirituals, and "The Battle Hymn of the Republic," strolled obliviously through town squares, blithely unconscious of the vicious stares, the barely concealed homicidal longings of the crackers who loathed them, loathed their sense of superiority, their northern ingenuousness, their smug, carpetbagging belief that *they* knew how white folks down south should live their lives. This was 1963, the year before those two Jewish boys—Schwerner and Goodman— would be murdered along with the black boy Chaney and two years before the massive escalation of the Asian misadventure, before white kids had the good sense to ignore other people's battles and fight for their own self-interest, to save their own skins, to risk the billy clubs of cops up north—preferable to the lynchings of the Klansmen down south—so as to avoid the bullets and booby traps of the Vietnamese. But down south, in deepest cotton country, in 1963, everywhere Melvin traveled with Herbert Montgomery, the northern white kids he met, *especially* the women, had this lack of fear—not courage, really; it was more a carelessness. They were, all of them, supremely careless. It was not, to Melvin's mind, that they bravely faced a danger they knew was there; it was that they didn't seem to know the danger existed. They thought they were invincible. It was this quality that astonished Melvin. These white kids had such a natural sense of entitlement, had led lives of such privilege and security, that they believed not only that they knew what was best for other people but that they themselves would never die.

This carelessness was something that Melvin and his fiancée, Dorothy, had never known. They managed their lives with care, judiciously plotted every career move—Dorothy, like her future husband, was a law student, one of the first black women to attend

New York University Law School—cautiously weighed decisions about when to get married, where to live, and considered how their families would feel about what they did. Melvin and Dorothy simply could not afford to be careless. But after traveling down south and seeing these bold, blind children of privilege, particularly these blithely committed white girls, these products of Barnard and Bryn Mawr, so convinced of their own righteousness, so reckless in the expression of their beliefs, Melvin came to envy and respect their diamond-hard obliviousness, their utter carelessness. He knew he could never be so careless. Neither could Dorothy. But he came to believe—a private idea, one he would never express to Dorothy or to anyone else—that one measure of his success, of his life's achievement, would be the carelessness of his children.

> > >

When, after three miscarriages in four years—causing Melvin and his wife to wonder whether they would ever be able to have children at all—Dorothy gave birth to Abigail, the new mother decided to forsake any ambitions she'd had for a career and devote herself to rearing her daughter. By the time Abby was born, Melvin had stopped worrying about the future personality of his progeny. He was just so relieved, so grateful that the baby was alive and healthy, that she wasn't missing an arm, that she didn't have twelve toes or a misshapen body or a retarded brain. The baby was okay. After Dorothy's string of miscarriages, Melvin had been tormented by nightmares of a stillborn child, horrifying visions of a lifeless, bloody bundle of flesh, dreams that jolted him awake in the middle of the night, dreams that, of course, he could never reveal to Dorothy. So Melvin's primary emotion when Abby was born was solace. *The baby is okay. The baby is okay.*

She was a beautiful child, which was rather mysterious to Melvin, since neither he nor his wife were, in his eyes, particularly attractive. She was brilliant, which was *not* surprising, since Melvin and Dorothy were both exceptionally bright. And she had, through her upbringing, through Dorothy's meticulous cultivation, that privileged sense of invincibility, that luxury of carelessness that Melvin had perceived in

< 58 >

those confident, committed white girls years earlier. Not that Abby was some imitation white kid! *That* was the last thing he or Dorothy wanted. When Melvin started working at Hull, Evans, Chamberlayne & Auerbach, Dorothy insisted that they get an apartment on the (somewhat) integrated, liberal Upper West Side of Manhattan, rather than moving to the suburbs. She wanted their daughter to have all the benefits of wealth, all the advantages of white kids, but she wanted her to know who and what she was, wanted her to have contact with her own people, wanted her to have a sense of history. When Abby wanted to become a Girl Scout, Dorothy insisted instead that she join Jack & Jill, the youth club for the children of the black bourgeoisie. When Melvin wanted to buy a summer home, Dorothy insisted that it be in Oak Bluffs, the black enclave on Martha's Vineyard. Dorothy wanted to make sure that nobody would ever be able to accuse the Hutchinsons of trying to be white.

Yet, because of his assumption of his own superiority, this was not an accusation that Melvin worried about much. It was, Melvin thought, his natural sense of self-worth that allowed him to get along well with his white colleagues and clients at Hull, Evans. He did not seek their approval or try to extract their guilt. He simply did his work, and did it as well as any of the Ivy League ofays at the firm. He was cordial with everyone at Hull, Evans, but he didn't socialize much with them. His courtly congeniality was designed as much to block intimacy as it was to invite respect. Melvin's minimal social life revolved around a ritual from which his Hull, Evans colleagues were strictly excluded: the Black Partners Lunches.

In the first two years of the monthly get-together, Melvin and Art Walker dined alone. They were an elite of an elite, the talented tenth of the twenty or so African-American attorneys at New York's most prestigious law firms, the only two to have made partner. Every few years or so, a new member would join the table. In time, the Black Partners Lunches acquired the aspect of a secret society, an exclusive club whispered about not only by black associates who yearned to be let in but by white attorneys who were intrigued (in the way white folks so often seemed intrigued by black folks, as if impelled by a sort of anthropological curiosity) by the monthly ritual. "So," a white partner at Hull, Evans once asked Melvin, as if gingerly inquiring about exotic tribal rites, "what do you fellows *talk* about at these lunches?"

After a moment's thought, Melvin knew the answer and had to restrain himself, practically had to bite down on his tongue to keep from blurting out the truth: What do we talk about? Do you really want to know what we talk about? Do you? We talk about *you*. About all of you. And how we despise you. Lord, how we laugh at you, mock and diminish you. All of you! Your arrogance and stupidity, your abysmal ignorance, your self-obsession. It's y'all, you silly white clowns, we talk about. So please dispense with the idea I know you harbor: that we wish to be like you. That we desire your approval, your patronizing pats on the head. No—we only want what you have: freedom, money, power, access. But as for you . . . don't you know we hate you, hate you all? That is what we talk about!

Of course, Melvin did not say this to the white partner. He simply shrugged and replied, "Business."

As the founders of the Black Partners Lunches, Melvin and Art Walker set the tone for the gatherings, and the two other early diners at the table were men who, temperamentally, were very much like Melvin and Art, serious-minded achievers who'd made good marriages to sensible women, men who were dedicated to their work while maintaining a somewhat wry attitude about the positions they held in these bastions of whiteness; men who had spent most of their lives setting good examples, who every day assumed the burden of a certain standard of conduct, negotiating the precarious balance of being their own men while having to serve as representatives of vague notions of dignity and competence and propriety not only to their colleagues and their families but—this idea had been drilled into them all their lives—to an entire people. And though they were far too unsentimental to talk about it, these earliest members of the Black Partners Lunches came to depend on one another for encouragement and support. They consulted one another on what moves to make at the office, on how to invest their money, where to buy property, where to send their children to school. Their families vacationed together. They were social pioneers and they knew it, venturing into territories where no black men—aside from those who were part of "the help"—had ever set foot before. And it was understood that they should never zealously seek the endorsement of whites. They didn't give a damn whether they were invited to join the white men's clubs. But if the ofays came a-courtin', well then, why shouldn't they join? Why *wouldn't* they? The four men who formed the nucleus of the Black Partners Lunches had only to answer to one another.

Eventually, two more members joined the table. But they would never share in the intimacy of the nucleus. As much as they had earned the admiration of the other men at the table, they would never be included in their social sphere. Their families would never become part of the loving extended family that the four earliest members had created with their wives and children. Though the fifth and sixth diners at the table were like their colleagues in their reasonableness and impeccable manners, in their bold ambition tempered by wry good humor, the two newer members differed from the nucleus in one critical respect: They had white wives. Not that they talked about it. They didn't need to. Their very reticence on the subject of their families instantly gave them away. And it wasn't that the members of the nucleus disdained the more recently minted partners for their choice of mates. They just didn't mix with the mixed families. The nucleus had the good taste to avoid making disparaging remarks about interracial couples. And the two most junior partners were polite enough not to make an issue of it.

Then along came partner number seven, Freddy Banks. Clearly a different breed of cat. In his first visit to the table, Banks dominated the conversation. It wasn't just that he was brash and cocky and lacked the sense to conceal his high opinion of his own intelligence. There was something else, something about his flat, slightly nasal voice, something about the way he constantly gestured with his hands, something about the way he seemed to stare right through you. A thought occurred to Melvin, but he quickly dismissed it, knowing it was inaccurate: It was not that Freddy Banks acted "white." It was more that he seemed like some new type of black man. Later that afternoon, long after the lunch was over, Melvin recognized what it was he had seen in the seventh partner: Freddy Banks was careless.

At the second lunch Freddy Banks attended, after he, the most junior partner at the table by two years in promotion and five years in age, held court for half an hour, Art Walker, the most senior member, the esteemed old lion of the group, the poker-faced mentor, asked Banks with a point-blank directness that startled everyone at the table except Banks: "So, tell me, is your wife white?"

Freddy Banks didn't bat an eye. "Oh, worse than that," he said with an insouciant grin. "She's blond."

Banks didn't return to the Black Partners Lunches after that. He wasn't missed, certainly not by the nucleus. Eventually, Banks moved out to LA, where he became very rich in real estate. Then he lost everything he had during the Great Recession of '91. Melvin heard he finally shot himself in the head.

And Melvin couldn't help but think—though, as with so many of Melvin's most candid thoughts, it was one he would never express to another person—that this was precisely the fate Freddy Banks deserved.

>   >   >

When Melvin's name was added to the firm's, when Hull, Evans, Chamberlayne & Auerbach became Hull, Evans, Chamberlayne, Auerbach & Hutchinson, a party was held at the Plaza. The giants of law and business in New York and a good many from Washington, Chicago, Boston, and LA showed up for the glittering fete. But the party that mattered to Melvin, the celebration he would truly revel in, would not occur until three months later, when in August, in Oak Bluffs, he would invite Art Walker and Hal Jones and Bill Stewart and their families to his place, when the members of the nucleus and their progeny—there were even a couple of grandchildren toddling about on this golden summer evening—would come together to rejoice in his—their—greatest triumph.

Melvin was a bit disappointed when Abby, home for the summer after her freshman year at Yale, told him she'd be late for the festivities. She was nineteen, after all, and had a social life of her own. Melvin understood. When he and the other members of the nucleus slipped away from the rest of the party and stood out on the deck of Melvin's oceanside home, in the gathering dusk, feeling a crisp, salty

< 62 >

breeze on their faces, the lingering pungent aroma of barbecued chicken and ribs in the air, and raised their glasses, Melvin felt such a love for his friends, *his* homeys, these happy few, the proud black warriors who waged battle with legal briefs and measured their victories in promotions and raises and partnerships and now savored this most historic of conquests, that he, perhaps the most stoic of them all, had to blink back tears of pride.

Then Abby, as ever, flighty, energetic, with her small, lithe body and quick birdlike gestures, burst into the circle, first throwing her arms around her father, then embracing Hal and Art and Bill, by turns teasing and complimenting these men she'd known all her life in her girlishly endearing, chirpy little voice, effortlessly exuding charm, intelligence, grace. Melvin watched her, his exuberant, beautiful daughter as she dazzled his brothers-in-arms with talk of her studies at Yale and her desire to become a lawyer—"You guys are my role models, really"—and as he silently sipped his gin and tonic and savored the presence of Abby and his friends in the orange glow of the evening, he felt as if his life had reached some perfect moment, some pinnacle, an apotheosis of success and affection and just plain good luck that few men, let alone black men, would ever know.

And it was at this very moment that Melvin noticed, striding onto the deck, this sandy-haired, green-eyed goon with the lopsided grin and upturned snout of a Rockwellian Little Leaguer, but with that swagger, that cocky spring in his step that bespoke not innocence but a sort of decadence, a taste for the freewheeling mischief of the rich and white; the flip side of the carelessness that Melvin thought of as a sort of freedom, the quality that he spotted instantly in this leering prep was a predilection for destruction.

"Daddy," Abby said, "I'd like you to meet a friend of mine from Gay Head—Tad."

And as she introduced this clown to Art and Hal and Bill and bubbled about how they'd met, Melvin couldn't even hear her, could only glare and think, How could you? Why the fuck did you, would you, do this, bring this fool in his alligator shirt and his khaki shorts, this socklessly moccasined, tan-ankled boob, this, this Tad—*Tad!*— to ruin my party, to embarrass me before my friends, my brothers?

"Daddy just had his name added to the firm's," Abby chirped, her voice sounding suddenly not charming but hugely irritating to Melvin, like the bland, happy squealing of a TV newscaster. "It's quite an honor."

Tad grinned his crooked grin at Melvin and said, "Good for you."

My God! Melvin wanted to explode, You dare to come into my home, into my town, you little punk from the *Vineyard,* 'cause you, *Tad,* are from the Vineyard, but *I* live in *Oak Bluffs* and am damn proud of it, and you have the audacity to come in here and condescend to me, to talk down to me! "Good for you." Why, I ought to kick your scrawny little ass all over this deck. *Good for you.* Well, I'd like to do something that would be good for *you,* Tad; I'd like to stomp on your jug-eared head till it's a mass of blood and—

"You don't mind, Daddy, do you?"

"Huh?" Melvin snapped out of his interior tirade.

"Tad and I are going out with some friends. But I'll be home by two."

"Home by two," Melvin said absently. "Ask your mother."

"And, Daddy, I'd like to be called Abigail from now on."

"Abigail," Melvin said without inflection, transfixed on Tad's jack-o'-lantern grin. "Abigail." He hadn't called her that since she was six hours old.

Abby and Tad disappeared from the deck and Melvin and the other members of the nucleus stood awkwardly in the faded denim blue twilight, shifting and coughing, commenting on the fineness of the weather, the food, the drink. A mosquito buzzed near Melvin's ear. He slapped his own face, missing the insect. "Well, gentlemen," he said hollowly, "shall we join the rest of the party inside?"

That night, after the party, Melvin and Dorothy, lying in bed, discussed the Tad situation. Dorothy, of course, had known about this white boy all summer, making Melvin realize once again how shut out he was from the special intimacy his wife and daughter shared; shut out by his own absorption in work and the mundane but essential details of supporting a family, focusing on mortgages and tuition and insurance premiums, but even more excluded by his simple maleness.

"But, but," Melvin protested impotently, "I thought she always liked Daryl," Bill Stewart's boy, a junior at Princeton, good-looking, smart, solid, like his father. "Didn't he take her to her prom last year?"

"Yes," Dorothy explained, "but the physical attraction just wasn't there." "Physical attraction": The words made Melvin shudder. It was the first time in nineteen years that he'd thought of his daughter as having a sexual appetite.

"She wants to go white-water rafting with Tad next week," Dorothy said.

"Next week! Where?"

"Colorado."

"It's out of the question. Has she ever been white-water rafting?"

"This will be her first time."

"No it won't. I won't allow it."

"I think we should let her do it," Dorothy said calmly. "Let her have this date with him. In another month, she'll be back in New Haven and he'll be back at William and Mary. Then I'll go to work on her."

"You don't approve of this guy?" Melvin said, suddenly nervous, wanting to make sure he and Dorothy were on the same page.

"What do *you* think?" Dorothy said piquantly. "Don't worry, honey. This will not stand."

Melvin and Dorothy spent the next hour together, lying in bed, man and wife, plotting. This was how they'd always charted the course of Abby's life. They never made demands, handed down ultimatums. They schemed together, and then Dorothy implemented their decisions, convincing, cajoling, and, often tacitly, bribing their child to do things their way. And, so far as Melvin could see, they'd been on a nineteen-year winning streak. There had been no adolescent rebellion from Abby. She had always, in the guise of exercising her own free will, done precisely what her parents wanted her to do. But the game wasn't over yet.

"Let her have this little excursion," Dorothy said. "Then I'll start working on her."

As he drifted into sleep, Melvin couldn't help but think how absurd it was: white-water rafting. What the fuck was a nigger doing white-water rafting? Runnin' the rapids? A colored person. Now, he was, of course, all for breaking barriers. No one could doubt it. But

Lord Almighty, what business did an Afro-American have runnin' the rapids? Like skiing. Why would any black person want to get on skis? And yet, Abby had done *that*, too. Even convinced Melvin to go cross-country with her one day, a couple of winters ago, upstate. Ridiculous. He must have fallen on his ass about forty times. But Abby—ahem, Abigail—loved it. Skied as well as any of the white folks out there. Amazing. Melvin just couldn't see why this was considered enjoyable. Well, he thought drowsily, let her have her white-water excursion. Just as long as Dorothy was right and this Tad liaison was doomed. He would, as he usually did on matters concerning their daughter, defer to Dorothy. Melvin was beginning to feel better, relieved.

> > >

Abby fell out of the raft. Melvin didn't know how it could have happened—didn't they strap you in or something?—but he didn't care to know the details, since any details were overwhelmed by one brutal fact. Abby fell out of the raft. Smashed her skull upon the rocks. Abby was dead. There was no getting around that fact. Abby was dead.

It was Dorothy who wanted, and handled, the details; Dorothy who went and saw the body when Melvin was too numb to leave their bed; Dorothy who demanded the autopsy that revealed traces of cocaine in Abby's body, a fact that, at the time, meant nothing to Melvin, so subordinate was it to the one huge fact, the fact that Abby was dead. It was Dorothy who first wanted to assign blame, who wanted to find someone—Tad, the trip leader, the company that built the raft, anyone—to sue; though with Melvin almost catatonic from shock, no charges were pursued. It was Dorothy who made the funeral arrangements and who dressed and shaved Melvin on the morning of the closed-casket—some of the best morticians in New York were unable to restore Abby's shattered face to anything like its original prettiness—ceremony. Dorothy was the one who greeted the guests and accepted the condolences while Melvin sat in a back room of the funeral parlor, alone, drinking Jack Daniel's from a pocket flask.

< 66 >

Melvin could not decide if the universe had been turned inside out, if life had ceased to make any sense at all, if everything he'd believed in—progress, destiny, the future—had turned out to be an ugly, hollow joke, or if there *was* justice in this life, justice of the most ruthless, exacting nature.

Ten years earlier, Athena had died of breast cancer, and less than a year later, Harry followed his wife to the grave, killed by cirrhosis of the liver. Melvin had grieved for his parents, but in an almost formal, slightly detached way. It somehow made sense that his parents had passed. He was a grown man, in his early forties; it somehow seemed to fit into a basic design of the universe that he should no longer have parents; he mourned their loss, but he could accept it. There was a logic, a natural order to it. But to lose a child! To have a child die before you did defied any sense of progress, any concept of a natural order. It was pure, cruel chaos; it mocked the future. "Children are the *point* of life," Athena had said. And now Melvin had lost the only child he would ever have.

Yet, when he would ask why, the thing that unnerved him most was that there might be a reason, that perhaps Abby's death was retribution for the one mistake, the one slipup he'd had in a lifetime of rigorous propriety. And it, his mistake, his single lapse, had happened in Gay Head, on the Vineyard, just a few years earlier. And now Melvin feared he had been cursed, that he had cursed himself with his one error of judgment and that Tad, that leering, freckled Howdy Doody, had been some sort of emissary of fate, that Tad—from Gay Head, the very town where Melvin had lapsed—was sent to be the agent of Melvin's retribution. But, good Lord, did the price have to be *that* high? Was Melvin's sin so horrid that he had to lose his daughter? *He* hadn't taken a life. Why did Abby's life have to be taken?

Over the next several months, a canyon opened up between Melvin and his wife. Dorothy joined the Organization for a Child-Friendly Society, a nonprofit group, and wound up working even longer hours than her husband. For the better part of nineteen years, the majority of Melvin and Dorothy's conversations had been about Abby. Now, with Abby gone, they had little to talk about. Melvin knew that Dorothy felt guilty, that she must have realized that, had

Melvin made the decision alone, Abby would never have gone on that rafting trip. He knew Dorothy feared that he blamed her for their daughter's death. But he didn't blame her. He wanted to tell his wife that. He never did. Because even to enter into a conversation about blame might reveal the extent to which Melvin blamed himself for the tragedy, might lead to a confession of his one mistake, that single lapse of judgment in what had been an exemplary life. And *that* he could never confess to Dorothy.

A year after the accident, Melvin felt a clammy intimacy with death. Not that he actively wanted to die. It was more that he simply no longer cared whether or not he lived. He could live; he could die; it didn't make a big difference to Melvin. Life and death had become equally (un)appealing options. (*Children are the point of life!* So what now was the point of Melvin's life?) There were nights when Melvin would sit alone in his study and stare at his heirloom on the desk before him, the one thing his father the mailman had bequeathed him, Harry Hutchinson's fondest possession: a .38-caliber Smith & Wesson. He remembered when Harry had taken him into the master bedroom of the old house on Largent Street and, with a ceremonial solemnity, opened the top drawer of the dresser, rummaged through some clothes, and carefully pulled out the gun. Melvin must have been about thirteen, fourteen years old. "I just want to let you know this is here," Harry said, an unmistakable trace of pride in his voice. "In case something ever happens and you need to defend our home." Melvin stared in awe at the big black hunk of metal. "Hold it," Harry said, placing the pistol in his son's hand, "feel its weight." Melvin was astounded by how heavy it was. He quickly grasped it with two hands to keep from dropping it. "I've never had to use it," Harry said judiciously, "but if the time ever comes, I'll be ready. And I want you to be ready, too, son." Melvin could still not get over the sheer heft of the thing. How did Alan Ladd and Humphrey Bogart and John Wayne handle these heavy hunks of metal with such ease? "And remember," Harry said sagely, "don't *pull* the trigger. Squeeze it."

Now, nearly forty years later, Melvin Hutchinson, by any measure a success in life, sat in his study on Central Park West—he was a wealthy man, a successful black role model—and considered how and when he would turn this ancient pistol on himself. Not that he *wanted* to do it. But he could sit alone in his study, clutching a tumbler of warm, thick Jack Daniel's, and think, reasonably, with his lawyer's mind—he was a great, a massively successful lawyer, one of the top lawyers in the whole country, maybe even in the whole world; who could doubt it?—what would be the best method for blowing out his brains. Would he hold the gun to his temple? Or put the barrel of the pistol in his mouth? Would he, if he was to choose this option, kill himself in his study, leaving his body—with perhaps half a head—for Dorothy to find? No, he didn't want to do that to Dorothy. So where—were he to do it, and he certainly wasn't thinking he *would* do it; he was just considering, just considering it—would he kill himself?

But no, he would think, he couldn't kill himself. Black folks don't commit suicide. We die of drug overdoses; we kill each other in fits of violence; we gradually self-destruct from booze and dope. But single acts of suicide, deliberate, dramatic one-shot acts of self-extermination: That's rare for us. That's what white folks do. Statistics bore it out. Black folks had too much to worry about, were too accustomed to, conditioned by, endurance to kill themselves. Though, Melvin remembered, his sister, Alma, had tried it, hadn't she, a lame, halfhearted attempt? But hadn't he always looked down on her for it? Not so much because it was weak but because it . . . well, it just wasn't what black folks were supposed to do. Swallow a bottle of sleeping pills, or antidepressants, or whatever the hell it was —that just wasn't black. Now, if she'd accidentally shot up too much junk . . . well, you could say that was foolish, crazy, self-destructive, but it wasn't like saying, Oh, I just can't take it anymore. I'll end it all. Good-bye, cruel world! So how could Melvin even contemplate, however reasonably, however practically, doing such a thing? He could never do it, Melvin told himself, could never actually pick up his daddy's gun and blow out his brains. But he couldn't stop thinking about it.

>   >   >

It was during one of his evening reveries in his study, sipping Uncle Jack and staring at Harry's .38, that Melvin received a call from Art

Walker telling him he was about to be appointed to a federal district judgeship. So far as Melvin could tell, this was something his friends in high places had wangled for him. He was more flabbergasted than excited by the honor. These judgeships usually went to people with long records as prosecutors or public servants. It had been more than twenty years since Melvin had worked in the U.S. Attorney's Office. (He still bristled over memories of how some of his friends from Rutgers, Columbia, and the NAACP gave him shit for wanting to be a prosecutor; in those days, it was far more trendy to be a public defender. As much as Melvin felt for those poor and innocent people who couldn't afford legal counsel, he knew he could never bring himself to defend someone who might actually be guilty, and, given Melvin's general attitude toward people, he felt that the majority of those charged with crimes probably *were* guilty. As far as Melvin was concerned, his decision to work in the U.S. Attorney's Office had nothing to do with politics. Melvin simply had the *personality* of a prosecutor.) He expected there to be some controversy over his selection, but none ever arose. Melvin's credentials, as they stood, were simply too impressive to quibble over.

Melvin loved his new job. He loved the splendor of a jurist's trappings: the flowing black robe; the bench, that exalted perch high above everyone else in the courtroom; the gavel—ah, that gavel!— that he relished slamming down with crisp authority. He loved deciding, discriminating, carving up a lousy lawyer's argument, ordering counsel to approach the bench, sustaining or overruling objections, and, most delicious of all, sentencing. Was there any greater pleasure than sentencing a murderer or a drug dealer—those who would steal other people's lives or who would work to distribute the sort of substances that had poisoned his daughter's body—to twenty-five years, life in prison, or death? To deal death to those who would kill —surely this was good and essential work Melvin did.

Melvin held an image of himself in his mind's eye. In this vision, he wore his judge's black robe and carried in his hands the sword of justice, an immense and heavy Excalibur-like weapon that he wielded with consummate precision, with conviction, marching forward through some vast white space, slashing away at killers, drug dealers, the dregs of humanity, cutting them down, slicing them in half with the sword of justice. Sometimes, in Melvin's vision, his foes were faceless, almost shapeless, virtually invisible; other times, they were actual defendants he'd seen in court, some white, some black, some Hispanic, some Asian, but all of them deserving of death. Forward he marched, wielding the sword of justice, slashing, slicing, hacking, dealing death with grim conviction, watching his foes fall beneath him, vanquished, deleted. By the sword of justice.

Becoming attorney general meant giving up the robes, the bench, the gavel. But still Melvin carried the sword. He brandished the sword of justice before all the American people. Once in office, Melvin realized he had become someone else. It hadn't happened overnight. It had begun with Abby's death. He withdrew from his friends, stopped attending the Black Partners Lunches, stopped socializing—except for a handful of one-on-one meetings with Art Walker—altogether, even with the nucleus. He stopped caring about, virtually stopped doing, the work he had once enjoyed at the firm that now bore his name. He spent evenings alone in his study, contemplating putting a bullet in his brain. This, Melvin realized in retrospect, was the first phase of his metamorphosis. Phase two began when he was appointed to the bench and took grasp of the sword of justice. The third phase commenced with his nomination to head the Justice Department. As attorney general, Melvin had become larger than the office, the title itself. He didn't give a damn about the day-to-day bureaucratic shit. Henry Beedle handled that. Beedle shoved papers, reports, memos, directives across Melvin's desk, some of which the attorney general read, most of which he signed, all of which he could feign a knowledge of if necessary. But it was rarely necessary. Melvin knew he was no mere cabinet member, no run-of-the-mill token Negro. He had become, as attorney general, the embodiment of law and order in the United States of America. He brandished the sword of justice, waved it about, twirled it above his head, and people, especially his own people, worshiped him for it. He was an orator, really. That had become his true vocation. Someone who inspired with words, with the timbre of his voice, the power of his rhetoric. Like a Douglass. Or a King. But as much as Douglass and King had been concerned with justice, they were, out of necessity, more concerned with freedom. Much as Hutchinson was concerned with freedom, he was more obsessed with justice. And he was an orator with real clout, genuine influence in the most elite circles in America. Melvin, in this third phase of his transformation, had found, much to his surprise, that he liked being a politician. He loved wading into a crowd of people, pressing the flesh, kissing babies, making irrelevant small talk with strangers. He, an essentially dour man who had always kept to himself, had the *touch,* that mysterious gift for the political game.

Now, today, on Melvin Hutchinson Day in Norris, New Jersey, he stood on the edge of history. He might very well become vice president, second in command of the greatest power on earth. And if he could do *that,* then what was to stop him from ascending to the very pinnacle? Melvin Hutchinson had the whole package: the civil rights experience, the corporate expertise, the respect accorded all judges in a society of laws, the knack for politics, the peculiar charm that all successful public figures needed. Sooner or later, Melvin had always believed, a black man would become President. But he'd always assumed it would be later rather than sooner. Now, here he was, poised near the vice presidency. And who—what African-American who had come before him, what black person in the entire history of this misbegotten nation—was more suited to the task than he? None, of course. But Melvin Hutchinson knew that no matter where life took him, no matter how turbulent the next phase of his metamorphosis might become, he would, from now on, for the rest of his life, be one thing above all: a man with a sword.

➤   ➤   ➤

Standing in the pulpit at the First Baptist Church, Melvin Hutchinson stared out at the congregation, all those proper, civic-minded ladies dressed in their Sunday best on this Friday morning, and realized that most of them were probably not as old as he'd first assumed, or, perhaps more accurately, realized that *he* was as old as many of them, that these were, for the most part, his contemporaries, people very much like himself, like Dorothy, like the members of the nucleus, and as he paused in the midst of the speech he knew by heart, his mouth feeling thick with gooey saliva from this morning's bourbon, he felt a wave of melancholy pass over him, recognizing that these folks who had come to hear him speak today—Melvin Hutchinson Day—were his true people, that they loved him, and he loved them more than he could say.

"Sometimes," Melvin said, his voice dropping to an intimate whisper, "I get tired. I really do. I go to these conferences on crime and I meet and consult with doctors and professors and sociologists, with lawyers and politicians, with preachers and community activists and plain old ordinary black folk. With people like us. And we struggle, we really do, to make sense of what's happening in our community. How can we deal with the crime and the violence and the drug abuse? With the teen pregnancy and the welfare dependency, with the hopelessness that infects so many of our young people? And, you know, I get tired." Melvin's voice began to rise, to take on an angry power. "I get tired of the conversations that go around and around in circles. I get tired of all the platitudes, the empty rhetoric that leads to nothing. I get tired of people like us, the people, good, strong, decent African-Americans, who pay the bills and play by the rules, having to take the rap, to bear the burden for that relatively small part of our community that just can't seem to get its act together."

"Amen," Melvin heard somebody say. A ripple of *Amens* spread through the congregation.

"I get tired . . . I get sooooo tired of the bad apples tryin' to spoil the whole barrel. I get tired of this responsibility that has fallen to me, that has fallen to each and every one of us in our community. I just get so *ty-uhd* sometime!"

"Tell it!" somebody yelled.

"Preach, brother," another called out.

"Amen!" many women—and some of the few men present—cried.

"But I have assumed this responsibility," Melvin said. "I have taken on this burden. This is the life I have *chosen*. And I do my best to reach those kids in our community who can be saved. Because I believe in redemption."

"Yes, Lord!"

"I believe in mercy. I believe in saving souls!"

"Speak!"

"But I am a realistic man. I am a clear-eyed man. A man of the law. And I know that not every soul can be saved. That not every young brother or sister can be redeemed. That not every lost youth is deserving of mercy. But those who *can* be saved, I will try to save. That's why I love these drug reeducation centers, where kids can still be rescued before they fall through the cracks. Where kids can make up for an early mistake. Where tender young souls, misguided by poverty and the twin devilments of drugs and crime, can still redeem their lives!"

"Talk about the redemption, brother!"

"Tell it!"

"Amen!"

"But my eyes are open," Melvin said to the blurry congregation. "My vision is clear. And I can see, oh, as much as it pains me, I can *see* that not all our people can be saved. That the cold-blooded killer, the money-grubbin' dealer, the vicious gang-banger is not *worthy* of our mercy, is not *capable* of redemption, is *immune* to rehabilitation."

"Mmmmm-hmmmmm. Mmm-mm-*mmmm!*" the congregation hummed sadly, emphatically.

"They've lost all respect for God's precious gift of life. And only their Maker can judge whether they can be saved. Only when they meet their Maker can the vicious parasites who would destroy our community, America's strong, proud black community, only when they meet their Maker can the killers be offered redemption. It ain't comin' to 'em in this world. Only in the next world. Only when they meet their Maker. So I say, let's help 'em get there!"

"AMEN!"

"I say let's send the killers on their way. Expunge them from our world and hurry 'em on over to the next one. We don't neeeed their kind here!"

"HALLELUJAH!"

"Those who take away precious lives, black people who kill other black people, who poison *our* community, have no place in this world. And I say, Hang 'em high! *Hang 'em high!*"

The congregation erupted in mad applause.

"Hang 'em high!" Melvin yelled exultantly.

And the crowd responded: "Hang 'em high, Hutch!" In seconds it became a chant, powerful, rhythmic, deafeningly loud. "Hang 'em high, Hutch! Hang 'em high, Hutch! Hang 'em high, Hutch!" All these proper black ladies, dressed in their Sunday finery, rose to their feet, pumping their fists in the air, screaming at the tops of their lungs: "Hang 'em high, Hutch! Hang 'em high, Hutch!"

And Melvin stood in the pulpit, thrusting his own fist in the air and calling back to them: "Hang 'em high!" Melvin heard the organ burst into a rousing, stomping gospel tune. He looked to the front pew and saw Henry Beedle and all the white agents and functionaries in his entourage glancing around the church, seeming at once frightened, awed, mystified. Beedle looked up at Melvin in the pulpit and smiled his rusty, feral smile, then gave the attorney general an exuberant thumbs-up sign. Melvin beamed, savoring the noise that washed over him, the cries and the music that felt almost like an embrace, like pure, ecstatic love. "Hang 'em high, Hutch! Hang 'em high, Hutch! Hang 'em high, Hutch! Hang 'em high, Hutch!"

(4)

SITTING ON THE EDGE of the bed he shared with Emma, still groggy and mucus-eyed at 7:30 in the morning, Seth stared at his girlfriend through the open doorway of their bathroom. Emma, her back to Seth, stood before the bathroom mirror, carefully applying eyeliner, wearing a cream-colored slip. Seth marveled at the twinkling of Emma's hair, still wet from her shower: the way the crystalline beads of water clung to the tight little curls of her Afro, glistening. He felt the familiar Emma rush, a peculiar mix of affection and sadness, surge within him. It was a feeling he had rarely experienced in the six months he and Emma had lived in the first-floor apartment of the two-family home Trudy Winkler owned in Blissfield, New York. Just as he was feeling warmed by the poignancy he associated with his lover, Emma, tilting her head slightly, saw him in the bathroom mirror, seeing her, and, still holding her makeup pencil in a steady hand, said, with consummate nonchalance, "So I think I'm pregnant."

Seth's first impulse was to pull Emma back into bed and make love to her. But in the next moment, fear gripped him and the first thing he thought to say was, Oh shit. But he didn't. Trying not to show any emotion in his voice, he asked, "Are you sure?"

"No."

"Have you done, you know, one of those home"—Seth stopped short, nearly stumbling over the word—"pregnancy tests?"

"Nope."

"Are you planning to?"

Finished with her makeup, Emma walked into the bedroom and wriggled into a black-and-white floral-printed dress. "I need to see a gynecologist soon. I haven't had a checkup since we left Vymar."

They were silent for a long moment. Finally, Seth asked, "You want some coffee?"

"I already made a pot. There's some left."

Seth sat motionless at the dining room table, staring vacantly at his untouched cup of coffee and the morning's *New York Times*, still folded up in its bright blue plastic wrapper. Emma walked into the room, dressed in the conventional office clothes that suited her personality so poorly they always seemed to Seth like a sort of costume. "So what would you want me to do?" Emma asked, maintaining a chilly, casual tone.

"What do you mean?"

"If I'm pregnant?"

That word again. Naked beneath his bathrobe, Seth nearly shuddered. "I don't know. That's up to you. *Isn't* it?"

"You mean to say you have no opinion on the subject?"

"Why don't you find out if you are—" Seth said, stopping short again. "And we can fight about it then."

Now Emma was pissed. She pulled on her trench coat with a haughty tug. She walked over to Seth and, leaning down, put her face close to his. "Whatever happens," Emma said in a quiet, even voice, "just don't fucking lie to me."

Emma kissed Seth gently on the forehead, then walked away, her heels clicking smartly on the hardwood floor. Seth continued to stare at his cup of coffee and the folded-up *New York Times*, thinking of nothing. He heard the door of their apartment swing open, then, in the next instant, heard Emma hiss, "Goddamn it!" upon, no doubt, discovering this morning's deposit from Scarlett. The door slammed shut.

Emma usually left for work at least sixty minutes ahead of her boyfriend, and Seth had come to relish that hour of solitude in the mornings. Getting prepared for another day at the office, gathering his energies, Seth often came up with some of his best ideas for the *Mavis!* show during his hour alone in the apartment. But on this particular morning, Seth went about his routine with a zomboid languor. Padding about the apartment in his bedroom slippers, he let his coffee grow cold, couldn't even bring himself to remove the *Times* from its plastic wrapper. Emma's bombshell had sent his thoughts swirling. Seth suddenly longed for a distant past.

>   >   >

He could still remember casual sex, those days when the worst thing you feared was herpes, when condoms were relics of the past, like girdles or sock garters. Seth hadn't carried around birth control. He'd rarely even brought it up on a one-night stand. Women were supposed to be responsible for their own bodies. That was feminism, right? If you were responsible for your own decision when it came to the question of abortion, then you should be responsible when it came to the question of conception. Right? Seth had heard that some women were offended if a guy didn't at least ask about birth control. So one night, with a new lover, he'd asked. The woman had actually seemed miffed. "Of course, I have *protection*," she'd sneered, seeming to mock the archaic word Seth had used, making him feel like Potsie, that dweeb on *Happy Days*, naïve, limp-dicked, and nebishy. After that encounter, Seth had never asked a woman about birth control again.

Back in the early and mid-eighties, Seth had what he termed "erotic friendships" with a number of women. He fell for Piper Laurie types—the Piper Laurie character in *The Hustler* to be exact —women who looked relentlessly straight, almost prim, but who bore a whiff of pathology. The type of women who, like that Piper Laurie character, might go to a bar at eight in the morning for a little pick-me-up; fragile as an eggshell, smart but unfocused, desperately lonely, famished for affection. They were brainy, high-strung women, plain Janes who fucked with a hungry intensity and fantasized about different methods of suicide. If you escaped from a Piper Laurie soon enough—that is, stopped sleeping with her before she began to think you had a "serious relationship"—that was an erotic friendship. That was casual sex. You didn't have to talk about it, didn't have to worry about it. Those days were gone, gone forever.

<   78   >

By looks alone, Emma Person was precisely the sort of woman who had always ignored Seth. She was anything but plain. Emma was, to Seth's eyes, stunningly beautiful. She reminded him of the black actress on *Room 222*, the smart, straightforward student with the "natural" hairstyle. Emma wore her hair in a retro 'fro and was gorgeously almond-toned. The type of girl who would never even say hi to Seth. Like those beautiful black girls who had blown right past him in the corridors of Blissfield High as he tried to make eye contact, condemning him to invisibility with their total lack of acknowledgment. He hadn't even been Potsie to them. He hadn't even been a blip on their radar screens. Promenading down the corridors with their haughty gaits. God, how he loved them, yearned for them. They were just cool as shit.

Yet, Emma was, spiritually, Seth's kind of gal. She was, he thought on the night they first met, the twofer of his dreams: a black Piper Laurie.

Seth's heroes had always been black. As a teenager in Blissfield, he had covered the walls of his bedroom with a collage of posters, publicity stills, and photos clipped from magazines of his racially homogenous idols: Muhammad Ali, Kareem Abdul-Jabbar, Donna Summer, Pam Grier, Lynn Swann, Martin Luther King, Jr., Richard Roundtree, Reggie Jackson, Walt Frazier, Angela Davis, John Coltrane, Stevie Wonder, Tamara Dobson, Malcolm X, Billie Holiday, Wilma Rudolph, Arthur Ashe, Miles Davis, Cicely Tyson, O. J. Simpson. . . .

Seth wished back then that he had more black friends, or, really, *any* black friends. While he was acquainted with a handful of the handful of African-American students at Blissfield High, those kids preferred to keep to themselves. Some of Seth's white friends teased him for his Afrocentricity, calling him a "Milano cookie," the inverse of an Oreo, white on the outside, black on the inside. Though Seth would laugh agreeably when his friends poked fun at him, he found their criticism ridiculous. Why would anyone think that he somehow "wanted to be" black? It always struck Seth as a bizarre concept, perhaps because of its total impossibility. Wanting to be black, to Seth, was like wanting to be a pigeon or a tablecloth. He didn't envy black people. He was just open-minded, like his parents. Lester and

Trudy Winkler had never tired of reminiscing about the summer of 1963, when they and baby Seth had attended the March on Washington, thrilled to be present at what they knew was an historic moment, listening, misty-eyed, as Dr. King delivered his most famous address. "It's up to us—white people—to make Dr. King's dream a reality," Lester would tell Seth.

Yet, many years later, after Lester Winkler had died, Seth had been reluctant to tell his mother about a woman he loved deeply. After five months together, Emma was about to move in with Seth and he had still not mentioned his lover to Trudy. Though he'd never heard his mother make an even remotely antiblack comment, Seth was worried. Not knowing what to say, he sent his mother a picture instead.

"You only like her because she's the blackest thing in Vymar!" Trudy screamed over the phone the day she received the photo of Seth and Emma. "You've always been obsessed with black people! It's unhealthy!"

"We're in love, Mom. Emma's moving in with me tomorrow."

"This is unacceptable! You have to find somebody else!"

"Sorry, Mom, but—"

"She will ruin your life! Don't you see you're just a *symbol* to her! That's how black people think!"

Though disturbed by his mother's reaction, Seth had to laugh. He realized that Trudy had never met anyone quite like Emma. As far as Seth could tell, Emma didn't even *know* she was black.

Or maybe it was just that Emma's race mattered less to Emma than it did to other people. Early in their relationship, Seth and Emma had attended a play written by a black senior at Vymar. In one scene, three prepped-out white girls sat in a dorm room, giggling as they discussed who their favorite Beatles were. A black student, dressed in colorful Afrocentric garb, walked onstage. "Who's *your* favorite Beatle?" one of the white girls asked.

"I don't *have* a favorite Beatle," the black girl said in a voice thick with contempt. As every other black student in the audience burst into laughter and applause, Emma groaned and shook her head.

"Oh my God!" Emma wailed in mock agony as she and Seth

walked home after the show. "I *do* have a favorite Beatle! I must not *really* be black!"

"That bugged you, huh?" Seth asked.

"It's just so ridiculous. I can't like Schubert, or Virginia Woolf, or Woody Allen movies, and now I can't like the goddamned Beatles and possibly be black at the same time."

"I don't know. I think the whole play was trying to be, you know, an expression of black pride."

"Why should I be either proud *or* ashamed of being black? It's not an accomplishment—or an embarrassment. It's nothing I've ever *done*. It's *just* my race."

➤　　➤　　➤

A child, a child. A *child.* His child. *Their* child. As Seth stood in the shower, jets of hot water splashing against his chest, he tried to imagine the reality of having a child with Emma. What, precisely, would the child be? Would the child consider itself half Jewish and half black? What would you call such a child in this day and age? *Mulatto* didn't seem quite right. *Biracial:* that was the word. But was it really accurate? Certainly, every biracial child Seth had ever seen *looked* black. And all the biracial people Seth had ever met seemed to consider themselves black—certainly more black than white. Because of the way they looked. So if Emma did indeed have a baby, Seth would be the white father of a black child. Though his genes would make up half the child, Emma's genes would make the child more hers than his. It didn't seem fair.

Stepping out of the shower, Seth remembered a card they had received the previous Christmas from a college friend of Emma's, Naima, and her husband, John. The card featured a photo of the little family: John, his skin the whitish pink of a slab of cold, rare turkey; Naima, darker even than Emma; and their parchment-toned baby boy. Under the photo, Naima wrote, "Have faith in your love no matter what anyone might say or do." Good God! thought Seth. She made it all sound so dangerous. Just what exactly might "anyone" say or do? Do! Staring at the family portrait, Seth felt as if he had received a correspondence from the future. There he was someday, battling ignorance, intolerance, and injustice every minute of his life, simply by virtue of the woman he had married, the child they were parenting. Everything Naima told Emma about life in an interracial marriage made the situation sound like some sort of disease or addiction that required a recovery program or support group. Naima and John belonged to an interracial couples group; most of their friends were interracial couples. Wouldn't anyone else, Seth wondered, tolerate their company? He admired Naima and John for their brave affirmation of love before a hostile world. But it was in the same way he admired people who joined the Peace Corps or became rabbis. Noble, sure, but could *he* ever do it? Wouldn't it just be *easier* to marry a white (which, inevitably, meant a Jewish) woman? Did he really want to be in the sort of marriage that might be a topic on the *Mavis!* show?

Actually, Mavis Temple had rejected, at least twice in the six months Seth had worked on the show, suggestions from producers for a segment on interracial marriages. "I do not wish, in any way, to be seen as advocating such a thing," Mavis had said with a frosty disdain the last time the subject came up in a meeting. Seth, fortunately, had not made the suggestion. And, though he worked more closely with Mavis all the time, he had never told her that the woman he lived with was black. In fact, his life outside the office almost never came up. Mavis didn't give a shit. But Seth certainly did not want Mavis to disapprove of his relationship. The thought made him laugh out loud as he toweled himself dry: Here he was, a white guy, living with a black woman but having to conceal that fact from his boss, a black woman. Postmodern times.

Seth was having a bad hair day. Most mornings, he manipulated his shoulder-length mane into the hip 'do of the moment, moussing his hair into a large bun atop his head, holding the bun in place with two ornately painted plastic chopsticks. Some days, like this morning, the process of getting the topknot just right could take as long as a quarter hour. But it was worth it to Seth. Adhering to the latest trend in androgynous multiculturalism, he often complemented his hairstyle by wearing a green plaid kilt. Here was the fashion statement as political statement. Seth got a kick out of riding the 8:49

< 82 >

from Blissfield station into Manhattan, surrounded by drab white men in their drab dark suits while he sported his bun and kilt. He liked being part of the workaday professional crowd, yet *apart* from it. Sure, he might, now that he'd received his promotion to associate producer on the *Mavis!* show, earn a lawyerly or bankerish salary, but he was still a rebel.

As he slipped into his kilt, Seth's thoughts turned to the painted cherub. He had recalled the mysterious young woman often in the weeks since he'd seen her in the Seventy-Second Street subway station. He'd been waiting for the downtown number 1 train. He couldn't even remember where he was going that night or why Emma wasn't with him. He only remembered the girl, the way she stared unabashedly at him, completely without subtlety. He had just been minding his own business, standing idly on the subway plat-form, leaning against a pillar and watching, absentmindedly, a tiny gray skeletal mouse racing in and out of the wooden slats on the subway track, desperately searching, Seth assumed, for something to eat, a scrap of discarded bagel maybe, or a cigarette butt. He was becoming almost preoccupied with musings about what this starving subterranean rodent was so maniacally darting about for when, sud-denly, he had the feeling that someone was staring at him, looked up, and saw her.

She couldn't have possibly been older than fifteen; heavily, almost clumsily, made up, her tight little mouth a gaudy slash of red, bisect-ing her Kabuki white mask of a face like a scar. She was all dolled up, going down to the Village, for a party maybe, struggling to look, if not of legal drinking age, at least like a college student. And she was checking Seth out. Perhaps she was not old enough, experienced enough yet to know how to conceal her lust. Seth thought at first that he must have been imagining it, because it was so baldly apparent. She was brazenly checking him out. Seth wondered if any woman had ever looked at him with such open carnality in her gaze. Probably it had never happened before, because when he was fifteen, the girls his age weren't checking *him* out; they were lasciviously eyeing guys in their twenties and thirties, just as this girl—he knew he should think "young woman," but that phrase barely suited this painted cherub—was currently appraising him. By the time Seth had started engaging in mating rituals, women were far more discreet. Seth tried not to stare back at the girl, letting his gaze drift down again to the subway tracks, looking for that filthy, darting little bone of a mouse, pretending he didn't know he was being watched. He knew he could probably walk right up to the painted cherub, initiate a conversation, and, at the very least, exchange phone numbers. But before he could take the scenario any further in his mind, Seth was overwhelmed by a sudden squeamishness. He glanced back at the girl, who was still staring brazenly at him, and knew he could never be with her—because he could no longer look upon such a girl as someone he might have sex with, only as someone who could be, almost, practically . . . his daughter! And the erection that was just arising beneath his kilt deflated like a rubber balloon. This was when Seth knew he was getting old.

No way he was going to make the 8:49 at this point. But, finally ready to leave the house, Seth grabbed the *New York Times* from the dining room table and removed the newspaper from its wrapper, figuring he'd skim it on the train. If he was lucky, he could catch the 9:04; that way, he could still get to the office before Mavis showed up and—

Seth's attention was seized by the front page headline: VICE-PRESIDENT EWELL COMATOSE AFTER STROKE, CONDITION CRITICAL; MCCRACKEN DECLINES TO NAME REPLACEMENT.

Below the headline was a large photograph—it looked as if it had been taken on the roof of a building—of white-haired Vin Ewell on a stretcher, oxygen mask strapped around his nose and mouth, being lifted into a helicopter. But even more compelling to Seth was the grave figure standing in the background—that increasingly familiar, scowling visage—peering out of the night sky: Uncle Melvin.

➣   ➣   ➣

Emma liked her job as a receptionist at the Miasma showroom because there was hardly ever any work to do. The phones rang sporadically, customers strolled in to stare dreamily at the sports cars they coveted, but an actual purchase, in the three months Emma had worked there, was rare. She spent much of her day reading books and magazines while sitting behind an enormous desk in front of an enormous window that looked out on Park Avenue. Her first day of work at the Miasma showroom, Emma had felt painfully self-conscious sitting in that window, exposed to the gaze of any passerby, as if she were as much a commodity to be gawked at as the shiny Japanese status mobiles. The cars, the girl. See the cars; see the girl.

"We like the Avelston Agency best," Tommy Coughlin, a thirty-five-year-old salesman at the showroom, told Emma on her first day. "They always send us beautiful temps. They understand the nature of the job. The visuals."

Emma eyed Tommy warily. "What do you mean?"

"It's a compliment," Tommy said quickly, flashing what Emma could tell he considered a winning grin, "not harassment."

By the time Emma started working at the showroom, the sales staff had been downsized from six to three. Tommy and the two other salesmen, Marv and Bob, were usually as idle as Emma, spending their long, empty days sitting at their desks toward the back of the showroom, reading the newspapers, talking on the phone. Most days, around eleven, Tommy, a red-haired, freckle-faced Irish Catholic, would saunter over to the front desk and, keeping half his attention focused on the street, always looking for the potential buyer who might drift into the showroom if he happened to make eye contact with a salesman half-sitting, half-leaning on the edge of the desk in the big picture window, flirt with the temp.

"Hard fucking times," Tommy Coughlin said on this dead Friday morning. "I can't even remember when my last commission was."

"Three weeks ago," Emma said.

"Was it? Wow. Well, maybe things will pick up. Ya gotta believe, right? I figure in another year, Troy will have the economy back on track."

"You think so?"

"He's a good man. He knows what he's doing. People expect the President of the United States to solve all their problems overnight. But these things take time. Why are you always so hard on the guy?"

"I told you, Tommy, I'm apolitical."

"Yeah, sure. Well, at least you won't have Vin Ewell to kick around anymore."

"Why's that?"

"Haven't you heard?" Tommy asked. Emma shook her head. Tommy walked back to his desk and returned with a copy of the *Daily News.* The front-page photo was a tight shot of Vin Ewell on a stretcher, an oxygen mask obscuring much of his face. Beside the picture was a large, blocky headline: TROY: "I'M PRAYING FOR HIM."

"Massive stroke," Tommy explained. "He's in critical condition."

"Oh well," Emma said, unfazed.

"He's a goner. Good as dead. Which leads to an interesting question. Who does Troy pick as his new vice president? Who do you think he should pick?"

"I told you, Tommy—"

"Yeah, you're apolitical, I know, I know. You know who I think he should pick? You'll like my choice. Melvin Hutchinson."

"Really?" Emma said, trying not to reveal anything other than mild curiosity in her voice. Emma had never been particularly fond of her illustrious uncle and she made it a point not to tell people that she was related to the attorney general.

"It's about time a black man was vice president. And Hutch is cool. He's serious; he's competent. He's like you. He doesn't wear his race on his sleeve."

"No, it's written all over his face."

"You know what I mean. He's not, like, an ideologue."

"And what if he became President?"

"I could live with that. But, hey, let's check him out as veep first."

"Take him for a test-drive?"

"So to speak."

The phone beeped and Emma answered it. "Miasma showroom."

"Hi, honey," Seth said.

"Oh, hi." Emma looked up at Tommy. He gave her a wink, then sauntered to the back of the showroom. "What's goin' on?"

"Did you hear about Vin Ewell?"

"Oh yes."

"Everybody's saying your uncle might replace him. Isn't that incredible?"

"Credibility is a constantly expanding field."

"So, I know I've asked you before, but is there any way you could hook me up with him? Mavis would love to have him on the show."

"I haven't seen him in years, Seth. Not since Abby died. I just don't know him all that well. And I've told you, he and Mom have some strange relationship, I just—"

"Okay. Okay. Don't worry about it, sweetie. So what are your plans for tonight?"

"After I leave here, I'm going to the darkroom for three hours, and then I'm going up to Mom's place. Her arthritis is bothering her and she needs me to help her fill out some kind of medical forms."

"That's good. I'll be working late tonight, so I can call a car to take me home. I'll stop at Alma's and pick you up on the way. How's that sound?"

"Sounds good."

"Are you mad at me?"

"No," Emma lied.

"I'm sorry about the way I reacted this morning. I just wasn't expecting that sort of news."

"Yeah, well, we don't know anything for sure yet. I think you're right. We shouldn't talk about it until we know more."

"Is that what you want? To not discuss it?"

"That's what I want."

"Well, I want what you want. I really love you, Emmy. I really do."

"Yeah, me, too. I should probably go. You wanna come by my mom's about eleven tonight?"

"Sure. I'll see you then, sweetie."

"Bye-bye."

"Peace."

Though she had no irrefutable proof that she was pregnant, Emma felt certain that she was and, without scrutinizing the diametric formula that was taking shape in her mind or considering other possibilities, she believed that her pregnancy presented her with only two options, each bearing a specific and inevitable result: She would either continue the pregnancy and marry Seth or she would abort the fetus and her relationship with Seth would be over. Emma found both possibilities almost impossible to imagine. After so many years of cohabitation, she could not really envision a life without Seth. But it was even harder for her to foresee a baby, a child, some odd little Emma-Seth hybrid who would rule the lives of its creators, a tiny bundle of fate, conceived in carelessness but requiring extraordinary care for years to come. Emma grew angry with herself, thinking that she had allowed this to happen, that, in order to force a resolution with Seth, she had let herself get pregnant, accidentally on purpose. Could she now bring into the world someone she might always regard, or resent, as a mistake?

"Help! They're after me!" The man was a blur of charcoal gray as he burst through the doors of the Miasma showroom, racing blindly past Emma's desk toward the back of the showroom, where he collided with Tommy Coughlin, knocking the salesman to the floor, then tumbling himself. "They're after me!" the plump, flushed Yuppie screamed again. "You gotta help me!" The terrified man squirmed and flailed about on the light gray carpet of the showroom, struggling to stand up, then bumbling and falling again as Tommy tried to get a grip on him. "Help! They're tryin' to get me!"

Marv and Bob grabbed the hysterical man and pulled him off Tommy. "Take it easy, fella," Marv said. "You're safe now."

"Don't let 'em in! They're after me!"

Emma stepped outside, glanced up and down Park Avenue, and saw only twenty or so disparate pedestrians, nondescript white professionals, each assiduously minding her or his own business, and the usual stream of passing traffic. Walking back into the showroom, she saw the three salesmen huddled around Marv's desk. The surprise visitor sat slumped in Marv's chair, swiveled all the way around, his back to Emma. Tommy looked up at Emma, then pointed to the water fountain. Wondering fleetingly why Tommy couldn't tear himself away to fetch the water, Emma went to the fountain and filled one of the tiny paper cups from the plastic dispenser.

"I-I-I-I-I'm so sorry," the stranger said, struggling to catch his breath. "They were closing in on me."

"I've heard about this sort of thing before," Marv said sagely.

"A gang of black kids, out on the street. I was just walking along and—"

< 88 >

"A group of them suddenly had you circled, like they'd come from different directions," Marv said.

"Y-y-y-y-yes."

"This thing is catching on. I read about it in the *Post* the other day. Five or six thugs surround you, one of them grabs you, another takes your wallet, then the whole bunch of them take off, scatter in different directions. So nobody knows who to chase."

"They were after me."

"Did they grab you? Did they get anything?"

"No, I saw what was happening and ran in here."

"Jeez," Bob said, shaking his head. "Right out on Park Avenue. Animals."

"Excuse me," Emma said, squeezing between Marv and Bob with the cup of water.

"Gaaaaah!" the Yuppie screamed when he saw her, raising his arms to cover his head.

"Water?" Emma asked as Tommy, Marv, and Bob stifled snickers.

"Oh, um, I'm sorry, miss," the man said, embarrassed. He gulped down the water. "Thank you, thank you, miss, thank you very much."

Emma returned to her desk as the men muttered about how the city became more dangerous all the time. Emma paid them no mind. She pulled a scrap of notepaper from her purse. She had scribbled the name and number of a gynecologist recommended by Naima. Maybe I'm not even pregnant, Emma thought. I haven't thrown up; maybe that's a good sign.

But even when she felt most certain that she was indeed pregnant, Emma could not accept the idea that whatever was inside her body was a person, a real human being. She remembered walking past the Planned Parenthood office in Vymar years earlier. A group of thirty or more activists marched in a circle, chanting, "We don't care if women die; right to life is still alive!" And Emma had wondered: If she was pregnant, could she bring herself to fight through a mob of sputtering, crimson-faced Christians shaking signs and waving jars of formaldehyde-soaked fetuses in her face just so she could have some squiggle of protohumanity vacuumed out of her? She knew she could not.

Today, there was a law on the books preventing protesters from blocking the entrances of abortion clinics. But the right-to-lifers had simply stepped up their terrorist tactics. In the past year, two clinics in Manhattan had been blown up. Who knew where a third bomb might be planted? Emma's mind was made up. If abort she must, she would do it pharmaceutically. Illegally.

>   >   >

"I'm a goddamned national institution," Mavis Temple liked to say, and though she used the word in its abstract sense, Seth had thought, ever since he met Mavis in person, that—with her epic girth and her stiff, unmoving, meticulously sculpted, nearly shoulder-width hairdo —there was something about the talk-show personality that was edificelike. Though sometimes, when Mavis came gliding down the producers' corridor, the flamboyant capes and oversized scarves and kente-patterned robes she wore to conceal her corpulence flowing, billowing, in her trail, Seth thought of his boss as a ship of state pulling majestically into harbor. Mavis Temple was a national institution, she would tell you, because she was entirely herself; infinitely more herself than most other people—especially those 50 million or so who watched her on television every afternoon—would ever be *them*selves. So it was difficult for Seth to see this institution as being really human. Not that he ever saw her as being subhuman or superhuman. As one of the most famous people on the planet, Mavis was somehow metahuman, less a person than a transcendentally fabulous personage.

Mavis was a temple of self-esteem. Seth could see, in his first face-to-face encounter with Mavis, that—unlike so many of the celebrities he had interviewed over the years—she thoroughly loved herself. Her manner, at once regal and bawdy, bespoke indulgence. Mavis seemed to indulge herself *with* herself, wallowing in her ineluctable Mavisness, indulging you with it in the same way that she indulged—when she was not prosecuting—the guests and audiences on her show. Sitting on the other side of Mavis's gleaming black-topped desk, scrutinizing his hostess, Seth was struck by the size of Mavis's head; that, in addition to having the biggest hair in show business—a swirling extravaganza of colliding shiny black ocean

<   90   >

waves and spiraling offshoots of slick ebony stalagmites frozen in space—Mavis's head itself, her face, was huge. It was a trait he'd noticed in many of the most successful TV celebrities—anchormen, game-show hosts, sitcom regulars. They all had these gigantic heads. All the better, Seth assumed, to fill the frame of your TV set, to dominate the medium.

Seth had been unusually nervous—clammy-palmed and cotton-mouthed—during his first meeting with Mavis. It was not merely Mavis's radiant presence that unsettled him. It was the fact that he was not sitting in Mavis Temple's office to interview her. *She* was interviewing *him*. Mavis had been impressed by an article Seth had published on the Opinion page of *American Century* magazine, an indignant screed condemning the nihilism of young black male rap stars. " 'Question authority' was the mantra of a more innocent time," Seth wrote. "Today's macho poseurs wish not to question but to obliterate all authority, moral or political, and to replace it with an oligarchy of rhymin', dissin' thugs—a fascism all their own, a dead-end street of nihilism and despair. They are the voice of yet another lost generation of African-American youth."

On the morning *American Century* hit the newsstands, Seth, sitting at his kitchen table in Vymar, brooding over his first cup of coffee, received a call from Alton Lewis, Mavis's swishy factotum, requesting that he fly to New York early the next day. For five seconds, the fantasy exploded in Seth's mind, the vision of himself sitting on that glittery stage, expounding his important views on the most popular talk show in the country—50 million viewers hearing his name, seeing his face! Then Alton said, to Seth's disappointment and dismay, that Mavis was bringing him in for a *job* interview. Mavis liked to do that sort of thing, Seth would learn, contacting a print journalist whose work she had noticed, summoning you to New York to check you out, see if you were her kind of person, then sending you away again, maybe never to call, or maybe to call in a year or two of she needed to bulk up her stable of producers and had decided in your interview with her that, if you were worth buying, you could be bought.

While Seth had often dreamed of being *on* television, he had never even considered working *in* television. But sitting across that enormous desk from Mavis Temple, Seth had found himself fervently wishing that the great lady would hire him.

"It says on your résumé here that you spent one year at the University of Michigan Law School," Mavis said. "Only one year. What happened?"

"I dropped out to follow my bliss."

"Say what?" Mavis said, scrunching up her face, seeming to josh Seth in a way that was at once avuncular and unmistakably hostile.

"Writing," Seth lied. "I wanted to move back east and establish myself as a freelance journalist. New York was too expensive. So was Boston. But I had friends in Vymar, Mass., so I moved there."

Seth was too embarrassed to tell Mavis the truth: that, after a year of law school, the lifelong urge to express himself, to get attention, to be seen, known, to become famous for anything, but just to be famous, to have people know his name, his face, had become so overpowering that he felt he had to find an outlet for it, a way to become famous for something—anything!—or he might die from longing. Just as Seth reached the point of desperation, his old friend Adam Landau from Blissfield High called to say that he was putting a significant fraction of his trust fund into a comedy club in Vymar. Knowing that Seth was bored with law school and that he had recently inherited a bundle from his father, Adam inquired if his buddy would like to put up 20 percent of the capital on this venture. Seth said he would, but on one condition: that he be allowed to perform two shows, one night per week, at the Laugher Curve. Adam, in need of Seth's investment, agreed (with the stipulation that the night be Tuesday).

Seth didn't tell Mavis how he'd packed his bags and driven out of Ann Arbor, speeding east to Vymar, singing triumphantly to himself the lyrics of an old Billy Joel song:

> Got a call from an old friend,
> We used to be real close,
> Said he couldn't go on the American way.
> Closed his shop, sold the house,
> Bought a ticket to the West Coast,
> Now he gives them a stand-up routine
> In L.Aaaaaaaaay . . .

Well, Seth was heading to the East Coast, and Vymar was no LA. But he sang the lyrics with passion and joy. Goddamn it, he was going to follow his bliss! He was going to live his life *his* way. He wasn't going to end up like Lester, who, three years earlier, had dropped dead at his desk, facedown in a bowl of soggy oat bran, which he ate—like clockwork, at 7:45 each morning, exactly fifteen minutes after he'd arrive at his law office—for his health.

Seth had never worked as a stand-up comic before, had never, in fact, performed onstage at all, but people had always told him he was naturally funny, and stand-up comedy seemed one of the fastest ways to become famous. Seth specialized in what he called "found humor," poking fun at those little quirks in everyday life that most people didn't notice but everyone would recognize. His onstage de-meanor—a fashionable persona at the time—was one of extreme agitation bordering on rage. Seth would shout out his punch lines, not merely observing life's little irritations, but reacting to them with sputtering indignation. One of Seth's favorite bits, which he practiced tirelessly before the mirror: "Ever notice the language we use to discuss relationships? I'm tellin' ya, it's all about MONEY! Think about it, folks. In a relationship, to be NEEDY is the worst possible thing. NEEDY—like a PANHANDLER! Undesirable. We talk about relationships being WORTH the effort, the VALUE we place on the relationship, about GETTING SOMETHING BACK, like a return on investment! Now, ya hear couples calling each other PARTNERS! Like they're in business together. Hey, I guess that's just the BOTTOM LINE!"

Seth didn't tell Mavis, would never tell her, about the excruciating humiliation of standing alone on a platform just a few feet away from an audience that hated you, about the singular hell of seeing these few faces—the ten or twelve or so people who would show up at the Laugher Curve on the nights he performed—contorted in scorn. He did not discuss the self-loathing he would feel rising up in him like a surge of vomit as audience members ignored him and talked loudly among themselves or got up and walked out of the club as he strug-gled to hold their interest or think of something cutting to say. He couldn't bring himself to tell Mavis how he felt like weeping, how he had to flee from the stage once the booing and hissing started.

After six weeks, a total of twelve performances, Seth couldn't take the abuse any longer and ended his stand-up career. While Seth had already blown a large portion of his inheritance on that one aborted year of law school and Adam's stupid comedy club, he still had enough left to live on. He started waiting tables at Vymar's Café Chier—just to have *something* to do—and pondered what he could do to obtain that elusive thing he desired, that measure of notoriety. Even if it wasn't on a huge scale—he was beginning to lower his expectations—he needed to have his name, his face, known.

He decided to become a journalist. Adam Landau, relieved to get his friend offstage, hooked Seth up with the editor of a small alternative weekly newspaper in Boston. The editor was always on the lookout for people who could produce readable prose for minimal pay. Soon after he started seeing Emma, Seth began publishing record reviews, then profiles of Boston's hipper performers. After the *Downtown Clarion,* based in New York's East Village, reprinted one of Seth's rock profiles, alternative magazines and newspapers around the country started giving him regular assignments. He submitted his rap piece to *American Century* on a lark. If he had known it would lead to a meeting with Mavis Temple, he'd have written it years earlier.

"You know, I've never worked in television before," Seth said as he watched Mavis flip through his stack of clips.

"Television's easy," Mavis said dismissively. "I can teach you television in two days. Two days max. What I'm interested in is what's in your head."

"Well, I gotta say, I'm a big fan of your show."

"Yeah? And what kind of shows do you generally like?"

"Uh, oh, I don't know. Something that's, er, generally stimulating."

"What do you think of junk?"

"Beg your pardon?"

"Junk. What do you think of junk? We put a lot of junk on the air. How do you feel about junk?

"Well, uh, I like to be entertained. I mean—"

"When you were at Michigan, make it into Detroit much?"

"Oh, yeah," Seth said eagerly, remembering that Mavis was from

Motown. "At least much more than most of my classmates. You know what I like about Detroit? It's a totally black-run city."

Without a moment's pause, Mavis said, "No wonder it's such a shithole."

Seth said nothing. He tried to maintain control of his facial muscles, not wanting to show how flabbergasted he was by Mavis's slur. Here was the most powerful—well, at least the most famous—black woman in America—and she said *that?* Suddenly, it occurred to Seth that Mavis was trying to trick him, maybe to see if he was some kind of closet bigot. He remembered that Emma had not been particularly fond of his rap essay. Though she never said it, Seth felt that on some level Emma had considered the piece faintly racist. So Mavis must have been trying to pull a fast one on him, waiting to see if he would counter her gibe with a racist retort. It would be a long time before Seth would recall Mavis's remark and realize that she had not been trying to psyche him out, that she had, in fact, said precisely what she thought.

"You follow politics?" Mavis asked in a brusque, uninterested voice.

"A little bit."

"What do you think of Troy McCracken?"

"I think he's the next President of the United States," Seth answered as quickly as he could, believing that a pause would suggest not thought but uncertainty, vacillation, weakness, and wanting, even if he might be wrong to at least seem sure, to project something like conviction, if an opinion could be a conviction.

"It's a crowded field this year," Mavis said. "Four candidates at least. Why McCracken?"

"One: He cultivates a compelling aura."

Mavis's magnificent head whiplashed back, a mighty roar of laughter bursting from her. The indulgence of Mavis's laughter, the sheer hedonistic pleasure she derived from her own guffawing, made Seth feel as if he was the thing he least wanted to be, the thing he feared he was: insignificant.

"Cultivate an aura!" Mavis jeered. "Lord, you *are* a journalist! Troy McCracken doesn't have to think about *cultivating an aura* any more than I do. *That's* why he'll win. Soon he'll be like me: a one-namer. Troy. Like Mavis. Say the name Mavis to any American above the age of three and they will know immediately to whom you are referring. You don't become a one-namer by *cultivating an aura.* Troy McCracken—soon to be simply Troy—is uncompromisingly *himself.* That's why he burns a hole through your fucking TV screen. Because he is so totally, so unpollutedly himself. In any case, you said, 'One.' What's reason number two?"

After a moment's hesitation, Seth, terrified and bedazzled, said the first thing that came to mind: "He's got great hair."

Mavis did not laugh. She eyed Seth for an unbearably long moment, then said, "I've got a taping to do. Ask Alton to get you a car back to the airport, or wherever it is you're going."

With that, Mavis rose and headed to the door, one of her garish, streaming scarves brushing across Seth's face as he sat frozen, wanting at least to say, Thanks for the interview, but unable to get any words out before Mavis Temple completed her grand exit, leaving Seth now trembling in his chair, wondering if he had somehow offended Mavis and fearing not that he wouldn't get the job he was no longer even sure he wanted but that, by possibly insulting this incredibly famous woman, he had invited something along the lines of cosmic retribution. Finally rising from his chair, Seth hurried to Alton's office and asked not for a car to the airport but for the location of the nearest men's room.

Seth dashed into the stall, fumbling to lock the door behind him. Falling to his knees, grasping the bowl, he waited for something to happen—but nothing happened. He coughed. A few drops of saliva made barely a ripple in the stagnant pool of water. Then Seth looked up and saw, scrawled in black Magic Marker on the white tile wall, just above the gleaming silver handle, a brilliant, hard-edged gem, redolent of primal terror and revulsion, a pithy masterpiece of toilet misogyny: "Never trust anything that bleeds for five days and lives."

>   >   >

A year and a half passed before Seth received his next call from Alton. Mavis, Alton reported, wanted Seth to show up for work as an assistant producer in one week. Alton was to make all the arrange-

< 96 >

ments for moving Seth—and any significant others—from Vymar to New York. After only two months on the *Mavis!* show, Seth demonstrated an uncanny knack for coming up with guests and topics that had an *edge*—which is to say that the subjects under discussion or the people Seth found to fuel the debates provoked a general anger and/or disgust in viewers that kept them from changing the channel. When he first joined the show, Seth felt a bit nervous about being the only white male on Mavis's staff. But to Seth's astonishment, Mavis Temple treated him not with the borderline contempt she displayed in their interview eighteen months earlier, but with an attentive generosity that was almost flirtatious. Faster than anyone who had come before him, Seth earned the status of one of Mavis's favorites.

Mavis was branching out, producing, in addition to her own program, a burgeoning batch of TV movies and news specials. But none of the new shows she'd produced had been a success. She needed something fresh, a grabber, something with an edge. One morning, Mavis summoned Seth and another hot young producer, Sophie Mendel, to her office. "Anyone catch the execution last night?" Mavis asked, clicking on the tape in her VCR before Seth or Sophie responded. Seth tried not to avert his eyes as the prisoner on the TV screen, strapped in a wooden chair, jerked and squirmed violently, eyes bulging, chest shaking as if he would burst at any minute, as carbon monoxide poisoned the air in his tiny room. Finally, the prisoner's eyes closed and his body stopped moving. The utter stillness of the prisoner was even more disquieting to Seth than his herky-jerky struggle. "What do you think?" Mavis asked.

"It's old hat," Sophie Mendel said crisply in that tone of hers that Seth had come to despise, that "I'm the smartest kid in the class and the answer is obvious to me; isn't it to *you?*" tone. "People are losing interest in it."

"And why?"

"One reason," Seth piped up, "is probably because they're not being marketed right."

"Good point," Mavis said. "But it's not just the marketing. They're not *producing* these executions. They're just showin' 'em. If they had any sense, they'd make every one of these an *event.*"

Mavis had a dream, and she assigned Sophie and Seth to bring it to fruition. The show would be called *Elimination,* a Pay-Per-View cable special in which an especially odious social parasite would be entertainingly eliminated. If the first show earned good ratings, Mavis hoped to turn *Elimination* into a regularly scheduled series. In record time, Seth, Sophie, and a small battalion of lawyers and facilitators had most of the pieces for *Elimination* in place. They had a cooperative state, Texas, whose governor and attorney general were pleased to exploit new habeas corpus laws that allowed them to select —in this case, at Mavis Temple's pleasure—which inmate on death row would have his number called next. They had the perfect venue for the event: Lone Star Stadium. And the ideal master of ceremonies: Nick Necropolis, former pro wrestler, aka the Greek Freak, a muscle-bound, curly-maned Adonis who had, with his first three blood-splattered features, become the number-one action-movie star in America.

But the critical element in the event was still missing. Mavis had a very particular set of qualifications she desired in a social parasite. From a large field of death-row inmates, Seth and Sophie had culled twenty candidates for the show. They split the cases between them, Seth examining the life stories and criminal records of ten, Sophie looking into the other ten. They felt confident that one of these convicted murderers would satisfy Mavis's standards. But the boss had turned down every one. Promos for *Elimination* had already hit the air. Each commercial featured an ominous voice-over of Nick Necropolis growling, "On April twenty-second, somebody's gonna pay." The day of reckoning was quickly approaching, and still no one knew who "somebody" was.

➤   ➤   ➤

Thank God, thought Seth, for Vin Ewell's stroke. Mavis would probably be so distracted trying to squeeze out a couple of shows from the vice president's tragedy that she might, for a day or so anyway, stop pestering Seth about his search for the proper parasite. Besides, as Seth walked into his office on this Friday morning, he couldn't stop thinking about Emma's possible pregnancy, that tidbit of news she had so casually presented to him barely three hours earlier. He called Emma at her current temp job and they had a brief, slightly stilted conversation. Sitting behind his desk, Seth stared forlornly at the stack of background files on ten members of Texas's death row. There had to be someone in this collection of wretched humanity who was wretched enough to meet Mavis's criteria. He decided to comb through each dossier again and make a final desperate pitch to Mavis. No sooner had he started thumbing through one of the dossiers than Sophie Mendel—wearing her usual antiquated yup-woman uniform: blue suit, blue-and-white bow at the collar, matching ribbon restraining her short chestnut hair in a tight little ponytail—appeared in his doorway.

"Hear about Vin Ewell?" Sophie asked.

"Gee," Seth said, "I'm just all broke up about that."

He was quoting Nick Necropolis, who, like all action heroes, had his trademark grisly death line, the little joke he cracked before killing his archenemy. In Necropolis's first movie, *Justifiable Homicide,* he played a cop who, in the penultimate scene, finally had his adversary, a black narco-terrorist—who had, of course, murdered Nick's black sidekick—cornered in an alley. The villain, sporting a white suit and dark shades, pleaded with Necropolis to spare him. "Yo, man, please, I beg you. I beg you! I got a wife and kids at home!"

"Gee," Necropolis snarled, "I'm just all broke up about that." He then unloaded his Uzi into the bad guy, causing his body to dance grotesquely like an electrified rag doll as splotches of blood exploded all over his white suit.

Sophie walked in and sat primly on Seth's couch. "What if I told you," Seth said, "that I'm going to be a father?"

"Do you know who the mother is?" Sophie deadpanned.

"You know, you're exactly the sort of woman my mother would want me to marry. When's the last time you went to synagogue?"

"More to the point: Did you happen to see any of the banquet where Ewell had his stroke?"

"No. Gruesome?"

"Oh yes. But more to the point: The banquet was in honor of Melvin Hutchinson. I watched the whole thing on the Politics channel. In his speech, Hutch mentioned a member of Texas's death row."

"Did he?" Seth asked hopefully.

"Jeremiad Hardee," Sophie said. "I called the Amarillo DA first thing this morning to check out the case." Sophie began reading from notes on the clipboard she always carried around with her. "Thirty-seven years old. A drifter. Raped and murdered a baby-sitter, then sexually abused and tortured the eighteen-month-old kid she was taking care of. Stuffed the baby's body in the freezer for his mother to find later."

Seth tried to contain his excitement. One of Mavis's key requirements was that the condemned man's crime be so unspeakably horrific that virtually no one would mind seeing him die. "Tell me more," Seth said.

"Jeremiad Hardee," Sophie said, still reading from her clipboard, "is a grade-school dropout, never been married, no children. His parents are both dead. No family ties that anyone knows of." Sophie looked up from her notes. "Your quintessential friendless psychopath."

Seth's excitement was evaporating. It was all too good to be true. How could they have missed this guy's case before? He could only think that this Jeremiad Hardee failed Mavis Temple's primary litmus test. Seth raised a skeptical eyebrow. "And . . ."

"And," Sophie said with a triumphant smirk, "he's white."

➤   ➤   ➤

Mavis Temple sat behind her enormous black desk, flipping through the dossier of Jeremiad Hardee. "I don't understand how we could have missed him before," she said pensively.

"I wondered the same thing," Seth said, "but—"

"But," Sophie quickly cut Seth off, "when we asked Texas to forward us the files on death-row inmates, Hardee's case had been lumped in the black group. Since we knew you didn't want a black parasite, we never even looked at his file."

"Okay," Mavis said, maintaining a thoughtful, somewhat distracted tone. "But how did he wind up in the black file?"

"It was because of his first arrest," Sophie said, "twenty years ago, in Conroe, Texas. Armed robbery. The sheriff who busted him evidently believed that Hardee's grandfather had been black. It was an old local rumor—that Grandma Hardee was running around with a black guy. So, on his first arrest form, Jeremiad's race was listed as black."

" 'Cause the cracker sheriff thought he was one-quarter Negro."

"Exactly. But that's the only time in Hardee's life that he's been classified as black. His birth certificate says white. He's been arrested four other times and every time he's been classified as white. And he considers himself white."

"He certainly *looks* white." Mavis held up Hardee's most recent mug shot. She paused, then said, "All right. This is my concern: I don't want any long-lost black relatives comin' outta the woodwork sayin' this Hardee's a brother. I'll be damned if I'm gonna have an authentic African-American executed on a show I'm producing."

"No living relatives that anyone knows of," Sophie said, now sounding so efficient and confident that Seth wanted to throw up. "But I plan to run a more thorough check. The sheriff who said he was black died eleven years ago."

Mavis leaned back in her chair and stroked her chins. "Well, boys and girls," she said finally, "I think we've found our parasite."

(5)

SAM ADAMS WAS BLACK, you know."

Henry Beedle stared curiously at Melvin Hutchinson for a moment, then broke into his feral smile, showing that mouthful of tiny brown teeth. "You don't say."

"He was," Melvin said. "Well, maybe I shouldn't say *black*. He was a quadroon, or maybe an octoroon. I can prove it to you."

They had been sitting in the back of the attorney general's Lincoln limousine for half an hour, parked in the middle of the playground of Samuel Adams High School, Melvin's alma mater, in Norris, New Jersey, the penultimate stop for the honoree of Melvin Hutchinson Day. The other limo and the two police cars in Melvin's motorcade occupied the center of the playground and were ringed by a small battalion of cops in riot gear, while outside the protective circle, students—some gawking, some glowering, some casting casual glances, pretending not to be curious—crowded near the back entrance of the school auditorium. The students in the playground would not be attending the speech to be given by Samuel Adams High's most illustrious alumnus. They were there just to get a look at him, Melvin assumed, when he would finally emerge from behind the darkened bulletproof windows of his car and enter the auditorium through the back entrance. His real audience, meanwhile, was waiting to enter the auditorium through the main entrance, inside the building. People were starting to pass through the metal detector while a handful of police officers and members of Melvin's own security team made a last-minute check of the space.

The logistics for the attorney general's appearance were all fucked up. The media—local New Jersey stations, plus the Politics channel —had finally caught up with Melvin at the previous event, a visit to Norris Children's Hospital. The camera crews had followed Melvin's entourage to Sam Adams, but the high school's principal, a jittery little man, said the auditorium would be too full to accommodate them. He assured the reporters, however, that Sam Adams High would be videotaping the attorney general's address and could provide them with excerpts if they needed them. So the media went on ahead to the Fort Brandriss Drug Reeducation Center, the final stop on Melvin's schedule. Minutes later, the nervous dwarf of a principal came out to Melvin's car to say that the school's video equipment had apparently been stolen that very day, so there would be no visual record of the attorney general's speech. Melvin graciously told the principal he didn't mind. But, of course, he was massively annoyed.

While Henry Beedle, chattering into his telephone, sat beside him, handling whatever mundane Justice Department business needed to be handled, Melvin pulled out his pocket flask and took a long swig of Jack Daniel's. He stared out the limo window, observing the kids in their oversized jackets, baggy pants, and baseball caps, their immaculate sneakers, their shaved heads and elaborate hairdos and gleaming gold chunks of jewelry. When did they, Melvin wondered, and why did they, the people who ran this school, ever give up the dress code? Feeling overtaken by another melancholy wave of nostalgia, Melvin heard himself murmur, "Sam Adams High." Beedle finished his phone call. That was when Melvin turned to his deputy and offered his historical factoid.

"Well," Beedle said, "I've never heard that before, but—"

"I can prove it," Melvin said, his tone going up a notch in adamance. "Sam Adams was black, an African-American. Look." The attorney general pulled out his wallet, removed a bill, and handed it to Beedle. It was a rare two-dollar note, printed, Beedle noticed, in 1976, with a picture of Thomas Jefferson on the front. "Turn it over," Melvin said. On the flip side was a famous depiction of the signing of the Declaration of Independence. "Look there," Melvin said, pointing to a figure in the left-hand background of the scene. "He's colored in." Beedle observed the somewhat heavyset figure in Colonial garb, whose face was indeed shaded a darker hue than those of the other men in the picture. "See. They had to color him. Because he was one-quarter or maybe one-eighth black."

"My, my," Beedle said quietly, staring at the bill. "And that's supposed to be Sam Adams?"

"It *is* Sam Adams," Melvin said in a deeper timbre, which Beedle had noticed was a feature of his boss's late-afternoon drunkenness, as opposed to the slightly higher, more convivial tone the attorney general's voice had during his usual late-morning drunkenness. "Little-known fact," Melvin added. "But it's part of history. A part of *our* history."

"Indeed," Beedle said, handing Melvin back his two-dollar bill, not quite sure whom the attorney general meant when he said "our."

As Melvin slipped the money back into his wallet, a sudden noise erupted in the playground, causing both the attorney general and his deputy to jump. Through the window on Beedle's side of the car, past the backs of the cops who surrounded the limo, in a far corner of the playground, they saw a group of kids gathered around a boom box begin to dance as the noise that had startled Melvin and Beedle, a driving, jangling, improbably up-tempo beat, grew louder. The girls danced, their backs to the boys, rhythmically gyrating their buttocks while the boys thrust their crotches toward the contorting behinds. A woman's voice began to wail over the compulsive beat. Melvin couldn't get all the words, but the singer was fervently demanding sexual gratification.

"Body, body, body," Melvin muttered. "Gimme yo body, gotta have yo body." He sighed, leaned back in his seat, and took another swig from his flask. "Black folks are still so damned obsessed with this body thang."

Beedle turned to him and cocked his head inquisitively. "Why do you think that is?"

Melvin wondered if this was a leading question. "I don't know," he said. "I mean, I have nothing against dancing. I used to cut a pretty good slice of rug myself, as they used to say. But . . ." Melvin paused, looked at Beedle, who was filling his pipe and still staring inquisitively at Melvin. And it occurred to Melvin, a bit sadly but not altogether unpleasantly, that Henry Beedle had become, in the two years and two months they had worked together, his closest confidant. He'd never really thought about it before. To Melvin, his conversations with Beedle had been all business, all orders and consultations. But somehow, between the cracks in all their occupational interchanges, an intimacy had evolved. And since he and Dorothy, what with his schedule and hers at the Organization for a Child-Friendly Society (she'd been too busy with her own work even to join her husband in Norris for Melvin Hutchinson Day), spent only one or two nights a week together and their conversations, especially since moving to Washington, tended to center on logistical details, planning for social obligations, the rearrangement of timetables, talk that was, on both their parts, deliberately devoid of real emotion, and since he had lost touch with the nucleus, seeing only Art Walker, and very rarely at that, Melvin had developed—with a gradualness so glacial that he'd been unaware of it until this very moment in the back of the limo—a *friendship* with Beedle. He had opened up to his deputy on many occasions, more than he ever had with any white person. And now, Beedle was the person he spoke to *most* openly. Not that he'd poured his heart out or made any significant confessions. But a trust that went beyond the professional had so firmly taken hold that Melvin had found himself blithely blurting out remarks to Beedle that he would, only a couple of years earlier, have kept entirely to himself. This bald-headed ofay with his Coke-bottle glasses and filthy little teeth, this arrogant, pipe-puffing, asexual egghead had a way of drawing things out of Melvin by simple, almost offhand, inquiry.

"Last week," Melvin continued, "I was spending the night at my place in New York. It was late and I had the TV on and I came across this show I'd seen a few times before, a local cable dance show, broadcast somewhere out of Brooklyn, *Dance Orgy* or *Dance Jam* or something like that, and some of the dancin' on this show, it gets pretty raunchy. Some of these women, the way they can shake their bodies, I mean really shake, like their whole body's going through orgasmic convulsions, their tits and their butts vibrating wildly, and, hey, man, I love the show, you know." Beedle laughed lightly, began puffing his pipe. "And I was happy I'd stumbled upon it the other night. But, usually, or at least the three or four times I'd seen the show before, all the dancers seemed to be twenty-one or older. Eighteen at the very youngest, but really, I think, in their twenties. Not last week. The dancers were, like, children. I'm talkin' eight, nine, ten years old. And they're tryin' to do the same lewd dances the grown-ups were doin'. These little boys— Boy Scouts! Some of them were actually wearing Boy Scout uniforms. Can you imagine? Instead of takin' them to Bear Mountain or some such place, the troop leader has them on *Dance Orgy*. And these little boys, they're rubbin' their balls and undulating their hips, and the girls, nine-, ten-year-old little girls, are writhin' around and strokin' the tits they don't even have yet and tryin' to make sexy faces at the camera, and I thought, My God, what are they *doing?* I wanted to find the parents, or whoever it is who takes care of them, and say, Why do you have your kids *here?* Why aren't they at the fucking library! Do your children really need to be learning this *now?*"

Even inside the sturdy casing of Melvin's limo, the beat from the boom box was thunderous. Melvin could see, through the window on Beedle's side of the car, four riot police approaching the dancing kids in the far corner of the playground. The couple at the center of the dancers actually seemed to be humping while standing more or less upright, the girl grinding her butt against the boy's thrusting pelvis. "Body, body, body," Melvin muttered. He could not hear any voices, but he could tell from the gestures of the people he watched through the window that the cops ordered the kids to turn off the music, that the kids made futile but obligatory gestures of outrage and uttered a few defiant but empty complaints before clicking off the music, picking up the box, and, with a few more perfunctory hand-flinging gestures of disgust, tossing a few more halfhearted protests over their shoulders, and making a great show of taking their time, sullenly left the playground.

Melvin slouched in his seat, took another swig. He didn't look at Beedle, but he could feel Beedle looking intently at him. "And watching these little kids on this dance show, I had the strangest thought occur to me. I thought, This is a tragedy. And they think it's a party. But this is a tragedy."

Beedle and Melvin were silent for a while. The sweet smell of Beedle's tobacco filled the Lincoln. "But does it have to be?" Beedle finally said. "I mean, kids can be saved. You, Judge, help save kids every day of your life."

"Yes," Melvin acknowledged instantly. "But I can't get to them all. Most of them, I'll never get to."

"But so many people respect you, Judge, so many of the kids look up to you. You give them the hope and the determination—"

"Blah blah blah," Melvin said. "Yes, I know, I try to do that. And some of them might listen, really listen to and believe me. But it just goes in one ear and out the other. A kid might listen to me this afternoon, but tonight he'll be out on the corner drinkin' forties wid da niggas."

"What are forties?"

Melvin laughed. "Forties? Beedle, you mean to tell me you live in Washington, D.C., on the border of the innermost of inner cities, and you don't know what a forty is?" Melvin always enjoyed an opportunity to seem street-smart to Beedle, or at least to make Beedle feel that *he* was about as hopelessly street-*dumb* as any white guy could be.

"You'll have to educate me, Judge."

"Forty-ounce bottles—of beer. Malt liquor, actually." Melvin took another swig from his flask of bourbon and grew solemn again. "They think they're partyin'. But it's a goddamned tragedy."

"Yet, I ask you again, Your Honor: Does it have to be? Tragedies can be averted."

"Who told you that lie?" Melvin asked in a flat, neutral voice. "You can't stop tragedy. Tragedy has a force, a logic all its own. Tragedy is inexorable."

Melvin looked out his window and saw the flustered little principal of Samuel Adams High School, accompanied by two police officers and two of Melvin's bodyguards, approaching the car. Melvin capped the flask, tucked it back into his pocket, and turned to Beedle. "Show time."

As Rashid Scuggs entered Benny D.'s barbershop and took his seat among the seven other brothers waiting for haircuts—you could always tell at Benny's place which customers, usually the older ones with the most nondescript hairstyles, were waiting for Benny and which, always brother Rashid's age and younger, with dreads, fades, top hats, an array of the wildest styles of the past twenty years, were waiting to get clipped by Calvin, Benny's young assistant—he couldn't help but notice that one of Calvin's tapes of the great spiritual leader was playing on the shop's TV.

"We don't know who we are," the spiritual leader intoned. "As black people, we need to find out who we are." The great spiritual leader, dressed in a sharp gray suit, immaculate white shirt, and a red-black-and-green bow tie, addressed an enormous crowd in an indoor sports arena. "The devil is everywhere. But he comes in disguise. If you knew he was the devil, you wouldn't be susceptible. But the devil is everywhere. The devil's in sugar. Because sugar is grafted. It's grafted from the sugar*cane*. Everything that's grafted is the devil. The white man is the devil. Because he's grafted from the black man. The original man. The African-Asiatic man. We're the original man. But we don't know that. We don't know who we are. We as black people need to be *told* who we are."

"You know, this fella sound like my grandaddy," Delroy said. Delroy was one of Benny's customers—he had to be at least eighty years old, Rashid thought—who seemed to be sitting in the barbershop jawboning every time Rashid came in for a haircut. "My grandaddy used to say, 'Don't ever eat the whitefish.' "

"Why's that?" Benny asked as he carefully guided his electric razor around the ear of a middle-aged customer who sat before him in the big barber's chair.

"Cuz the whitefish is the only fish with a *human* head."

"Say what?" Benny said.

"A *hyoo*-man head," Delroy repeated portentously. "I mean features like a man. The whitefish got a head like a man. You ever see a colored person eatin' whitefish?"

"Can't say I have."

"That's the reason why," Delroy said like a prosecuting attorney driving home a point in his summation.

"The white devil has got us brainwashed," the great spiritual leader thundered on TV. "He's got it so we believe only what he wants us to believe."

With the flourish of an old pro who loves his work, Benny removed the white apron from his customer's neck and waved it, matadorlike, shaking free tufts of salt-and-pepper hair. Displaying just the slightest twinkle of pride, he held up a rectangular mirror behind his customer's head. The fiftyish brother in the barber's chair stared into the huge wall mirror in front of him, turned his head this way and that, admiring the back of his skull in Benny's rectangular mirror. "Nice," the customer said quietly, "nice."

"The white man has us living in a topsy-turvy world," the spiritual leader pronounced, "where everything we do is wrong and every-thing *he* does is right."

"Well," Delroy said with a sigh, "you can say all you want about white folks, but they need us and we need them. Ain't no way around that. They need us and we need them."

"That's true," Benny said as his customer placed several bills in his palm. Rashid thought he could detect a slight grimace on Calvin's face as he concentrated on the head in front of him.

"The white man," the leader continued, "has us thinking *his* woman is superior to our own. That's why you see these brothers, troubled, confused brothers they are, chasing after the white man's women. Don't even matter what she look like. She may be uglier than nine miles of dirt road!"

Everyone in the barbershop burst into laughter. And Rashid laughed louder, more ostentatiously, than anyone. " 'Uglier than nine miles of dirt road!' " Rashid repeated, guffawing. "Ain't it the truth!"

"It's time we stopped doing what the white man tells us to do!" the great spiritual leader exhorted. "It's time we stopped chasing after his women. Time we stopped buying what he tells us to buy. Time we stopped eating what he tells us to eat—his filthy, unhealthy *pork,* the flesh of the disgusting pig!"

"Well, I don't know about *that*," the man who had just had his hair cut by Benny said as he slipped into his jacket. "I'm on my way to get me some ribs right now."

All the older men in the shop—Benny's rather than Calvin's customers—laughed heartily.

"Why don't you turn on something else?" Benny said as another customer sat in his chair.

Without saying a word, Calvin walked over to the television, clicked off the videotape, and punched in a different channel. Mavis Temple appeared on the screen, standing amid her studio audience, speaking into a cordless microphone. "Welcome back. We're talking today about strokes and comas. My guests are"—an elderly white couple appeared, seated in swivel chairs on a platform in front of the audience, both the husband and wife looking ruddy and spry— "Horace Campbell and his wife, Irma. Horace suffered a massive stroke and spent six months in a coma. But after reawakening two years ago, he has made an almost total recovery." Horace smiled and nodded to the audience. "Also joining us are Frederick Gummer and his wife, Denise." The Gummers appeared on the screen. The husband sat, seemingly frozen in his chair, eyes staring eerily, lifelessly, straight ahead, his mouth slack. His wife, sitting beside him, was wrinkled and haggard; she looked as if she were actually worrying herself to death. "Mr. Gummer," Mavis Temple said, her voice dropping an octave to convey her concern, her compassion, "also emerged from a six-month coma a while back, but, as you can see, he has not fully recovered."

"Not fully recovered!" Delroy said. "The man's a goddamn vegetable."

"And joining us from our Washington studio," Mavis continued, "is the surgeon general, Dr. Arthur Spooner." The familiar figure, dressed in his blue naval officer's jacket with the gold trim on the cuffs, appeared. Stolid, white-haired, bespectacled, Arthur Spooner reminded Rashid of Marcus Welby, M.D., or one of those other TV doctors. This, it occurred to Rashid, was the reason why the surgeon general was so popular, why he had achieved a quasi-celebrity status in the country: He *looked* the part. Rashid and the other customers waiting their turn in the barber's chair watched Mavis Temple on the shop's TV as she walked up to another TV on which Dr. Spooner appeared, a box within a box. "I know you're pressed for time, Doctor, so thank you so much for joining us."

"My pleasure, Mavis," said Arthur Spooner in a tone of gruff but benign authority, just the sort of tone one would admire in a busy doctor who knew what he was doing and had a lot to do but who was nevertheless attentive to an individual's emotional needs.

"Vice President Ewell," Mavis continued, "has been comatose for more than sixteen hours now. What can you tell us about his condition?"

"The vice president's status is still critical but stabilizing."

"Tell me, Dr. Spooner, is Vin Ewell aware of what's going on around him? Can he hear voices? Is it possible that he knows what has happened to him?"

"Possible, but, at this stage of the game, difficult to say."

"Has anyone tried to communicate with him?"

"Certainly his wife, Muriel, has been speaking to him. She has been at his bedside since last night, and I must say Mrs. Ewell has shown tremendous strength and fortitude in this difficult time."

The studio audience applauded, and Rashid wondered why. Muriel Ewell wasn't there to receive their support. So were they simply applauding Spooner for complimenting her in absentia?

"Now, Doctor," Mavis said, furrowing her brow, "I hope you'll be candid with me here. What are the vice president's chances of making a full recovery?"

"Well, as you know, Mavis," Spooner said with a gruff little chuckle, "I am known for my candor." In an instant, he turned infinitely more serious, almost grim. "But it's just impossible to say. As your guests today can attest, no one knows for certain when, if, or how a patient will emerge from a comatose state. But we are monitoring the vice president's condition very carefully."

"I thank you for your candor, Doctor. Now, this is a touchy question, I realize, but how long can Troy—that is, President McCracken —how long can he afford to wait before appointing another vice president? Aren't we facing a crisis of succession right now?"

"There is *no* crisis in the U.S. government," Dr. Spooner said sternly. "All of us are praying for the vice president's speedy and full recovery."

"Prayin'!" Delroy hooted. "Prayin'! When your *doctor* say he's *prayin'*, that mean you ain't *got* a prayer. That cracker's a dead man. Ain't no hope for him a-*tall*."

"Before I let you go, Doctor," Mavis Temple said, "I have just one more question, on a different topic. When will the renewed ban on the abortion pill be lifted?"

Spooner cleared his throat uncomfortably. "Well, Mavis, as you know, the pill was found to have some very dangerous side effects. We're studying the case very carefully. But at the present time, we must uphold the ban."

"Yet, there are some American women who have continued to use the abortion pill illegally."

"Yes, and I would say that those women are putting themselves at tremendous risk. These contraband abortion pills, some of them aren't the real pill at all, and they are extremely dangerous."

"And what do you say to critics, Dr. Spooner, who charge that, with the ban, the McCracken administration is simply capitulating to pressure from the antiabortion lobby?"

There was a smattering of applause from Mavis's audience.

"This is not," said Spooner, his voice becoming even more sonorous, "I repeat, *not* a political decision. The President, the attorney general, the Food and Drug Administration, and I have only one concern here, and that is the safety of American women."

Now the bulk of the studio audience broke into enthusiastic applause.

"Thank you, Dr. Spooner."

"Thank *you*, Mavis."

Mavis turned to the camera. "Don't go away. We'll be right back." The *Mavis!* theme music rose as Mavis Temple's image faded from the screen and was replaced by a laxative commercial.

"I'm tellin' y'all," Delroy said. "Vin Ewell is *out*. They already talkin' about replacing the man. You know what I heard 'em say on the news this morning, Benny?"

"What's that?" Benny said.

"They talkin' about making Melvin Hutchinson the new vice president."

"Well, it's about time."

The older men in Benny's shop nodded and muttered their agreement. Calvin, who hardly ever said a word except to ask a customer how he wanted his hair cut, looked up from his work—he was meticulously buzzing a young brother's initials across the back of his head—glanced at Rashid, and rolled his eyes in exasperation.

"Hutch is just the man for the job," Delroy said proudly.

"Somebody ought to shoot that nigger," Rashid said, the comment blurting out of him before he could think the better of it.

"Why you say that?" Delroy asked, looking hurt and bewildered.

"He's just another Uncle Tom," Rashid said.

"Naw, that ain't true a-*tall*. I known Hutch since he was knee-high to a grasshopper. Knew his daddy, too. Used to play cards with Harry Hutchinson."

"Yeah, well, I still say somebody ought to shoot the nigger."

"Well, you got your chance," Benny said as he snipped at his customer's hair with a pair of scissors. "He's speaking at Sam Adams High."

"Today?" Rashid asked.

"Don't you know it's Melvin Hutchinson Day?" Delroy said. "There's signs all over town: HONORING NORRIS'S NATIVE SON. He gave a damn fine speech this morning at First Baptist. Damn fine."

"When's he speaking at Sam Adams?" Rashid directed his question to Benny.

The barber looked at the clock on the wall. "Spozed to be talkin' at two o'clock. It two-thirty now. You mighta missed him."

Rashid quickly rose from his chair. "Catch you later, Calvin," he said. Rashid strode out of Benny D.'s barbershop as the remaining customers looked at one another quizzically.

Finally, Delroy broke the silence. "That nigga ain't gonna *really* shoot Melvin Hutchinson, is he?"

Calvin let out a hollow laugh. "Well, if anybody was gonna do it," he said, speaking clearly for the first time that afternoon, "Rashid would be the man."

Melvin was midway through one of his greatest hits, a reliable standard for youngish audiences about the importance of personal responsibility, respect for one's ancestors, our rich cultural heritage, the need to dream great dreams, to have the discipline and the self-respect to pursue those dreams just as the people who came before you—

And then he froze. Standing at the lectern, onstage in the same auditorium at Samuel Adams High School where decades earlier he'd addressed his peers—all of them, or most of them, anyway, conscientious young Negroes, the boys in jackets and ties, every girl present wearing a dress or a skirt—as president of the student body, Melvin Hutchinson stopped cold in midsentence and gazed at the subtly swimming audience before him. He felt himself wobble ever so slightly and wondered if he'd edged past the threshold, that slender line indicating that other people could tell he was drunk. Melvin, in the years since Abby's death, had become expert at going right up to the threshold, standing with his toes touching that barrier, but rarely crossing the line. When he did tiptoe over the threshold, it was always late at night, at some jolly gathering where most everyone was tanked. But now, standing frozen on the Sam Adams stage, Melvin worried that maybe he'd gone too far today, that maybe by starting his drinking two hours early this morning with that splash of vodka in his orange juice at 8:00 A.M. aboard *Justice One,* he'd hastened his approach to the threshold and had now, carelessly, stepped over it.

But almost as quickly as that fear entered his mind, it disappeared and Melvin suddenly felt the full force of his anger, the rage careening inside him as he stared at his audience. It wasn't the entire audience that maddened him. But it was the majority, all those young faces he saw out there slack with boredom, or twisted in sneers, or, worst of all—these were the faces his gaze flitted to, dispersed as they were throughout the crowd—stuffed with gum. He fixated on those mouths, lazily masticating, cracking the gum, popping it loudly, blowing pink balloon-sized bubbles. Here he was the most prominent man—let alone *black* man—these kids had ever seen in the flesh, an

alumnus of their school, coming back to give them a significant message, a message that, if only they would heed it, might save their
wretched lives. And they weren't even listening to him! It was so
obvious from their blank stares and sleepy expressions that nothing
he'd said had even registered. Why had they bothered to show up?
Why were they wasting his precious time? Why couldn't they even
show the common fucking courtesy to *pay attention,* simply to pay
attention for half an hour? Melvin Hutchinson—who knew he had
to be the most famous role model ever to show up at this school, who
had come here, back to his alma mater, returning, as black people
were always being urged to do, constantly being criticized for *not*
doing, to his roots, to his original community, who had taken time
out of his schedule to try to reach out to these kids—stared at the
multitude of dull, uncomprehending, gum-cracking faces and felt
nothing but disgust.

"What is wrong with you all?" Melvin said in a voice brimming
with resentment.

Surprised murmurs rippled through the audience.

"I said," Melvin fairly shouted into the lectern's microphone,
"what in the *hell* is wrong with y'all?"

The crowd came alive with shocked and indignant whispers, buzzing like a swarm of bees. Melvin looked to the front row, to his
entourage of white agents and functionaries, and spotted Henry
Beedle, who looked positively stricken. Melvin quickly glanced
around the auditorium. There wasn't a camera or a tape recorder in
sight. The absence emboldened him.

"I come here to give you people a valuable message and you can't
even be bothered to listen to me! What *is* the problem with you
people?"

"Maybe the problem ain't with us!" a voice called out from the
crowd. "Maybe the problem is with you!"

"Who said that?" Melvin shot back, feeling more primed to do
battle than he'd ever felt in his life. "Stand up. I wanna see who said
that."

While the crowd continued to buzz, a young man (obviously not a
high school student; he looked at least twenty-five; a teacher perhaps?) rose in the center of the auditorium. He had a tangle of coiled

braids on the top of his head, little hair at all on the sides, a scraggly goatee, and a red-green-and-yellow earring in the shape of Africa. He wore a Technicolor dashiki—probably, Melvin thought, made in Hong Kong. "Yo!" the young man said, and the kids in the audience applauded.

"And who are you?" Melvin asked.

"I'm Rashid Scuggs, director of the Norris Center for African-American Arts and Culture. Located at Sixty-six Jefferson Avenue. *Dat's* who I am!" All the gum-cracking students cheered their approval.

"And you have a problem with me, Mr. Scuggs?"

"Yeah, I got a problem witch you! Cuz you say *you* got a problem wid my homeys here. And the problem ain't wid us. Da problem is witch you! The problem is witch your message. Cuz your message don't address *our* cause. The *black* cause!"

While the kids cheered again, Melvin stared hard, though more analytically than angrily, at the young man in the audience. What was the strange incongruity he detected in this Rashid Scuggs? There was something in his demeanor, in his voice, that rang discordantly with Melvin. It wasn't his hostility. At this moment, Melvin didn't give a damn about that. It was something else. Melvin felt intuitively that this Rashid was an exceptionally intelligent person. But something in his voice seemed false. It seemed as if he were trying to assume a voice that was not his own, as if he was trying to sound the way a black man was *supposed* to sound.

"I've been fighting for the black cause my entire adult life," Melvin said slowly, forcefully.

"Yeah? Watchoo ever do for the black cause?"

"I risked my *life* for the black cause, for every single one of you in this auditorium today. I risked my life for you!"

Now a good portion of the audience, led by the principal of Sam Adams and the teachers in the auditorium, applauded for Melvin.

"Yeah?" Rashid challenged. "I know about choo. I know *all* about you."

"What do you *know* about me?"

"I know you call yourself a civil rights fighter. But you ain't never been in no fight. All you ever been is a lawyer in a suit!"

"And all Thurgood Marshall ever was was a lawyer in a suit," Melvin intoned. The crowd responded enthusiastically, but he did not hear them anymore, barely even saw them. It was just Melvin and Rashid now; he was all alone with this arrogant little punk. "And no, I didn't join in mass demonstrations. I didn't get hosed down in the street or have German shepherds snappin' at my Johnson or get firebombed out of my home. No, I didn't take part in the March on Washington. I was, in fact, in Hazelton, South Carolina, the day of the "I Have a Dream" speech, putting *his* words into action, doing the indispensable scut work of the movement, in short, makin' it law! And no, I shed no blood for your freedom. I just made it *legal.* I just made the shit *stick!* But you better believe I was at risk, cuz wasn't nothin' *less* nonthreatening than a black man, let alone a *blue-black* man like yours truly, wearin' a *suit*, drivin' a *car*, and callin' hisself a lawyer, let alone a *civil rights* lawyer, in Hazelton, South Ca'lina, in the summer of nineteen hun'red and sistee-*tree!*"

"Yeah, yeah, yeah," Rashid scoffed. "All you old-timesy niggas gotta talk about Dr. King. I don't even respect your Dr. King. Cuz all he ever did was let black people get beat up!"

"That's just about the stupidest shit I ever heard."

"It's the truth. And I defy you to tell me one lasting, concrete thing your Dr. King ever achieved, aside from makin' liberal white folks feel good about themselves. What did he ever accomplish?"

"One: He secured for you, and for every African-American, the most sacred right of democracy—the right to vote!"

"Hey, man, I don't even *use* my right to vote. I'm thirty years old and I ain't never voted in my life."

"What?" Melvin said, finding Rashid's comment almost unfathomable.

"I said, *I don't vote.* Ain't no real options for black people out there, anyway. The white politicians are just out to exploit us and the black ones are just a bunch a Uncle Toms!"

"Do you mean to say that after I worked my butt off, after people *died* to get your sorry black ass the vote, you're gonna go and *not* vote?"

"Votin' don't make no difference for black folks. Democracy for black folks does not exist in America."

"That is an untenable position, Rashid. Don't you have anything constructive to say?"

"I say it's time to be *de*-structive. If the system ain't gonna do nothin' for black folks, I say tear it down!"

"Don't you know that's suicide?"

"Don't *choo* know black people are gonna burn this country down?"

"Do you think, do you really *believe* that I have worked this hard, that I have come this far to have crazy ignorant niggas like you make a mockery of my life's work? Do you think I'm gonna let poisoned little shits like you destroy everything I've staked my *life* on?"

"You ain't nothin' but a Uncle Tom!"

Melvin could no longer ignore the crowd. The entire auditorium seemed to be rocking, the whole audience on its feet, alive with brutal energy. Melvin saw Beedle standing in the front row. The deputy quickly drew an index finger across his throat. *Cut it short; we're outta here!*

"Uncle Tom!" Rashid screamed, and suddenly the whole crowd seemed to be chanting it: "Uncle Tom! Uncle Tom! Uncle Tom! Uncle Tom!"

Then something grabbed Melvin's gaze, something sailing in the air, spinning end over end above the crowd, now hurtling toward the stage. When the object was no more than six feet above his head, Melvin could see that it was large, that it was made of clear glass but streaked with yellow, with liquid; it was—could it be?—a forty! The nearly empty bottle of malt liquor shattered at Melvin's feet. In an instant, Melvin's federal agents were onstage and the attorney general was surrounded. Melvin saw riot police burst through the front entrance of the auditorium, billy clubs in hand, fighting their way through the crowd, which seemed to surge in all directions at once. Agents on either side of Melvin grabbed his arms. Next thing he knew, he was running; no, his feet were barely touching the floor—agents were practically carrying him, rapidly through the back entrance of the auditorium, out into the playground. He saw the door of his limo in front of him. Seemingly out of nowhere, a white hand grabbed the handle and flung open the door. Melvin felt another hand, fingers spread, grip firm, come down with a powerful pressure on the top of his head. He felt still another hand on his back, shoving him into the car. He tumbled into the leather seat. Christian Emerson, his chief bodyguard, jumped in and sat across from him, gun drawn. Suddenly, Beedle appeared in the seat beside him. The limo door slammed shut. Sirens screeched. The car lurched forward, pitching Melvin back deeper into his seat, and now all he felt was velocity, almost as if he was in a jet taking off, as he and his entourage sped away from Sam Adams High.

➤   ➤   ➤

Trembling and disoriented, Melvin couldn't be sure how much time had passed. Five minutes? Ten? With a shaky hand, he raised his flask to his lips. Bourbon dribbled down his chin. The sirens were still going, but the limo now felt as if it was moving at normal cruising speed. The agent sitting across from Melvin, the strapping, Aryan Christian Emerson, stared straight ahead at nothing. Sitting beside Melvin, Henry Beedle spoke with uncanny calm into his telephone.

"No, no, we're fine. Were any arrests made? . . . Okay. No one has spotted this Rashid person? . . . No, do not, repeat, do *not* allow him to be detained. We don't want any headlines on this. There was no media present at Sam Adams and we want to downplay this as much as possible. . . . Yes, of course, something will come out, but the story is that a few hecklers disrupted the attorney general's speech. . . . Yes, fine. But again, we don't want this Scuggs arrested. Call the bureau and pull his file, and if he doesn't have a file, open one— today. We want surveillance, but what we do not want is an arrest. The last thing we need right now is a Free Rashid Scuggs demonstration. . . ."

Staring out the window of his Lincoln, Melvin finally realized where he was. He could tell by the boarded-up, defunct textile factories, the factories that had once made Norris, New Jersey, a magnet for migrating southern blacks. They were on the very edge of town, no more than fifteen minutes from Sam Adams High. Up ahead, Melvin saw Norris Bridge.

"We're on our way to Fort Brandriss," Beedle said into his phone, "and we're expecting several camera crews there, including POL.

We don't want anything intruding on this story. . . . Yes. A model drug reeducation center, blah blah blah . . . We should be there inside of fifteen minutes. . . . What's the latest on Ewell? . . . Goddamn it, I wish that son of a bitch would die already. . . . Okay. Talk to you after we leave Fort Brandriss." Beedle pocketed his phone. He looked at Melvin. "You still with us, Judge?"

"Yes, I'm all here, Henry." Melvin sighed. "Sorry about that. I don't know what came over me."

"For goodness sake, don't blame yourself, Judge. It was that would-be Black Panther who started it. But there was no media there. That's the important thing. We'll be able to squash, or at least finesse or control this story, if it gets out. But there *will* be media at Fort Brandriss and we should be arriving soon. So put your game face on."

Melvin took a final swig of Jack Daniel's. "I'll be ready," he said.

At Fort Brandriss, Melvin Hutchinson was as "on" as he'd ever been. Even the sight of pudgy little Wendy Hoffman, special correspondent for the Politics channel, with her piggy face and Shirley Temple curls, shoving a mike at him and asking her typically inane questions, couldn't rattle the attorney general. The near riot at Sam Adams had pushed Melvin several feet back from the threshold. He now felt quite pleasantly inebriated and thoroughly in control. He toured the former army base, praising the success of DRCs, complimenting staff members. He spent a long time talking to one female inmate, Tamika something or other, listening to her tale of woe, telling her of the benefits of sound punishment and discipline, even hugging her for the cameras—a shot that he was certain would be broadcast by every network present.

As the visit was coming to a close, the chief commandant of Fort Brandriss led the attorney general down two rows of some of the younger inmates, males on one side, females on the other. Melvin felt buoyed by the spectacle of all these young first-time offenders, the boys with their heads shaved clean, forced to get their lives together, compelled by their time in this boot camp to reform themselves, to become the decent, productive citizens he knew they could be. Most of them, at least two out of three, were black. And that only made Melvin feel more inspired. Because these were the young

African-Americans who could be saved. If only every one of those gum-cracking idiots at Sam Adams could spend three months in a DRC, that would get their stupid asses into shape. Maybe if that Rashid character had done some hard labor here when he was younger, he'd be doing something productive with his life today instead of inciting youngsters to riot. Filing past the row of brown, pink, and tan heads, Melvin was beginning to feel that the whole afternoon had been redeemed, was beginning to feel once again that his life had a special purpose, that in some way he had rescued these teenaged inmates. He imagined himself tapping each of them lightly once on each shoulder with the sword of justice. "Yes, you are saved," he would say to each of them as they received the blessing of the sword of justice.

Then came the shock. It was one of the whitest faces in the line: a young man—he couldn't have been older than fifteen—with a pallid complexion but with facial features, the nose, the lips, that were unmistakably Afroid. And more than that. More than that. Features so familiar that Melvin abruptly stopped and stared, stared hard in sudden, stomach-turning recognition. Were it not for the youth, and the pallor, he might as well have been looking into a mirror. And he could not stop himself, could not prevent the question from tumbling out: "What is your name, young man?" And before the inmate could answer, before he could utter the two words that would confirm the apparent, Melvin knew. He knew it was his son.

PART TWO

Mongrels

(6)

EMMA COULD SEE THEM coming as she turned the corner and began walking up Riverside Drive. There were two of them, swaggering insouciantly, casually twirling their nightsticks, the light from a streetlamp casting a gleam on their beige helmets and their black knee-high boots, their khaki uniforms looking bulky from the neck-to-knee bulletproof lining. Emma had lived in Washington Heights until she'd gone to college; she'd been visiting her mother in the crumbling old neighborhood for years; she'd walked down many a darkened street on many a late night, had passed by packs of young toughs and stumbling men in rags who had leered and called her names—and she'd never felt threatened. But the sight of these two young men in their riot gear, the red letters spelling FYC on their helmets, faces barely visible behind their visors, made Emma shiver with dread. As they saw her coming, their gaits became more languid, as if they were about to savor this encounter.

"Halt," one of the young men said, his voice slightly distorted by the tiny microphone installed in his helmet. Emma stopped. The two officers stood about a foot in front of her. They were the only people on the street. Emma could see the officers' faces clearly now. They couldn't have been much older than twenty-one or twenty-two; one of them still seemed to bear a layer of baby fat on his cheeks. "Federal Youth Corps," Baby Fat said. "Please state your name."

"Emma Person."

"I'll need to see some ID."

Emma groped through her purse, found her driver's license, handed it to the officer. He scrutinized the laminated card while his partner stared stonily at Emma. Baby Fat handed the license back to her. "What are you doing here at this hour?"

"Visiting my mother."

"You *are* aware of the curfew?"

"The curfew's at ten," Emma said, glancing at her watch. "It's only nine-forty-five."

Baby Fat looked her up and down. Emma felt suddenly as if she were standing naked on the sidewalk. She wondered what sort of weapons the officers were carrying. The FYC officers patrolling Washington Heights had once been armed only with billy clubs and stunners. They were considered policemen's helpers, simply keeping watch, supplementing the forces of law and order. But three months earlier, two FYC kids—one in Bed-Stuy, one in Washington Heights—had been killed by snipers. Soon thereafter, the young community servants were given bulletproof uniforms. It was rumored that some of them were now packing automatic weapons.

"We *know* what time it is," Baby Fat sneered. "You're not tryin' to get smart with us, are you? Not tryin' to give us some sass?"

Emma stared evenly at the officer; said nothing.

"We don't want to have to discipline you," Baby Fat said.

"And we could, too," the other officer chimed in, speaking for the first time. "Ain't no video cameras around."

Baby Fat stepped aside, presenting a clear path to Emma. "You can go," he said. "But don't let us catch you out here after curfew."

Walking up Riverside Drive, Emma could feel the eyes of the officers on her back. Sometimes, she thought, I could kill you all. Every last one of you.

>   >   >

As Emma entered her mother's apartment, Alma Person was in the kitchen, banging furiously on the ceiling with a broomstick, clutching the stick just above its straw sweepers and raising it rhythmically up and down in a pumping-piston motion, the rounded wooden handle thudding against the ceiling, threatening to crack the plaster. "You stop it with that fucking noise, you skanky white bitch!" Alma yelled at the ceiling. "You no-class tramp! Shut the hell up!"

"Hi, Mom."

"Oh, hi, honey," Alma said, setting down the broomstick, her voice becalmed. "I didn't expect you so soon."

"Neighbor bugging you again?" Emma asked, kissing Alma's damp cheek.

"Nonstop," Alma hissed. "She and her fucking illegitimate little animals, tromping around up there all hours of the day and night, blasting her music." Alma was speaking rapidly, in a low voice, as if trading confidential information with her daughter, trying not to be heard upstairs, just in case, Emma assumed, the neighbors might be eavesdropping. "They've got a dog now. And they run that dog around the apartment, from room to room, just to bother me. They can hear which room I'm in down here. So if that fucking bitch hears—"

"Which bitch?" Emma asked, trying to lighten the mood. "The woman or the dog?"

"The woman," Alma said, barely missing a beat. "If she hears me watching TV in the living room, she brings the dog into *her* living room so I have to hear the damn thing barking and running around and smashing into furniture. Then, if I turn off the TV and move into my bedroom, she listens and follows me into the bedroom above mine and lets the fucking dog run around up there!" Alma stopped suddenly. "Listen," she said, raising a hand as if to silence Emma, though Emma had not made a sound. "Can you hear that?"

Emma shook her head no. Though Alma had been complaining about the racket caused by her neighbor for two years, becoming increasingly agitated by it, threatening physical violence and lawsuits against the single mother and her unruly brood, Emma had rarely heard a peep from upstairs.

"Listen," Alma said impatiently. "Lis-sssseeennnnn . . ."

For Alma's benefit, Emma cocked her head and scrunched up her face as if straining to hear. "Ah, yeah," she said, nodding.

"That fucking cow!" Alma fumed. "She can hear me in here talking to you. Can't even leave me in peace to have a conversation with my own daughter." Alma grabbed the broomstick and commenced her banging again. "Shut the fuck up, you skanky, no-class bitch!" The handle of the broom thudded rhythmically against the ceiling. Several chips of plaster fell with a crackle on the linoleum floor.

"Yo, Mom," Emma said, taking hold of Alma's arms, "let's just forget about it for a while. Come on, let's go sit in the living room."

They took their customary spots, Emma on the couch, Alma in her rocking chair. Emma picked up the remote control and clicked on the TV. A commercial. She flipped the channel. A Tom and Jerry cartoon. Click. The Weather Channel, a plasticine man standing in front of a multicolored map of the United States. Click. *M°A°S°H.* Click. A black-and-white movie with Bette Davis. Emma didn't recognize it. Seth would know.

Alma rocked slowly, grimly. "It's because I'm black and she's white. So she thinks she can just walk all over me and get away with it. I complained to the landlord, again. Did I tell you?"

"Uh-huh."

"He didn't do a damn thing, of course. 'Cause *he's* white. Go ahead, trample on the black woman, you fucking—"

Alma stopped short, ceased rocking. "Do you hear that?" she asked, her voice quivering. "The vibrations. It's so loud, there's like a rumble." Alma held out her hand, palm facing the floor. Her hand trembled. "Do you see that? Do you see how it's making me shake? And this is my *good* hand!"

Emma nodded gravely.

"Can you hear it?" Alma said.

"Not right now, Mom. I think maybe you're just feeling an aftershock."

Alma started rocking furiously. "I'll fix her ass."

"You better let me take a look at those medical forms, Mom. Seth's gonna be here to pick me up soon."

➤　　➤　　➤

By the time she was pregnant with her only child, Alma Person had become acutely attuned to a certain quality in certain people, an incandescence behind the eyes, a subtle magnetism that made others want to emulate, to be near, and often to destroy them. All the great leaders and performers had it, of course, but so did countless anonymous people in all walks of life—this . . . not charisma, a cheap and trendy word that folks were tossing around a lot in those days. No, it was something else, this quality. Alma called it radiance. And she knew, long before she had given the quality a name, that she didn't have it.

Athena, her mother, had it. Athena's radiance was the type that manifested itself in an imperious, impatient demeanor. Nearly six feet tall and smarter than just about anyone she came in regular contact with, Athena seemed to inspire an instant deference from people—even from white people. Harry Hutchinson didn't have it. Alma's father was an easygoing mailman whose major passion was growing tomatoes in the Hutchinsons' small backyard garden and whose grandest ambition in life, he liked to say, was "to make it to the next day." Though she didn't have the words to express it, Alma sensed, by the age of five, that she was like her father: nobody special. She recognized this the day Athena brought home her new baby brother. Alma would stare at Melvin in his crib, as if trying to absorb some of the specialness that Athena said emanated from her son. Transfixed upon Melvin—who, when awake and alert, exhibited an almost eerie, distinctly unbabylike repose—Alma felt neither love nor hate for her brother. She simply wanted whatever it was he had.

Over the years, Athena doted incessantly on her gifted little boy, while seeming to regard Alma with an attitude that fell somewhere between the perpetual air of stern disapproval she presented to her pupils at Samuel Adams High School and the critical, frowning, appraising, yet grudgingly proud countenance she displayed when polishing her "heirlooms," the precious pieces of furniture, china, crystal, and silverware she had inherited from her mother. She criticized Alma, an excruciatingly shy child, for having "no get-up-and-go." Finally, at eighteen, attempting, if not to please, then, at least, to appease her mother, Alma got up and went to Columbia Teachers College.

As if by some perverse design, it was during her senior year at Columbia—just a few months before she would earn her degree and start a career in her mother's profession—that Alma fell in love with precisely the sort of man Athena Hutchinson despised. Rodney

Person, a sweet-natured, moonfaced young man, played the saxophone in Riverside Park. Alma had been sitting alone on a bench one afternoon, eating a ham and cheese sandwich, when Rodney, tenor sax strapped around his neck, carrying case in hand, seemed to appear out of nowhere. "Hello, beautiful lady," he said. "May I have the pleasure of serenading you?" Alma could barely listen as Rodney played, so thrilled was she by the unprecedented compliment he had paid her. Thin and flat-chested, Alma had never even been called attractive, let alone beautiful.

A weekly ritual developed. Every Friday afternoon, Alma would meet Rodney at the same park bench, bringing a sandwich for him and one for herself. They would eat and talk, then Rodney would play his sax, usually attracting a small crowd of passersby who dropped quarters, and the occasional dollar bill, in his open case. One day, after he finished playing "Stardust," an elderly white woman Alma had noticed in the park before dropped a twenty-dollar bill in Rodney's case. "You're a wonderful musician," she said, adding, as she glanced at Alma, "and you have a lovely wife." Rodney smiled and, staring rapturously at Alma, simply said, "Thank you." At that instant, Alma knew: It was just a matter of time.

Rodney Person, talented as he was, did not possess radiance. Alma didn't care. All she knew was that Rodney, for whatever reason, gave her love; and she was happy to give it back to him. Athena, after meeting Rodney, called him "an aspiring gigolo." Alma didn't care. The day after her graduation from Columbia, Alma married Rodney at city hall. Until that time, Rodney did not even have an apartment in New York—he slept on a friend's couch in Harlem. After the wedding, he moved into Alma's tiny one-bedroom place on Broadway and 110th Street. Alma was the breadwinner, supporting herself and her husband with the salary she earned teaching at Harriet Tubman High School. Rodney, meanwhile, tried to make a name for himself, playing with different bands around Manhattan, composing sporadically. Alma felt proud that she could help Rodney in his pursuit of a creative career. She felt that, together, they were building something, something important, something that would endure. In the early years of their marriage, Alma loved hanging out with Rodney and his musician friends, drinking, smoking reefer, even occasionally playing poker with them. For the first time in her life, she was hanging with the cool people. Years later, when she looked back on her twenties, it amazed Alma, the things she didn't worry about. Even when she became pregnant—carelessly, accidentally—Alma never worried. Rodney was playing gigs regularly, bringing in a little cash. Alma could see that her husband was less than enchanted by the idea of fatherhood. But, somehow, she just didn't worry about it.

Alma Justine Hutchinson Person knew if she had a daughter what her first name would be. Flaubert had his Emma; Austen had hers; Alma was going to have an Emma of her own. She had not given any thought to a middle name until she held her newborn daughter in her arms and felt her powerful, unmistakable aura, certain that it was not simply the joy of first-time motherhood she was experiencing but the recognition of that particular, ineffable incandescence, and so she named her child Emma Radiance Person.

Rodney was so moved by his daughter's birth, he went home that night and composed a song that came so easily to him, it seemed miraculous, cascading from his saxophone, almost all in one piece, unutterably gorgeous and heartbreaking and, he knew, probably the best song he would ever compose, because he recognized, before anyone else, of course, just how good this new song, "Radiance," really was. He played it over and over, until the neighbors, banging on his door at one in the morning, made him stop. Six months later, Rodney, backed by a loose-knit band, recorded his first album, highlighted by the title track, "Radiance." Within a year, "Radiance" began to take on the trappings of a standard. Other musicians recorded their versions of the tune. Royalties began to trickle in. Rodney signed a contract with a major jazz label. The Person family moved into an airy, high-ceilinged apartment on northern Riverside Drive in Washington Heights. "Radiance" was used in a perfume commercial and suddenly Rodney was making enough in royalties from this one song to support his family. Whenever she heard "Radiance," six-year-old Emma would say to her parents, "They're playing our song," then burst into delighted giggles.

Yet, gradually, a vague dissatisfaction, inexplicable and impossible to pinpoint, grew within Alma. She couldn't understand its cause until one night when she and Rodney went to see the Jimmy Higgins

Quartet play at the Village Vanguard. Between sets, Rodney disappeared backstage to talk to the band, while Alma—motherhood had distanced her from and made her somewhat self-conscious with Rodney's old musician friends—remained at the table, nursing her scotch and soda. Looking up from her drink, Alma saw Rodney, heading back to the table, intercepted by Miles Davis—a man who was pure, raw, blinding radiance. Miles Davis said something to Rodney in quiet, grave tones, then went backstage to greet the band. When Rodney returned to the table, he was bubbling. "He dug 'Radiance,'" Rodney exclaimed. "Miles dug 'Radiance'!" Alma smiled and offered her husband congratulations, but something about the incident annoyed her. There was something almost distasteful about Rodney's joy over another musician's approbation, even the approval of someone as undeniably great as Miles Davis. Why, Alma thought, couldn't Rodney Person be the man whom other musicians were eager to impress, instead of this grateful admirer?

Six years after recording his masterpiece, Rodney had not composed another song that was even in the same league with "Radiance." Nor did he really seem to want to. He rarely wrote new songs at all. He recorded three albums, made up almost entirely of other people's songs, in the three years after "Radiance." All three were weak. Rodney couldn't get another recording contract, but it didn't seem to bother him. Royalties from "Radiance" were still coming in, and Rodney earned more money playing occasional gigs. But he lacked the discipline and leadership to keep a band of his own together, so he generally sat in with other groups whenever he could. And to Alma's growing dismay, this situation did not trouble Rodney in the least. For years, Alma had believed she was supporting, encouraging, nurturing a man who aspired to gianthood, a man who had the talent and the courage to produce a major body of work. But Rodney was completely satisfied to have produced a single tune of import. He didn't care about having another. Alma began to feel the same bitter disappointment in Rodney that she knew Athena felt in Harry. Rodney Person had peaked at twenty-eight, and it did not faze him at all. Long after their divorce, Rodney's lack of ambition would still disgust Alma more than anything—save the fact that he named his second child, the son he fathered with Willow Cushing, Miles.

➤   ➤   ➤

It was the voices inside her head that told Alma Rodney was running around. Alma did not so much *think* her husband was cheating on her as *hear* it, and she did not so much hear the voices inside her head, the vague whisperings and urgent murmurs, as *feel* them, the way one can almost feel rather than hear the subtle waves of sound when a radio is turned on, with its volume extremely low, in the next room. The voices told her to confront Rodney with her suspicions, and she did. He denied being unfaithful. On one level, Alma knew Rodney was conning her, but on another level, she wanted to be conned. Rodney was so sweet, with his moony face and almost perfectly round childlike eyes—he'd always struck Alma as being practically ethereal in his lack of human spite and cunning—that Alma wanted to believe him more than she wanted to believe the far more convincing voices inside her head. And so she became a collaborator in her own deception.

But the voices would not cease. They told her that she needed to catch him, that she needed, just once, to have proof, evidence of his infidelity, that she could see with her own eyes. And they told her that if Rodney was indeed carrying on an affair, it had to be with Lucinda Robbins. New York's jazz vocalist of the moment, Lucinda Robbins had it: radiance. She was everything that Alma was not— flirty, gregarious, casually profane, the center of attention at any gathering. And Lucinda was voluptuous, while Rodney had been teasing Alma more and more about being "so bony," complaining that her elbows and knees were stabbing him in bed. Lucinda Robbins, the voices whispered feverishly. She was the culprit. Lucinda Robbins. Lucinda Robbins. Lucinda Robbins.

One weekend, Alma took Emma to Norris to visit Athena and Harry, telling Rodney they would return to Washington Heights Sunday afternoon. Instead, Alma and her seven-year-old daughter returned at ten o'clock on Saturday night. Entering the dining room,

Alma saw the snuffed-out candles, the smeared plates and empty cartons of Chinese takeout, and two empty wine bottles littered across the table. But no wineglasses. Those, Alma assumed, were in the master bedroom, from which the sound of "A Love Supreme" blared. Alma did not think; she reacted, obeying the fevered murmuring inside her head, the voices urging her to go on: *You must know, must see, with your own eyes. Go—now!* Grasping Emma's hand, dragging her daughter behind her, Alma marched down the long hardwood floor of the hallway toward the master bedroom, toward the sound of Coltrane's blaring saxophone, and flung open the door.

It is difficult, perhaps impossible, to say what precisely set Alma off, whether it was the simple fact of catching Rodney in the act or the discovery that it was not Lucinda Robbins but this pale, long-haired skeleton of a woman she saw squirming beneath her man. Just as Coltrane's sax reached a piercing crescendo, Alma unleashed a horrific, nerve-jangling scream. Alma turned and ran, ran from the apartment, down the six flights of stairs, ran out onto Riverside Drive and continued to run down the avenue, shrieking and flailing her arms about, running crazily for eight blocks before two policemen tackled and subdued her.

In her frenzy, Alma had forgotten about her seven-year-old daughter, who stood frozen in the doorway of her parents' bedroom, watching her nude father and this nude woman fumbling and writhing atop the bed, sheets and blankets strewn on the floor, while Rodney yelled, "Let go a me, lemme go!" and the strange white woman, seemingly terrified, clung to Emma's daddy, digging her nails into his fleshy back, staring at Emma with huge yellow eyes and looking, Emma thought, like her cat, Sissy, when Sissy was frightened, gasping for air and clutching Emma's daddy against her body as Emma's daddy struggled to tear himself free, yelling, "Let go a me, woman, lemme go!" And Emma stood perfectly still in the doorway of her parents' bedroom, staring, unblinking. Years later, Emma still could not say what she was feeling at that moment. She only knew she had to watch. Couldn't take her eyes off it.

Everyone has a private dread they are reluctant, if not unwilling, to admit, even to themselves, and this was Emma Person's: a terror of living alone. Life was so hard; life could be so arbitrary and cruel. How did anyone endure it alone? People had to go through life in teams. How, Emma wondered, could you *not* need someone to cry to, someone to tell about your day? How was your day? Emma loved that question, loved asking it, loved being asked it. How did people live, for years on end, for their entire lives, without someone to tell about their day? How else did you even know you were alive? That question was what she missed most terribly when she and Seth were living together in Vymar and he would have to leave town on story assignments, flying to New York or Los Angeles to interview some celebrity or another. When Seth was hired by the *Mavis!* show, requiring his move to New York, the first thought that flashed through Emma's mind was: Who will I tell about my day? Emma never told Seth how terrified she was at the thought of his leaving her alone in Vymar, loveless, emotionally unmoored. Seth would never know how much Emma needed his contact, how he gave her a comfort no one else could provide. Family and friends just didn't cut it when it came to intimacy. You needed someone to talk to in bed.

Absence of touch was what Emma had found so difficult about her early adolescence. How she missed it, the physical attention one got as a baby and during most of childhood, a contact that was seemingly banished from one's life at about ten or eleven and did not return until one entered a deep sexual relationship with another: the tender intimacy of someone caressing you, comforting your body, rubbing and kissing you where it hurt. It was so hard to live without that when she was thirteen, fourteen, fifteen, sixteen. Then she started seeing Keith, then Alec, then Seth. In twelve years of having sex, Emma had had only three lovers, and no more than three months had passed between each relationship. But those periods without physical intimacy and the emotions that came with it, those droughts, as Emma thought of them, had been torturous. The droughts made Emma feel as if she was fifteen again, lying alone in bed, needing so badly to feel another body touching hers, needing to talk to someone in the middle of the night, someone to whisper to and caress.

Yet, Emma thought, nostalgically, that at fourteen and fifteen she was tougher, hardier than she was as an adult. She remembered a song she wrote in the ninth grade, "I Don't Need No Man." Though she struggled to recall all the lyrics, only the first line, a line she would sing to herself from time to time in later years, stuck in her mind:

"I don't need no man/To send me flowers . . ."

It was a doo-wop feminist ditty that Emma performed in an all-female revue titled *Girls No More!* at Common Community High School—aka Commie Commie High—an alternative school in Greenwich Village that encouraged such political work, though Emma had written the song less out of any ideological commitment than the anger she felt toward Rodney, who, at that time, had just married Willow after seven years of cohabitation and announced that his new bride was pregnant. From that point on, Alma refused to let Emma spend time with her father. Leaving her for that white woman was bad enough; fathering a child with her was unforgivable.

Emma did not object to her mother's ban. In the first two years after her parents' divorce, Emma saw Rodney, alone, every weekend. Then Willow, finally recovered from the embarrassment of her first encounter with Emma, started joining Rodney and his daughter on their weekend excursions to museums and movies, amusement parks and zoos. Emma did not dislike Willow Cushing, but she did not like her, either. Tall and spindly, with an unusually pallid complexion and lank mousy brown hair, Rodney's lover had been christened Wilhemina and grew up on Sutton Place, the daughter of some rich guy. Though Alma was always urging her daughter to find out where the Cushing money had come from, Emma didn't know or care. In 1969, Wilhemina had her name legally changed to Willow, dropped out of Sarah Lawrence to try to make it as a folksinger, and was summarily disinherited by her father. Willow managed to produce just one album. Emma had heard it at her father's apartment, a compendium of morose love songs and earnest pleas for world peace, the album cover featuring a gauzy portrait of the wan, pasty singer staring glumly out a rain-streaked window. As a follow-up to her little-noticed debut, Willow ventured into something she called "experimental" jazz. A fan of "Radiance," Willow asked Rodney to play on her avant-garde record and Rodney, in his amiable, scattershot approach to his career, was pleased to oblige. The record company, unimpressed by the effort, refused to release Willow's second album —"I was way, way ahead of my time," she would explain to Emma. When her further artistic endeavors failed to earn her another recording contract, Willow wound up doing most of her singing as a background vocalist in television- and radio-commercial jingles.

Trying to keep her mother's spirits up, Emma regaled Alma with tales of Willow's hippy-dippy shallowness, her terrible cooking, her dumb jokes. And Alma did indeed seem cheered by Emma's stories. But Willow stopped being funny once Rodney married and impregnated her. (Or was it impregnated and married? No one was quite sure.) Alma grew more withdrawn and reclusive, and more dependent upon Emma for companionship and support. That was what people did, wasn't it? Emma thought years later. If you couldn't find the affection you needed in a lover, you had to find it in a child, a pet, something, anything! (Emma thought of Trudy Winkler, widowed, her precious sons away from home, cuddled up with Scarlett, kissing the Doberman's sleek brow, closing her eyes in pleasure when Scarlett licked and lapped at her, loving the feel of that huge tongue, that canine saliva, on her face.) Perhaps, Emma thought, you had this store of love within you and you needed to give it to someone or else it, and maybe *you,* would die. So you seek someone to give your love to. Sometimes you had to force it on them, sell it to them, beg them to take it from you. But you needed someone, anyone, to share your love with. Wasn't it after Emma left for college that Alma's most severe deterioration began? Wasn't it the four subsequent years of isolation, of feeling her love wither and die, that culminated in Alma gulping down a bottle of antidepressants? Wasn't it solitude as much as anything that had nearly killed Emma's mother?

No, Emma didn't need a man to send her flowers. She needed a man to save her from the empty, aching horror of aloneness.

➤   ➤   ➤

The first time Emma met Miles, her half brother was on a rampage. More than two years had passed since Alma forbade Emma to see her father. Despite the ban, Rodney was scrupulous about child-support payments and he and Emma exchanged cards and letters on a regular basis. But Emma and her father would not meet face-to-face again until Rodney's sister, Ernestine, invited Emma to her fiftieth birthday party. Ernestine's apartment in the Bronx was packed with relatives Emma had not seen since her parents' divorce. Willow was there, looking as wan and pasty as ever. Rodney, after giving Emma a long, affectionate bear hug, seemed a bit awkward in his daughter's presence. It seemed difficult for him to look Emma in the eye. He stared sheepishly into his glass of beer as they talked, giving short, vague answers to Emma's casual queries about work and family. Chill out, Daddy, Emma wanted to tell him. You don't have to feel ashamed. But she didn't. In a way, she liked seeing him squirm.

Enter Miles. Emerging from one of the back rooms in Ernestine's apartment where several of the children present were playing, eighteen-month-old Miles burst into the living room, screaming at the top of his lungs, running wildly, seeming to bounce like a human pinball off the legs of the grown-ups standing around Ernestine's living room. Miles's skin was as mayo white as his mother's, but he had a full, thick head of kinky black hair. Miles was not crying or throwing a tantrum; he was simply screaming as loudly as he could.

"Is anything wrong with him?" Emma whispered to her stepmother, unable to conceal a squeamish catch in her voice.

"Just getting out his aggressions," Willow said with a long-suffering fall in her voice that made Emma think Miles's behavior was routine.

As Miles scampered in Emma's direction, she scooped him up and held him above her head. "Hey, li'l bro," she said. Miles, laughing giddily, kicked her in the face.

"He kick hard," said Emma's cousin Tony, who was standing nearby. A hulking twenty-five-year-old high school dropout whose occupation, so far as Emma could tell, was beating up his wife and taking her money, Tony gazed admiringly at Miles. "Tough guy," Tony said, grinning like the half-wit that he was.

Emma set Miles down and he continued his shrieking. "Maybe he's just hungry," Willow said with a nervous flutter, handing Miles his bottle. Still screaming, Miles, bottle full of milk in hand, charged over to his cousin Angela, a four-year-old who was sitting quietly in a corner playing with a Barbie doll. Miles snatched the doll from Angela, tore the head off the toy, hurled it to the floor, and began battering the severed plastic Barbie head with his bottle.

Emma looked at her father. Rodney shrugged haplessly, as if to say, What do you want *me* to do about it? Following the lead of Miles's parents, the other adults in the room just shook their heads and smiled wryly or sucked their teeth and said, "That boy's somethin' else."

Finally, Aunt Ernestine, standing across the room from Miles, yelled, "You stop that actin' up, boy, you hear me!" All the party chatter stopped cold. Miles, frozen in midstrike, baby bottle full of milk poised above his head, looked up at Ernestine. Suddenly, he threw his bottle to the floor and started yelling back at her: "Ar-rahr-rahr! Agh rahr rahr rahr RARH!" Miles couldn't even form words yet, but, clearly, he was cursing out his aunt. "Don't you talk back to me, boy!" Ernestine shouted. Miles planted his little feet firmly on the carpet, jutted out his chin, pointed a finger at Ernestine, and started yelling anew: "Ya bahr yabba ba. Yabba babba BAH!" God only knows what names he would have called her had he the benefit of language. "Yabbaraaaarrrh! BAH!"

The room burst into laughter, more out of tension than anything resembling amusement. Miles, ignoring the response, ran over to his cousin Karen, who had been sitting at the dining room table with a puzzle book. Miles snatched Karen's pencil from her and raised it above his head as if he was about to stab his cousin. "Aiiieeeeeee!" Miles screamed. In a flash, Ernestine and Rodney converged on the toddler. Crying hysterically, he refused to relinquish the pencil. It took the two adults a full minute to wrest the pencil from Miles's tiny fist. "I think it's time for a nap," Willow said in a brittle singsong, picking up her bawling child and carrying him into one of Ernestine's bedrooms.

How, Emma wondered, did an eighteen-month-old child act like that? Surely, Miles's rampage exceeded normal infantile rambunctiousness. Emma's first assumption was that Miles must have been displaying learned behavior, that he must have been imitating what he saw at home. But Emma had never known her father to be violent. Rodney was so generally lethargic that she doubted he would even want to expend the energy required to hit Willow or anybody else.

So where did Miles's madness come from? Had Miles, somewhere in the genetic crapshoot, inherited the traits of violent creep relatives like Tony? Or did this weirdness come from Willow's side of the family? Or perhaps Miles was simply born evil? Maybe he was just some biological quirk, a random psychopath emerging already deranged from his mother's womb. Were such things possible? Did Emma even want to risk it? At sixteen, the notion was beginning to take hold: Emma would never have children.

>   >   >

Seth had never believed in love at first sight until he spotted Emma curled up in the fetal position on the floor of Café Chier, her slender body practically wrapped around the metal leg of the table she trembled and moaned beneath, looking less like someone who had just had her heart broken than someone who had just been shot in the belly and prompting Seth, who felt a sudden swelling of mingled emotions (empathy, pity, lust, a peculiar instant intimacy), to think ruefully, She's just the type of girl who'd never go out with me.

Café Chier was a one-of-a-kind establishment in Vymar, Massachusetts, a small college town that seemed to have precisely one of every kind of urban establishment: one jazz club, one gay bar, one (thanks to Adam Landau) comedy club, one expensive French restaurant. Café Chier was the sort of large, glossy and airy, overpriced coffee and pastry shop frequented by couples who were either just beginning or finally ending their romances. Seth had been waiting tables there for nearly two months, needing the money he earned less than he needed something to fill the empty hours he had on his hands now that he had abandoned his brief stint as a stand-up comic and no longer spent hours practicing his routines in front of the mirror, honing the act he had performed one night a week for six weeks at the Laugher Curve. On a typical evening at Café Chier, Seth shuttled between tables where couples who barely knew each other engaged in tentative conversation—trying to get acquainted without revealing too much too soon or saying something that might be stupid or offensive—after viewing whatever obscure foreign film or popular classic was showing at the Vymar Playhouse (the town's one revival house) and, not yet intimate enough to go directly to the apartment of one or the other and not wanting to go to a bar (there was something a little too indiscreet, a little too seventies, about sharing a late drink on a first date), considered a cup of decaffeinated cappuccino or espresso or a tall glass of either fizzy or noncarbonated mineral water a somehow safer option and tables where couples who knew each other all too well dealt long good-byes and recriminations, having chosen Café Chier as a "neutral turf," a place where they might weep and seethe but where, because of the bounds of public propriety, their emotions might not become too turbulent.

Seth had not been serving Emma's table that night—she was seated in another waiter's station—but he noticed, out of the corner of his eye, a tall blond guy striding angrily through the door of the coffee shop. Then, glancing at the table the angry young man had just vacated, Seth saw Emma, her back to him, fall, as if in cinematic slow motion, from her chair and crumple on the black-and-white chessboard-patterned floor. Though he had not even seen her face, there was something about this strange black woman (who, Seth guessed, accurately as it would turn out, was a student at Vymar College) that stirred him profoundly. He felt a sudden rush, as if he was a passenger in an elevator that had just shot up ninety stories without stopping. As he squatted beneath the table and lightly touched Emma's shoulder, Seth experienced a bittersweet sense of inevitability; it was as if he knew, through some previously untapped instinct, that he was about to embark on something of significance.

➤   ➤   ➤

Seth and Emma had spectacular sex in the early days of the hyper-war. The first night of the bombing was their fourth night sleeping together. They had just finished making love when, at about nine o'clock, Seth turned on the TV—he was always turning on the TV, Emma noticed—and they saw the map of Iraq and heard the voices of the reporters trapped inside the hotel, the sounds of explosions in the background. Seth popped a huge bowl of popcorn and he and Emma sat mesmerized for hours that night, listening to the trapped reporters, watching the replay of President Bush's speech from the

Oval Office: "The liberation of Kuwait has begun." *Let the games begin!* Finally, Emma could stand it no longer. They turned off the TV and had exultant, feverish sex the rest of the night. They slept the next morning. Emma cut classes. Seth called Café Chier and told the manager he was quitting—something he said he'd wanted to do for a long time. That afternoon, they made sweaty, pounding love with transcendent abandon. Then they watched more TV.

Holy shit! Tel Aviv gets Scudded! Everybody's waiting for some kind of response. Good God, was this how it would start? Was this how World War III would commence? We attack Iraq. Iraq attacks Israel. Israel attacks Iraq. More Arabs get pissed off and side with Saddam. The Soviet Union backs up the Arabs. The coalition bombs Moscow! The Soviets bomb New York! Was this the beginning of the end, the fate we had all dreaded but secretly longed for? Was the *pre*apocalyptic period suddenly over? Was the motherfucker of all wars finally here? Were we actually going to watch it on TV?

Seth and Emma watched, entranced, for hours. Finally, Emma could stand it no longer. They turned off the TV and had screaming, loin-bursting sex. Seth made more popcorn. Lying naked and exhausted in the bedroom, Emma could hear the kernels frying in oil, ricocheting off the sides of Seth's big black iron kettle, slamming like gunshots. Seth returned to the bedroom with a heaping bowl of the stuff. They turned on the TV.

Reporters speaking through gas masks! Jesus Christ. Nerve gas. Mustard gas. Something Seth had always associated with *All Quiet on the Western Front,* with some type of warfare that had passed into history along with those old-fashioned aeroplanes like Snoopy's *Sopwith Camel.* But no. In this Mideast conflict, nerve gas—not nukes—was the ultimate weapon. Seth imagined Tel Aviv, all of Israel even, turned into one gigantic gas chamber. He thought of all those Soviet Jews who, just a few months earlier, had fled the specter of civil war in the U.S.S.R. to go to the country that had been marked for Armageddon. Talk about out of the frying pan and into the fire.

Seth had recently started keeping a journal. What he really wanted, Seth told Emma, was to be a novelist, but he was still casting about for a story. "A journal," he said, "might give a wake-up call to my muse." But he had found making journal entries as dull and fruitless as trying to find "good grist" for a novel—until the bombing started.

"Suddenly, it feels like we're living in history," Seth wrote. "Or I realize for the first time, the first time in my adult life, anyway, that we have been living in history all along. But now I *feel* it. The last time I felt it this strongly was in the sixties, when I was a grade-schooler and Bobby Kennedy and Martin Luther King, Jr., were assassinated and there was Vietnam and the Black Panthers and all that shit on TV. And Watergate. Though that was the seventies, wasn't it? But now, this moment feels historic. The music I'm listening to now—I always obsess on one record for two or three weeks and play it over and over again, and the one I'm bingeing on now is *Heaven or Las Vegas* by the Cocteau Twins—suddenly seems *historic,* or it has historic resonance. Whenever I hear it from now on, I'll think, Oh, yeah, I was listening to that during the war period. The War."

The next night, Seth and Emma, eating popcorn compulsively, watched Patriot missiles blast Scuds out of the sky for hours. And it was—there was really no other word for it—thrilling. Seth and Emma talked solemnly about the futility of it all, the senselessness of all this killing. But they were exhilarated by it. They turned off the TV and threw themselves into body-slamming, come-splashing, cathartic fucking.

The following evening, Seth and Emma went out to eat at Vymar's one Chinese restaurant. Seth ordered steamed shrimp, with steamed vegetables and brown rice, no sauce, hold the MSG. As for Emma, she loved monosodium glutamate, enjoying the buzz it gave her, the tingly, prickly, slightly sweaty, shivery sensation, making her feel both calm and alert as she savored her General Tso's chicken—she had just a taste of Seth's dish and he declined to share hers (Great, Emma thought, one of those dietetically correct types)—and listened to the conversations, or the *one* conversation, the one about the war, swirling around her. She eavesdropped on the edgy voices pondering the bombs, the nerve gas, the weirdness of it, nobody really sure where it was all going to lead, and, yes, things were pretty easy from the air, but what about the ground war? Looking up from her plate, Emma saw Seth gazing lovingly at her. She smiled. He seemed like a sweet man. She wiggled slightly in her chair, relishing the delicious achy feeling between her thighs. They went back to Seth's apartment and made slow, gentle, languorous love, shuddering and hanging on to each other as if for dear life as they came in precise simultaneity. Then they turned on the TV.

The newscasters weren't wearing gas masks anymore. A big, beefy general with a buzz cut and some incredibly Nazi-like name showed videotapes of targets getting blasted. In ghoulishly cheery tones, he described the missiles and their various targets as Seth, Emma, and much of the rest of the world watched. They were ghostly, infrared images, taken from cameras placed in the noses of missiles, so that watching the videotape you felt as if you were riding with Slim Pickens in *Dr. Strangelove,* just a-ridin' that missile as you zeroed in and then—POW!—the big jizz in a flash of light. News commentators said it over and over, but that didn't make the observation any less true: It *was* like playing a video game. That was the clearest point of reference Seth had for watching these missiles zoom down chimneys and explode before his eyes. He was reminded of his friend Phil from college, a smooth and urbane dude, a very mellow guy— except when he played Space Invaders or some such game. Seth used to watch him at their favorite burger joint. Phil would thrust his pelvis against the machine, twisting the controls violently in his hands, banging down hard on the buttons, screaming, "Come on you bitch, you fucking bitch!" Kicking the machine when he got blown out of the sky. "You fucking bitch! Fuck you!" Pushing against the machine and punching the air with his fists when he scored high. "Aaaaarrrgh! Yes! Yes! I love it! Aaaaaarrrgh!"

The jovial general with the SS name and the bulky, neckless punching-bag body showed a clip of a bridge in Baghdad, overhead view, shot from a camera in the belly of an airplane. "Watch very carefully," the general said. Suddenly, a little rectangular spot, like a white radioactive cockroach, scooted from the bottom of the screen and disappeared at the top. A bomb is dropped from the plane, then: the startling flash of light. "That was the luckiest man in Baghdad today," the general said dryly. "Imagine what he saw in his rearview mirror." The roomful of reporters and soldiers at the general's briefing burst into laughter. Seth and Emma laughed, too.

As they fell asleep in each other's arms that night, their naked bodies entwined, noses just barely touching, Emma thought, This is it. This is the best feeling in the universe. Nothing can compare with this feeling.

The next morning, life seemed to have returned to some semblance of normality in Vymar. The tension, the rippling waves of anxiety Seth and Emma had felt the night before in the Chinese restaurant, had evaporated. Walking through the snowy, blindingly white streets on this sunny, blustery morning, Seth no longer felt the intense connection he had felt with other people—with all these strangers—the night before. Last night, as he and Emma had walked down these same snow-laden streets, Seth had felt a strange bond with everyone. He had never known such a feeling of mass connectedness, as if everyone in the world were going through the same trauma. The war was a global experience. We were, all of us, living in history together. But this morning, that awesome bond—those millions of invisible umbilical cords that Seth had imagined attached him to every living human—was severed. Each person had slipped back into his or her own individual cocoon, reencapsulated, safely sealed off again.

"We're all getting kind of used to it now," Seth wrote. "The war is on, that feeling of significance is gone. Oh, yeah, the war. Nobody knows where it goes from here, but we do seem to be kicking the bloody shit out of this country, so we might as well start the ground war and get it over with. The war's gotten, well, almost boring. And we're glad for the boredom, glad to be rid of that sense of living in history. Would it even be possible to live day to day, to get on with the tedious daily business of life while being so intensely aware of history? And, by the way, doesn't that Tariq Aziz guy, the Iraqi diplomat, look like he's being played by Peter Sellers?"

Six weeks later, it was all over. Iraqi soldiers emerged, shellshocked, from their trenches in the middle of the desert and fell to their knees before the U.S. ground troops, evidently embarrassing their conquerors. Saddam Hussein surrendered. Baghdad was a crater: ruins flowing with filthy water, garbage, blood, and shit.

On Main Street in Vymar, Massachusetts, joyful citizens decorated the primary artery, the financial center of the town, where the main branch offices of every bank, the snazziest restaurants, and fanciest shops had always been located, but where in the last two years one franchise after another had closed. A smattering of business failures was, in itself, not so unusual; aside from Main Street's ancient institutions, there had always been—for Vymar—a relatively high turnover rate on the strip. What had been weird, though, about '89, '90, and now '91 was that no new stores took the places of the old ones and today Main Street was speckled with darkened windows and huge black-and-white or red-and-white GOING OUT OF BUSINESS signs. But after the hyperwar, Main Street looked more bright and festive than it had since Christmas. Little yellow ribbons and American flags decorated every lamppost and storefront. A giant red-white-and-blue banner was suspended over the boulevard: VYMAR SUPPORTS THE TROOPS!

Walking down Main Street, Emma felt as if she had had her guts ripped out. One hundred thousand people had been killed in the hyperwar. One hundred thousand. More even. It was unimaginable. She could not get her mind around a number like that. She just couldn't comprehend it, visualize it. One hundred thousand people. "That's the size of the University of Michigan football stadium," Seth said. A giant football stadium full of people. Obliterated. In a half-dozen weeks or so. And more dead to come. And Saddam Hussein still in power. But out of Kuwait, which now looked like hell on Earth: A-bomb-sized clouds of billowing black smoke, huge oil refineries aflame, the entire landscape blackened, on fire; enormous patches of land resembling a garbage-can fire in a dark alley.

But . . . one . . . hundred . . . thousand . . . people. An ungraspable number. How many Americans had died in Vietnam? Half that, maybe? How many had died of AIDS at that point? Was it more than five figures? One hundred thousand!

And the Vymarians seemed to be gloating over it. There was a malevolent sheen in their grins: *Hey, we kicked butt, didn't we? Didn't we!* We had unleashed the most efficient killing machine in the history of civilization and had slaughtered more people in the shortest span of time since Nagasaki. And we couldn't stop congratulating ourselves for it.

"It's just inconceivable," Emma said to Seth over dinner that night. "And for what? The guy is still in power."

"Well, we lost a lot of people, too," Seth said.

"Nowhere near as many."

"But our share. Would it be better if they had killed more of us? We'd have lost. That's war. It sucks."

"But at least the people we lost were *soldiers*. I mean, if you're a soldier, you know that part of the job is that you might have to die at any minute. But the people in Iraq, these weren't just soldiers."

"Mainly."

"Mainly, sure, but a lot of them were women, children, old people, babies—civilians."

"Civilians dying in war is nothing new. Sad to say, but it's true."

"But it's still revolting. One hundred thousand individuals. One hundred thousand lives."

"Yes," Seth said, "but they were *Iraqi* lives."

Emma was too stunned to respond. After almost two months of sleeping with Seth, she was suddenly struck by the thought: I don't know this person.

➤ ➤ ➤

Sixty people dead in LA. Now *that* was a number that could freak Seth out. He could understand the outrage. He felt it, too. He remembered turning on the TV soon after the hyperwar and seeing more ghostly, infrared footage, this time of a group of men with clubs mercilessly beating an unarmed man as he writhed on the ground. "Damn," Seth said, "things are really out of control in Kuwait." He turned and looked at Emma, who was sitting beside him on the bed, staring at the TV, her mouth agape.

"Turn up the volume," Emma whispered urgently. "I think this is America."

A year later, after a white jury acquitted the white cops who had attacked the black "motorist" (as the media referred to him), Seth and Emma watched the ensuing insurrection, rebellion, uprising (or, as the media referred to it, "riots") with an exponentially increasing horror. It was the randomness of the violence that terrified Seth. The Rodney King beating had been heinous. All reasonable people agreed on that. But even Rodney King had had some interaction with his attackers, some exchange with the police before the assault. Of course, that didn't justify what the cops had done to him. But still, it wasn't as totally arbitrary as black people dragging innocent drivers from their cars and attacking them simply because they were white.

"They're not comparable situations," Emma said hotly. "These are enraged citizens, not cops. The people assigned with maintaining law and order aren't supposed to go out and beat people with clubs just because they're black!"

Well, Seth thought, two wrongs don't make a right. He and Emma both knew that. Still, the sight of that one white guy getting pulled from his truck and stomped on by black thugs was infinitely more disturbing to Seth than 100,000 Iraqis getting blown up. To be beaten within an inch of your life—just because you're white! Seth began to worry about things that had never concerned him before. Were he and Emma, as an interracial couple, at particular risk? He felt fairly safe living in Vymar. But what if they had been living in New York when the series of Rodney King–related revolts broke out around the country? Hadn't there been a white casualty in Manhattan already? Days after all the violence had died down, Seth was still fretting about his safety with Emma. "It just makes you wonder," he said to her as they lay in bed late one night. "I mean, what could happen to us?"

"You know, I'm getting really sick of this," Emma said, sitting up. "What do you want me to say? When you keep telling me how worried you are about us being an interracial couple or how scared it makes you, you're putting me in the position of having to reassure you. You want me to tell you, Oh, don't worry, I won't get you killed. And I am just not gonna waste my breath trying to convince some frightened guy that he should go out with me. Either you have the courage or you don't. If you don't have the balls to be seen with me, let's not waste any more time. Let's end the relationship— now!"

Seth knew Emma was right, and from that moment on, he kept his fears, which refused to disappear, to himself. Besides, he thought, *most* of the victims of the rioting weren't white. Most of the casualties had been blacks and other minorities. The crazy irony of it! Most of the people the blacks in LA killed were their own people. The neighborhoods they torched were their own neighborhoods. Seth hated to think it, but sometimes black people just didn't seem very *logical.* Seth was surprised to find himself even entertaining such a bigoted thought. But he thought it nonetheless. And something about the thought, something about the raw honesty of it, gave Seth a frisson of guilty pleasure, like jerking off to a porno video or laughing at a really crude ethnic joke. And the thought, that little flicker of racism in his consciousness, touched off a puzzling question. He had always been so fond of black people and, though he never asked explicitly, he always wondered what it meant to Emma, to be black. Suddenly, Seth wondered, What does it mean to *me*—that is, being white?

➤ ➤ ➤

December 1959. Lester Winkler was finishing his first semester at the University of Pennsylvania Law School. He and Trudy, his bride of six months, lived in a four-flight walk-up a few blocks from campus. Money was tight, but, with Lester's parents paying his tuition and Trudy's parents paying for their rent, the newlyweds weren't complaining. Trudy earned money for all their other expenses by working as a receptionist in the university's admissions office. Though he felt pressured with final exams coming up, Lester wanted to do something special for Trudy to show how much he appreciated her support. He left the library early one frigid evening and bought a tall, gorgeous Christmas tree. He hurried home to start decorating it. He wanted to have at least the tinsel and lights in place when Trudy walked in the door. Then, together, they could add the shiny spherical ornaments and the gossamer angel he had bought.

"Surprise!" Lester whooped as Trudy walked in the door with a bagful of groceries. He plugged in the lights. They began flashing in a jagged pattern, red, green, and yellow explosions seeming to ricochet off the branches of the tree. Trudy stood in the doorway, aghast. "Merry Christmas, honey!" Lester sang.

Trudy, her face ashen, walked into the kitchenette and set the sack of groceries down on the counter. The whole time, she kept her eyes focused on the flashing tree. She seemed in a trance. Lester, uncomprehending, asked, "Don't you like it?"

"How could you do this?" Trudy asked in a low rasp that made the hairs on the back of Lester's neck bristle like a dog's. "Have you no respect for our religion?" Trudy said in the same gravelly voice that Lester had never heard come out of her before.

"It's just a Christmas tree, sweetie," Lester said nervously. He shrugged and smiled. "Just think of it as a decoration."

"A decoration?" Trudy said, her voice returning to its normal high-pitched timbre before, in the next instant, she shrieked, "A decoration! How could you bring this into our home!" Before Lester could stop her, Trudy lunged at the tree, screaming hysterically. "Have you no respect for our religion? You have no respect for our religion!" As Trudy took hold of the tree, Lester tried to take hold of his wife. "You have no respect for our religion!" Lester felt lost in a spinning whirlwind of arms and branches and electrical wires, feeling the scratch of both pine needles and Trudy's nails on his face and hands. Trudy now had a firm grip on the tree and, with a ferocious tug, pulled it away from Lester, ripping the cord for the lights from the wall socket. Dragging the tree across the floor, fumbling through the doorway, Trudy struggled to the edge of the staircase.

"You're crazy!" Lester heard himself yell as he rushed after his wife, slipping in the bits of tinsel and pine needles scattered across the floor. With a mighty heave, Trudy lifted the conifer and hurled it down the stairs. She ran down to the third-floor landing, where the tree lay awkwardly on its side. She picked it up again and hurled it down the next flight of stairs, the lights on the tree clattering and shattering on the steps.

"You don't respect our religion!" Trudy screamed over and over as she hauled the tree through the tiny lobby of their apartment building, Lester, his knees sprained from the several spills he'd taken on the stairs, hobbling in pursuit. Trudy shoved the tree through the front door, out onto the street, and, with one last burst of furious energy, hurled it into the gutter.

>   >   >

The earliest known human inhabitants of the vast expanse of wilderness that included the area that would someday be called Blissfield were the Mohican people. Long after the natives had been chased away or exterminated by waves of Europeans—the first of these led by an especially bloodthirsty Dutch fur trader named Pieter Bliss—the woodland along the Hudson River remained largely unsettled. Only late in the nineteenth century did wealthy New Yorkers—almost all of them white Anglo-Saxon Protestants—begin building country homes in the area. The suburbanization of Blissfield began in the 1920s as a new generation of WASPs who could afford to escape the congestion of New York City created a pleasant little hamlet for themselves. Quaint general stores popped up; a band shell was constructed in the center of town. The commute into Manhattan —it was a two-hour train ride in those days—was a small sacrifice for the doctors, lawyers, and bankers who wished to provide a safe haven for their families in Blissfield. In the thirties, the Irish began to infiltrate the town. Then, after World War II, the Jews started moving in. By the end of the fifties, the wealthiest WASPs had fled Blissfield, moving farther north or leaving New York State altogether for places like Princeton and Greenwich. There remained a number of Irish families in Blissfield and a few Italians. But everyone who knew anything in New York knew by 1962—the year Lester Winkler, law school diploma in hand, and his pregnant wife, Trudy, moved into the suburb of their highest aspirations—that Blissfield was a Jewish town.

Later in the 1960s, two wealthy Negro families moved into town; in the 1970s, two more arrived. Blissfield residents prided themselves on their lack of prejudice and welcomed the black families. If there were no more blacks moving into town, the white residents reasoned, it was simply because real estate prices were too high. Blissfielders did not discriminate. Blissfield had been a Jewish town for so long that Trudy Winkler and her friends imagined it would always be a

< *151* >

Jewish town. The change came gradually. In the eighties, many of Trudy's friends moved away. Couples whose children had already graduated from college sold their homes at massive multiples of their original costs and bought condominiums in Manhattan. Some in Trudy's circle, those she called "the old at heart," actually moved to Florida. A few couples divorced and fled in opposite directions from Blissfield. An unnervingly large number of homes were vacated. Trudy and her remaining friends wondered—a bit nervously, though they tried to conceal the squeamishness that laced their speculations —if perhaps more black families would start moving in.

But there were no new black faces in town. In fact, two of Blissfield's original four black families had moved away. Trudy wondered why. Perhaps, she thought, the blacks who were wealthy enough to live in the suburbs simply wished to live among themselves. She knew that Hallisbury, about twenty miles southwest of Blissfield, was gaining a reputation as a black suburb, just as Blissfield was known as a Jewish suburb. Trudy could empathize. It was the desire to live among her own people that had led her to Blissfield in the first place. Let the blacks have Hallisbury. Trudy had noticed, in recent years, that Hallisbury's downtown area had become just a bit . . . well, shabby. And, when passing through the town, didn't it seem that there were more and more young people loitering in the streets? And the noise from the car radios had grown significantly louder. Few Blissfielders talked about what they saw happening in Hallisbury, but they all noticed it.

Meanwhile, the people who took control of all the beautiful old houses that had once belonged to Trudy's friends weren't black— but they weren't white, either. They were the sort of people Trudy and her friends had encountered only in restaurants and laundries. They were *Orientals*. And, distressingly, it wasn't just the houses these people started taking over. First came the fruit and vegetable stands, then the video store, then more laundries and restaurants. And the final outrage: a barren-looking little food shop with strange victuals that Trudy would never even consider buying, fishy sauces and mysterious brown things packed in jars, floating in hideous brown juices. The sign on the storefront wasn't even in English! It was just a bizarre jumble of spindly, indecipherable characters, a mess of calligraphy that seemed to disinvite any white person. Lester Winkler died around this time, and Seth began to notice some troubling attitudes in his mother. Whenever Seth returned from college for a visit home, Trudy griped about what was happening to the neighborhood. "What am I, living in Tokyo?" Trudy fumed. "Chinatown? Soon we're gonna be the only round-eyes left on our block!"

But with the nineties came the former Yuppies, refugees from Manhattan, couples with children just starting grade school. Though Trudy had hoped a new generation of solid Jewish citizens would move into Blissfield, the new residents came in every brand of white: WASP, Irish, Italian, Jewish, and so on. With Blissfield almost 20 percent Oriental—or, as Seth was always reminding his mother to say, *Asian*—Trudy was relieved to see what she had called "the yellow tide" stemmed. And though she was less than pleased to be living amid so many goyim, she had to admit that Blissfield's mix of white ethnicities seemed to work well together. Because they were all bound by the same principles: the desire to keep their streets safe and their schools sound and their parks clean and their property values high. And, though it was rarely stated bluntly, they all wanted to keep Blissfield from turning into another Hallisbury.

➤   ➤   ➤

Yes, Seth was willing to concede, his mother could be insensitive; she could blurt out prejudiced comments. But a racist? Yes, she had flipped out when she learned Emma was black. But she had apologized to Seth and retracted her unpleasant remarks. And she'd never said anything racist to Emma herself. In fact, Trudy went out of her way to show that she accepted Emma. Whenever she called Vymar and got Emma on the phone, Trudy would tell her about the work she had done—her first forays in fund-raising—for the civil rights movement. Or she would tell Emma about the latest novel by Toni Morrison or Terry McMillan she was reading. Emma responded to Trudy's overtures with a glacial indifference. This was what Seth found most exasperating. How could you be so cold to someone who was trying so hard to be nice?

Even playing host to Balford for an entire school year was an attempt by Trudy to feel closer to and understand Emma. Balford was a poor black kid, the son of a preacher, from some godforsaken town in Mississippi. During Trudy's last year in the old Blissfield house—before she moved into the two-family home on the other side of town—Balford lived in Seth's old room, attended Blissfield High, and basically became a member of the Winkler family. Trudy wrote a letter to Emma telling her how excited she was to be "exposing this young man to a whole new world." Trudy added, "I might even learn a thing or two myself (smile)."

Typically, Emma did not respond to Trudy's letter, but she let Seth know how she felt. "It's inverted missionary work. Instead of going out to educate the noble savages, she's bringing the savage to her. Don't you see the assumption of superiority? She's assuming that her wealthy white suburban way of life is inherently better than this kid's. I just find something really cloying and condescending about the whole thing."

"Why," Seth asked, "can't you think of it as a cultural exchange program?"

"Cultural exchange would be if your mother or your brother went and lived in Mississippi. As it is, this is a one-way deal. Let Trudy go work as a sharecropper for a year."

"You'd probably criticize her for that, too."

"Probably."

"You really hate my mother, don't you?"

Emma paused, seeming to consider Seth's question carefully. "I don't think hate," she said thoughtfully, "is a strong enough word."

While Trudy provided Seth and Emma with regular updates on how successfully Balford's year up north was progressing, Eric, a senior at Blissfield High, told them a different story. Balford, he said, was incredibly weird. At home, he stayed in his (Seth's) room every evening, reading the Bible. He never went out. At Blissfield High, Balford had no friends. Even the handful of black students—most of them bused in from other communities—avoided him. At lunchtime, Balford would sit alone in a corner of the cafeteria, reading the Bible. "I've been living in the same house with this guy for six months," Eric said, "and I don't think I've heard him say six sentences."

Seth didn't meet Balford until late in the school year, when he had to go to New York on a story assignment and decided to pay a visit to Blissfield. Sure enough, Balford, on this Friday evening, was holed up in Seth's old room. "Come in please," Balford said, almost inaudibly, when Seth knocked on the door. Balford was a lanky kid with a long, solemn face, hooded eyes, and a grimly quiet demeanor that made Seth think there was either a lot going on inside him or nothing at all. Seth did most of the talking for the five minutes he spent with Balford, standing awkwardly, barely inside the doorway, feeling like an alien in the very room he had grown up in, while Balford sat, virtually immobile, at Seth's old desk.

"So, uh, how have you liked your stay here?" Seth asked.

Balford stared at him, with no trace of emotion in his sleepy eyes. "I just put my trust in Jesus."

"Oh. That's good. Well, see ya around."

Closing the door on Balford, Seth almost had to laugh at the notion that Trudy might somehow understand Emma better by bringing this poor slob into her home. As far as Seth could tell, pigmentation was the only thing his girlfriend, a quick-witted atheist, had in common with Trudy's guest. Seth even wondered if maybe Balford was a little bit brain-damaged.

"I've done everything I can to reach out to him," Trudy said as she adjusted and readjusted her pillows, trying to get comfortable as she talked to Seth, who sat on the edge of her bed just after he'd met Balford. "There's no getting through to him."

"But you always said things were going well with him."

"And they are! Look where he's living. Look where he's going to school. For him, this is a great experience. All I'm saying is that he lacks good interpersonal skills."

"Maybe he's just shy. He's probably never been around so many white people before."

"Another thing I just don't get. Every night, all he ever wants to eat for dessert is fruit cocktail—every single night. I have presented him with these amazing desserts. Homemade rugulah, mandelbrot. At Purim, we had a hamantaschen to die for. To die for. And all he wants to eat is fruit cocktail from out of a can. Now what kind of cultural exchange is that?"

"Well, the semester is almost over. Just a few more weeks."

"Thank goodness. So how's *your* schvartze?"

"She's fine."

"So can I just ask you one question?"

"I doubt there's anything I could say to dissuade you," Seth said, thinking, I'm beginning to sound like Emma.

"What does it mean to you to be Jewish?"

"Look, Mom, could you just lay off Emma—"

"Who's talking about *her?* My question is to you, about you. What does it mean to you to be Jewish?"

"Aw, Mom, I don't know. How could I even begin to answer such a question? It's complicated."

"Is it? I mean, should it be? Why isn't it more simple, more clear to you?"

"I just don't—"

"It must be something I did. But I cannot, for the life of me, see where I went wrong. I mean, your father and I, we sent you to Hebrew school, we had you bar mitzvahed, you spent that summer on the kibbutz, we celebrated holidays—"

"Mom, look, I appreciate all that, but, you know, well, let me put the question to you: What does being Jewish mean to *you?*"

"Survival," Trudy said instantly, in a voice of steel. "That above all else. Survival."

Though Seth had not anticipated any particular answer, the one his mother gave shocked him into silence.

"Perhaps your father and I didn't teach you well enough," Trudy continued quietly, "didn't *instill* it as we should have. But, my God, Seth, you had aunts and uncles and cousins you will never meet because they were systematically murdered, exterminated, annihilated. Because of what they were. Just because of what they were. Maybe you're just too young for it to mean much to you. You're too removed, too distant. But the survival of this line, the endurance of our people, means everything to me. Because if they had had their druthers, *none* of us—not *you,* not any one of us—would be alive today. Because of what we *are.* And that's why I have trouble understanding you, Seth. How can it not matter to you what you *are?*"

Seth could not answer, could not think of anything to say. His mother's words had touched him in an unfamiliar way. Trudy seemed to have reached into him and stirred something, something that seemed strange yet utterly basic, utterly fundamental, something that was purely, inescapably Seth. He didn't know what it was his mother's words had done to him. He only knew that he had to leave her room at once, before he started crying.

>   >   >

"I think I'll always feel like a kid," Seth said, "until I have a kid of my own."

Emma and Seth were sitting on a hill in Blissfield Park, just before dusk on a mid-October evening, two weeks after they'd moved into Trudy Winkler's home, watching a father and his son trying to get an enormous, brightly colored kite aloft. Emma was just beginning to understand the deep affection Seth had for his hometown, the nostalgic way he viewed his childhood, the loss he must have felt, but rarely discussed, when his father died. Still, his comment annoyed her. If Seth really meant what he said, what, then, was Emma to him? The vehicle for his personal growth, the vessel of his maturity? As for Emma, she stopped feeling like a kid the night she caught her father in bed with Willow Cushing.

Though the breezy weather was perfect for kite flying, the father and son were having trouble getting the kite to take off. The son, a bouncy, chubby ten-year-old, was particularly hapless when holding the spindle. Finally, the dad, a bespectacled, fortyish man with gray-flecked hair and a budding middle-aged paunch, took charge. With the father holding the spindle, the wind carried the kite high into the air. The little boy cheered and applauded. The dad stood motionless at the top of the hill, watching the kite, now suspended high in the orange sky, the string taut as he gripped the spindle in his hands. Emma kept waiting for the father to turn over the spindle to his son, but he just stood there, staring serenely into the sky, admiring his accomplishment. He said something to his son and the kid went running eagerly from the park, disappearing into one of the neighboring houses. Two minutes later, the son returned with a video camera. That's nice, Emma thought, now he'll turn the kite over to his son and capture the fun for posterity. "Go down to the bottom of the hill," the father said. "You can get a better shot from down there." The son dutifully scooted to the bottom of the hill, pointed the camera at his father, and started shooting. The dad stood at the top of the hill, grinning childishly, admiring his feat of flight. "Get a shot of the kite!" he called out to his son. The kid obediently pointed the camcorder at the airborne toy.

"That's sweet," Seth said.

"Sure," Emma replied archly. "Always nice to see a man getting in touch with his inner child. I can't imagine it's too much fun, though, for his *actual* child. I mean, who is the grown-up here? Whose kite is it, anyway? Is the son supposed to look at that video-tape someday and remember fondly how cute his middle-aged father was flying his kite?"

Seth gave Emma a wounded look. "Yeah, well, maybe we better head home," he said.

Sitting behind the wheel of the car, Seth took the long route back to Trudy's, driving languidly through the twisting roads of the woodsy suburb, calling Emma's attention to some of the more sprawling homes, to the vast lush lawns that impressed him. "It's really a great town," Seth said. "So close to New York but so insulated from the craziness of the city." He glanced hopefully at Emma. "Don't you like it?"

"I don't dislike it," Emma said. "But I can't really say I like it, either."

"What's not to like?"

"I don't know. I just feel like you and I, we stand out so much here. You don't see many black people in this town."

"Well, you're helping integrate it. There'll be more."

"I guess. It's not just that, though."

"What then?"

"This whole—I don't know . . . this way of living, it seems to re-quire a lot of . . . maintenance. Like you really have to *want* it. Be really committed to it, to maintain it all. I just don't know if I want it that much."

"You mean you don't know if you want *me* that much."

"No, that's not what I meant."

They drove the rest of the way home in silence.

"You're dead inside," Keith said through angry tears. "You're selfish. And you're coldhearted. And you don't even know it."

Listening on the other end of the phone as she sat in her dorm at Vymar College, Emma apologized for hurting Keith's feelings. She tried to explain that after Keith graduated and took a job in Seattle, she'd simply gotten lonely. It wasn't anything personal. She had not set out to fall in love with Alec, but she had. It did not mean that she didn't still love Keith. She would always love Keith.

"You sound like you're reading from a script," Keith said, strangling on a sob. "He's white, isn't he?"

"Yes. But that's got nothing to do with it."

"I always knew you'd leave me for a white boy."

"Oh please."

"You're dead inside," Keith cried. "Don't you see it? Don't you know this isn't normal? You're dead inside."

Emma sighed. She had been faithful to Keith for three months after he moved to Seattle. Finally, she had just gotten lonely. She explained that to him over and over. If that made her a coldhearted bitch, if that made her "dead inside," so be it. Besides, Emma couldn't take a weeping man seriously.

But now, years later, lying in bed beside Seth, wide awake, three hours before she would have to get up for work, four hours before she would tell Seth that she thought she was pregnant, Keith's words gnawed at her.

Dead inside.

Seth had often criticized Emma for being "antisocial." But, really, she was more asocial. She didn't hate people. It was just that she could take or leave most of them. Once Rodney gave her a Nikon for her twelfth birthday, Emma discovered something far more absorbing and pleasurable than an active social life.

She wasn't coldhearted. Was she? If anything, she was overly sensitive. There were times when Emma felt so vulnerable, so painfully attuned to people and the world, that she imagined she had no skin, that she was all exposed muscle and bone, tissue and nerves. She just wasn't weepy and girlish. That's what men couldn't handle. But she loved. She loved intensely. When she loved a man, whether it was Keith or Alec or Seth, she drew a circle around herself and her lover. She befriended the friends of her boyfriend. Even Naima, her closest confidante, she had met through Alec. What was coldhearted, what was selfish about that?

You're dead inside. Dead inside.

Emma turned on her side and, eyes adjusting to the darkness, stared at Seth, his long, dark hair spread across his pillow. How many years had she stared at that face? How could she even think about not having this man in her life? They had their problems, yes. But all couples did. Seth was generous. She could not deny it. And he had saved her. He had saved her.

He saved her that night in Vymar when, a year after she had swiftly dispatched Keith Reynolds for Alec Larsen, Alec swiftly dispatched her, telling her as they sat in Café Chier that it just wasn't working, that they just didn't have enough in common, that he just didn't love her anymore, and she, unable to believe it, making him say it again and again because she still could not believe it, could not fathom that this man for whom she'd sacrificed so much, for whom she'd endured the scorn of Vymar's black community, *her* community, a man she had made the focus of her life, this beautiful man with his yellow hair and blue eyes—"Hitler's wet dream," she had teasingly called him—could drop her, just like that, without warning, in a coffee shop. "Who will I give my love to?" she asked, barely audibly, as Alec got up and walked away from the table, through the glass doors of Café Chier.

The next thing Emma knew, she was on the floor, under the table, and when she looked up, feeling unable to speak, unable to answer the waiter's question ("Are you all right?") but touched, touched deeply by his kindly, quizzical face, she realized that, yes, she would be all right. Because she knew, just from looking at Seth, that he would accept her love.

>   >   >

Seth was, he had to admit, a little bit afraid of Emma's mother. As he settled back into the richly upholstered seat of the chauffeur-driven black sedan—a perk Mavis provided to any producer who worked past 9:00 P.M.—Seth recalled one of the weirder stories Emma had told him about Alma Person. It had happened during the brief period between Alma's discovery of Rodney's affair with Willow and the day Rodney decided to pack his bags and move in with his mistress. Alma heard through a grapevine of old friends that Rodney would be attending a costume party at the home of one of Willow's cronies. Alma stormed into the party, sans costume, and began pushing through the crowd, looking for her husband. A young white partygoer, made up as a cat, smiled at Alma and asked innocently, "What are you dressed as?"

"An angry black woman," Alma replied.

Alma found Rodney and Willow—dressed, respectively, as a bear and Goldilocks—talking in the host's bedroom. As soon as she saw Alma, Willow leapt out the window and went running down the fire escape. Alma grabbed Rodney by one of his bear ears and dragged him home.

An angry black woman. No matter how kind Seth was to her, Alma regarded him with an attitude only slightly more gracious than contempt. Emma told Seth that he tried too hard, buying Alma expensive presents and flattering her extravagantly. She told him just to lay back, to be himself. There was something patronizing, Emma told him, in his excessive magnanimity toward Alma: Look how *nice* I am to you! Don't you appreciate it? Yes, I know you're an angry black woman, but, look, I *like* you. And you should like me, too!

When Seth arrived at her apartment, Alma treated him with her usual frostiness. "Is the car waiting downstairs?" Emma asked, giving Seth the chance to let Alma know that they would have to leave soon.

"Oh, yeah," Seth said, "but he can wait." Then, trying to be polite, not boastful, trying to let Alma know he wasn't in a hurry to get away, but sounding obnoxious in spite of himself, Seth added, "Mavis pays him well."

Alma snorted derisively. Seth sat down in a musty armchair, quickly surveyed Alma in her shapeless, dirty-looking housecoat and, not knowing what to say but wanting to say something, blurted out the first thing that came into his mind, a transparent lie: "You look lovely tonight, Mrs. Person."

Alma coughed, seemed to swallow back some phlegm.

"Seth," Emma said as a commercial ended and the Bette Davis movie reappeared on the TV screen, "what is this?"

"Oh, this is *The Little Foxes,*" Seth yelped, like a schoolboy rushing to provide the correct answer to the teacher's question. His eagerness made Emma smile and think, with a sweet resignation, I *do* love this guy. "Great movie," Seth added, making a merry little bounce in his chair.

"Oh, yes," Alma said. "I remember. Lillian Hellman. I saw this about a thousand years ago."

"It's shot by Gregg Toland," Seth said excitedly. "He was the cinematographer on *Citizen Kane.* And he uses the same deep focus technique in this movie. Great, great camera work."

"I love the voices of the actors," Alma said. "Especially the fella playing the older brother. He must have been a stage-trained actor. The richness of his voice, those inflections. A great old Broadway voice. 'Well, Regina,' " Alma said, imitating the actor with a sinister lilt in her voice.

"Yeah, really. And look at how this scene is shot, Alma," Seth bubbled. "The angle from the top of the staircase. You can tell Toland *loved* that banister!"

"Ooooh, you're right," Alma fairly cooed, "that's a gorgeous shot."

Emma silently reveled in the exchange. She had never seen Alma and Seth so loose and undefensive with each other. Emma knew her mother was loony and could be difficult to deal with, but she'd also felt that Seth could see only the looniness, couldn't get past it. But here they were, seeming to enjoy each other's company thoroughly. Maybe, Emma thought, they should just watch more movies together.

A commercial came on and Alma and Seth continued talking, Seth bringing up other films Toland had shot, *The Grapes of Wrath, The Best Years of Our Lives, The Long Voyage Home,* prompting Alma's reminiscences of her favorite scenes from those movies. The series of commercials ended and *The Little Foxes* resumed. The story took place in the late nineteenth century, in the South, and in this particular scene, one of the black servants tried, with idiotic ineptitude, to deliver a message he'd received from one of his employers to a group of white men who sneered at his bumbling. The black actor stammered, elongating his words, mugging grotesquely.

"Oh God," Emma groaned.

Alma, who had been sitting still as she chatted with Seth, now began her slow, grim rocking again. "You know, there isn't a single goddamned reason for this shit."

Seth squirmed in his armchair. "Comic relief," he said angrily.

"Well it certainly isn't comic to me!"

"Oh, no, not to me, either," Seth said hurriedly. "I mean, that's how it was intended, in its day."

"Well it wasn't funny in its day, either. Take it from me."

"No, I didn't mean—"

"He's not excusing it, Mom," Emma interjected.

"Not at all," Seth said.

"Good," Alma muttered, grimly rocking.

The warm mood was shattered. The scene dragged on excruciatingly. "I'm gonna turn," Emma said, picking up the remote control. She began idly flipping channels, past a game show, a wrestling match, a preacher, basketball. Seth leaned back in his chair, not knowing what to say, not wanting to say anything that might set Alma off—and he never could tell what might set Alma off—pretending to pay close attention to the rapidly flashing images on the screen, feeling an itch developing in his lower back, wondering when Emma would give the signal that it was time to leave, knowing that she— not he, never he—would have to be the one to say that it was late and they should go, stifling his urge to hurry the end of the visit, even though he was beginning to worry about the car waiting downstairs, realizing that each minute they lingered in Alma Person's apartment was costing Mavis Temple Productions money but, on some level, not really minding that, wanting, actually, to take advantage of the perks that came with his position on the show, wanting to see just how much he could get away with when it came to the price of his privileges but, all the same, wanting to get the hell out of this crazy woman's apartment and away from Washington Heights—who knew, after all, what danger the driver might be in down there on that treacherous street? Still, Seth kept his mouth shut. He didn't want to offend Alma, or Emma. Seth wanted to be polite. He was nothing if not polite.

Emma turned to the Politics channel. A camera panned across a row of army barracks as the offscreen newscaster—it sounded to Seth like Wendy Hoffman—said, "So Tamika Graham wound up here, at the Fort Brandriss Drug Reeducation Center." The scene changed to a medium shot of a young black woman dressed in olive drab fatigues, her hair braided, her face gaunt, prematurely middle-aged. "All I cared about was that pipe," she said in a weary voice. Behind Tamika were rows of metal bunk beds bearing sheets but no blankets, the mattresses looking like slabs of white stone. "Bein' sent here was the best thing that coulda happened to me."

Cut to a shot of Tamika running an obstacle course, climbing a rope ladder up a brick wall, falling to the ground on the other side, struggling to her feet, and running toward the next hurdle as a black female drill instructor, eyes in shadow beneath the flat brim of her Smokey the Bear hat, barked, "Don't you drag your ass, Graham! I've got my eye on you!" Tamika fell to the ground again and crawled beneath a menacing-looking wooden apparatus. Wendy Hoffman's voice-over drowned out the drill instructor: "At the end of Tamika's six-month sentence, she must fulfill another six months in a job assigned to her by the government before she can be reunited with her four-year-old son, Malcolm, who has been placed in a temporary foster home."

The scene switched back to Tamika sitting before the rows of unwelcoming mattresses. "I hope I can be with my little boy again," she said in the same exhausted voice. "But the fack is, I just was in no shape to take care a him. I have to earn the right to be his mother. And I haven't earned that right yet. So Malcolm had to be taken away from me. But I wanna do my time, get a good job, and earn the right to be a mother to my little boy. When I was on crack, I just wasn't a fit mother. But I hope I will be again. That's my goal."

"God, this is so pathetic," Emma said.

Wendy Hoffman, with her pudgy face and curly blond hair, appeared on the screen, standing in front of a barbed-wire fence. "Here at Fort Brandriss . . ."

"Brandriss," Alma said quietly. "Isn't that where they sent Miles?"

"I don't know," Emma said. "I know he's in some DRC, but I don't remember where."

A distinguished-looking black man appeared on the screen. Dressed in a blue serge suit, he walked between two rows of ramrod-straight, fatigue-clad inmates, women on one side, men on the other, inspecting the troops, as it were.

"Lord save us," Emma said.

Alma: "Hush up now."

"Isn't that—" Seth said, stopping short as the identification appeared at the bottom of the screen: "Melvin Hutchinson: Attorney General."

"Today," Hoffman's voice-over continued, "Fort Brandriss, one of the nation's most effective drug reeducation centers, was visited by the man in charge of the DRCs."

Melvin Hutchinson walked slowly down the line, hands clasped behind his back. His attention was focused on the male inmates. A tall man, he towered above the seemingly endless row of skulls, all of them as round and bald as bowling balls. Melvin paused in front of one of the paler domes and seemed to strike up a conversation, but the only sound coming from the TV was now Tamika Graham's voice-over: "I see this is as a second chance. I mean, I'm not like a violent criminal or anything. I was a drug addict. I didn't need to go to, like, a serious prison. I just needed a chance to get my life together."

Cut to a shot of Melvin embracing Tamika, a bit gingerly, Emma thought, outside her barracks. "This young woman," Melvin said to the camera, "should be a role model to every person who goes through a DRC of what sound punishment and discipline can accomplish."

The newscaster: "As he left Fort Brandriss, the attorney general was asked about a new dilemma facing the administration."

Cut to a tight shot of Melvin, a microphone being shoved in his face. "Judge Hutchinson!" Wendy Hoffman shrieked. "Would you accept the vice presidency were it offered to you?"

"We're all praying for the vice president's recovery," Melvin said with an iciness so similar to Emma's and Alma's that Seth shook his head at the jolt of recognition. "Any speculation beyond that is unseemly." With that, Melvin disappeared into his waiting limo and Emma changed the channel.

"What do you think, Mrs. Person?" Seth asked. "Your brother could be vice president." Alma shrugged. "We were saying at the office today that he gives off a great air of authority."

"He never got over Abby," Alma said flatly. "Abby died and Mellie wants to punish the whole world for it."

"But most people," Seth said, "think that his daughter's death made him more compassionate."

"Sometimes x equals x," Alma said. "But oftentimes, x equals y. *Most people* don't know *that*."

On that cryptic note, Alma fell silent. Seth said nothing; neither did Emma. Seth tried not to stare at Alma as the three of them sat mute. She must, in her early days, Seth thought, have been a real Piper Laurie type, attractive without quite being pretty, seemingly solid but bearing that unmistakable whiff of pathology. Now, the madness had taken over. Alma pulled a pack of cigarettes from the pocket of her shapeless, dingy housecoat. Clutching the cigarette between bony, wrinkled fingers, Alma moved with the slow-motion effort of a junkie, and Seth wondered if perhaps she'd had too many late nights, too many wild and druggy times in the sixties, hanging out with jazz musicians and other denizens of the black bohemian demimonde. Emma's mother still had a bit of the bohemian about her, sometimes sporting a chic black beret—that was, when she left the house. Since her attempted suicide several years earlier, Alma had become an almost-total recluse, locked behind the door of her crumbling cavern of an apartment, living off disability payments from the board of education and alimony from Rodney. Alma didn't seem to do much but sit around watching TV all day. In a way, Seth thought, it wasn't all that different from what Trudy did, was it? But Trudy at least had her fund-raising job with the Jewish Heritage Foundation. She got out of the house and functioned in the real world for several hours each day. Only then would she come home, pour herself a glass of wine, pop a Seconal, curl up in bed with Scarlett, and turn on the TV. Seth had always been reluctant to introduce his mother to Emma's. Alma seemed, at times, truly to hate white people, and Seth feared that, despite her very best intentions, Trudy might let slip some comment that would offend Alma. And yet, they were, in some creepy way, very much alike.

That led Seth to wonder about Emma. She had a self-sufficiency that could easily turn into isolation, reclusion. What did Emma like to do, anyway? She always told Seth how she preferred developing her photos to shooting them, how she loved the cocoonlike feeling of the darkroom, the red light, the pungent smell of the chemicals, the solitude of the tiny space. So how different was she, really, from her mother? Or from *his* mother? Was that why Seth loved her? On the surface, Emma seemed so unlike Trudy. But maybe that was just the facade? Were their interiors far more similar than Seth dared imagine? He remembered something Mavis Temple had once said on the show, a wry little rhyme: "One way . . . or another . . . every man . . . ends up with his mother. . . ."

Just as Seth was beginning to feel unbearably claustrophobic, just as he was about to break the sacred protocol, Emma said, "Well, Mom, it's late. We better get going."

As they emerged from Alma's building, Seth was relieved to see that no harm had come to the company car or to the driver, who sat complacently behind the wheel, listening to a Knicks game on the radio. Looking down the block, Seth spotted a couple of FYC officers standing on the corner, keeping a lookout, he assumed, for anyone who might try to approach the black sedan and chauffeur. "Thank God for the FYC," he said, pointing to the two kids in their riot gear. Emma glanced at them, said nothing, and slipped into the backseat of the car.

They rode in silence for a long time. The one thing Seth wanted to talk about was the one thing they had agreed not to talk about— at least not tonight. Emma stared out the window of the car as they cruised up the parkway. Seth knew that she would not be the one to break the silence. Emma could go for hours without saying a word. Seth could stand it no longer. Even as he opened his mouth to speak, he didn't know what would come out. "Well, your mom was in rare form tonight, eh?"

"What do you mean?" Emma asked suspiciously.

"I mean, actually, we seemed, she seemed, you know, in pretty good spirits, at least when it came to talking about movies."

"Hmmmm."

"Didn't you think so?"

"I guess."

"She didn't even mention her upstairs neighbor tonight."

"Oh, that was before you got there. Apparently, the woman has gotten a dog that's been driving Mom nuts."

"A dooooooog . . ." Seth said, and Emma knew exactly what was going through his mind.

"Yeah," she said, "evidently the dog runs around the apartment and makes even more noise than the kids."

"I seeeee," Seth said with a knowing inflection that made Emma cringe. She knew that Seth was making one of his characteristic false connections, feeling, in his smug way, that he had discovered some core secret, some essential clue to a person or situation that explained everything. But his equations were always so facile, so shallow. He was always looking for the easiest connection, the straightest line between two dots. And he was so often dead wrong.

"I know what you're going to say." Emma sighed.

"The dog living above your mom—it isn't a *Doberman,* is it?"

"I don't know what it is, but the situation is very different from the deal with Scarlett. Okay? So let's just drop it."

"I just wonder," Seth said slowly, like a bad TV detective unraveling a mystery, "if there isn't some dog thing running in your family."

"No, Seth, I generally like dogs. You know that I generally like dogs. I just don't like dogs that are almost two years old, *still* not housebroken, and shit on my doorstep on a daily basis. Are you able to comprehend this distinction?"

"*Your* doorstep?" Seth said.

Emma did not reply. She stared out the window as the car entered Blissfield, thinking, It's over. It's over. Over. Over.

Seth immediately felt the need to apologize. But he didn't. He knew it was unfair, referring to Emma's living arrangement in his mother's house, playing that card. But she'd asked for it. They were quiet for a long time again. Seth wondered nervously what the driver was thinking about all this, but he decided the guy was probably too absorbed in the Knicks game to eavesdrop on his passengers. Seth glanced at his watch. "God, it's after twelve. I hope Mom isn't worried."

"You hope Mom isn't worried," Emma said nastily. "What are you, fifteen years old?"

Seth ignored the comment. "Actually," he said, "she probably thinks we're already in our apartment, already asleep."

As the black sedan pulled into the Winkler driveway, Emma noticed the two lights that were always the last to go out in Trudy's home: one in the upstairs bedroom, the other in the vestibule on the first floor. Seth and Emma entered the house through the side door and stepped into the vestibule, the narrow passageway that included the front door of the house, the side door, the door to the first-floor apartment, a staircase going down to the basement, and the staircase leading up to Trudy's apartment. There, under the soft light of the vestibule, right in front of the door to Seth and Emma's apartment, was Trudy Winkler, squatting, her Laura Ashley nightgown hitched up over flabby knees, feet, covered in fuzzy pink slippers, planted firmly on the cool tiles and, between her feet, a coiled dark brown mound of shit. Emma and Seth stopped dead in their tracks, staring aghast at Trudy, who reflected their horror in her own face, her mouth agape, bright blue eyes wide behind her glasses, her hair a Medusan tangle. The three of them were frozen in a moment of mutual, inexpressible shame, Seth and Emma, the guiltless parties, feeling monumentally ashamed by the monumental shame that Trudy at that moment must have felt. Trudy emitted a sound, something like "Haaaaaarrrrrrgggghhh!" She bolted upright, in middefecation, a grotesque schlurping sound seeming to echo off the walls of the passageway. A splash of shit fell from her nightgown and splattered on the tiles. She turned and blundered up the stairs, a trail of feces spilling from her, sprinkling the birch-wood steps of the staircase in a Pollockesque pattern as Scarlett began barking crazily in the apartment upstairs. The door to Trudy's apartment slammed shut. Emma and Seth stood silent and still, staring at the initial turd and the zigzagging trail of muddy drippings that crawled up the staircase.

(7)

S HE WAS EVERYTHING HE hated. A soulless deb trying to be hip, smoking Gauloises and speaking with an almost imperceptible English lilt, though you knew damn well she probably hailed from Winnetka or Sherman Oaks or some such place. She looked just like Elizabeth Taylor in *National Velvet*—the first movie, to Rashid's later mystification, that his mama had ever taken him to see—with her violet eyes and black hair, though this woman's hair had a fine silken texture that was almost Asian—jet black sort of Thai hair, cut in a modified bob that you could tell she liked swinging, swinging back and forth across her face as she shook her head whenever she adamantly disagreed—and she seemed to adamantly disagree quite often—with the two men sitting across from her, who spoke in authentic English accents as they both leaned forward in their chairs, trying to get as close to her as possible, wanting to touch her, to take in the smell of her, seeming to sniff the air just to get a whiff of her, her shampoo, her perfume, her pheromones, while she leaned farther back, occasionally blowing vile streams of smoke in their faces, laughing her contemptuous little laugh, brazenly mocking them. Rashid had seen her on campus many times, walking with Euro fags, who weren't necessarily European or faggots but who had that Continental air about them in their long black coats, their long, gaunt, pale, almost womanishly delicate faces and their spiky haircuts and slicked-back ponytails. One Sunday morning, Rashid had spotted her walking down 110th Street. In her right hand, she clutched the leash of a fluffy little squat-legged dog. Her left arm was linked with the black-clad arm of one of those skinny Euro fags, who, with his free hand, held some pretentious Euro butt to his lips, taking long, eye-squinting drags. They were having a serene little coupley outing together, probably, Rashid guessed, after a languorous morning of cunnilingus—the Euro fag had an "I just ate pussy" leer on his face. The Elizabeth Taylor bitch didn't even look at Rashid, of course; women like her, if they noticed him at all, what with his fearsome dreads and scary black skin, immediately averted their eyes. He began to notice her more and more around Columbia—probably they had classes that began or ended at the same time—and the more he saw her, the more he felt he knew her, knew what she was all about, feeling his disdain for her grow every time he spied her. It was all there in her bearing, in the haughty tilt of her head. Just by looking at her, Rashid Scuggs knew what she was: a pillar of impenetrable solipsism, a creature with no social conscience, no sense of feminist pride, no political convictions whatsoever; a Scarlett O'Hara wanna-be who thought she could rule the world with a toss of her locks and a flutter of her lashes. It was Rashid's belief that the world would be a better place without her kind in it. And he wanted desperately to fuck her.

At the beginning of the new semester, Rashid noticed her in a class he was a teaching assistant for, one of those bullshit theory courses where the professor spouted pompous notions about the chairness of the chair, how the chair beckoned your butt to sit in it; the type of Europhile garbage Caucasian American academics got off on. Zoning out during yet another tedious lecture on Derrida, Rashid spotted her toward the back of the classroom. She glanced at him, freezing him for a second or two in her purple eye lock, then glancing back at the lecturer. Rashid's fantasies about her grew more sweaty and specific. He began to imagine which particular items of her wardrobe he would tear off as he ravaged her. He could hear the exact sounds she would make when she came.

Now she sat in the very same pew with him at Carbunkle's, a pseudo-English pub that Rashid frequented in the early evenings when it was usually sparsely populated. Rashid was closing in on a first draft of his dissertation, "Niggas and Bitches: Rap's Problematic Terms of Endearment," and he enjoyed poring over his manuscript while treating himself to a burger and a beer at the end of a particularly productive day. Carbunkle's had a churchy atmosphere, dark and woody, with stained-glass windows and, in Rashid's favorite corner of the pub, an old pew serving as a bench for customers. The Euro fag hag and her two British suitors sat at the table at one end of the pew, Rashid at the other end, an empty table between them. They were having some sort of a . . . a *row*, Rashid guessed they would call it, about life in New York, the significance of the city's cultural artifacts or something like that, and though he couldn't help stealing glances and half-eavesdropping, Rashid was far more focused on the dissertation in front of him.

"Pardon me." He turned and saw her, only inches away, tossing a shiny hunk of hair away from her face, practically stretching out in the pew as she leaned toward him. "I hate to interrupt you while you're enjoying your beef burger, but what is the name of those blokes in the little red caps, not the Hell's Angels, but . . ."

"The Guardian Angels."

"Right. The Guardian Angels. Thanks. Carry on."

She turned back to her companions and Rashid returned to his dissertation, and his "beef burger."

"They're this roaming freelance mob," she said.

"Like the skinheads?" one of the authentic Brits asked.

"No, no, no, these blokes in the little red caps, these Guardian Angels, are like an unofficial arm of the police. They're a law-and-order mob. You never see fewer than seven or eight of them roaming about looking for crime, on patrol as it were. They're very highly respected here. Their leaders are celebrities."

"And they, the leaders, they wear little red caps, too?"

"Of course."

"So these are the community-service recruits, then?" the other Englishman asked.

"No, that's something else. Those kids in the khaki uniforms are the Federal Youth Corps, an *official* arm of the police. And the government helps pay your tuition after you serve. Some people think, though, that the Guardian Angels should be included in the community-service program."

"Amazing country."

They continued their jolly bantering for a while longer, then paid their bill. The two English guys rose from the table, but the girl stayed in the pew. "Go on ahead," she said. "I'll meet you out on the sidewalk."

Rashid, pretending to be absorbed in his dissertation, felt the Brits glance at him. "There she goes again," one of them said. They laughed and left the restaurant.

"Morgan Bradstreet," the girl said.

Rashid turned and saw her holding out her hand. He shook it. "Rashid Scuggs."

"Pleased to meet you, Rashid. So tell me, are you just going to keep staring at me or are you going to ask me out?"

"I wasn't staring at you."

"Maybe not tonight. But you certainly have been in Professor Nathan's class."

"Really? I thought *you* were staring at *me*."

"Guilty as charged. So how about a cup o' tea or"—she faked a harsh outerborough accent—"kawfie? Tomorrow. After class."

"All right."

Morgan rose to leave. "Until tomorrow, then."

➤   ➤   ➤

The whole time Rashid sat across from Morgan in the tiny, chichi coffee shop she had selected, he was worried that someone he knew —one of the brothers or sisters from his department or, worse yet, one of his black students, one of those kids who looked up to him— might see him with this white chick and think she was his girlfriend. He couldn't help but glance around the place, looking up every time someone came through the door, as he talked; and it was Rashid who did almost all the talking, wanting to make sure that this chick knew what he was about, telling her of his commitment to the African-American community at Columbia, about his devotion not to "multi-culturalism" in academia—"It's already multicultural," he explained impatiently, "in that you have a mix of people from different back-grounds already at universities. You have a few token courses mixed in with the mainstream stuff already"—but to "ethnocentrism." "By which I mean a total concentration on one's own culture, whatever it may be. African-Americans don't need to study Eurocentric white culture. We swim in it every damn day. We've had it shoved down our throats all our lives. What I'm saying is forget *multi*culture. Know your *own* culture. I am an ethnocentrist, an Afrocentrist. And I make no apologies for it."

"Then why are you TA'ing for Nathan's class?" Morgan asked matter-of-factly.

"Hey, gotta pay the rent. I don't have a rich mommy and daddy paying to put my ass through grad school. Anyway, classes are not as important to college students as the socialization process they go through at the university. Now, if it was up to me, every black undergraduate in the humanities here would follow an exclusively Afrocentric curriculum. But even if they absorbed all that I wanted them to learn, I still have a responsibility to them as people. I still have to get them to know, by my example, who and what they are in a social framework—which means that I have got to be a role model every minute of every day."

"My God," Morgan said evenly, "that must get rather exhausting."

"Don't mock me," Rashid snapped.

"I'm not mocking you. I'm entirely serious."

Rashid scrutinized her face. By conventional Eurocentric standards, she was beautiful. There was no doubting it. But what did he care about conventional Eurocentric standards? "So what are *you* about?" he asked.

"I'd love to tell you, but I've got another class in five minutes. I guess you'll have to ask me out to dinner and a movie."

"You ask me."

"How 'bout dinner and a movie?"

"All right."

Morgan scribbled her address and phone number on a napkin. "You can come by my place Friday night, seven o'clock."

"Make it Saturday."

"Saturday. Seven o'clock."

➤   ➤   ➤

Broken mugs in Morgan's cold, empty, useless fireplace—a "non-working" fireplace. Only in this city, Rashid thought, would you hear of such a thing—fireplaces that were solely for decoration, often sealed up with bricks, as Morgan's was, its useful function canceled out, its existence now somehow considered a perk, a decorative fixture worth an extra hundred dollars or so in rent. Or a place to hurl your crockery. The shattered earthenware was the first thing Rashid noticed when he entered Morgan's living room at eight o'clock Saturday night. "Did you have an accident?" he asked, pointing to the glistening ceramic shards scattered in front of the brick wall that substituted for a roaring fire.

"Oh, that," Morgan said, pooh-poohing it with a flip of her hand. "No, no. No accident."

"What happened?" Rashid asked, suddenly wondering if he really wanted to know.

"I got mad and broke some mugs. Just letting out a little aggression." Morgan opened the closet and grabbed her coat. "I'm starving," she said. "Where do you want to eat?"

"You must have been pretty mad," Rashid said. "How many mugs did you smash?"

"I don't know. Three or four? We all have to deal with our anxiety somehow," she said prettily. "Let's go eat."

It would have been wack enough, Rashid thought, if she had just *told* him she hurled mugs against the wall, but obviously, that was not sufficient. She wanted him to *see the shards*. Why hadn't she swept them up before he arrived? Rashid imagined Morgan systematically picking up each mug, then crazily pitching it into the brick. And leaving the shards behind. As if to say, Look, now you see how crazy I am.

This time around, during dinner at Carbunkle's on Saturday night, it was Morgan who did the talking, telling Rashid about her "beautiful" mother, an Oklahoman who went to London to work as a fashion model and met her father, "a beautiful man," who was teaching at Cambridge University. Morgan lived in Cambridge with her parents and her older brother—"a lovely guy, my best friend, truly; he plays in a band now, Intifada, kind of grunge; they play downtown a lot"—until her father transferred to Princeton when she was ten. Morgan told Rashid about her love of writing, about how she could feel the writing, the talent, growing inside her. She knew it sounded silly. No, Rashid did not think it did. (Though he didn't tell Morgan—would never tell anyone—of his own literary aspirations.) "I think I could be a very good novelist," Morgan said, blushing slightly. "I really do."

"Too many artists are irresponsible," Rashid said.

"I know." Morgan smiled mischievously. "Isn't it delicious?"

"Do you write much?"

"Constantly. I already know what my first novel will be. It's called *The Philosopher's Daughter.* But I can't publish it until my father is dead."

Rashid made a sour face. "Autobiographical?"

"Naturally. I shouldn't worry, though. I don't say anything so scandalous about him. I love my father. He's a beautiful man."

"Everybody in your family's so beautiful. You should meet some ugly people once in a while."

"I don't discriminate."

>   >   >

"I hated that movie," Morgan said as she and Rashid shared a bottle of wine at Carbunkle's after the show. "The woman's character is such a male fantasy."

A typical feminist debate-stopper, Rashid thought. Just say that the women are stereotyped and you could therefore dismiss the entire body of work of a Spike Lee or a Martin Scorsese. Morgan wanted to kill all argument about the movie they'd just seen by accusing the filmmaker of being a man. "Of course, she's a male fantasy," Rashid said. "Every woman character created by a male artist is a male fantasy. Because men can only *fantasize* what it's like to be a woman. It's beyond us in any way except imagination—or very extensive and costly surgery."

Morgan laughed. "You're a bigot, Rashid, but you're funny."

"Me and Archie Bunker."

"And Malcolm X," she said, winking at him. "All you lovable bigots."

As they started on their second bottle of wine, Rashid used a line

< 176 >

he'd always wanted to try out on a woman. "So what were you like as a child?"

Morgan looked startled. "I had a very happy childhood."

"It's interesting," Rashid said, "how often when someone makes a flat statement about themselves, the opposite of what they say is the real truth. Think of Nixon: 'I am not a crook.' Of course, he was, in fact, a crook, and he knew it, too."

"So when I say that I had a very happy childhood, you assume that I'm lying to you?"

"Or to yourself. Do you not like delving into the past?"

"My past is fine!"

" 'My past is *fine*,' " Rashid said skeptically.

Morgan laughed and lit another cigarette.

As they left Carbunkle's, she invited him up to her apartment for a nightcap. Rashid told her he wasn't a big drinker. "Just my luck," Morgan said. They stopped at a liquor store and Morgan bought a pint of gin. Walking back to her apartment, Morgan gazed at a shiny dark green sports car that was—incongruously, given the neighborhood—parked on her corner. "I want that Jag," Morgan whispered throatily, an edge of lust in her voice.

"You want that Jag," Rashid said incredulously.

"Don't mock me. I know it sounds terrible. But you know, mister, you're a bigger snob than I am."

"I am not a snob!"

>   >   >

"You're a pious, moral snob," Morgan said. "The worst kind of snob. Even your ethnocentrism is a form of snobbery."

"Yeah, yeah, yeah," Rashid said.

They were sitting on her futon now, sipping gin and tonics. The ceramic shards glittered in the nonworking fireplace. "You *know* it's true," Morgan said, leaning forward, showing Rashid her cleavage. She wore a deep-cut V-necked sweater of light gray cashmere. Her brassiere, Rashid could not help but notice, was black lace. "You judge people entirely by how they look, what they wear, the way they talk, how much money they have."

< *177* >

"Well, I have standards, dear. Just like anybody else." *Dear?* What was Rashid saying? He was drunk—a rare occurrence.

"But you *hate* anyone whose tastes and attitudes are not your own. And so much of it is just fashion. Another fashion will come along; you'll adopt it and hate anyone who doesn't wear what you wear or *say* they believe the same things you *say* you believe."

"Where is all this shit coming from?"

"Sorry," Morgan said with a small laugh, leaning back and away from Rashid as casually as she'd gotten in his face. "I'm usually much more circumspect in conversation. I save my directness for my writing. But I don't know. You seem to bring this out in me."

The next time Rashid looked at his watch, it was after two. They had finished the pint of gin and had moved on to the bottle of Cointreau Morgan kept stashed in her kitchen cabinet. "Look at this!" Morgan marveled, pulling one notebook after another from one drawer after another. Most were spiral-bound, though there was one fancy leather-coated diary with Morgan's initials engraved on the cover and even a couple of those marbly black-and-white-covered cardboard notebooks of the kind Rashid had used in penmanship class. "How could someone keep this many journals? And I'm only twenty-one! This is insane. Only an insane person would write this much, don't you think?"

Rashid didn't know *what* he thought. Thinking, rationality, had evaporated earlier in the night. He had reverted to pure feeling, gripped by a powerful intimacy.

> > >

"You don't know what it's like, injecting drugs. It's the most intense feeling in the world. It really is like going to heaven." Rashid ran his finger across the hollow of Morgan's arm. Her vein stood out like a cord of thick electrical wire beneath a thin layer of yellowish masking tape. The vein felt ropy as Rashid gingerly stroked it. The flesh around the vein was tender, membranous. "You can die this way," Rashid said.

"No shit," Morgan sneered. "Of course, we're careful. And I only do it with my brother. He knows what he's doing."

"Have you been tested?"

"Six months ago. Negative. Two years after I started shooting up. If you're careful and in the least bit sanitary about it, there's nothing to worry about—except OD'ing. And that's also just a matter of common sense."

"Damn," Rashid said, transfixed on that cord buried in the crook of Morgan's elbow.

"Listen to Hendrix. Listen to Charlie Parker. Kurt fucking Cobain. What do you think: It's a *coincidence* that they sound the way they do and just happened to inject drugs?" Morgan stared at Rashid. "God, I'd love to shoot up with you. But you'd never do it, would you?"

"Hey, reality is tough enough as it is. I don't need no hallucinations."

"Sensible boy."

Rashid paused, tried to defog his brain. He looked at his watch: 3:15. "Well, it's late, I should probably—"

"You can stay if you want."

"Oh, I don't know, I—"

"Stay. I want you to. Stay."

➢   ➢   ➢

They huffed and they puffed, they sweated and strained, him on top, her on top; his dick flopped around like a fish in her palm, sloshed about like a giant mussel in her mouth; and the harder they tried, the softer he got. Finally, rolling off his body, Morgan said, "This isn't working."

"So you noticed."

"It happens to other guys, blah blah blah."

"Guess it just wasn't meant to be."

"Maybe you're thinking about someone else."

And only then did Janet enter Rashid's mind at all that night. In fact, in the four days since Morgan had introduced herself to him at Carbunkle's, Rashid had not thought of Janet once. Bizarre. He knew that they'd been growing apart for a long time, but shit, he'd gone out with this woman for years. You'd think she'd have entered his mind once. Thoughts of Morgan had totally eclipsed thoughts of Janet. It made Rashid angry, the extent to which he could not control his thoughts.

"Yeah," he said, "there is someone else."

"There always is."

"For you, too?"

"Sort of," Morgan said.

"Oh," Rashid said, not surprised and trying to show it in his voice.

"He's married."

"Oh," Rashid said, surprised, and trying not to show it in his voice. "I think I saw you with this character, walking a dog one Sunday morning."

"Not *him*. That's Alain. The *only* thing I like about Alain is his dog."

"Then who are you talking about?"

It was a sordid little tale, Rashid thought, the story of Morgan's affair with Kent, a banker or some kind of executive, the father of one of her former best friends from high school whom she ran into on Fifth Avenue the day before Christmas, thirteen months earlier. Kent had divorced his first wife, the mother of Morgan's friend Amanda. He had two young children with his second wife, but that didn't stop him from propositioning Morgan right there on the street, his arms full of F.A.O. Schwarz shopping bags stuffed with Christmas presents for the little ones. Nine months later, Kent was ready to leave his wife for Morgan. But after a tearful confession to his spouse, Kent returned to his senses. He showed up at Morgan's apartment for one last fuck, then told her it was over.

"You seem to have recovered pretty well," Rashid said.

"Actually, I've been dreaming of killing him, with a gun, ever since he broke up with me."

"Really?"

"In the dream, I shoot Kent, then put the pistol to my own head. I always wake up before the gun goes off."

"Well," Rashid said, rising from the bed, "on that note . . ."

Five minutes later, Rashid was dressed, standing, with his coat on, in front of the door to Morgan's apartment. Morgan stood naked before him, her skin looking almost eggshell white under the too-bright light of her foyer. "We'll have to try this again sometime," she said coyly.

"I don't think so," Rashid said.

"Oh, don't be a spoilsport."

"You have Kent to deal with. I have Janet. I don't even know what I'm doing here." Rashid smiled. "You got me drunk and tried to take advantage of me."

"I'm a notorious date rapist."

"But I'm serious. We won't do this again."

Morgan stuck out her lower lip, like a petulant child. "Okay."

"Good night," Rashid said, beginning to unlock the door.

"Complete this sentence," Morgan said. "When I can't get what I want, I . . ."

"Give up," Rashid said instantly.

Morgan laughed. "I was asked to complete that sentence in a psychiatric test once, and do you know what I said?"

"What?"

Morgan eyed Rashid carefully, as if she were memorizing him. "I want it *more.*"

>   >   >

The very idea of an interracial relationship had never occurred to Rashid until he and his mama got "nigger-rich." That was what his mama, Lorena, called it. Lorena's father was a butler, a man Rashid would grow up to consider one of those grinning, shuffling house niggers. Grandaddy had spent his whole life taking care of some Miss Daisy type of rich cracker who never did get married—probably no man in his right mind would have wanted her (she was a cold, brittle woman), even though she was sitting on a fortune—and who spent her last years as a recluse in her South Carolina mansion with Grandaddy taking care of her as he always had. Even though he was twenty years older than she, Grandaddy was a spry old servant at eighty-five, while the dowager aged at an accelerated pace, ravaged by Alzheimer's, a shrieking, incontinent hag, ending her life as she had begun it, screaming for Grandaddy's attention—just as she had when she was a newborn and Rashid's grandfather had just started working for the Perkins family—and Grandaddy having to wipe her old woman's ass just as he had wiped her ass when she was a baby. Yet, when the old bitch finally died, Grandaddy was devastated. Lorena said she figured her father and Miss Perkins had been in love and, maybe, she once speculated, even lovers. No, that was too strange to imagine. Yet, Grandaddy's first and only wife had died giving birth to Lorena. All of Grandaddy's children and the members of the Perkins family had left the plantation a good ten years before the old bitch died. So she and Grandaddy had a full decade alone together, though, for the last three years or so, the woman was senile. The week after Miss Perkins's death, Lorena's father was more depressed than she had ever seen him. Then he learned that the old bitch had left him $1 million in her will. And even that didn't cheer him up.

Rashid's mama told him that Grandaddy was acting like many a widower she had known. "You see it all the time," Lorena said. "A husband die and the widow blossom, get some new interests, make new friends, start her life over. A wife die and the husband be dead six months later. Didn't happen to Daddy when my mother died—I guess 'cause he had four children he had to raise and couldn't afford to let his wife's death defeat him. But when Mizz Perkins die, Daddy just shrivel up, disappeared. Men die, women blossom. Women die, men fall apart. Just show you who need who in this life." (Her own husband had disappeared before Rashid was born. Lorena never talked about him. Rashid learned in his childhood that his mother didn't want to hear any questions about the man. And through a potent instinct for denial, reinforced by Lorena on a daily basis, Rashid had, by early adolescence, stopped thinking about his father altogether.) Grandaddy was in the ground less than six months after Miss Perkins died. Fortunately, he'd had the presence of mind to draw up a will about a month before his death. He must have known he was slipping away. He hadn't even spent any of the money Miss Perkins had left him. The million dollars was to be split among Grandaddy's four children.

"We're rich, we're rich!" Rashid screamed when his mama gave him the news. He was twelve years old at the time and he and Lorena had been scraping along on her salary as a file clerk in the Norris

City Department of Records and living in a tiny apartment in the Norris, New Jersey, projects for as long as Rashid could remember. "We're rich, Mama! We're rich!"

Lorena was nonplussed. She must have figured that, after taxes, her inheritance wouldn't be so spectacular. "We ain't rich," she scolded Rashid. "J. Paul Getty rich. Rockefeller be rich. We nigger-rich. Just nigger-rich."

Still, they had enough money to move out of the projects and into a neat little row house on one of the few blocks along Largent Street that had been spared the wrecking balls of urban renewal. And, at the beginning of eighth grade, Rashid switched from Norris Junior High to Benson Country Day School in Benson, New Jersey. He endured the ninety-minute bus ride to this green and hilly suburb that might as well have been in a completely different country from the one he inhabited in Norris; withstood the slights of the white kids, who simply assumed they were smarter than he was, who spoke casually of their country homes, their horses, their boats; and suffered in silence when his old friends from Norris warned him that prep school would turn him into a white boy.

Nicole was the only thing that kept him going during eighth grade. There were only six black kids in Rashid's class at Benson, three boys and three girls. Darius, the star athlete of the class and about as hip a young dude as you could hope to find in prep school, was already dating Sharon, the best-looking of the black girls. Lloyd, Rashid's best friend at Benson, was basically a nerd and too shy to have a girlfriend. But Rashid figured Lloyd could hook up with Sereeta, the best black student and one of the two or three smartest students in their class—period. Unfortunately, Sereeta was hugely fat and prodigiously pimpled. Lloyd could have her if he wanted. Rashid, meanwhile, set his sights on Nicole, who was just bright enough, just pretty enough, just attentive enough to him to fuel his fantasies for the better part of the school year. Rashid felt confident that she liked him as much as he liked her. And, given the racial makeup of their class, Rashid felt that a romance with Nicole was virtually preordained. Who *else* would she go out with?

The answer: Barry Janeway. In May, Nicole started dating—publicly holding hands and (barely) surreptitiously sneaking kisses with

—Barry Janeway, who was not only white but buck-toothed, freckle-faced, with shaggy red hair that hung in his eyes, and not even *smart*—in fact, probably one of the worst students in the class! But he was rich, and he was white, and Rashid, for the first time, felt real heartache, that sickening, plummeting sensation, that deep hurt that can only be dealt by someone you love. The hurt was compounded by the fact that Rashid had never even contemplated dating a white girl at Benson and so had never dreamed that Nicole might go out with a white boy. What the fuck did she see in this clown, anyway? It could *only* be that he was white, and rich. There could be no other reason for Nicole rejecting Rashid for Barry Janeway. At the end of the school year, Rashid told his mama that he wanted to leave Benson Country Day. He wanted to attend Samuel Adams, the huge, and all-black, high school back home, in Norris, New Jersey.

➤   ➤   ➤

It was during Rashid's first year at Sam Adams High that the whippings began. Lorena had never wanted her son to leave Benson Country Day and get corrupted by the "hoodlums and hos" she said attended Sam Adams. If Lorena heard through the grapevine that Rashid had stayed out late after school, hanging out with hoodlums, she'd give him a whipping. If she discovered he'd been talking to some trashy young ho, she'd stride into his bedroom while he was studying, a thick belt in her hand. "Drop your drawers," Lorena would command before flaying Rashid's quivering buttocks. As Rashid grew older, Lorena stopped whipping his behind and chose to lay the strap to his bare back instead. When Rashid received an A— rather than an A or an A+ in one of his courses, Lorena lashed his naked shoulders until she could see welts rising. But Rashid's mama saved the most severe beatings for those times when her son seemed genuinely interested in some ho. "You ain't gonna get one of them bitches pregnant and ruin your life! Not as long as I'm around! Take your damn shirt off." Rashid would endure his whippings in silence, gritting his teeth and fighting back tears. Even though by seventeen he knew he didn't have to submit to his mama's attacks, he put up with them nonetheless, closing his eyes tight, grinding his teeth, struggling not to cry out in pain as Lorena seemed to grow more frenzied with each slap of the strap. When she was done, Lorena would collapse in her favorite armchair, dripping with sweat, breathing heavily, lustily, her body limp, spent. "Bring me a glass of water," she would order Rashid; and he would obey.

The whippings finally ceased when Rashid was accepted at Rutgers University. Lorena had achieved her goal. Her son had gotten into a good college and could escape Norris (though she insisted Rashid return home to visit every weekend; and he obeyed). Rashid made fast friends with other black students at Rutgers, but he found it painfully difficult to come on to women, to pursue sex, even if he was very attracted to a girl. He knew that his mama had somehow thwarted him, sexually stunted him. When women made overtures to Rashid, he retreated, afraid to acquiesce. But afraid of what? Rashid could not say. He wondered for a few weeks if perhaps he was a homosexual. But he ruled out that possibility. When he masturbated, it was always women he fantasized about. When he tried to imagine a man in bed beside him, his erection promptly expired. Rashid didn't know what to make of his dilemma, so, with his massive propensity for denial, he put it out of his mind. Still, he was quietly haunted by the fact that at the end of his first year of college, he was still a virgin.

Then his mama hooked him up with Janet. She was the daughter of a friend of Lorena's. Janet lived in Brooklyn and worked as a secretary at an insurance agency. At twenty-one, she was two years older than Rashid. And Janet was . . . normal. Rashid had never met anyone so *normal*. Attractive—but certainly no fox—practical and extremely quiet. Rashid and Janet spent long evenings during which she barely ventured an opinion. On their first dinner date, Rashid suggested they get ice cream for dessert. "You like ice cream?" he asked. "Do you?" was Janet's reply. "Yeah, I do," Rashid said. "Me, too," Janet said. During his last three years at Rutgers, Rashid alternated weekend visits, spending one weekend in Norris with Lorena, the next in Brooklyn with Janet. Rashid like being able to say he had a girlfriend; he liked the fact that he could have regular sex, if only every other weekend. His great powers of denial prevented him from ever wondering if he was actually in love with Janet. Being "in love"

—Rashid, in his mind's eye, always saw the expression surrounded by sardonic quotation marks—was inconsequential. Janet was his woman. And someday, silent, reliable, normal Janet would be his wife. Lorena, Rashid thought, put it best: "Janet is a woman who will never leave you."

Lorena had wanted her son to become a lawyer, but instead he enrolled in Columbia's graduate program in Cultural Studies. Rashid's mama was disappointed, but she was still proud to see her son in the Ivy League. And then she died, all of a sudden. The year after Rashid received his master's degree. Lorena just dropped dead of a heart attack—she'd always suffered from hypertension—one night while sitting in her favorite armchair, watching television. Lorena left her son the house on Largent Street (which, while he continued living in Manhattan, pursuing his doctorate at Columbia, Rashid maintained as a sort of shrine to his mama, virtually everything in the house remaining precisely the way Lorena had left it) and the remainder of her inheritance from Grandaddy: approximately fifty thousand dollars. Rashid was too shocked by his mama's death to really grieve. A single thought kept running through his mind: Now it's just me and Janet. . . . Now it's just me and Janet.

➤   ➤   ➤

Janet was not very intelligent. The realization came to Rashid slowly, grudgingly. He didn't judge people by silly, arbitrary standards of intelligence, standards that had been set up mainly by white society. And he'd never spent much time—except during his year at Benson Country Day—wondering if someone was smarter than he was or if he was smarter than somebody else. He was the best student at Sam Adams High, but he didn't look down on the other pupils. And, intellectually, he'd always held his own with his friends from Rutgers and Columbia. He had never given any thought to Janet's brainpower until after his mama died and they began spending every weekend together in Brooklyn. Rashid began to realize how bored he was by the content of their conversations: stories about relatives and friends, what happened at Janet's office that week, what would they eat for dinner, and, increasingly, what sort of wedding they would have.

They never discussed politics, literature, or—in anything but the most mundane, personal, everyday terms—race and culture. When Rashid tried to broach such topics or talk about his work, his studies, his dissertation, Janet would abruptly cut him off. "Don't come at me with that uppity talk," she would scold him. "I ain't no scholar. Talk to me like normal folks." But, really, they didn't talk much at all. Mainly, they watched TV. Janet loved situation comedies, especially the ones featuring black actors. Occasionally, Rashid would get angry, damning the programs as minstrel shows that depicted African-Americans as buffoons.

"How can you stand these stereotypes?" he would ask Janet.

"I know it's bad," Janet would say, "But it's *funny*. And they're not all stereotypes."

"Of course they are! And these shows are usually written by white writers!"

"But they're *funny*. Why can't you just chill and enjoy it?"

Watching Janet as she stared at the screen—she even gazed fixedly at the commercials—laughing at inane jokes, sighing at the manipulative tender moments, Rashid imagined his girlfriend's mind as a TV test pattern—static, neutral. The longer he stayed with Janet, the more he felt that he had to put a straitjacket around his own intelligence, keep his thoughts to himself, restrain himself from using the words that might best convey what he wanted to say, lest Janet snap at him, "Stop talkin' white!"

One Sunday night as he was about to leave Janet's place in Brooklyn and head back to Columbia, Rashid suggested they "take a little time off," maybe not see each other for a while. Janet sat at the kitchen table, putting on nail polish as Rashid spoke, barely looking up to acknowledge him. "I just don't think I've been myself since Mama died. I just need some time alone to get my head together."

"You don't wanna come around, don't come around," Janet said, blowing on her fingertips to dry them.

"That's not what I'm saying."

"Tcch." Janet sucked her teeth, started painting her other hand.

"Well, I'll call you when I'm feeling more straight, more clear about everything."

"Lemme tell you something, Rashid," Janet said, looking up and pointing the nail-polish applicator at her man, "ain't *nobody* ever gonna love you the way I love you. 'Cept maybe yo mama." She executed a little waggle with her head, a gesture of blasé indignation. "And she's dead."

Rashid considered going out with other women. Mentally, he went through all the possibilities open to him, considered every available sister he knew. But for one reason or another—too fat, too thin, too bitchy, too bourgeois—he ruled out every option. Then, out of the blue, Morgan spoke to him at Carbunkle's. Next thing he knew, they were drinking cappuccino together and he was telling her about all his deepest convictions. A few days later, he was in her bed. Now, almost a week after he fell down on the job, was unable to finish what he—or was it she?—had started, Rashid couldn't stop thinking about the way he'd been able to talk to her. And she had engaged him, not merely listened, or agreed, or told him to shut up, but countered, challenged, absorbed his statements. Sitting alone in his apartment Friday afternoon, Rashid wanted to call Morgan. But he decided not to. He decided to call Janet instead. Morgan was a crazy white bitch. She would only cause him trouble. Janet was good for him. Whatever her flaws, she was good for him. It was Janet he would call. It was Janet he would sleep with tonight. Rashid was reaching for the phone when it suddenly rang. Morgan was on the line. One of her creative writing professors was having a book party that night. Would Rashid like to attend it with her? Rashid said yes, instantly.

➤   ➤   ➤

"Sometimes—I mean, it's probably just me," Morgan said as she and Rashid climbed the stairs to the apartment where the book party was being held, "I think that maybe Michael Mayhew is coming on to me." Morgan went on to point out that she would never even dream of touching her writing teacher. But Mayhew, she thought, had made some comments that seemed . . . "inappropriate."

"Lemme tell you something," Rashid said sagely, "if you *think* a man is coming on to you, he is."

"Really?"

"Men are dogs. That's what women always forget. You learn it once, maybe, then you forget it. Like you learned it with your married man—what's his name, Clark?"

"Kent."

"Yeah, him. All men are dogs."

Rashid didn't have to *wonder* whether Michael Mayhew was coming on to Morgan when he saw the balding, potbellied writer beam as he spotted his pupil walk through the door. Mayhew grabbed Morgan by the waist, putting his arm all the way around her and pulling her toward him, pressing his aged pink mouth against her tightly puckered lips, as if he might try to force his tongue down her throat. That was sickening enough; but Rashid had seen lots of men, and women, force themselves on their objects of desire in a party setting. It wasn't until a moment later, when Michael Mayhew introduced Morgan to a circle of his wrinkled, white-haired cronies, that Rashid felt he understood, for the first time, what the feminists were always bitching about.

"Gentlemen," the aged writer said, pulling Morgan into his body, crushing her slender frame into his tweed, "I'd like you to meet my most beautiful student." A small hand grenade of rage exploded inside Rashid. Here was Morgan, by every indication an extraordinary writer, probably the *best* student this motherfucker had ever had, and yet he introduced her to these leering old men by talking about her looks—by *bragging* about her looks, as if he had had anything to do with her beauty. At that moment, Rashid felt disgusted to be a man.

Maybe, it occurred to Rashid, Michael Mayhew wanted his fellow geezers to think he was boning Morgan, implicitly boasting of a conquest by flaunting his "most beautiful student" before them. Looking around the party—which was being held in the loft studio of some ancient Abstract Expressionist and his (young and beautiful) wife—Rashid noticed that he was not just the only African-American present but the only male under fifty and that most of the old men at the party, celebrating the publication of Mayhew's latest collection of short stories, were accompanied by beautiful young women. Mayhew was one of the few who had shown up solo. Perhaps this was why he'd invited Morgan—to save face by impressing the other wizened lechers. Rashid might as well have been invisible at the gathering. The only person there who seemed to notice him at all was a sweet old poet, who, Morgan later informed him, was gay. It figured: All the geezers there, homo or hetero, craved young flesh.

Rashid and Morgan didn't stay long. But just before they left, Morgan pulled Mayhew aside and asked if he would write recommendations to graduate school for her. Mayhew suggested they meet for dinner to discuss it. Morgan agreed.

"How could you do that?" Rashid asked scoldingly as he and Morgan stepped out of the converted TriBeCa warehouse and started walking down the windy, trash-strewn sidewalk.

"What else am I going to do?" Morgan said. "Michael Mayhew is the most prominent writer I know. *And* the best. And he likes my work. I'm not an idiot. It's not like I have to suck him off or anything. He'll continue to flirt. I'll continue to be polite. Harmless. So give me a break. I've dealt with far more threatening men—far more— then Michael Mayhew."

➤   ➤   ➤

"I slept with a black guy once," Morgan said casually. It was late Friday night, three hours after they'd left the Mayhew party. Morgan and Rashid were sitting on her futon, polishing off another pint of gin. "Well, I guess *slept* with isn't quite accurate. This was a couple of years ago, in a writing seminar. His name was Trelaine—which I thought was just so cool. Like *your* name. *Rashid.* Makes one think of a windswept desert. Trelaine. Rather dashing, don't you think? Anyway, he was an undergraduate, but he was much older than the rest of us, older than you even."

"Shocking."

"I mean, like thirty or something. Not that it matters. Age doesn't matter. Anyway, I liked Trelaine's stuff, though Michael Mayhew obviously didn't think much of it. And I started talking to Trelaine once after class. The next time class met, he gave me a story of his, one he hadn't presented in the seminar. A good story. I really liked it. Then, about two days after he'd lent it to me, he called and said he needed it back—immediately. I thought it was a bit odd. It was about nine o'clock in the evening. But then, I thought, Well, perhaps he just wants to see me. He lived about five blocks away, so I asked if he wished to come by and pick it up. He said, 'No, I want you to bring it to me.' So I arrived at his flat, and I thought I looked pretty good. I was wearing this Christian Dior trench coat I have. And Trelaine looks like he just got back from working out. He greets me at the door, wearing a sweaty T-shirt and sweatpants. After he closes the door behind me, he just walks over to his desk, sits down, and starts reading a book—as if I wasn't even there. I went and stood over him. 'I really liked your story.' I said. And he just sort of grunted at me. I'd always thought he was a bit sullen in class, but when talking to him alone, I'd found him quite charming. 'Here it is,' I said, and dropped the manuscript rather nastily on the desk. Trelaine jumped up, and the next thing I know, we're on the couch and my trousers are around my ankles and Trelaine is just pounding and pounding into me. And when he's finished, he walks across the room, picks up this ugly white gym towel, and wipes himself off with it. Then he throws the towel across the room—right in my face. He pulled back on his sweats, returned to his desk, and started reading again. And I'm just sitting there, or lying there, on the couch. I hadn't even taken my trench coat off. I didn't say a word. He didn't say a word. I pulled up my trousers and left."

Morgan took a long drag on her cigarette, exhaled slowly.

"So he raped you?" Rashid said.

"I wouldn't say *that.*"

"What *would* you say?"

"Only that . . . it was . . . memorable."

"What happened when you saw him in class?"

"I was too embarrassed to go to the next class. And, the one after that, Trelaine didn't show up. He never came to class again. Someone said they had heard he'd dropped out, that he had a kid somewhere that he needed to support and couldn't afford to stay in college. I never saw him again. Never particularly wanted to." Morgan and Rashid were silent for a long moment. "I think I'm going to put on some music."

So that was what this bitch wanted, Rashid thought as he watched

< *191* >

Morgan walk over to her CD player: to be taken by the big black bruiser. Well, maybe tonight, he was drunk enough, full of enough fury at her and her whole fucking world, to be up to the task.

➤   ➤   ➤

Rashid knew, the morning after he and Morgan finished what they'd started a week earlier, that they would never spend another night together. He wouldn't allow it. Not that the sex had been unsatisfactory. On the contrary, the fucking had been almost too intense. In the middle of the act, Rashid felt as if he had not only entered Morgan but that somehow *she* had entered him. There was some bizarre sense of fusion, a terrible intimacy, that moved Rashid to his core; an intimacy that he found almost unbearable. There was no way he could permit this to happen again. Not with any white chick.

For several days after that night, Morgan called Rashid, but he wasn't answering his phone. So she left tender, flirtatious messages on his answering machine. "I'm beginning to think you're avoiding me," he heard Morgan say on Thursday evening. He finally picked up the phone. She wanted to see him that night. He said he was busy. Rashid suggested they get together Saturday afternoon, go to a movie. "As long as I get you for the night, as well," Morgan said. "Come over Saturday at two o'clock," Rashid said. They would see what happened from there. "You make it sound rather ominous," Morgan said, but she agreed to his terms.

As Morgan sat across from Rashid on his couch Saturday afternoon, pouring herself a glass of wine and talking about different movies they might consider seeing, Rashid stared at her and tried to block out thoughts of how astonishingly beautiful she was. It was only by white Eurocentric standards that Morgan was beautiful (wasn't it?), and what use did he have for such standards? None!

"We can't see each other anymore," Rashid said.

Morgan took a sip of her wine, stared at Rashid. "I thought you might say that. . . . Why not?"

"I'm still involved with Janet. She's my girl. I'm committed to her."

Morgan's eyes turned glassy. "That's not all there is to it. You're lying to me."

"That's the reason."

"No. There's something else. It's because I'm white, isn't it?"

"There's that, too. I need to be with a sister."

A single tear rolled down Morgan's cheek. She didn't bother to wipe it away. "I really care about you, you know. And I know you care about me. I can feel it. I felt it the other night. The other night was . . . significant."

"Maybe for you. But I won't let it happen again. I'll go with you to a movie today. But after today, we can't see each other anymore."

"I *know* you feel for me."

"Finish your wine. Pick a movie. I'll see whatever you want. I don't care."

"How can you deny your feelings?"

Rashid felt as if *he* had just drunk a glass of wine, vaguely light-headed, though he hadn't touched a drop. "I'm not gonna get into a big, long hassle about this. We had one night together. We satisfied our curiosity. That's it. Now, let's go."

"Curiosity!" Morgan laughed bitterly. "You're lying to yourself more successfully than you're lying to me, Rashid."

➤   ➤   ➤

"Popcorn?" the pimply theater attendant asked.

"Jumbo," Morgan said, almost seductively. "With butter. *Lots* of butter."

Rashid paid no attention to the film that flickered before them. He stared at the screen, but the images hardly registered. He couldn't even remember what movie they were watching. He kept glancing out of the corner of his eye at Morgan. While Rashid barely touched any of the popcorn in the huge cardboard barrel, Morgan gobbled it greedily, scooping up fistfuls and stuffing them in her mouth, devouring the butter from her fingers with sucking, smacking sounds. Morgan polished off the entire bucket, then, licking the last salty trace of butter from her thumb, said urgently, "I'll be right back."

Fifteen minutes passed before she returned. As Morgan slipped back into her seat, Rashid could detect the faint, at once sweet and medicinal smell of one of those breath-freshening sprays. Morgan slouched, seemingly exhausted.

"Are you all right?" Rashid asked.

"I am now."

At that moment, Rashid understood. The very idea disgusted him. Bulimia. What an insanely bourgeois disease! You just have access to so much food that you have to stuff your face with it, then puke it out. The arrogance of it! Bulimia, Rashid thought, could never exist in the Third World. It couldn't exist in most of the first or second worlds, either. Most people could never even imagine having so much easy access to so much food that they just couldn't help gorging themselves and then regurgitating it all. But quantity was no problem for rich bulimic bitches. There would be more food where that came from. All you can eat, you vomit queens!

And yet, contemplating what he knew Morgan had just done, Rashid still had to fight the urge—that swelling pain, that need—to wrap her tenderly in his arms, to embrace her madness.

After the movie that neither of them had really seen, out on the darkened sidewalk, Morgan said she was going downtown to visit a friend. Rashid was heading back uptown.

"Okay," Morgan said. "I'll see you when I see you."

"Later," Rashid said.

>   >   >

It would be a long time before Rashid and Morgan spoke again. Morgan stopped showing up at the bullshit theory lectures. Rashid didn't see her around campus anymore. Rashid had almost stopped socializing altogether, spending his evenings alone, reading, grading papers, working on his dissertation. For many weeks, someone kept calling and hanging up on his answering machine without leaving a message. Sometimes, Rashid thought it was Janet, but that wasn't her style. It had to be Morgan. But why wouldn't she *say* anything? Rashid often thought of calling Morgan, but he couldn't bring himself to do it. Instead, he fantasized about her every night when he mastur-

<   *194*   >

bated, reconjuring in his mind the one time they'd had sex, when he had set out to take her violently but instead found himself consumed by affection. Finally, one evening, he turned off his answering machine. The phone rang almost immediately and it was all he could do to stifle a little yelp of excitement when he picked up the receiver and heard Morgan's voice. After a couple of minutes of strained small talk, Rashid said, "So where have you been hiding yourself?"

"I've been hanging out a lot with my brother," Morgan said, sparking Rashid's memory of her thick yellowed vein, "and with Kent."

"The married man."

"Yes. We meet at night—in hotel rooms. All rather illicit."

"And you enjoy this?"

"Well, *you* won't have me."

"And how does Kent's family feel about this?"

"I don't know. We don't talk about his family."

"Just pretend they don't exist, huh? You think what they don't know won't hurt you?"

"We should stop this conversation. This is misplaced."

"Misplaced?"

"It's a misplaced conversation. It should never have taken place."

"Okay. It's deleted from the record."

"I just hate it when you put on your moral, judgmental tone."

"I'm always judgmental. It's my salient feature."

"Is it? Well, what you did with me wasn't so generous to Janet, was it?"

"No. It wasn't."

"I'm sorry, but you deserved that."

"Yeah, well, I still feel bad about what we did to Janet."

"Well, I don't feel bad about anything I've done."

"I know."

"You think I should. But I don't."

"I guess that's the difference between you and me."

"God, you are too smug for words. Listen, I'm going to go. We shouldn't be saying these things. I'm going to go."

"All right."

"Call me later(?)"—at once a question and a command.

"All right."

Naturally, Rashid did not call Morgan. And after she told him she was seeing Kent again, he stopped thinking about her. But even more disturbing to Rashid than his past thoughts about Morgan— the obsessive memories and fantasies that sometimes made him wonder if he might actually be "in love" with her—were the thoughts that occupied his mind all of the following summer, thoughts about white women in general. Walking the streets of Manhattan, he couldn't stop looking at hair; his eye seemed compulsively drawn to the backs of heads, heads of long, straight hair, to strawberry blondes and chestnut browns. He couldn't stop himself from checking out women with pastel eyes, peaches-and-cream complexions. What was happening to him? He couldn't get his mind off these fucking Christie Brinkley bitches! But, then, Rashid would think, why *should* he? Why *couldn't* he find such women fetching? Why must he dismiss his attraction to them as some form of Eurocentric cultural brainwashing? Maybe it was the other way around; maybe his shunning of these women, his blocking them out of his vision (until Morgan), maybe *that* had been due to cultural brainwashing. Just thinking such things unsettled Rashid. These thoughts, so different from any thoughts he'd had before, seemed almost not his own. Where were these thoughts he couldn't stop, could not control, coming from? Here he was, pushing thirty, a righteous brother, dedicated to the black cause, thinking that it was his *right* to be attracted to, even to date, to fuck, perhaps to fall "in love" with white women if he chose to do so. What the hell was happening to him?

Rashid remembered an afternoon a couple of years earlier when he sat in a Columbia cafeteria with one of the more scrupulously correct sisters in his department, openly scoffing at a brother they spotted eating with a white woman.

"I just hate seeing that shit," the sister said.

"Me, too," Rashid said. "The only thing I hate as much is seeing a black woman with a white man."

"But that's *different*," the sister said.

Rashid knew that by "different," she meant less objectionable. And he didn't challenge her, didn't doubt what she said. But now he wondered *why* it was different. There were, of course, the obvious rationales, always cited: the preponderance of black males who were in prison or unemployed or otherwise undesirable to black women. But why—it suddenly, jarringly, occurred to Rashid—should *he* feel responsible for this situation? And why did this situation make it so "different" for black women? Why, because of numbers, because of statistics, should they have the freedom to date whomever they chose while *he* had to limit himself, be forced to place constraints on human possibility? Rashid, unable to squelch the thoughts that seemed to be exploding in his mind, decided that numbers, the statistics on "marriageable" black men, the raw data of only the last thirty or forty years or so, didn't explain it, didn't justify why it was "different," why it was acceptable for black women to be with white men but *not* acceptable for black men to be with white women. The reason went deeper, far deeper into the American psyche, into American history. The fact of the matter was that it had *always* been acceptable for white men to have black women, ever since the days when the plantation owners and even their lowliest white male underlings felt it was their privilege to prowl the slave quarters, plucking the ripest female chattel for their carnal pleasure. White men fucking black women was as American as apple pie! But if a black man—be he a slave in the seventeenth, eighteenth, or nineteenth centuries or a young, allegedly "free" brother in the twentieth—even glanced at a white woman, that was grounds to have him strung up. How little times had changed. Only today—Rashid could not control the idea, could not stop it from bursting in his brain—black folk had internalized the twisted double standard that had been part of our oppression, granting white men a freedom that black men had to be, if not denied, then excoriated for. History was what made white male–black female relationships "different" from black male–white female relationships. All the other rationalizations were lies. Therefore, it occurred to Rashid, a black man loving a white woman was a radical act, a political statement that was truly subversive, truly counter to all forms of establishment thought—white *or* black—in America. That was why, in an era of resurgent conformity, so few black men dared do it.

Rashid knew he had to stop thinking such thoughts, but he could not dispel them. They came to preoccupy him. That summer, he hardly saw anyone. He tried to work on his dissertation, but to no avail. He wandered the streets all day thinking his blasphemous thoughts and checking out tawny, corn-husky manes. He supported himself with the money he had inherited from his precious mama, who had inherited it from her Uncle Tom father, who had inherited from his Miss Daisy boss lady, who had inherited from her forefathers, who had made it off the backs and the sweat and the toil of Rashid's forefathers and foremothers. Late in the summer, one of his aunts, Lorena's older sister, called to tell him—to taunt him, really, with the information—that Janet was engaged to an accountant. And Rashid was happy for his former lover, glad that she'd found a successful black man to marry. But the news made him feel all the more isolated, all the more sorry for himself. Was there anyone in the world—anyone other than that crazy, Anglophile, heroin-addicted white girl—for Rashid to love?

Then, one morning, just a week before the start of the new semester, Morgan called. There was no small talk, no little niceties. "I need to see you," Morgan said. "Please." They met that afternoon at the tiny chichi coffee shop where they'd had their first date. Morgan looked like shit: drawn, pale, with dark circles under her eyes. Her hand trembled when she raised her cup of cappuccino to her lips. Her voice quavered slightly when she spoke.

"What's happened to you?" Rashid asked.

Morgan told him. Earlier that summer, she'd OD'ed. Had to be rushed to the hospital. Spent twenty-four hours in an intensive care unit, then six weeks in a drug rehab center. "Really," she said, "an asylum for rich people. In Connecticut. Rather posh, actually." Now she was preparing to leave for London. Today would be her last full day in the States. She was going to live with her uncle and his family. Try to get well again. Didn't really know what the hell she was going to do there. "I just have to get out of New York. Out of America. America's insane."

Or maybe, Rashid thought, *you're* insane. But he didn't say that. Instead, he asked, "This OD, was it about Kent?"

Morgan shrugged weakly. "Maybe it was about Kent. Or maybe it was about my brother. Or my father. Or maybe it was about you."

"I don't want that responsibility."

"I assume you're still with Janet."

"Yes," Rashid lied.

"Are you in love with her?"

"No."

"Better that way, eh?" Morgan said. "Stick to yer own kind."

"Yo, baby, what's love got to do with it? We need to dispense with these ridiculous Western ideas about 'true love.' Like God, like communism, like capitalism. These second-millennium ideas should be tossed onto the ash heap. Does that sound harsh to you? I don't care."

"You know the last time we saw each other? That afternoon last winter when we went to the movies? A friend of my mother's saw us walking down the street. I saw her at a dinner party at my parents' place a couple of months later. Naturally, she assumed you were my lover. She kept saying, 'He's got such beautiful skin. Such beautiful skin.' 'Yes,' I finally said, 'and it's as cool and smooth as marble.'"

Rashid thought of the way Morgan had clutched him when they made love, her fierce tenderness.

"You and me, Rashid. The timing will just never be right, will it?"

"It's not a question of timing."

"I'm thinking of converting to Catholicism."

"What the fuck for?"

"I need faith. I want to have faith in my life."

"You want reassurance. There's a big difference between reassurance and faith. But you'll never understand that," Rashid said reproachfully, "will you?"

"Look," Morgan said, holding out her hand delicately. "I painted my fingernails. All by myself. Specially for you. My mother took me to have my hair cut yesterday."

"Are you fading on me?"

"I am very heavily medicated. I thought the caffeine would perk me up."

"If you were any more perky, you might be able to pass for comatose."

Morgan smiled, her genuine smile; it was the first time Rashid had seen it that afternoon. "I should get a cab. I have to go home."

Out on the sidewalk, Morgan kissed Rashid, gently, once on each cheek, European-style. "I'll see you when I see you." Watching the taxi disappear down Broadway, Rashid knew he would never see Morgan again. He would not allow it.

➤   ➤   ➤

Rashid had to get out of Manhattan, out of New York altogether. He burned to get as far away from white people as he could. He needed to go someplace where there were no white faces in sight, no crazed Morgan Bradstreets, no sleazy Michael Mayhews, no heads of crimson and golden hair. Rashid wanted to be in a world that was totally black. He returned to Norris, New Jersey.

Rashid spent weeks cleaning up the old house on Largent Street, throwing away some of Lorena's ancient, musty furniture, replacing it with his own stuff. He felt tremendously relieved to be away from Columbia. There was really, he decided, no reason for him to be there. All he needed to do academically was finish his dissertation and take his final oral examinations. Rashid was no longer even certain he wanted to pursue a career in academia. He needed to do something that would help his people more directly, in a more immediate, profound way. And he wanted to help not only those black folk who could make it into top universities. He wanted to help the people on the street. The real, the authentic African-Americans. And, by the end of the fall, he found a way. Using fifteen thousand dollars of what was left of his inheritance from Lorena, Rashid bought a small, decrepit, abandoned office building on Jefferson Avenue, one of the main drags of midtown. The space would need a great deal of work, a great deal of cleaning and refurbishing, before it could match his vision. Still, the first thing he did on the day he took over the property was to paint a large sign and put it in the window:

NORRIS CENTER FOR AFRICAN-AMERICAN
ARTS AND CULTURE
DIRECTOR: RASHID SCUGGS

➤   ➤   ➤

"I heard you kicked the motherfucker's ass," Eugene Little said.

"Well," Rashid said with a self-effacing laugh, "it was an ass that needed kicking."

Nearly a week had passed since Rashid's confrontation with Melvin Hutchinson at Sam Adams High, and word of the encounter was spreading through Norris. The big disappointment to Rashid was that the story hadn't made it into the media, but at least the folks in his hometown knew what he had done.

"We need more brothers and sisters to take a stand like you did," Eugene said. "We need more protests. We gots to get organized. Like in the sixties, man. Know what I'm sayin'?"

"I hear ya."

"And that's what I try to do with my art, you know what I'm sayin'? Send out a positive message to people. I mean, far as I'm concerned, I don't even really make art. It's propaganda. That's what I'm about. Propaganda for the people."

"Right on."

Rashid and Eugene Little were sitting in the director's office of the Norris Center for African-American Arts and Culture. In two and a half weeks, the NCAAAC would officially open with an exhibition of Eugene's photographs. Rashid had hoped to display the work of a younger, hipper photographer, but of all the sample pictures he'd seen, only Eugene Little's were good enough for a solo show. Eugene, a fiftyish brother who taught at Norris Community College, had shown a lot of promise as an artist back in the seventies, but his career had never really taken off. Still, he was fairly well known in Norris and had last shown his work two years earlier at the college. In January, he had eagerly agreed to produce a new series of pictures for Rashid's gallery. It was now April. He sat in Rashid's office, a black leather cap pushed down over his brow, a portfolio resting on his lap. Rashid wanted to ask him to open the portfolio and show him the new work. But Eugene Little seemed more interested in talking politics.

"I mean, where is the movement today?"

"Folks feel defeated. They've gotten so accustomed to their disenfranchisement, they don't have any fight left in 'em."

"It's a damn shame." Eugene Little shook his head woefully. "Not like in the old days, when everybody was down for the struggle."

"Well, I like to think we can revive the spirit."

"We gots to!"

"And artists like you have an important role to play," Rashid said, looking for a segue into a discussion of Eugene's new work. With so little time left before the opening, Rashid was getting nervous. He'd already sent out invitations to a hundred of Norris's most important residents. Advertisements for the show would start appearing in the local press any day now. And, in a major coup, Kilarti Mufoso, critic at large for the *Downtown Clarion,* had agreed to review the exhibition. All the pieces were falling into place. But Rashid still had not seen the photos that were going to be displayed.

"Yeah," Eugene said, "but I don't even like to call myself an artist. You dig? *Artist.* I don't go for the connotation that word has. It sorta places you above the people. You dig? I make propaganda."

"I hear ya. Well, hey, Gene, let's take a look at some of your propaganda. Why don't you open up that portfolio and show me what you got?"

Eugene sighed heavily. He placed the portfolio on Rashid's desk and flipped it open. "Here it is, brother." There was nothing inside.

Rashid felt suddenly nauseated. He looked up at Eugene. Little was staring at the floor, his eyes concealed by the bill of his leather cap. "What's the deal, Gene? Is this some kinda joke?"

Eugene squirmed in his chair. "Well, man, you know, makin' strong photographs, work that really talks to people, I mean, you gotta have the fire. You know what I'm sayin'?"

"No. I don't know what you're sayin'."

Eugene looked up again, a helpless expression in his eyes. "I just ain't had the fire, brother. I don't got the power."

Rashid clenched his fists. He could feel his dormant hysteria, the hysteria he knew he'd inherited from his mama, the hysteria he'd rarely unleashed, beginning to stir inside him. "Why didn't you tell me this before?" he said quietly.

"I kept waitin' for the fire. I thought it would come, but, well, I, er . . ."

"You've had three months, Eugene."

"Well, that ain't so much time, man. You gotta understand, I have other commitments."

"All right, all right, all right," Rashid said, trying to steady his nerves. "Don't you have anything recent, maybe not from the past three months, but stuff from the past year or so that I could put up?"

"Well, there's the stuff I showed at the college two years ago."

"Eugene, I can't show work you've already displayed in Norris. Haven't you shot anything since then?"

Eugene stroked his chin as if trying to remember, then, after a few seconds, said, "Um . . . no."

"You haven't taken any photos in the past two years?"

"That's what I'm trying to tell ya, brother. I ain't had the fire."

"And I don't suppose there's any chance you're gonna *get* the fire in the next two weeks."

"Um . . . well, brother . . . I . . . well . . . no."

Rashid put his elbows on his desk and buried his face in his hands. "I'm dead."

Eugene Little rose, picked up his empty portfolio. "Well, brother, I gotta run. Gotta meet my ol' lady. But, hey, man, if I get the fire, I'll be sure to give you a call."

Rashid continued to hold his face in his hands. "I'm dead," he whispered.

"Okay, man," Eugene Little said. "I catch you later." He hurried out of the office.

"I'm dead," Rashid said to no one. "I'm dead."

(8)

MELVIN HUTCHINSON: the headline read, HE'S DONE WELL, BUT HAS HE DONE GOOD?

The attorney general sat in one of the sleek, oversized leather armchairs in the dim light of the Eagle Room, that intimate den in the Millennium Club, a glass of cognac in one hand and, in his other hand, which fairly trembled with indignation, a copy of the offending article, ripped from that morning's *Washington Post*. The only other person in the Eagle Room was Henry Beedle, who sat across from his boss in an identical thronelike armchair, sipping cognac, puffing on his pipe, and trying, in his calm, steady manner, to soothe Melvin's rattled nerves. Occasionally, ancient Clarence would enter the room to refill their glasses, empty Beedle's ashtray, and ask if all was well before shuffling away again. Beedle was starting to worry about Hutch. A week had passed since Vin Ewell's stroke. With each day, Hutch drew closer to winning Ewell's job. But the nearer he got to the prize, the more agitated Hutch became. Beedle had thought the boss's outburst at Sam Adams High had been an aberration. Now, it seemed that that was only the start of a strange unraveling. He'd never seen Hutch so distracted and edgy, so ill-tempered and insecure. Beedle's sources at the White House told him that Muriel Ewell was getting ready to pull the plug—all she needed was a little prodding, someone to persuade her that Vin's condition was hopeless. The scuttlebutt was that Hutch would be Troy McCracken's choice to replace Ewell, just as Beedle had as-

< 204 >

sumed all along. Beedle figured the attorney general would receive a summons from the President any day now. It was up to him to make sure that Hutch had his wits about him when the call came.

"Can you believe this shit?" Melvin growled, shaking the newspaper article. "The implication of that headline. The fucking condescension. Who the hell is some slimy reporter to judge me? And by what standards? It's a fucking outrage!"

"It's because you're the man," Beedle said in his unflappable drone. "Everybody knows you're the man. So they're hitting you a little harder these days. You've been exceptionally lucky with the press, Judge. More than two years in office and hardly anybody's laid a glove on you. Now that you're in line for the vice presidency, you're going to come under tougher scrutiny. It's merely a sign that your star is ascending."

Hutch seemed not to have heard a word Beedle had said. "I bet you anything this reporter's black. That name, Russell Davis. Use a nigger to attack a nigger. Ain't that always the way? Just listen to this shit." Melvin read the passage from the article in a jeering, stentorian voice: " 'The attorney general's tenure has been marked by half measures, an inability to fulfill promises that some might have considered dubious in the first place.' Okay, you get that, don't you? He accuses me of making *dubious* promises, then criticizes me for not fulfilling them. I can't win!"

"He's an insect, Judge. An insignificant insect."

"Get this now: 'While Hutchinson claims to support affirmative-action policies that honor "quality over quotas," none of his top deputies is an African-American. While the attorney general has famously proclaimed that the country needs "not more prisons, but more executions," the number of death-row inmates who have been executed has only'—only!—'risen by ten percent in the past two years. The attorney general has supported the controversial forced closings of two photography exhibitions in New York City, but he has been curiously lax in enforcing the new obscenity codes elsewhere. And while Melvin Hutchinson claims to support a woman's right to choose, he has threatened prosecution of any woman who violates the renewed ban on the abortion pill.' Well, Jesus Christ, it's the goddamned law! I'm the fucking attorney general of the United

States. It's my *job* to enforce the law. What is this clown bashing me for?"

"On the other hand, Judge, he does praise you for the administration of the DRCs, for your handling of the Federal Youth Corps, and gives you big points for your inspirational rhetoric."

"But, but, but," Melvin sputtered in rage, "would you just look at this!" He held up the second page of the article, which displayed a chart titled HUTCH'S CORPORATE BOARDS. The chart listed the seven companies for which Melvin had served on the board of directors and, in a separate column, the annual payments he had received from each corporation in the last year he served. "I resigned from every one of these boards the day I was appointed to the bench. So what is the point of this chart? They're trying to make it seem like I'm some sort of criminal!"

"Well, Judge, I don't know, I—"

"Have you *ever* seen this done to a white public official?"

"Er, well, actually, I—"

"You know what this is about, don't you? They're saying, Look at all the money that nigger pocketed. Can you believe a nigger made *all that money?* He couldn't a *deserved* it! What do they think, that I showed up at board meetings and *mugged* the other directors?"

Beedle laughed, trying to get Hutch to laugh along with him. But it was no use.

" 'He's done well,' " Melvin sneered, " 'but has he done good?' You get the inference there, don't you? Like all I wanted to do was line my pockets. I was the *only* black member on five of those boards. Does this Russell Davis think corporate America would be better *without* black representation at the highest levels? Does he have his head that far up his ass? What should I have done—spent my career working in some urine-stained community center?" Melvin downed the last of his cognac, then slammed the glass down on the side table. "Have you ever heard this question asked of a white public official? Ever?"

"It's because you're the man," Beedle droned soothingly. "You're the man. Just a heartbeat away. You're just one very irregular heartbeat away from being a heartbeat away from the presidency." Beedle leaned forward. "Do you realize, Judge, that you could make history?

History! It's within your grasp. But it won't come without a price, sir. Everybody has to take their licks, especially from those idiots in the press. It happened to Lincoln. To Roosevelt. To Dr. King! Every great leader has to put up with these stings from these . . . these . . . mosquitoes. But you can take it, Judge. You're a giant besieged by pygmies. Pygmies! But you can handle it. You shall prevail. History is within your grasp, Judge. Dare I say it? Dare I say the words? *Vice President Melvin Hutchinson."*

Melvin stared at the ornate pattern on the rug beneath his feet and chewed the insides of his cheeks. For a week now, everyone he came in contact with was kissing his ass. He was accustomed to deference, of course, but this was getting ridiculous. The solicitous grins, the obsequious pleasantries—it was all so excessive. Even Dorothy was treating him differently. "Have I told you recently how much I love you?" she'd said the other night. She even had sex with him. The first time in—damn, how long had it been?—at least six months. Yes indeed, everyone wanted to smooch the behind of the man who might be second in command of the only superpower on earth. Melvin knew he should be enjoying, relishing, this, but all he felt was dread.

Something is about to happen to me. Something terrible is going to happen to me. Four of the past seven nights, Melvin had returned to New York, to his apartment on Central Park West, just to escape the Washington buzz. All that gossip—and so much of it about *him.* Better simply to fly *Justice One* back to New York. *Something is about to happen to me. Something terrible is going to happen.* Melvin reverted to his old habit, sitting in his darkened study, laying Harry's .38 on the desk, staring at the shadowy shape of the revolver, sipping Jack Daniel's. In his mind's eye, he saw the sword of justice. But now, he no longer wielded the sword. Instead, he was kneeling in some vast empty space and the sword was poised above him, directly over his head. *He* was the one the sword would smite. All because of his one mistake, his single lapse in judgment. For this grave error, the sword of justice would come down on him. Sometimes, in this vision, as he stared up at the sword of justice, a face would take its place: that shaved head, the black features with the white skin; he'd see those hazel eyes that stared at him from the line of inmates at the Fort Brandriss Drug Reeducation Center and hear that voice, that adolescent twang, which sounded neither white nor black when it told him the name, the two words that Melvin knew would doom him. "Something is about to happen," Melvin would whisper, alone in the darkness of his study. "Something terrible is going to happen to me."

"Will there be anything else, Your Honor?" Melvin heard someone say. He looked up, suddenly aware again of where he was, feeling the cotton of his suit pants, itchy, pressed between his sweaty hamstrings and the hot leather of his armchair in the Eagle Room. Standing over him was white-jacketed, white-haired old Clarence with his grinning mouthful of white teeth. Clarence was waiting for an answer.

"No," Melvin muttered. "No, nothing else tonight."

"Yes, *suh!*" Clarence sang.

"Don't you mock me, boy!" Melvin exploded, slapping his palm down on the arm of his chair.

A look of sheer terror came across Clarence's face. Wordlessly, he stumbled out of the Eagle Room, closing the door behind him. Melvin looked at Beedle. His deputy stared at him in openmouthed astonishment, all his little brown tobacco-stained teeth showing. Finally, Beedle shut his trap, cleared his throat, and said quietly, "I think you could use a good night's sleep, Judge."

Melvin crumpled the *Washington Post* article in his hand, shaped it into a ball, and tossed it into the fireplace. "I know who I am, Henry," he said flatly. "I know exactly who I am."

➤ ➤ ➤

"The darker the berry, the sweeter the juice: That's your motto," Willow Cushing's girlfriend Melissa teased her when she caught Willow checking out Rodney Person across a packed artist's loft at one of those chaotic Greenwich Village parties—the air thick with marijuana smoke, cacophonous jazz playing on the stereo—that seemed to consume Willow's nights back in the good ole seventies. Willow knew that some of her friends thought she had a thing for black men. But the truth was, Willow just liked *men*. And men liked *her*. Men had always liked her. She counted on it. Willow had become, at this point in her life, a sort of collector of men. She reveled in the vast variety of maleness. All manner of men intrigued her, from the wispy, long-haired boys who loved to give her massages during—as far as Willow was concerned, excessively—prolonged foreplay to the middle-aged rich men who would take her anywhere she wanted to go and insist on paying for it all, wanting nothing in return but a whiz-bang session in the sack. Black men were, to Willow, just another novelty. But simply because she'd slept with a few at all—something that even some of her most self-consciously adventurous white girlfriends had not done—she had acquired this reputation. At this particular party, though, it was not Rodney Person's blackness that attracted Willow. It was the fact that this black man was *Rodney Person,* an ass-kicking saxophone player, the composer of a classic, "Radiance." Talent—whether it was talent in business, the arts, or in bed—was the biggest turn-on to Willow Cushing.

As she gently pushed her way through the crowd, moving toward Rodney, she *knew* she could have him. That was how confident Willow could be in those days. She knew it was simply up to her whether she and this man would spend the night together. When Willow saw the way Rodney Person lit up as she introduced herself, she was certain that, yes, it would be only a matter of hours, that later that night, she would take him to bed.

How things had changed in a little more than twenty years. Willow was, if anything, even hornier than she'd been as a young woman. But long gone were the days when she could hit a bull's-eye on any target. For a woman who was—God, how she winced at the term, how she fairly gnashed her teeth when she read in a magazine article someone who was born in precisely the same year as she described as—middle-aged, she still looked good. She knew that. She had kept her figure. And men still liked her. She had that spark, that good-natured flirtatiousness that men responded to. But she couldn't seem even to *buy* a fuck anymore. Like an aging athlete, she'd felt her powers receding for five, ten, almost fifteen years now. The desire to bed any man she chose, like the desire to hit a tennis ball, was still there; but she just couldn't get the ball over the net anymore. She associated her decline to the birth of Miles and the chopping off of her hair. Like so many women after their first baby, Willow had dispensed with her long locks and opted for a short, sensible, low-maintenance haircut. Life was complicated enough with diapers and 2:00 A.M. feedings—who needed to worry about their hair? Mother-hood was anything but sexy. In retrospect, though, cutting off her hair, and keeping it short, was akin to Samson willingly letting Delilah clip him. Somehow, motherhood and a drastic haircut had, in tandem, diminished Willow's prowess.

Now, as she gazed across the cramped little recording studio at Kenny Carter—God, he was so fine, with his mocha skin and long, exquisitely curled eyelashes and his angel's voice—Willow felt a sad resignation in place of the cockiness that had come naturally to her during her peak years, two decades earlier. Willow, Kenny, and four other singers stood in front of microphones, headphones secured snugly over their ears, trying to get just the right harmony for a radio commercial. Over and over again, they sang the closing lines of the upbeat little jingle, wearing out their voices hitting the high notes, until, at last, the producer was grudgingly satisfied with the effort.

"Metro-pol-i-tan Sa-vings . . . /'Cause all good things in life/Have a price."

There were three male singers and three females. Except for Willow and one of the men, all the singers were black. At the end of the session, Willow suggested everyone go out for a bite to eat. The white guy said he was late for an appointment with his therapist and took off. The rest of the group went to a coffee shop around the corner. Willow felt awkward throughout the meal. She felt as if none of the other singers were acknowledging anything she said. The talk was all about music and various gigs and Kenny, Juhwan, Nadine, and Michelle bantered easily among themselves. But whenever Willow got a word in edgewise, no one really responded. She felt almost invisible. It was all the more frustrating because she felt that Kenny was right there for the taking. If only he would *notice* her. Willow felt that even if she *was* middle-aged, she was still the best woman for him at the table. Nadine was way too fat and Michelle, like Juhwan, had let it be known she was gay. Willow was certain that Kenny was straight. She was certain they could connect. If only he would acknowledge her. Come on, people! Willow wanted to shout. I am here, you know! You don't have to freeze me out just 'cause I'm white. Do you have to be so small-minded? What did I ever do to you? She didn't cry out, though. She just kept trying to engage them, kept banging her head against their wall of indifference.

Willow could remember a time when it was actually *cool* for black people and white people to talk, to hang out together. It hadn't been so long ago. Had it? In her early days with Rodney, they almost always hung out in mixed circles. Sometimes, Willow was the only white person in a group. Sometimes, Rodney was the only black person in a group. But there was never any strain. As long as the folks possessed a certain measure of bohemian savoir faire, as long as nobody was too uptight—uptight only in the bourgeois, middlebrow sense, not uptight about race; nobody was ever uptight about that—everything was mellow. Willow knew that things had changed, but she could never pinpoint when the change had occurred. Sometime during Miles's early childhood, she and Rodney had stopped socializing together. Though they stayed married, continued sharing the same apartment, he went his way, hanging out till all hours of the night with whomever it was he hung out with, and Willow went hers, though going her way meant being the primary caregiver to Miles. When Willow did go out for a drink with a friend, or attend the rare party, or indulge in a brief affair—she'd gotten lucky with four men since Miles's birth, though none of those liaisons had occurred in the last half decade—the company she kept was invariably white. But why did it have to be this way? Sitting in the coffee shop with the four black singers who refused to acknowledge her, Willow now had to fight the urge to scream, *It doesn't have to be this way, people! I have a black husband, you know. You don't have to alienate me. For God's sake, I have a black child. I'm not your fucking enemy!*

After the late lunch, Willow and the other singers caught the number 1 train. Willow got off the subway at Eighty-sixth Street. Everybody else, who bid her cursory good-byes, was going farther uptown.

➤   ➤   ➤

"Is Daddy black?" Miles asked Willow one spring morning as they sat on a bench in Riverside Park. Miles was three years old. It was the first time he'd ever said anything about race.

"Yes," Willow said.

"And you're white?" Miles asked.

"That's right, Miles. And what are you?"

"Miles is gray," Willow's little boy said.

Actually, in terms of pigmentation alone, Miles was, to Willow's surprise, as pale as she. He'd been born pale, but Willow had always thought he'd darken as he got older. He didn't. Yet, somehow, in the contours of his face, in the texture of his hair, it was clear to the average American eye that Miles was not quite "white." But he wasn't "black," either. Willow could detect the curiosity of other mothers when she took Miles out in his stroller. They were too polite to ask, but Willow could see the question in their faces: What *is* he? She had to laugh when she finally asked Miles the question and heard his reply. It reassured her. During her pregnancy, she'd never worried about having a mixed-race child. It wasn't until she saw the puzzled faces of the other mothers in Riverside Park that she thought her son's in-betweenness might be a problem. But when Miles told her he was gray, Willow considered it a positive answer, a self-identification that showed her son could appreciate all the ambiguities of his peculiar situation in this peculiar society. So there would be no problem. There was no problem now; there would be no problems to come.

➤   ➤   ➤

"You have a complete lack of foresight, Wilhemina," Danforth Cushing had told his daughter in the last conversation she would ever have with him.

"But I have a plan," she insisted. "It's just not the plan you would like me to have." Once again, she outlined her scheme to her father. She was going to drop out of Sarah Lawrence, have her name legally changed to Willow, live on an ashram in Vermont for a while—just to get her head together—then try to make it as a folksinger. "It's a good plan, Father. And all I'm asking you for is an allowance. A thousand dollars a month, that's all I'm asking you for."

Danforth refused. He refused his daughter the allowance, refused to speak with or see her, refused, when discussing her with other family members, to call her by her new name. He refused to include her in his will, refused a visit from her when he was on his deathbed. And Willow didn't really care. Each refusal made her, briefly, angry. But she was never wounded by them. She realized that she'd never loved her father enough to be hurt by him.

Still, over the years, Willow would think about that one thing he'd said to her, that remark about the foresight. For some reason, it registered deeply with her. There were times when she thought foresight was completely irrelevant. "How can you worry about the future," a Buddhist friend once said to her, "when the future doesn't exist?" Those words seemed so true, so profound to her. *Of course* there was only the now. Now was the only time that ever really existed. And yet, Willow could never stop dreaming about the future, hoping that someday she would arrive at some point of ultimate fulfillment. She thought the moment would occur when she produced her first album. But it didn't. She thought moving in with Rodney Person would bring her to that special destination. It didn't. She believed, for a while, that motherhood would be the greatest fulfillment she could ever experience. And again she was disappointed. By the time she hit her mid-forties, Willow was castigating herself almost daily for not having planned her life better, for not having had some foresight. Then again, she would muse, what difference would more planning have made in this random universe? "Everything happens for a reason," her Buddhist friend had said and, for a time, Willow believed him. Not anymore; not now that she was middle-aged. She believed just the opposite: that *nothing* happens for a reason. We all just blundered along, hoping for the best amid the chaos.

Foresight! How could she ever have foreseen that someone with a talent as big as Rodney Person's would want to spend his life eating, sleeping, smoking dope, watching TV, and scrounging for gigs with lesser players? How could she have foreseen that someone with as much conviction as she had once had would end up singing commercial jingles? How could she have foreseen that after giving her child all the love and attention she had never received herself, he would end up resenting her? How could she ever—even with a crystal fucking ball—have known that in a world that at one time actually seemed to be growing more tolerant, more communal, more racially mixed than ever before, her own son would someday hate her for being white?

In middle age, Willow Cushing—she'd never taken her husband's name—found herself contemplating alternative scenarios, unknowable what-ifs. And as the years passed by, one person became the obsessive focus of her speculation, her might-have-been fantasies: Melvin Hutchinson.

> > >

When Willow arrived home from her recording session and the late lunch with the black singers who refused to acknowledge her, she found Rodney in his usual four o'clock mode, asleep, fully clothed, on top of their unmade bed, snoring. On this particular afternoon, Rodney had fallen asleep with the television on, tuned to the Politics channel, and Willow paused as she entered the bedroom to watch, for the fourth time in the last several days—POL always repeated certain features, seemingly ad infinitum, if news was slow—the same clip of Melvin Hutchinson touring the Fort Brandriss Drug Reeducation Center, just outside Brandriss, New Jersey, the very place where Miles had been incarcerated for three months; and seeing this feature yet again, Willow felt certain that it had been shot on Miles's last day at the DRC, the previous Friday, exactly one week earlier. And the serendipity of it seemed just too weird for her. Did Melvin know Miles was there? He *must* have. He was the attorney general. He was in charge of the DRCs. He had to have known that Miles Person was an inmate at Fort Brandriss. Why else would he have chosen that particular DRC to visit, on what just happened to be Miles's last day there? He had to have known. And that, Willow assumed, was why he'd chosen to visit Fort Brandriss. Just to get a tacit look at his son.

< 214 >

While Rodney snored obliviously, Willow removed her hidden scrapbook from the bottom of the big oak dresser in the far corner of the room, then sat beside her unconscious husband and began flipping through the thick, clear, plastic-jacketed pages. The book was devoted entirely to items about Melvin Hutchinson, from tiny clippings about the attorney general's announcement of some change in an obscure Justice Department policy to the photo from the cover of *American Century* magazine, a startling shot of Melvin, wearing a dark suit, arms folded across his chest, glowering straight into the camera, the headline in bold white letters at the bottom of the page: HERE COME THE JUDGE. She ran her fingers over the plastic jacket of the scrapbook page, wanting to stroke the face in the photo, fearing, fleetingly, that Rodney might wake up and catch her, then realizing that Rodney would only wake up if she physically roused him or clicked off the TV, ending the white-noise sound track of his dreams, and that, even if he did suddenly awaken, he wouldn't even notice or care what Willow was doing. So Willow continued to stroke the plastic and stare at that dark, iron face, a face she knew so well because, even though the coloring was different, it was the same face her only child was slowly developing.

Willow thought of all the letters she'd sent to Melvin—never to his home, of course, always to his office at Hull, Evans—making herself vulnerable to him in a way she'd never made herself vulnerable to any man, telling him about the consuming power of her feeling for him (even though they barely knew each other, the depth of the feeling, the love for him, was unmistakable, overwhelming); telling him that she was absolutely certain that the child growing inside her was his; letting him know that she would accept any decision he came to about this situation, that he could acknowledge this responsibility or reject it but that the responsibility would always be there, that *she* would always be there, ready to share a life with him if he wanted, accepting his decision if he chose not to. Willow continued to write Melvin during the first year of Miles's life, sending him pictures, giving him details of the baby's development. And not once did Melvin reply. Maybe he thought Willow was crazy. Maybe, being a lawyer, he had decided that any sort of response would make him susceptible to a paternity suit. But Willow didn't want to sue Melvin.

She didn't want to hurt him at all. She wanted to share this tremendous love with him.

Melvin's silence became punishing. After a while, Willow wanted only for him to acknowledge her, to send even a perfunctory note back to her. He didn't have to return her love. He didn't have to admit that, yes, he was Miles's father. He only had to acknowledge that Willow, and Miles, existed. That was all. If he had done just that much, in just one short note, perhaps, the entire situation would have been resolved for Willow. But she never heard so much as a word from Melvin. And so the pain went on and on.

What would have happened if Melvin Hutchinson *had* written her back? What would have happened if they'd met again, just two or three weeks after their first (and only) encounter, before Willow even knew she was pregnant? Melvin would have felt the love she felt; Willow was sure of it. He would have left his wife, she would have left Rodney, and they would have been married by the time Miles was born. The whole course of her life—or at least the past fourteen, fifteen years—would have been different. She'd have had money, *real* money—and respectability. And today she'd be the wife of the attorney general. Maybe on her way to being the wife of the vice president. She'd have lived out the sort of life she'd been born to, but with such a delicious twist: the fact that her rich, powerful, eminent, and distinguished husband would be an African-American. Ha! Take *that*, Danforth Cushing! How painful it would have been for you to see your flaky, flighty daughter with a man who was, well, not as rich as you, but at least as powerful, and far more famous, and a *black man*. What a kick in the balls that would have been to the great white Father!

Instead, Willow was left with the smelly residue of her bohemian dreams. She'd committed to another type of life entirely, with an entirely different sort of (black) man, an artist, a romantic renegade. Willow had thought, when she first moved in with Rodney Person, that it was a bold act of self-assertion and, as such, the perfect revenge against her father. Willow would be, in her own contemporary way, as untamable as her mother had been. Danforth, as much as he had tried, had never been able to crush his wife, Bettina, with propriety and domesticity. Bettina had lived her life her way, going off with friends to ski in Gstaad, leaving Danforth to his stultifying business deals and country clubbing while she flew down to Rio de Janeiro for Carnaval. Because Willow could barely even remember her mother—she died in a plane crash in Brazil when Willow was three—Bettina loomed as an almost mythical figure in her daughter's life. When Willow dropped out of Sarah Lawrence, when she embarked on a creative career, when she moved in with this black genius of an artist, she was, in her way, emulating Bettina, living the even bolder, even *more* nonconforming life she was sure her mother would have lived if only she'd been born in the age of liberation.

How everything had turned to shit. Willow had never had the adventure, the success, the happiness she'd felt entitled to. She hadn't outdone her mother. At least Bettina had had the good fortune to go out in a blaze of glory at twenty-eight instead of living on to endure the grinding insults of domestic life. And instead of shaming Danforth with a life that had fulfilled her perfect plan, Willow had given her father ample opportunity to gloat over her misfortunes, to shake his head scornfully when he discussed her with other family members (how eager they all were to tell Willow of Father's feelings) and decry her "complete lack of foresight."

But things might have turned out so differently. If only Melvin Hutchinson had answered her letters. Why couldn't he acknowledge her, acknowledge their son? Just once.

Willow tucked the secret scrapbook back in its hiding place. On the television, a newscaster was talking about the President. "With an eighty percent approval rating, Troy McCracken is more popular at this point in his first term than any other President except George Bush."

"That Troy," Willow muttered. "Everybody loves the guy." She had never been able to see the appeal herself. She picked up the remote control and clicked off the television. Rodney immediately awakened.

"What? Wha-wha-wha?" Rodney said, glancing around the bedroom.

"Nothing, Rodney," Willow said. "I just turned off the TV."

"Oh, okay. I got a gig tonight. I don't want to oversleep."

"Don't worry, I'll wake you."

Rodney smiled his big loopy smile. Even now, his grin radiated a childlike innocence. There was a time, fifteen, twenty years ago, when Willow had found innocence endearing. Now, it disgusted her. "Thanks, baby," Rodney said. His head fell back on the pillow and within a second, he was unconscious again, snoring obliviously.

>   >   >

Melvin Hutchinson was incredibly straight—that was the first thing Willow noticed about him as they were introduced. So straight that he was actually wearing a tie, and a neatly pressed sky blue button-down shirt beneath a white cardigan sweater, to a midnight beach party. There were about a dozen people sitting around the bonfire that unusually chilly night in late June in Gay Head, just behind the summer home of a divorced lawyer named Stanley, who was having an affair with Willow's friend Melissa. Stanley was a partner at Hull, Evans and, a couple of hours earlier, he thought of giving his colleague Melvin a call and inviting him over. Willow thought that, since most of the guests were friends of Melissa's, Stanley had wanted to have a little more representation on his side. He was a good ten years older than Melissa and perhaps feeling a bit unhip and outnumbered. "He's a black cat," Stanley had said–that "cat" clanging awkwardly —directing his comment to Willow, seeming to want to impress her, knowing that she had just married—and had been living with for years—an Afro-American. On this night, Rodney was in Japan, touring with the Jimmy Higgins band. Willow had never felt so dispirited about their relationship. Maybe it was the marriage that had done it —that contractual obligation. She didn't know why Rodney had been so eager to make their love official, legal. But she had acquiesced. And from the moment she said her vows, the staleness she had felt only vaguely before in their relationship became overpowering. She grew more and more bored, agitated. She began to feel that her career was going nowhere, that Rodney's career was going nowhere. Their sex became rote. Willow feared that by getting married she'd willingly locked herself in a cage. She wanted release. If nothing else, she wanted another lover.

Now here was this outrageously dignified black man in his

cardigan and tie, apologizing for arriving so late, explaining that he'd driven his wife and daughter to the airport earlier that evening— they were off to Paris for a three-week vacation—before coming out to Oak Bluffs, which Willow remembered was the "black section" of Martha's Vineyard. There was occasional movement around the bonfire, people getting up to refill their drinks or stretch their legs, and, in the rearrangements of the circle, Willow subtly made sure that she eventually wound up sitting beside Melvin. What was it that intrigued her about him? "The darker the berry, the sweeter the juice." Yes, Willow was drawn to Melvin's blackness, loving the way his oak-toned skin shone in the orange glow of the bonfire. But there was—as always—more to it than that. An air of accomplishment clung to him like cologne. He had the same casual self-confidence, the self-confidence of someone who was accustomed to giving people orders, that the rich, white, older men Willow used to date had, that Danforth Cushing had. Uh-oh, Willow thought, that surrogate daddy thing again. But there was something else about Melvin, a quality that Willow could not define that set him apart from other wealthy, accomplished men she had known; and here Willow could not decide if his race was part of that quality or irrelevant to it. Still, she sensed something, something unquiet about Melvin Hutchinson. Was this a racist thought, Willow wondered: that there was something danger- ous about Melvin? Was it simply because he was black that Willow sensed a sexy viciousness beneath that tidily knotted tie? Willow remembered something Danforth had said many years earlier, ad- miringly, about a business associate: "He's a killer." Perhaps that was the quality—a quality having nothing to do with race—that Willow saw in Melvin. He was a killer. A stone-cold killer.

Feeling simultaneously chilled by the ocean wind and warmed by the bonfire, Willow flirted extravagantly with Melvin. As they drank and talked, she felt the old confidence building up. Rodney was the only man she'd slept with for a long time. But, tonight, she felt she could have another. Melvin was leaning closer and closer to her; their knees were touching; the rest of the conversation around the bonfire faded into meaningless sound, as undistracting as the breeze; the other guests were simply shapes, shadows on the periphery. Then Melvin asked, "What did you say your name was?"

"Willow."

"Willow?"

"It's unusual, yes."

"Oh no."

"What?"

"You don't happen to know a man named Rodney Person?"

"He's my husband."

"He's my sister's ex-husband."

"Oh no."

They both broke into giddy, jittery laughter. "Small world," Melvin said.

"You must have heard such awful things about me."

"Nothing but."

Still, Willow thought, he didn't seem discouraged. Perhaps his interest had been piqued even more.

A joint was passed around the bonfire. Melvin drew on it. He was obviously not accustomed to this. He coughed. "I'm gonna report you to old man Hull," Stanley called out from the other side of the fire, wagging his finger reproachfully. Melvin laughed, took another drag, coughed again, and passed the joint to Willow, who, of course, handled it expertly. Melvin removed his tie.

Soon they were brazenly coming on to each other. Melvin put his face close to hers, his eyes bloodshot. "My mama warned me about girls like you," he said.

Where, Willow wondered, could they do it? Not in Stanley's house. She didn't even have a room to herself there. She was sharing one of the guest rooms with another female visitor. And she couldn't very well invite herself to Oak Bluffs. Though maybe Melvin—what with his wife and daughter, at this moment, somewhere over the Atlantic Ocean, on their way to Paris—might invite her. But Willow knew from experience that some married men—Rodney had been an exception—didn't like having sex with extramarital lovers in the same bed they shared with their wives. "Let's go for a walk," Willow said.

They wandered along the beach, occasionally bumping into each other in a stoned sort of stagger. After a while, they were far from the party. Willow gave Melvin a playful shove, sending him stumbling into the foamy tide. He rushed toward her. She ran away. He had his arms around her. They were tumbling in the sand. Tongues entwined. Fumbling with buttons and zippers. Bodies grinding against each other. Willow felt the sand under her—suddenly—bare butt. Unlocking her mouth from Melvin's, she whispered, "I'm not on the pill."

Then Melvin said the strangest thing. "Just let me put the head in." Willow laughed, and so did Melvin. The next thing she knew, all of him was in, with such power, such magnitude, that she came almost instantly and, hips still bucking uncontrollably ten minutes later, came again, this time in explosive synchrony with Melvin.

Afterward, as they lay in the sand, Willow started to laugh, a laugh of pure joy. Melvin laughed, too, but only for a moment and not as freely. He sat up and started groping for his clothes. "I have to get you back to the party."

"What's the rush?" Willow said, running a finger down Melvin's spine.

"I'm sorry, I—shit—so this is what people mean when they talk about being stoned."

"Do you mean to say you've never—"

"We have to go," Melvin said, pulling on his shirt. "My mind, my thought patterns are weird. This is fucked-up."

Willow laughed again, though her feelings were wounded. "Wham bam thank you, ma'am, eh, Melvin?"

"You don't understand what we've done."

"What do you mean?"

"We have different concepts. I know we do. We have different concepts about what just happened."

Willow leaned into Melvin and licked his earlobe. "Different concepts, huh? Well, to me, that was just about the best sex I've ever had."

"And to me," Melvin said, "it was a sin."

>   >   >

Willow had heard about the "terrible twos" and she could only hope that they had arrived early for her son and would pass quickly. But

< 221 >

Miles's extreme misbehavior began at twelve months of age and it seemed a breed apart from normal infantile antics. There was a strange edge of malice to Miles's misdeeds, a deliberateness that made them all the more disturbing—like the afternoon little Miles dragged a chair across the bedroom, climbed atop it, snagged one of Rodney's cigarette lighters from the top of the dresser, then ignited his parents' bedsheets. Willow smelled the fire—Rodney wasn't home at the time—and managed to put it out before the entire mattress went up in flames. Miles began bullying other little children, but not in the clumsy, reactive way of other toddlers. There was something distinctly premeditated and sadistic about the way Miles —still under the age of two—tormented his diaper-wearing peers in the playground. No amount of discipline from Willow seemed to work. When she yelled at Miles, he yelled back. When she hit him— which she could rarely bring herself to do—he hit her back. Rodney, usually dazed, always indifferent, was no help. Willow read all the child-rearing literature she could get her hands on, talked to all the young mothers she knew. But no advice seemed useful. Melissa suggested that perhaps Miles was possessed by a demon and Willow should take him to an exorcist. Instead, Willow took her son to see a psychic.

After examining Miles alone while Willow sat in a waiting room, the medium gave the anxious mom her assessment: "Your son is suffering from a severe identity crisis."

"Identity crisis!" Willow scoffed. "He's not even two years old!"

"Nevertheless," the psychic said, "he does not know who he is."

"No *baby* knows who they are," Willow protested. "All they do is cry and eat and shit and sleep. They don't think about identity."

"You asked for my opinion and I am giving it to you. Your boy does not know who he is and he suspects that the truth of who he is is being kept from him."

"I don't know how you could discern this. Miles doesn't even speak in full sentences yet."

"You brought the child to me and I have given you my reading," the psychic said serenely. "Will you be paying by cash, check, or credit card?"

What rattled Willow about the psychic's reading was its likely accuracy. Did Miles know, on some subliminal level, that Rodney was not his father? Was that the source of his rage?

Miles continued his bizarre rampages for another eighteen months, right up until the day he asked Willow about black and white and told her that he was gray. After that, he calmed down, became a seemingly well-adjusted kid. Willow was mystified. Perhaps Miles's weirdness had nothing to do with the secret identity of his father. Perhaps it had been a racial thing. Maybe the knowledge that he was different from other children, a knowledge that might very well have come over him at one year old, the recognition of the curious looks from other kids' mothers, had caused his malicious behavior. Once Miles realized he was a borderline case, a denizen of the gray area, he could relax and be happy with himself. This, in any event, was Willow's hope. And for almost ten years, Miles—ignorant of who his real father was, untroubled by racial ambiguity—displayed a normal, even admirable, equanimity. Maybe, Willow thought, her son really *had* just suffered an early and extended bout of the terrible twos. That—until the rages returned—was what she liked to believe.

>   >   >

Though his parents never raised their voices, never had what you could really call fights, young Miles was painfully attuned to the tension between them. Their long silences at the dinner table, his mother's snappish tone, his father's distant, distracted air: They all registered with Miles. And so by the time he began the first grade at Common Community Elementary School, he was grateful for the time he could spend away from his parents. Life at home was, in a quiet way, difficult. School, on the other hand, was easy. He made friends easily. He excelled at his courses with ease. School didn't become hard until he got to Common Community Junior High. He noticed the change on the first day of class in the seventh grade. Suddenly, as if by some secret decree, some tacit set of instructions that Miles had not been made privy to, the black and Latino kids stopped socializing with the white kids. An ethnic awareness that had not seemed to exist in Miles's previous six years at Commie Commie spread throughout the class. Miles saw friendships between black and Jewish, Irish, and Puerto Rican kids end overnight. At twelve years old, he felt he had to choose sides.

Miles chose white. For no other reason than that he liked to study, he loved getting A's (he had, at this point, never received a grade lower), and his Jewish friends were the most serious students. His very best friend, since the third grade, had been Max Friedman, and Miles could see no reason why he had to stop being friends with Max. Miles still tried to maintain his friendships with the black and Hispanic kids in his class, many of whom he'd known since he was six, but they grew hostile toward him. "He think he white," Miles heard his former friend Randall say as he walked past a group of black students in the corridor. "There go the zebra," Miles's ex-playmate Yolanda sneered as he passed by a table full of black students in the cafeteria. Miles was hurt, and he found the kids' anger hard to grasp. Where had it all come from, and why now? What specifically had changed? Just two years earlier, he and Randall and Max—a black guy, a white guy, and an in-between guy—used to play together all the time. Now Randall seemed to hate Max. And, though Max never said anything about it, Miles felt his Jewish friend was as confused by Randall's hostility as he was.

Then one day, late in his first semester of seventh grade, during a phys ed session, Miles stood, in T-shirt and shorts, with Max and three other Jewish guys, under a basketball hoop in a far corner of the gymnasium. "Hey, Miles," Max said, "how do you stop five black guys from raping a white woman?" Miles was stunned by the question. Was this supposed to be the setup for a joke? Miles let out a single, uncertain laugh, almost more of a cough, and shook his head. "Throw 'em a basketball!" Max said, breaking into an enormous grin, his braces glittering under the fluorescent lights of the gym. The other guys burst into high-pitched pubescent laughter and Max, grinning at his biracial friend—his *best* friend—seemed to expect Miles to laugh, too. But Miles felt something churning inside him, a weird sensation that he could not consciously remember having had before but that felt scarily familiar. His heart was pounding rapidly. He felt, at once, as if he was about to get an erection and about to throw up. He feared that he was going to start screaming and crying like a baby, and the next thing he knew, he was on top of Max, straddling the

Jewish boy's scrawny chest, and there was blood smeared all around Max's mouth and Max was the one screaming and crying and both Miles's hands were full of Max's curly brown hair as he methodically slammed Max's head against the slick and shiny hardwood floor of the gymnasium.

➤   ➤   ➤

Miles chose black. After a one-month suspension from Common Community—only his high grade point average saved him from expulsion—he returned, to find he'd become a hero to Randall, Yolanda, and all the black students who had shunned him before. He soon learned from Randall and the others that there was a specific code for black authenticity and that any black student who did not follow it was acting white. Studying hard was acting white. To hang out with any white kid was to act white. Being genuinely black meant not studying hard. Being an authentic black kid required speaking in "black English" and keeping up with the latest slang. To be black, one had to wear the right thing: the right baseball cap, the right jewelry, the right sneakers. And most of all, being black meant hanging out exclusively with people who were black. Miles was happy to follow the code. During his second semester of seventh grade, his GPA plummeted. But he was popular. He'd found a comforting acceptance from a group he could proudly call his own. And walking the black walk, talking the black talk won him respect not only from black students but from white students, as well. Even though he rarely spoke to white kids anymore, Miles could see the way they gawked admiringly at him as he swaggered through the halls in his new hip apparel. He relished the way white kids stepped out of his way when they saw him coming. Everyone, it seemed, preferred Miles now that he was acting black. This was the way all his peers, black and white, wanted him to be. And acting black was so easy. The code of black authenticity was so free of complexity, of contradiction, that Miles Person was actually relieved to follow it.

Randall, Miles, and four other black guys from the junior high school became a crew, hanging out in the East Village after school, playing basketball, standing on corners drinking forties, calling out to the pretty brown girls who walked by, and, increasingly, looking for other crews to hassle. The crew was essentially Randall's and, following the leader, each member adopted a street name. Randall, though he had never deejayed anything, called himself D. J. Ransom. And Miles, still revered for his assault on Max Friedman, was dubbed "Hair Trigger." It was a name that, in scuffles with other young crews downtown, Miles did his best to live up to.

> ➤   ➤   ➤

At first, Willow told herself it was just typical adolescent aggression: Miles's fight with Max at school, his sullen silences at home, the way he'd sneer and suck his teeth in irritation anytime she asked him a question (the most common being, "Where were you tonight, young man?" when Miles would walk in the door at eleven o'clock on a school night). She'd given up trying to get Rodney interested or involved in what was happening to Miles. "He's just raisin' hell," Rodney would say with his usual hapless shrug, "sowin' some wild oats. I did the same shit when I was his age. It's just a stage he's going through." Willow wanted to believe that, too. But then, in the eighth grade, Miles started coming home with black eyes, scars on his face, dried blood on his clothes. When Willow tried to talk to him, he'd stalk into his room, slam the door, and start smashing things. In the morning, after he'd left for school, or wherever it was he spent his days, Willow would pick up the debris in Miles's bedroom, the pieces of shattered glass; the twisted carcass of a clock radio that had been hurled against the wall, then stomped on; the tattered pages of books Miles would rip apart in his rage.

Willow knew that Miles was the only person she could ever take this kind of shit from. She had never tolerated this type of behavior from a lover, a relative, or a friend. But motherhood, she'd discovered as soon as Miles was born, was a different planet of love. Willow simply did not have it in her to lash out at, to really punish, her son. For most of Miles's life, Willow had given *all* her love to him. She had shared her love with nobody else. Her love had been good enough to sustain Miles all these years. She believed that now, in this trying time, only through her love could Miles be redeemed.

One morning, sitting across the breakfast table from Miles—Rodney could be heard snoring in the master bedroom on the other side of the apartment—Willow stared beseechingly at her son—the entire left side of his face was red and swollen from yet another fight—and said, "I want to understand you, honey. I don't want to argue with you. I don't want to discipline you. I just want to . . . to try . . . will you please just help me to understand you?"

"Don't you talk that shit to me!" Miles exploded. He was on his feet now, his puffy face contorted in rage, thrusting a finger at his mother. For a moment, Willow feared he might strike her. "You can't fucking understand me! You will never ever fucking understand me! Cuz you're nothin' but a stupid white bitch! You're just a stupid white honky bitch!"

Willow sat rigid in her chair and felt the tears sting her eyes. "Oh, honey," she whispered. "Oh, my child." She could feel the tears rolling down her cheeks now, taste them, warm and salty, in her mouth. Miles stood over her, seeming, for a second, not to know what to do. Then, when he noticed his mother's tears, Miles burst into shrill, mocking laughter. Seeing that he had hurt Willow, he wanted to let her know how much he enjoyed it. There was something forced about the laughter, but Miles kept it up, cackling, jeering with self-conscious indulgence. And the self-conscious effort of the laugh, the fact that Miles was working hard to let his mother know how he relished her tears, made Willow cry even more. Miles, still cackling, walked over to the hallway closet, grabbed his jacket and baseball cap, and, slamming the door behind him, left the apartment. Willow could hear his strained laughter echoing through the corridor of the apartment building.

>   >   >

Had Willow Cushing possessed even a month's worth of foresight, she wouldn't have been surprised when her son was busted. As it was, Miles's arrest for drug dealing came as a shock. Drug possession would have been bad, but understandable. Willow had indulged in drug use—and never with unfavorable results—right up until the day she discovered she was pregnant with Miles. But *dealing!* It

< 227 >

made no sense. Their family lived, if not affluently, then comfortably. Miles had never had to do without any material thing he desired. And he'd never been a particularly materialistic kid. It was only in hindsight, after Miles's arrest, that Willow could see the pattern that had been taking shape for a year, the way that Miles and Randall and these other relatively privileged black kids from Common Community Junior High had made the effort to become street thugs, to affect the manners of kids from Bed-Stuy and the South Bronx—though they assiduously stuck to a far safer turf, in the East Village—getting into fights, staying out late, and, now, selling dope.

But what upset Willow even more was her suspicion that Miles had gotten the marijuana from Rodney's private stash. "No way!" Rodney protested. "I keep my dope locked in a strongbox on the top shelf in the bedroom closet. Besides, I don't even get high that much —and then only during the day, when Miles is still at school. Even if he knew the dope was there, he'd have to be a safecracker to get into that strongbox!" When Willow inspected the strongbox, she could see that the mangled lock had been jimmied.

In a way, Miles had been lucky. It was only grass he'd been caught selling, not crack, and the amount was fairly small, a half an ounce. And instead of being sent to some awful prison or reform school, Miles was sentenced to three months in a "boot camp" for first-time offenders, the drug reeducation center at Fort Brandriss, in New Jersey. Maybe, Willow thought, three months in a DRC would be a good thing for her son. After all, Melvin Hutchinson, as attorney general, was in charge of the camps, and even though his silence, his rejection, had hurt her, Willow still trusted Melvin's judgment. If he thought the DRCs served a good purpose, then they probably did. Willow decided that she wouldn't visit Miles during his time at Fort Brandriss. "Sometimes, you just have to practice tough love," her friend Melissa said. Willow silently scoffed at the term. Tough love! Love was supposed to be tender, not tough. What a classic American euphemism. "Tough love" enabled people to feel justified in hurting, in punishing their children. Was Danforth practicing "tough love" when he cut Willow out of his life? Willow had no use for such linguistic fig leafs. By declining to visit Miles during his three months at Fort Brandriss, she was punishing her son. And that was precisely what she wanted to do.

> > >

Willow nearly gasped when Miles walked in the door after his stint in the DRC. He was completely bald. He'd grown at least two inches, and the additional height accentuated his gauntness. His cheeks were so hollow that the curve of his cheekbones looked forbiddingly sharp, like prehistoric carving tools. And his hazel eyes, which had always been alive with mischief, looked like a sad old man's eyes. "Hi, Mom," Miles said wanly, setting down his duffel bag. Willow put her arms around her son and clutched his body tightly against hers, afraid that if she let go and looked at him again too soon, she would burst into tears. Miles had grown so thin, Willow felt as if she were embracing a skeleton. She could feel Miles's long arms drooping limply down her back.

Rodney stayed home for dinner that evening—it was the first time in more than a year that the three of them had shared a meal together. Rodney had been cranky for a week, ever since Willow threw out his strongbox full of dope. "You're lookin' good, my man," Rodney said to Miles, who was listlessly chewing a mouthful of mashed potatoes. "Howdja like the program there?"

"The program is as hard as you make it," Miles said in a dutiful tone, as if responding by rote.

"Do you think it helped you?" Willow said, struggling to keep her voice from shaking, still disturbed by Miles's haggard appearance, his weary demeanor.

"I caused problems," Miles said. "There were traumas I inflicted on myself. I had a negative self-image. I was a very negative individual."

"And you're not anymore?" Willow asked.

"The program has helped give me a positive image," Miles said robotically. "I have a good sense of self-esteem now. I'm ready to be a positive role model to the people in my community."

"I think that's great, brother man," Rodney said. "A little discipline was just what you needed. I wish I'd had more of that when I was

< 229 >

growing up. Maybe if my folks had sent me to military school like they did my older brother, I wouldn't be such a fuckup today." Rodney laughed dryly.

"I caused problems," Miles said again. "Traumas I inflicted on myself. I let myself be swayed by my so-called friends. But I won't let that happen again. From now on, I will be a positive role model."

Miles enrolled at Harriet Tubman Junior High School, near Columbia, and began studying hard again. But, while in his younger days Miles had been excited by his schoolwork, fueled by intellectual curiosity, he now went about his assignments with a humorless resolve, a grim sense of obligation. Each day after school, he attended a Bible study class, then immediately returned home, disappeared into his bedroom, and plowed away at his homework. After dinner, he cleared the table and washed the dishes. Miles did not listen to music anymore. Nor did he watch television. He went to bed at ten every night and rose at six. He made his bed every morning and kept his room relentlessly tidy. And each night, during Miles's first week back home, Willow wept for her new son.

At two o'clock one morning, Willow rose from bed to go to the bathroom. As she was heading back to her bedroom, she sensed another presence awake in the apartment. She walked into the living room and found Miles sitting on the couch in the dark. She sat down beside him. "What's the matter, honey?"

"Can't sleep," Miles said.

"Why not? Are you feeling okay?"

"I've been having nightmares."

"What kind of nightmares?"

"I forget them as soon as I wake up."

"Miles, honey . . . what did they do to you . . . at Fort Brandriss?"

Miles stared blankly at his mother, then shook his head. "I can't remember."

(9)

LOYD WAS GETTING MARRIED to a white chick. No big surprise there. Rashid would have been more surprised if his old
friend from Benson Country Day—one of the six black kids in
Rashid's class during the misbegotten school year he spent there and
the only one he'd kept in touch with—had decided to marry a black
woman. Rashid had considered telling Lloyd he couldn't make it to
the wedding. It had already been three years since he and Lloyd had
last seen each other—he figured maybe it would be best just to let
the friendship fade away. But then, Rashid thought, he didn't want
to dis Lloyd like that. They'd grown in different ways. After Lloyd's
freshman year at Benson, his family had moved to California. Lloyd
went to Stanford, then to Stanford Law School. Now he was a lawyer
in San Francisco. And, despite his fondness for white girls, Lloyd was
basically a good-hearted brother. The wedding was going to be in
Long Island. The bride's name was Amy Miller—a JAP, Rashid figured, one of those secret Jews whose family had adopted an ethni-
cally neutral name after arriving on Ellis Island. Driving to the
wedding on a balmy Sunday afternoon in April, Rashid found himself
fantasizing about going home with a Jewish American Princess. He
hadn't gotten any play at all since Morgan—hadn't really sought any
—and he was horny as a motherfucker.

Rashid got lost on his way to the wedding and missed the ceremony. The reception was just getting underway when he arrived at
the Golden Knolls Country Club. He was sipping his first glass of

champagne when he saw her, standing in the center of the ballroom, snapping photos as people milled about, lean and lithe in her gray tunic, black jacket, and black pants, her hair short and natural, her complexion rich and dark, a radiance emanating from her such as Rashid had never felt before. He knew at once that she was it, the woman he'd been waiting for, his shining black heroine, his African queen.

> ➤   ➤   ➤

Emma had noticed him when he entered the ballroom in his colorful kufi hat, a kente cloth draped over the shoulders of his dark suit. She wanted to get a picture of him, but every time she started to move in his direction, he seemed to drift away, ambling to another area of the ballroom or stepping outside, where guests gathered under an enormous tent. Finally, she gave up. Simon and Emma had a routine they followed on every wedding shoot. They'd get all the wonderful pictures of the couple stuffing cake into each other's mouths. They'd shoot the next dance. Then get a few final shots and start packing up before the reception wound down. That gave them time to grab a couple of drinks before last call and get the hell out of there before drunken guests started demanding more photos. After helping Simon stuff equipment in the back of the Honda, Emma got a glass of champagne and walked out to the veranda, which overlooked a brilliant emerald golf course.

She took a few sips of champagne, then had one of those scary vomit burps, a deep belch accompanied by the feeling of a surge of liquid burning in her throat, then subsiding, leaving a stale aftertaste. Emma was relieved that she didn't puke right there on the veranda. She had been throwing up at least once a day for nearly a week now. When she and Simon arrived at the Golden Knolls Country Club early that afternoon, the first thing Emma did was race to the ladies' room and regurgitate her breakfast.

"Well, you're definitely pregnant," Dr. Marcia Goldman had told Emma five days earlier.

Emma sat in the young OB-GYN's cluttered office and fought the impulse to cry. "I knew it," she said quietly. "I mean, when my period was just a few days late, I *knew* it. I guess you really do just know."

"Sometimes," Dr. Goldman said.

"I don't know what I want to do. I only know that if I abort, I want to do it with a pill."

"I understand."

"God, what a mess."

"I have to tell you, Emma, that I'm happy to administer the procedure with you. But I'm only doing this because you're a friend of Naima's. You have to realize how important secrecy is in this matter. If you decide to terminate your pregnancy and I administer this procedure and the wrong people find out about it, you could end up in a drug reeducation center and I could be sent to a federal prison."

"I understand."

"I hope you do. Because this is a very serious matter."

"I just don't know what I want to do yet. Can I take some time to think about it?"

"Well, don't take *too* much time."

"A week. Can I have one week?"

"Yes, I'll expect to hear from you a week from today—at the latest."

Standing out on the veranda at Golden Knolls, Emma began to feel, for the first time, that there really was something—someone—alive inside her. Was it a sensation or a sentiment?

For someone who regarded marriage with an attitude that fell somewhere between ambivalence and terror, Emma had found, on these shoots with Simon, that she rather enjoyed weddings. There was something contagious about the outlandish optimism of two people vowing to live together forever, or at least until death. Deciding to link your fate with another person's required such blind faith that Emma couldn't help feeling buoyed by it. Still, she was not convinced that marriage was for her. But this particular ceremony—no doubt because it was the first interracial wedding she had shot with Simon —touched her deeply.

One week and a day earlier, Emma woke up on a Saturday morning and found herself alone in her bed in Blissfield. She walked into the dining room, where Seth sat at the table with a cup of coffee. His long brown hair hung loose over his shoulders. When he saw Emma, he gestured for her to come sit on his lap. Seth seemed shell-shocked as he spoke. "I want to say, sweetie, that I'm really sorry about what happened last night." Only a few hours had passed since Seth and Emma had caught Trudy squatting on their doorstep.

"It wasn't your fault," Emma said.

"I know," Seth said, "but I don't think I've appreciated, up until now, what you've been telling me about my mother. But now I understand. I'm going to start looking for an apartment in Manhattan this week. I'll be really tied up at work until *Elimination* airs, but I'm gonna make a couple of calls to real estate agents, anyway."

"All right."

"You think that's a good idea?"

"Yes."

"I just think we need to get away from here. I think my Mom has a lot of problems."

"I agree."

"I really want things to work out with us, Emma. And, I know you don't want to discuss this, but, whatever you decide to do, if you really are pregnant, I want you to know that I will be supportive of any decision you make. I really want to make this relationship work."

Emma said nothing. She drew Seth's body closer to hers and they held each other for a long time, rocking gently back and forth in the dining room chair.

Over the following week, Emma continued to hold the diametric equation in her mind: Either she would continue her pregnancy and marry Seth or abort and break up with Seth. She could imagine no other outcome. The problem was that one day she would believe that marrying Seth and having the baby was absolutely the right thing to do; and the next day, with equal conviction, she would be certain that aborting and breaking up with Seth was the best course of action. But she did not discuss the quandary with Seth. They didn't even see much of each other that week, what with Seth working past midnight almost every night, preparing for the live telecast of the execution of Jeremiad Hardee. And Emma continued making an effort to return to Blissfield late in the evening and leave as early as possible in the morning to avoid seeing Trudy. Seth's mother, meanwhile, stayed in her apartment upstairs in the two-family home. The turds stopped appearing on Emma and Seth's doorstep. But Trudy had not apologized for her revolting deposits. Emma didn't care. She just wanted to get the hell out of this woman's house as soon as possible. Emma wondered to what extent Seth wondered what was going on with her: whether she was really pregnant and what she would do if she was. She had not told him about her visit to the OB-GYN and he had not asked. Emma understood that Seth was trying to be considerate, letting her know that the decision was hers and that he would not try to interfere. Emma supposed that she should feel empowered by such independence. Still, she wished Seth would show more of an interest.

"So," Emma heard a voice on the country club veranda say, "you must really hate this."

She turned and saw that cool-looking guy in his kufi and kente cloth. He was even more attractive up close.

"Hate it?" Emma said. "No, it's just a job. I mean, I'd rather be taking pictures of something else. But this isn't so bad. Anyway, I kinda like weddings."

The young man chuckled slightly. "No," he said, "I mean you must hate seeing a couple like this getting married. A successful brother like Lloyd . . . marrying a white woman . . . I *know* that must bother you."

Emma felt an anger bubbling up inside her. "Why would that bother me?"

The young man seemed perplexed. "Why *wouldn't* it bother you?"

"Because it's got nothing to do with me. I don't even know Lloyd."

"Well, you must wonder why a brother like Lloyd couldn't find a sister to marry?"

"You know, that idea has always mystified me. Why can't someone *find* a person of their own race to hook up with? I mean, do you really seek out people to fall in love with? Do you actually *choose* the person you fall in love with? *I* don't. I never have. People come into your life, and if you're lucky, you find love."

The young man stared strangely at Emma, almost as if he was trying to decipher what she was saying, as if she was speaking to him in a foreign tongue. "I've never heard a black woman say that."

"Well," Emma replied tartly, "maybe all black women don't think alike—shocking as that may seem."

"But by marrying a white woman, Lloyd is rejecting black women."

"That's ridiculous."

"I should think an interracial marriage would offend you just as a point of pride—of black pride."

"Why should I be either proud *or* ashamed of being black? It's not an accomplishment, or an embarrassment. It's nothing I've ever *done*."

"It's who you are."

"It's *just* my race. Why must my race sum up everything I am? You're a cultural determinist."

"But culture determines, to use your phrase, everything."

"If you believe it does, then it does. That's just your worldview. You want a single view to explain everything in human society."

"It is not a view. It is reality."

"*Whose* reality? Yours! Why must your reality be everyone else's? I have my own reality." The young man was staring hard at her now, just a bit too intently for comfort. "Why are you looking at me like that? We're just having a debate."

"I'm sorry. You just remind me of someone I used to know."

"Heeey, that's original," Emma said with a laugh. Rashid laughed, too.

"I don't think I got your name."

"Emma Person."

"Rashid Scuggs."

They shook hands. "So what do you do, Rashid?"

"That's a good question."

"That's a bad answer." They laughed again. Even though Emma was making fun of him, Rashid detected a generosity in her teasing. He knew that, on some level, she was digging him. "I just got my Ph.D. in Cultural Studies from Columbia."

"So you're an academic?"

"Hell no! I mean, I'm not teaching anywhere. I guess you could call me a freelance ethnocentrist-intellectual."

"Sorry, you can't be both."

"Both what?"

"Both an ethnocentrist and an intellectual."

"Why not?"

"Because ethnocentrism is, by its very nature, anti-intellectual. Ethnocentrism is an ideology of blood and skin. And, as a great man once wrote, 'Blood and skin do not *think.*' If blood and skin—or to use the fashionable euphemism, culture—determine all, then where does that leave the *mind?* You see, this is what ethnocentrism always leaves out. The mind. The mind! So that you, Rashid, can only see that Lloyd and Amy have different blood and skin. You can't imagine that they might relate on a level of consciousness, that maybe their *minds* are in tune."

"Now, hold on a minute—"

"I'm not finished."

"But I—"

"Let me finish, brother."

Rashid held up a palm in surrender. "You have the floor."

"Another thing that pisses me off about ethnocentrism is that, insofar as it is anti-intellectual, it is also an assault on that most miraculous function of the intellect: imagination. It limits sympathetic imagination. If blood and skin determine all, it becomes impossible to appreciate—to imagine—the human complexity of someone whose blood and skin—whose culture—are different from your own. You can't imagine otherness, so you can't have compassion. If you can't have compassion, you can't believe that people of different ethnicities might actually love each other. Ethnocentrism isn't really an ideology at all. It's more like a religion—a religion of blood and skin. You, Rashid, are like some fundamentalist Christian who believes that his religion explains everything and therefore everyone should believe what he believes. So since Lloyd doesn't let his ethnicity dictate whom he falls in love with or how he lives his life, he's somehow impure to you. Like someone who didn't go to church was to my grandmother. A nonbeliever. And by your standards, by the religion of ethnocentrism, insufficiently black."

"May I speak now, please?"

"Go right ahead."

"Ethnocentrism is not a religion and it's not an ideology. Ethnocentrism predates both religion *and* ideology. People were joined by blood and skin, by tribe, first, not by belief. You simply deny that it's *always* been this way. For you, some color-blind 'We Are the World' fantasy is a religion, the opiate of the integrationist masses. 'I Have a Dream' and all that bullshit. I say, let's stop dreaming and deal with *reality.*"

"But if tribalism is the basis of human reality and reality is as narrow as you make it out to be, how do you explain the fact that we're both here at this wedding? How have Lloyd and Amy managed to transcend the reality you describe?"

"They may have managed to escape reality for the time being," Rashid said soberly, "but it will catch up with them. Sooner or later, reality will bash them over the head. It happens to every interracial couple."

"Do you speak from experience?"

Rashid's mouth twitched into something that resembled a smile. He took a gulp of champagne. "So what do you do when you aren't taking pictures of weddings?"

"I take my own pictures."

"Of what?"

"Whatever happens to be obsessing me at a particular time."

"So you're an artist?" Rashid said uncertainly.

"As far as I'm concerned, yeah, I am."

"Have you had your work shown in any galleries?"

"Not yet."

"Well, Emma, I think it's fate that has brought us together." Rashid pulled out his wallet and handed Emma one of his business cards. "I've been searching for an artist for the first show at my cultural center. But, as of yet, I haven't found anybody good enough."

Emma read Rashid's card and laughed. "Norris, New Jersey."

"What's wrong with Norris, New Jersey?" Rashid said defensively.

"Nothing's wrong with it. That's where my mother is from. I know it well. Though I haven't visited in at least ten years. Not since my grandfather died."

"Well, maybe it's time to get in touch with your roots, homegirl? How'd you like to have your first show at the Norris Center for African-American Arts and Culture?"

"You've never even seen my stuff. What if you don't like it?"

Rashid waved his hand dismissively. "Just from talkin' to you, I'm sure your work is *deep*."

"It's not terribly ethnocentric, though."

"Look, why don't you call me. We can get together and I can check out your stuff. And if I'm into it—which I'm sure I will be—we can get a show up in two weeks."

"Two weeks?"

"Two weeks max."

"Well, Rashid, maybe you're right. Maybe this *is* fate."

"I feel a providential vibe. Don't you?"

Emma shot Rashid a skeptical look. "You *are* for real, aren't you?"

"Call me up, we can get together, and you can see for yourself," Rashid said, a nasty edge to his voice. "Anyway, don't sound like nobody else is offerin' to show your shit. So you can call me or you can go on shootin' weddings."

Emma stared at Rashid, a faint, inscrutable smile on her lips. "I told you, I *like* weddings."

"Yeah, but I don't see no ring on your finger."

"When the time comes . . ."

"What are you waiting for?"

Emma looked away from Rashid and stared out at the vast golf course. She'd never seen anything so damned green. "You got any kids, Rashid?"

"None that I know of. You?"

"No." Emma was quiet for a long moment. "You know what my grandmother used to say? 'Children are the point of life.' Do you think that's true?"

"I don't know. Ask me when I've had a couple. . . . Do you think it's true?"

"Most of the time, I think Philip Larkin had it right." Emma returned her gaze to Rashid. "Ever read any Larkin? English poet."

"Wasn't he a Nazi or something?"

"Not quite. A racist. A misogynist. And a great fucking poet. But not a Nazi."

"Naw, never read him."

"Yo, man." Lloyd, resplendent in his bridegroom's attire, stepped out onto the veranda. He put an arm around Rashid. "I haven't even had a chance to talk to you."

"Yeah, well," Rashid said with a shrug, "Emma's been monopolizing me."

"Oh, puh-leeeze," Emma said, with her laugh that was at once mocking and generous.

Lloyd smiled broadly. "I think this fella belongs in the dog pound, don't you? Come on, man, let's go talk."

"Call me," Rashid said to Emma. "I'll be at the center all day tomorrow. I'm serious."

"All right."

Lloyd and Rashid disappeared into the ballroom. Emma finished her glass of champagne and decided to take a short walk around the grounds of the country club. She knew Simon would be looking for her soon, but she didn't care. Rashid had put her in a nostalgic mood. She remembered her sophomore year at Vymar College, when she moved into Marcus Garvey House, the designated black dorm on campus. There she was surrounded by people like Rashid, young African-Americans enjoying the privilege of a superior education, brimming with contempt for anyone who wasn't like them, staying up late together recounting indulgently, almost cherishing, every slight they had ever been dealt by the white world, exchanging war stories about the insults, the oppression, they had suffered, nursing each other's wounds, reinforcing each other's prejudices, hunkering down, exulting in the safety, the solace, of self-segregation. And Emma could see the appeal. She enjoyed the bunker mentality of Marcus Garvey House. There was something bracing about living one's life in a permanent snit.

Yet the only reason Emma had moved into Marcus Garvey House, the only reason she'd enrolled at Vymar College, was to be with her boyfriend Keith Reynolds. Then Keith graduated and moved to Seattle. And Emma started seeing Alec Larsen, whom she teasingly dubbed the "Norse God," "Hitler's wet dream," and her housemates in the black dorm let her know she was no longer welcome. One of the few African-Americans at Vymar who associated with Emma was Naima, who had never lived in Marcus Garvey House and who also had a white boyfriend.

Emma had wandered to a shady area behind the main building of the country club. There was a small pond, its glassy surface shimmering in the glow of the sunset. Beside a stone bench stood a gray-haired woman, holding in her arms a child who looked to be about a year old. Emma had noticed both of them at the reception, but in the swirling mix of guests, she could not remember who was related to whom. Here, beside the pond, she assumed that the woman was the grandmother of the curly-haired little girl, but she had no way of being certain. More strikingly, she could not determine the race of either the woman or the child. They both seemed to have somewhat tan complexions, but, standing several yards away, in the gathering twilight, Emma couldn't be sure *how* tan. From this distance, one would have assumed they were both white. But to peer just a bit more sharply, one might guess they were both black. Or perhaps they were biracial. Or one of them was biracial and the other black—or white. It was impossible to tell.

Random thoughts and images were popping in Emma's mind like flashbulbs. She thought of Seth, remembered holding him in the dining room chair, remembered how kind, how gentle, how considerate he could be. She thought of Rashid and wondered why she was so attracted to someone who was so pigheaded. Perhaps it was his very certainty, that airtight lack of doubt, that appealed to her. Emma had told Rashid, bluntly, what she believed. But her beliefs were based on ambiguity, on an appreciation of life's contradictions, while his were grounded in the impregnable soil of pure conviction. She thought of the baby growing inside her and felt overwhelmed by tenderness.

"Chee," the infant in the woman's arms said, pointing.

"That's right," said the gray-haired woman of indeterminate ethnicity, her voice, like her skin tone, failing to give a hint of her race. "That's a tree."

"Buhr," the child said, pointing to a robin that alighted on the stone bench.

"Yes, sweetie, that's a bird."

"Kai." The little girl pointed heavenward.

"The sky. Yes, that's the sky. And it's *all* wonderful. It's all wonderful."

"Ottur."

"Water. That's right. That's the water. And it's all wonderful. *It's all wonderful.*"

Emma felt her eyes filling with tears. Damn, she thought, this pregnancy was making her awfully emotional. But at least, at last, she had a sense of resolution. She knew what she had to do.

> > >

On nights alone in his New York apartment, Melvin Hutchinson no longer sat in his darkened study drinking bourbon and brooding over his father's .38-caliber Smith & Wesson. Now, he carried the pistol with him from room to room. If he was making a sandwich in the kitchen, the gun lay on the counter beside the bologna and mayonnaise. When Melvin sat on the toilet, the pistol rested near him on the edge of the bathtub, just in case he should have the sudden urge to insert the barrel of the .38 into his mouth—he imagined the cold, metallic taste of it—and blow his brains out through the back of his head. And on this particular evening, as he sat on his living room couch, glass of Jack Daniel's in one hand, television remote control in the other, flipping through the five hundred channels his cable service offered him, the .38 lay on the coffee table, within easy reach. He was considering carrying the gun with him everywhere. There was nothing to stop him. A recent antiterrorism law permitted authorized members of the three branches of government to carry a firearm at all times, leading Melvin to wonder during his meetings with officials in the Justice Department, in the Capitol, and in the White House just who was packing. Melvin, what with his security detail, had never felt the need to arm himself. But tonight, he thought, Why not? Though he would eschew the weapon of choice for most government officials—a 9-mm semiautomatic—and tote instead Harry's ancient .38.

Melvin turned to the Politics channel. F. T. Lieberman, Speaker of the House of Representatives, appeared on the screen, railing from the floor of Congress against the attorney general. "I knew Melvin Hutchinson when he was a good man, a righteous man, a fighter for civil rights. But I've seen him become contaminated by the barbarism that pervades this administration. It's a barbarism that is affecting us all. We are becoming a nation of barbarians!" A chorus of boos resounded throughout the House. F. T. Lieberman, his frizzy white hair and unruly white beard giving him the look of an Old Testament prophet, began shaking his fist and yelling over the disparaging cries of his fellow lawmakers. "Yes! Yes! We are becoming a nation of barbarians! For years now, we have been lurching into fascism. We have a Supreme Court that considers no punishment too cruel or unusual. And Melvin Hutchinson, once a good man, is now a grotesque, a jocular barbarian. We are all becoming barbarians!" The booing finally drowned out Lieberman's tirade.

Melvin chuckled quietly. The more Lieberman raved, the better it was for Melvin. To the shock of the nation and the world, the Democrats, during the past year's midterm elections, had squeaked out a two-seat majority in a House of Representatives that now included members of five different political parties. Even more shocking, the Democrats had narrowly elected Lieberman, a dinosaur of the American Left, to the Speaker's chair three months earlier. With Vin Ewell incapacitated, F. T. Lieberman would be the one to ascend to the presidency should Troy McCracken suddenly die. And, as nobody wanted to see that happen—even Lieberman's allies had to admit the man was something of a crackpot—Troy was going to have to name a new vice president soon. But what the fuck, Melvin wondered, is taking him so long? Despite the conventional wisdom that said Melvin was in tight with the President, the attorney general had had only a handful of private meetings with McCracken—six maybe—in two and a half years. And Troy had not even phoned him since Vin Ewell's stroke. So maybe Troy didn't want to give the vice presidency to Melvin. Maybe the ofays didn't want to see a man like Melvin in such a position of power after all. Well, fuck 'em. Fuck 'em all. Maybe Troy would have a sudden heart attack, or get struck by a bolt of lightning on the golf course. And F. T. Lieberman, the raving Jewish anachronism, would become President of the United States. Good! He'd be just what all those assholes deserved.

Wendy Hoffman's pink, piggy head—with its squinty eyes and fat little nose—appeared on the screen. How Melvin loathed her.

"Washington insiders," Wendy Hoffman squealed, "say that the attorney general and California senator Brad Blythe are the two favorites to be named vice president. The two men have employed different strategies for dealing with all the recent speculation. While Senator Blythe has been more visible than ever, Attorney General Hutchinson has kept a scrupulously low profile over the past week, scaling back public appearances and spending most of his time locked behind the door of his office at the Justice Department." Yeah, yeah, yeah, Melvin thought. If he hadn't cut back on his appearances, Hoffman and the rest of the media would accuse him of campaigning for Vin Ewell's job. A bar graph appeared on the screen. Directly above the first and tallest bar, labeled HUTCH, was a photo of Melvin's head. Above the second bar, marked BLYTHE, was the head of the California senator. The shadowy outline of a man's head topped the bar designated SOMEBODY ELSE. And a question mark rested above the last and shortest bar: DON'T KNOW. "According to the latest Politics channel poll," Wendy Hoffman said, "thirty-eight percent of Americans would like to see Melvin Hutchinson named vice president; thirty-five percent chose Brad Blythe; fifteen percent wanted somebody else; and twelve percent don't know whom they would want to fill the veep position should Vin Ewell die or be judged permanently incapacitated. With a margin of error of plus or minus three percentage points, there is, statistically, little difference between the standings of Hutchinson and Blythe."

"Yeah, sure," Hutch yelled at the TV screen. "Unless I really got forty-one percent and Blythe really got thirty-two percent! I'd say *that's* a statistical difference!" Melvin downed the last of his Jack Daniel's, then swished the bourbon around in his mouth before swallowing. He could feel that the press had been turning against him in the days since Ewell's stroke. Beedle was right: Now that it looked like Melvin was the man, the long knives were coming out. But what Beedle couldn't see was the racial aspect. The real deal was that nobody in power wanted to see a black man rise to the vice presidency. Melvin sensed that the media was now building up Blythe, a white nonentity. Blythe and Troy McCracken, with their bland "big man on campus" looks, could have been twins. So what the fuck, Melvin thought, pouring himself another glass of Uncle Jack, let the ofays have their blue-eyed bookends, their white-on-white ticket for the next election. Melvin decided that he didn't want the vice presidency anyhow. He didn't need the aggravation. What the fuck.

The downstairs buzzer sounded, giving Melvin a start. "Hello," he said into the intercom.

"Good evening, sir," Winston, the doorman, said in his colonial lilt. Melvin had rarely heard Winston say more than those three words. As a servant, Winston was the antithesis of Clarence Eldridge, the Millennium Club's butler. Raven-dark and possessing an air of aristocratic haughtiness, Winston sat in his blue cap and uniform behind the front desk in the lobby of Melvin's building on Central Park West, greeting the residents as they came and went with the same two salutations, in a tone that managed to convey both politeness and a sense that Winston could not give a shit—as was clearly the case, and why not?—whether you lived or died: "Good evening, sir." "Good evening, ma'am." "Good evening, sir." "Good evening, ma'am." In the four years that Winston had worked as one of the night doormen in his building, Melvin had never had a conversation with him. But Dorothy had. And it was through Dorothy that Melvin learned that Winston hailed from some African country—Melvin could never remember which one—and had been trained as a surgeon in England. After years of practicing back in his own country, Winston had been forced to flee in the wake of a coup d'état that resulted in the ascension to power of a general with proletarian roots who set about torturing and executing the best and brightest minds of his nation. No wonder then that Winston could barely manage to offer the minimum level of solicitousness of the average Manhattan doorman.

"Good evening, Winston," Melvin said into the intercom.

"There is a woman here to see you," Winston said, his voice laced with a vague disdain. "A Ms. Cushing."

Melvin heard the sword of justice slice through the air, just above his head. "Send her up."

>   >   >

She didn't look bad, Melvin thought as he stared at Willow across his dining room table, for an old white broad. He, of course, was older than she by a good ten years. But men always aged better than women. And black folks always aged better than white folks. Her hair was short. The only other time Melvin had seen her, it hung almost down to her butt. And she had accumulated quite a few lines on her face. But there was still something sexy about Willow Cushing. She had some good fucking left in her. Melvin could see that. Though Melvin would never allow himself to give in to temptation. That one lapse had caused him enough trouble already—and, with Willow here tonight, after all these years, that single mistake stood to cause him even more grief. What an outrageous thing for her to do, Melvin thought as he sipped his Jack Daniel's, to show up on his doorstep like that. What if Dorothy had been home? Well, no point in worrying about that. Melvin was certain that his wife was in Washington—or, more accurately, in their home in Elyssia, the Virginia suburb just outside Washington—that night. Willow took a sip from her glass of white wine and stared back at Melvin with her big—what color were they?—almost yellowish, it seemed, like a cat's—eyes.

"I can't tell you," Willow said, "how many times in the last fifteen years I've passed by this building, hoping I might just happen to catch you going in or coming out. You know, I live only about twelve blocks from here."

"I know," Melvin said.

"New York." Willow shook her head and let out a short, brittle laugh. "Twelve blocks. Fifteen years. And we never so much as run into each other." She paused. "I was really sorry to hear about your daughter . . . Abby?"

"Yes."

"Well . . . I want you to know . . . I was really sorry to hear about that."

"All right."

They were silent for a long time. Melvin was determined not to speak first.

"Miles is your son, you know." Willow said. "I know you probably don't believe me. But I'm sure of it. You're a lawyer, so you would probably want concrete proof. But I'm sure DNA tests would prove it. He's yours. Do you believe me?"

Melvin sipped his bourbon. He did not reply.

Willow let out a long, slow sigh. "Miles . . ." She hesitated, took a drink of wine, and began her sentence again. "Miles was in a drug reeducation center. At Fort Brandriss. I think you must know that."

"I know," Melvin said. He could feel his anger, the old familiar violence—never expressed physically, never—rising within him. "Have you come here to blackmail me?"

Surprise flashed in Willow's yellow eyes. She laughed incredulously. "No, Melvin, I'm not here to—"

"Name your price. I know Rodney hasn't been doing all that well lately. You must have a figure in mind. And you know I can't risk a paternity suit. So name your price."

"Melvin," Willow continued, acting as if she hadn't heard what he'd just said, "do you know what goes on at Fort Brandriss?"

"Well, I *am* the attorney general. I ought to know."

Willow inhaled, seemed to sniff back a tear. "Then I have to ask you, Melvin: How could you let them do what they did—to your own son?"

PART THREE

MANIFEST DESTINY

(10)

"C AN YOU HEAR ME?" Muriel Ewell leaned over, putting her mouth close to her husband's ear. "Can you hear me, Vin?" She stood upright again, crossed her arms. "I don't know why, but I think you *can* hear me. I just have this feeling that you can." Arms folded across her chest, Muriel Ewell walked slowly around the hospital room, which had the feeling of a luxurious hotel suite, the walls cream-colored rather than antiseptic white, an enormous television suspended from the ceiling, a cushy couch and armchairs in the corner, a large window, with bright, lovely curtains, overlooking the hospital courtyard. "You should see your digs, Vin. I think even you would approve." Muriel returned to her husband's bedside. He lay utterly motionless, a tube shoved in his mouth, going down his windpipe, more tubes running into his arms, his bed surrounded by an array of high-tech machinery, buzzing, beeping, whirring. What were all these gizmos *for,* specifically? Muriel wondered. She glanced toward the floor, to the tangle of wires and the heavy-looking plug in the wall socket. One of those bleeping machines, she'd been told, was an emergency generator, designed to keep the vice president's life-support system running in the event of a blackout or the inadvertent pulling of the plug. But how, Muriel speculated, did you turn off the emergency generator?

"Well, Vin, it's been over two weeks and I still can't get a straight answer as to your chances. And the whole country is waiting. You've never gotten so much press in your *life,* and all of it favorable. Everybody is pulling for you. At least they *say* they are. But you know what's funny? *I'm* the real focus of this story. Every morning as I leave the house, I walk past this pack of reporters and cameras and whatnot and into the limo. Sometimes they call out questions. But I don't answer 'em. Most of them are ever so respectful. I tell ya, Vin, I feel like Jackie Kennedy! For the past two weeks, everyone has forgotten about Dawn McCracken. That tawdry li'l piece a trash. *I* might as well be the First Lady. And here's the kick, Vin. I get to be treated like First Lady, but you don't get to be President! Ain't that a pip! Nobody thinks you're gonna pull through, honey. You know what I hear the reporters sayin'? 'The Vin Ewell deathwatch.' That's what they're calling this. 'The Vin Ewell deathwatch!' And I am more the focus of attention than you are. Imagine. If you could see this, oh, Lord, you'd just . . . you'd just shit your damn pants, Vin!"

Muriel pulled a chair to her husband's bedside and sat down. "Lord, I think of all those years I followed you around, all over South Carolina. I'm talkin' about the early days now. All those rubber-chicken dinners. And me having to smile and be all polite and singing your praises. My God, what a performance I've put on—back home, then in Washington, then trailin' you all over the world, nice little wifey. Havin' to grin and choke back my pride and deny and deny and deny. To lie for you. To scoff when reporters would come up to me and ask about whatever little slut you happened to be stickin' it into at any given time. And me, chokin' back the bile, smilin' as I lied. 'Vin is the most devoted husband and father I know.' My God! The *lies* I told for you. Devoted father! The only person you ever shat on as much as you shat on me was our son. Don't you know he *hates* you? Don't you know your own son hates your guts? The press can't even find Jody. And I ain't tellin' 'em nothin'. But I talked to Jody. He's in Alaska—Anchorage, if you care. And you know what he told me, Vin? You know what your only child said when he heard you were in a coma? He said he thought it would be a good thing for the country if you died. This is your *son* speaking, Vin. Your only child!"

Muriel Ewell walked over to the full-length mirror that was screwed into the bathroom door. She took a tube of lipstick from her handbag and applied a fresh coat to her mouth. She gently patted her crown of silver hair. "Do you know, Vin, that in the past two weeks I've taken calls from ten literary agents? And not just any agents. The best in the business. They want my life story. Not *your* life story, sweetheart. Mine! And get this, Senator—oh, I'm sorry—Vice President Ewell: We've gotten feelers from Hollywood. Hollywood!" Muriel walked back to the bed. "Who do you think should play me, Vin, honey? I'm partial to Meryl Streep myself. Though I'm told Glenn Close has expressed interest. And for you—well, who gives a shit? It's *my* story. But we don't have an ending yet. That's what one of the literary agents from New York said to me. 'It's a terrific story, but, of course, as of yet, we don't have an ending.' Well, I'm just going to have to provide them with an ending, Vin, honey. A real tearjerker. And when folks see the movie, see how I stood by you in these final days—oh, there won't be a dry eye in the house!"

Muriel stared at her husband, who lay as still as a statue, or a corpse. She leaned down again, putting her face close to his. "I'm gonna pull the plug, Vin," she whispered, almost lovingly. "I'm gonna pull it. I'm just waiting for the right moment. You're causing a lot of problems for a lot of people, you know. Lingering like this. Figures you couldn't just have a heart attack and die like anybody else. You just have to be a goddamned pain in the ass for everyone. But not much longer. I'm just waitin' for the word, Vin. You know how these things work. I'm just waitin' to get the go-ahead. But I'm gonna do it, honey. I'm gonna pull the plug."

Suddenly, Muriel Ewell noticed her husband's eyelid twitch. She thought, at first, that she was only imagining it. Then it happened again. And again. It was unmistakably twitching. The eyelid, wrinkled and leathery, discolored to a shade of gray, like an elephant's skin, began to rise. The heavy fold of skin began flapping up and down furiously. Then it stayed open, and Muriel could see her husband's eyeball, his blue pupil seemingly coated with a layer of yellowish gunk.

"Oh, no, Vin," she heard herself say, feeling as if she'd been plunged into some weird dream. "Oh, no, Vin, oh noooo."

Vin Ewell's eyeball began swimming about, rolling around searchingly, the only living thing in this immobile head. The wrinkled, leathery eyelid flapped up and down.

"Don't you do this to me, Vin!" Muriel hissed. "Don't you *dare* do this to me, you bastard! You owe me. You *owe* me!"

As suddenly as it had begun, the angry blinking ceased. The mucousy eyeball stilled. And the heavy grayish eyelid slowly dropped like a stage curtain.

There was a knock at the door. Muriel stood up, tried to adjust her face, putting on a careworn expression. "Come in please," she said meekly.

Arthur Spooner entered the room, followed by a nurse. The surgeon general walked over to Muriel and took both her hands in his. "How are you, Mrs. Ewell?" he asked warmly.

"Oh, I'm hanging in there," Muriel replied in a weary voice. "Somehow, I'm hanging in there."

"Yes," Spooner said, "I can see that you are."

He was a kind man, Muriel Ewell thought. And not a bad-looking man, either. Wasn't he a widower? Or maybe he was divorced? But the surgeon general was definitely single. She remembered that much.

"I'd like to talk to you, Mrs. Ewell," Spooner said gravely. "In private."

"About Vin?"

"About the future of our country."

➤　➤　➤

Henry Beedle never imagined that such a thought would occur to him, but after five days at the American party's strategy conference in Chicago, he realized how good it was to get a break from Washington. The Vin Ewell deathwatch was dragging on; Melvin Hutchinson had been growing ever more neurotic. It had been a relief to mingle among all the lawyers, lobbyists, legislators, and leeches who had gathered in Chicago to plan for the next campaign. But rather than a real strategy session, the five-day conference had become an orgy of self-congratulation. With the leader of their party, the President of the United States, riding high at 80 percent popularity in the polls, how could they not feel good about themselves? The participants at the conference didn't discuss the precarious global situation, the continuing economic decline, the fissures that ran throughout American society. They talked about the greatness of Troy McCracken, about how popular their man was. Because popularity was power. And holding on to power was the primary concern of the folks at the American party's strategy conference.

In the entire five days, Henry Beedle had telephoned the Justice Department only once, just to check in. And even that one time, he did not call Melvin Hutchinson. He called Assistant Attorney General for Public Security Dean Rockport. He and Dean went way back—they had attended Yale Law together—and Beedle knew that if anybody was up on what was happening inside the Beltway, it would be Dean.

"Well, I'll tell ya," Dean said, "ol' Hutch has become rather diligent in your absence."

"What do you mean?" Beedle asked.

"He's been in his office all week, ordering in reams of files."

"Files? What kind of files?"

"I dunno. I'm just going by what the secretary told me. And he's been on the phone a lot, too. Guess Hutch figured with you gone, he might as well do his job himself!"

Dean Rockport laughed. Beedle did, too, but only for a moment. "Listen, Dean, I'm flying back to Washington tomorrow morning. I'd like to know exactly what files Hutch has been calling up. Okay? I want to know as soon as I step into my office. Right?"

"Check," Dean said.

>   >   >

After the call, Beedle returned to the orgy of self-congratulation. Everyone at the conference talked about how much the *mood* of the country had changed. How, if nothing else, Troy McCracken's presidency had altered the spirit of the nation.

It was, Beedle recalled, only five years ago that America was turning to shit. Most citizens agreed on that one fact—all the polls said so, if not in so many words. But what could anybody do about it? The immoral coward who then occupied the White House refused to admit that his personality and policies might have been largely to blame. Instead, he blamed Congress, the media, the usual suspects. But The People kept demanding that he *do* something. Finally, some White House wiseacre suggested a New Constitutional Convention, where delegates from across the country would congregate to figure out how we got into this social morass and what could be done to get us out. The implication of the convention was that the Constitution, our most sacred of documents, might not be up to snuff anymore; that perhaps we needed to make a few alterations in order to contend with the problems of modern times. It was a desperate ploy, this New Constitutional Convention, but the President then was a desperate man. Unfit for the office he held, bereft of conviction, he was prepared to embark on any scheme that might deflect attention from his own shortcomings and the wretched incompetence of his administration. No one really believed that the delegates would tamper with the Constitution. The White House only hoped the convention would turn out to be a good, diverting television show.

So one sweltering July evening, Henry Beedle and a couple thousand delegates and reporters crammed into Independence Hall in Philadelphia for the opening ceremonies of the New Constitutional Convention. Beedle sat high above the crowd in a portable glass booth. As a prominent political consultant, he'd been asked to comment on the festivities for the Politics channel. There was nothing for him to do, really, until the end of the evening, when he would go on-camera to interpret "what it all means" for viewers around the world. So he just sat back and prepared to enjoy the show. First up was a small battalion of multiracial American kiddies who joined pink and brown and yellow hands and commenced with their ear-shattering squealing: "O, byoodiful for spacious skies . . ." Then, placing tiny palms over their hearts, they recited the Pledge of Allegiance. Yawn. It's going to be a long night, Beedle thought.

Then the keynote speaker took the stage. After weeks of debate, the convention's steering committee had decided on the young governor of Colorado to deliver the address. Reasons: He was supremely telegenic, he had not yet acquired too many enemies, and, most important, as a member of the American party, neither Republican nor Democrat, he was the perfect "nonpartisan" choice.

"Ladies, gentlemen, friends," Troy McCracken began, "I am here to say to you tonight that the Constitution of the United States of America . . . is good."

Thunderous applause. This was to be expected. Beedle figured the convention would end up being a celebration of the Constitution. And why not? There wasn't much else to feel good about in those days. But he was struck by McCracken, his demeanor, his aura. It had been a year or so since Beedle had last seen a McCracken speech, and in that time, the governor seemed to have become, somehow, more substantial. There was something about him that reminded Beedle of Kevin Costner in *The Untouchables*, that potent mix of innocence and righteousness.

"What the Constitution really offers us is protection," McCracken continued. "It protects our precious liberties so that we can be free to fulfill our human potential."

Trite, Beedle thought, but not a bad theme, protection. Americans were all feeling a bit helpless and vulnerable back then; they *wanted* to be protected. But trite as the words were, Troy spoke them with a conviction that was gripping. Looking down from his perch in the POL booth, Beedle could see that the crowd was absolutely focused on the speaker—they seemed to be *concentrating* on him. Extraordinary.

"What the good and decent people of the United States need are protectors—not programs. We need our neighborhoods protected from crime and the menace of drugs and homelessness. We need our jobs protected so that we don't lose our livelihoods to foreign competition and ugly quotas. We need to have our children protected in their homes and schools, protected from the drug dealers, the abusers and molesters, the scourge of AIDS and welfare, the Stalinist doctrines of political correctness. We need protection from the pornographers and the serial killers and the mass murderers and the narco-terrorists. We need to eliminate the parasites who eat away at the healthy body of the United States of America. We need protection from the greedy bankers and thieving politicians who would steal from the pockets of real, hardworking, good people. . . ."

One would have anticipated bursts of applause throughout McCracken's speech, but instead, the entire hall sat perfectly still, silent and enraptured. What was it that held their attention? There was something real, something authentic about Troy. He did not seem to be consciously projecting an image. He had that peculiar radiance that all great performers had. It was something impossible to describe. But you knew it when you saw it.

"And we need protection from a federal government that intrudes in our lives, squanders our money, and tries to rob us of our precious liberties. We need protection from the chaos and madness that rule over so much of our planet."

Even when the words were angry, Troy McCracken never fumed. Perhaps it was his beauty that blunted the rage—the smooth, clean looks that gave him a boy-next-door appeal. Then again, so many of Beedle's contemporaries were boy-men in their features. No wonder that, even deep into middle age, his generation was still characterized by the word *baby*.

"We need leaders strong enough to protect us. Not to burden taxpayers with more costly and destructive social programs. Not to provide us with handouts. We're proud. We're Americans. We shall provide for ourselves on the level playing field that free trade creates in the enlightened, civilized world. I say to you tonight, my fellow Americans, we are still the best! And we shall *never* be defeated!"

Pandemonium. People were clapping, whooping, hugging one another, and weeping with joy. It was as if the home team had just won the seventh game of the World Series. Beedle sat in the glass booth, leaning forward in his chair, awestruck. He had a stiffy.

> > >

"Troy understands religion!" Henry Beedle said, perhaps a bit too emphatically. He was sitting around a table in the lounge of the hotel in Chicago, surrounded by a familiar array of lawyers, lobbyists, legislators, and leeches at 11:45 on the final night of the American party's strategy conference, the last man in the circle of men to offer his theory on the enduring popularity of the President. "Everybody thinks," Beedle continued, "that America was founded by freethinking products of the Enlightenment. But America was founded—settled—a hundred and fifty–odd years earlier. By *my* people, if you will. My ancestors. And these were not men of reason. They were religious zealots. Today, we would call them *fanatics*. America was founded by religious fanatics! And this strain of zealotry lives on—in all of us!" Beedle realized, with a start, that he was pounding on the table with his fist. He had had too much to drink. Better shut up. "That's all," he said. "Troy gets it."

The table full of men muttered their agreement. The conversation then turned to women, the subject of who, among all the women at the conference, had the highest degree of fuckability. Beedle rose from the table and bid everyone good night. He knew only too well that there might be some whispering about him afterward. He was aware of all the speculation about his sexual orientation. Well, let them talk! The truth was far more simple than any of the gossipers could ever glean. Henry Beedle was an irredeemable, and unrepentant, onanist. He had never felt particularly attracted to any woman or man—at least not enough to go to bed with them. Beedle had no interest in intercourse. When it came to orgasms, he was entirely self-reliant. Yes, he had been aroused when he witnessed Troy McCracken's speech at Independence Hall. But it was not Troy's *flesh* that excited him. It was his radiance.

Another reason—other than the crass discussion of female anatomy—why Henry Beedle left the table: He had, earlier that evening, taped a segment for *Nightchat,* and the show would be broadcast at midnight. Beedle, sitting in a studio in Chicago, had debated an opponent sitting in a studio in Washington; the debate was moderated by the host of *Nightchat,* who sat in a studio in New York. Beedle liked the topic for debate: Has television gone too far in sensationalizing live executions? What pleased Beedle was that nobody even questioned whether or not executions should be televised. The only question was whether or not television had "gone too far." The peg for the *Nightchat* segment was the execution of Jeremiad Hardee, which was scheduled to be broadcast the following evening.

Lying back on the bed in his hotel room, watching himself on television, Beedle was pleased with his performance. "America's squeamishness about capital punishment is a fairly recent phenomenon," Beedle said authoritatively on TV. "Why, in the early twentieth century, families used to bring picnics to hangings. The whole town would gather together to see justice meted out. It was not unusual at all. Children viewed the executions and were not traumatized. In fact, they may have gained a good sense of right and wrong, of the consequences of crime. People will not watch *Elimination* tomorrow night to get their jollies. They will watch in order to see justice done. That is what Americans desire: a revival of our traditional values."

Watching himself on the screen, Beedle had to admit that he had gotten pretty good at this TV game over the past five years. He spoke in measured tones. He looked directly into the camera and didn't blink too much. Knowing that he had somewhat unattractive teeth, he was careful not to open his mouth too wide. When he smiled, he did so with lips pressed together. And in this segment of *Nightchat,* Beedle was thoroughly thrashing his opponent. Henry Beedle wriggled out of his pajama bottoms and, watching his image on the television screen, enjoyed a luxurious wank. The show ended and Beedle was just falling asleep, sated and exhausted, when the telephone beeped. "Hello?"

"Henry," a voice said raspily, urgently. "It's Melvin. Melvin Hutchinson."

Beedle was flustered. "Yes, well, hello, Judge." Trying to gain some composure, he asked, "And to what do I owe the pleasure of this call?"

"Henry, I need to talk to you. Something's happening at Brandriss."

Still groggy, it took Beedle a moment to realize what Hutch was talking about. Brandriss. Fort Brandriss. The drug reeducation center. "What? What's happening?"

"Something—" Melvin stopped short, seeming to search for the right word. Beedle waited silently, with a sudden sense of dread. "Something . . . ghastly."

(11)

THERE WAS A PARTY atmosphere in control room number one at Mavis Temple Productions. Seth Winkler sat quietly among his jubilant colleagues, staring at the twenty small television screens before him, beaming different pictures from Lone Star Stadium in Dallas, Texas. While the dozen other producers and assistants in the room burbled excitedly, Seth listened to the byplay of instructions and nervous chatter coming through his headset. There was really nothing for him or anyone else in the New York control room to do except stand by for some unforseeable emergency that might require the intervention of Mavis's staff at headquarters. The real action was down in Dallas, being coordinated by Sophie Mendel in a control room in a trailer. Though Seth and Sophie had both been immersed in arranging the telecast of *Elimination,* it was Sophie whom Mavis wanted down in Dallas with her. Seth was relegated to the role of fireman—essential in a crisis, useless otherwise—in New York. Seth couldn't believe it. He had simply *assumed* that he would be the one to accompany Mavis to Dallas. But these days, a lot of Seth's assumptions were turning out to be false.

"She's a fucking monster now!" Seth heard one of the other producers in the New York control room exult. "Mavis Temple is now, uncontestably, the biggest star in television. Who can touch her now? She's bigger than a star. She's the sun! She's a goddamned galaxy unto herself!"

The day before, at the end of a one-hour program on infertility, the hostess of the *Mavis!* show spoke quietly, directly into the camera. "This has been a very difficult segment for me to do," the talk-show queen said. "Because I have a confession to make. Like several of our guests today, I, too, am infertile." The studio audience broke into nervous babble. Mavis continued: "I can't have children. I know a lot of you wondered why Dennis"—Mavis's ex-boyfriend— "and I never got married. Well, that's the reason. I've tried every fertility drug on the market. But to no avail. I know there are other options open to me. I know there are a lot of dear, dear children out there who need to be adopted. But I will never be able to experience the joy of childbirth. And I just wanted to share that with you."

Seth had sat in his office, stunned, watching the taping of the program on his closed-circuit TV. What amazed him even more than the revelation, a jolt in itself, was Mavis's performance. Her voice quavered. Her eyes were watery. But she never actually wept. Seth remembered something that some actress—was it Katharine Hepburn?—had once said: "If the actor is crying, the audience can't." Mavis was right on the verge of tears, but she didn't succumb. Her confession—on her own show, America's favorite arena of confession —was a masterpiece of controlled anguish. "Thank you," Mavis said, "for letting me share my pain with you. See you next time." With that, the *Mavis!* theme came up and the show was over.

After the taping, producers hovered outside the closed door of Mavis's office. Some wanted to console her; others wanted to commend her for her courage. Seth wanted to ask her—though he knew he didn't dare—if what she'd said was true. When Mavis finally emerged from her office, Alton Lewis, her favorite minion, was by her side, carrying her suitcase. Mavis was her usual brusque self. She was off to Dallas to prepare for *Elimination*. She didn't have time to talk with anyone. The limo was waiting. The next morning, Mavis's confession made the front page of newspapers across the country. Seth could only marvel at his boss's genius. With *Elimination* airing that night, Mavis's revelation of her barrenness had to rank as one of the most impeccably timed publicity stunts in years. The numbers for the execution of Jeremiad Hardee—already anticipated as unusually high—were bound to be stratospheric now.

"Seth? Are you hooked up, Seth?" Sophie Mendel's voice came, anxious and squeaky, over Seth's headset.

"Yes, I'm listening."

"God, Seth, I wish you could be here."

"Yeah," Seth replied stiffly, "me, too."

"You should see this. It's like the Super Bowl or something."

Actually, the scene had more the feel of a patriotic heavy-metal concert. On one of the TV screens before him, Seth looked at the stage that had been set up in the center of Lone Star Stadium. Decorating the platform was a mammoth American flag, or a backdrop painted like the American flag, that extended from the floor of the stage up into the rafters. It reminded Seth of the giant American flag that George C. Scott gives his opening speech in front of in *Patton.* On another screen, the camera panned across the faces in the crowd. Seth saw elderly couples, beer-chugging young biker types, clean-cut Christian-looking folks who'd brought their children with them. A pretty diverse crowd, except for the fact that all sixty thousand spectators were white. On yet another screen, he watched Mavis Temple—who would only appear before TV audiences briefly that night, at the beginning and the end of *Elimination*—chatting backstage with the real emcee for the execution, America's box-office champ, star of *Justifiable Homicide, Justifiable Homicide II,* and *Justifiable Homicide III,* the Greek Freak, Nick Necropolis. Seth watched Mavis and Nick—shooting the shit as casually as two ordinary, completely anonymous little people, neighbors, say, who'd bumped into each other at the supermarket—with a deep, painful longing. Their conversation was not being transmitted over his headset. What could they possibly be talking about, these two megastars? How he would have relished the chance to eavesdrop.

"Seth?" Sophie asked nervously. "Seth? Are you listening? Am I coming through?"

"Yeah, I'm here."

"Shit, sorry, I'm just really hyper. I've never done live TV before. I've never been—I don't know . . . in charge like this before."

"You'll do fine. You're a pro."

"You're the one who should be here."

It was all Seth could do to keep from agreeing with her. But he had to be gracious. He had to learn humility. There were plenty of people these days who seemed eager to teach it to him. "Well, I'm not there," Seth said, trying not to sound bitter. "I'm in New York. Just remember I'm here if you need me. But don't worry. You'll do just fine."

"Thank you, Seth. You're a mensch."

"Gee, thanks. Soph." A mensch, that was all Seth would ever be. But how he burned to be something more than that.

Eight hours earlier, Seth had treated his college buddy David Katz to an expense-account lunch at La Connerie, the hot place for media biggies. David was a corporate lawyer who rarely went out for lunch at all, let alone to a restaurant as chic as La Connerie, and Seth tried to suppress a smirk of pride as Laurent, the maître d', welcomed him exuberantly and showed Seth and David to one of the corner tables, Seth—one of the hottest young producers on one of the hottest shows on television—swaggering across the dining room, feeling the breezy swish of his kilt against his thighs, nodding to the table full of other young producers—each of them, like Seth, wearing topknots and kilts—who waved eagerly to him, all of them, Seth knew, fairly drooling with envy for his position, his place, and trying to be blasé about all this attention, though he felt certain that David Katz, dressed in his square dark suit and white shirt and striped tie, and unaccustomed to glamour of this sort, had to be pained with awe of his old roomie. But it was a frustratingly brief high, the thrill of having the maître d' kiss your ass, the triumphant walk across the floor of La Connerie. As much as he cherished his status, Seth feared that his life was unraveling. Yes, he had money, perks, the envy of his peers, but he was beginning to realize that he might never possess the thing he coveted most. He would never be famous. How many famous TV producers had there been—ever? Maybe ten.

Looking back, it dawned on him that he had once possessed a measure of notoriety, and the potential for true fame. Working as a journalist, especially as a rock critic, had brought him far more atten-tion—though far less money and far fewer perks—than his job on *Mavis!* Every time he panned a new album in the *Downtown Clar-ion,* Seth was deluged with angry mail, letters that made it plain he was being widely read, that his name, if not his face, was known. Seth found that it was rather easy to become famous as a critic if you simply trashed, in a snidely entertaining way, at least 80 percent of the records you reviewed. There were three varieties of pan Seth reveled in. The first and least satisfying—though still hugely enjoyable—was the trashing of an older, established artist, a legend even, someone who still had the nerve to try to produce relevant work. Seth would damn the aging giant for failing to make music as good as his old stuff: "He has simply never lived up to the promise of his early masterpiece . . ." and so forth. The second, more delectable pan was the denigration of an artist who had recently made a mark for himself and now threatened to expand his range, to explore new musical territory, to try something that required genuine ambition. What delight Seth took in slapping down these overachievers. His primary weapon in such attacks was that deadliest of American critical epithets: *pretentious.* Best of all, though, was the assault on the first album of a newcomer. To crush someone just as they came out of the gate, to destroy an artist in the first days of his career—that was a special thrill. *How dare you attempt to express yourself! You shall be banished to the world of silent anonymity. Just like every other schmo.* An essential element of a pleasurable pan was that the artist you were attacking had to have real talent. Seth didn't even bother reviewing musicians who truly sucked. And he doled out his favorable notices to the mediocrities: journeyman singers who had never had a hit record; obscure acts who were beloved only by other rock critics; one-shot wonders who he knew didn't have the tools for the long haul; white rappers. On such people, Seth lavished praise. He saved his abuse for the gifted.

The bummer was when artists who'd been trashed managed to succeed anyway. One reason Seth and David were having lunch at La Connerie that afternoon was to commiserate over an unlikely success. After Joe, their friend from college, had had his first novel trampled on in the *New York Times,* Seth started calling everyone he knew from Colgate to alert them to the bad news. "It's really a shame," Seth would say. "I hear the guy is living hand to mouth. I don't know why he doesn't get a real job. You just have to let go of these artistic fantasies. I really feel sorry for Joe." Seth was perplexed to hear from several old friends that Joe was unfazed by the bad notice, that he was actually hard at work on his second novel. Seth figured that Joe was probably just putting up a brave front. How could anyone *not* be destroyed by a bad reception? He remembered all too well his six-week stint as a stand-up comic. Without the approval of other people, how could you possibly persevere? Then, just three weeks after the devastating *Times* review, Seth heard that Joe had signed a contract—and a fairly lucrative one at that—for his second novel. And this morning—outrage of outrages—David Katz called Seth to tell him that he'd heard Joe had won a literary grant and was planning to move to Prague to write! As Seth and David sat at their corner table, sickened by their friend's good fortune, they had to find another ground—other than artistic delusion and lack of money—on which to condemn him. The solution came easily to them. Joe was no longer a struggling, pathetic fool, a failure. Now, Joe was pretentious.

"Prague!" Seth snorted. "How pseudobohemian can you get?"

"Maybe I'll buy him a beret for his birthday," David sneered.

"And it's not even like he got this grant on merit. Didn't you say he knew someone on the board of the foundation?"

"That's what I heard."

"Sneaky little shit."

In control room one that night, Mavis Temple's magnificent head filled five of the twenty TV screens. She was just finishing her introduction of the festivities. "And the crowd here is going wild!" Mavis beamed. "Let's join them." Spotlights swirled crazily around the American flag backdrop on the stage in the center of Lone Star Stadium. "Ladies and gentlemen!" Mavis's voice boomed over the loudspeakers. "Please welcome America's number-one box-office star and your host for *Elimination*—Nick Necropolis!" The Greek Freak strode onto the stage, looking so buffed out that he threatened to burst his tuxedo. He stood at the podium stage right and leaned toward the microphone.

"Are you ready?" Nick Necropolis rasped. The crowd howled. "I said, Are you ready?" Whoops and shrieks resounded through the stadium. "Are you ready to see justice done?"

On one of the TV screens, Seth saw a beefy guy in his twenties, wearing a John Deere cap and pumping his fist and chanting, "Yes! Yes! Yes!" Seth could hardly concentrate as the folks in Dallas turned their attention to the stadium's enormous TV screens and the tens of millions of people watching at home and the buzzing crowd of producers and assistants in the New York control room were treated to a ten-minute minidocumentary. He barely heard the kudos of his colleagues as they congratulated him on his artful editing of the footage of Barbara Mae Jenkins standing teary-eyed in a cemetery, before the tombstones of her husband, Earl, killed in a car accident, and little Earl Junior, tortured to death at eighteen months of age. He was hardly paying attention when the parents of Tiffany Snopes, the baby-sitter who'd been raped and murdered by Jeremiad Hardee before he killed Earl Junior, appeared on the screen to express their grief. How many times had he already looked at this videotape? He knew what effect the pitiful Snopeses—with their old weatherbeaten faces, faces right out of *The Grapes of Wrath,* their drawling inarticulate musings on why this tragedy had befallen their daughter, their struggle to make sense of it all—would have on an audience. But had Seth ever really been able to sympathize with them? Yes, it was terrible what had happened to their kid, but, *come on . . .* Tiffany? What would a woman named Tiffany Snopes really have amounted to, anyway?

Barbara Mae Jenkins was back on the screen. "Jeremiad Hardee has made me suffer like I've never suffered before. He made my baby suffer. He made Tiffany suffer. Now, I want *him* to suffer." The crowd in Lone Star Stadium roared its endorsement. She was good, this Barbara Mae. Seth had been thrilled when he saw the raw footage of her interviews. Bland-looking, but telegenically bland, a redneck Everywoman. He felt bad for her. She was just poor white trash, but a more compelling image than the Snopeses. Still, Seth had never really been able to *connect* with her, either. Certainly not in the past week. However bad Barbara Mae's pain was, Seth could not believe it was any worse than the pain he was feeling.

While Barbara Mae prattled on about her loss, it was Emma's face Seth saw, Emma's voice he heard. He replayed the scene over and over in his mind, remembering how surprised he was to see Emma awake, sitting on the living room couch, waiting for him, when he got home from work at one in the morning. He'd been doing his best, trying so hard to let her know how much he loved her. He knelt in front of her, put his hands on her thighs. "You all right, honey?" She looked as if she'd been crying. Had Trudy said—or done—something again?

"Seth," Emma said softly. "I know now."

"Know what?"

"I know that I want to have a baby."

Seth felt warmed with joy. He was not relieved, or surprised. Because he had known that Emma would come to this decision. He felt, rather, like a boxer who'd just won a match he was expected to win. It was the soothing joy of having an imminent desire fulfilled, the comfort of having one's surest faith reaffirmed. And this joy of reassurance lasted for two seconds, right up until the moment Emma uttered her next sentence.

"But I don't want to have a baby with you."

On the giant TV screens in Lone Star Stadium and on the screen directly in front of Seth in the New York control room, the haggard, ghostly face of Jeremiad Hardee appeared. He resembled the actor Harry Dean Stanton, only swarthy, with an olive-toned complexion; and even crazier-looking than Stanton, with the familiar psycho killer's deadness in his eyes, the blank gaze of derangement. "I pleaded not guilty," Jeremiad Hardee said. "And even though now I say, yes, I did kill them young folks, in my heart, I still don't believe Ah'm guilty."

"This guy is perfect!" Seth heard one of the producers standing behind him say.

"Straight from central casting," another chimed in.

"A cornpone Hannibal Lecter."

"What people don't understand," Jeremiad Hardee said in his low, emotionless voice, "is that Ah'm a victim, too. I had a very abusive childhood. That's what led me to do the things I done. So I can't say Ah'm sorry for what I done. Cuz Ah'm a victim, too."

On the twenty screens in the control room, Seth saw the faces in the crowd, some of them puffy and scarlet with rage as they yelled at the image of Jeremiad Hardee, others aghast by the killer's gall. Yet, in a weird way, Seth could see Hardee's point.

Seth had spent two hours trying to reason with Emma, trying to get her to see that marrying him and having their baby was the only right decision, even though he wasn't sure he believed it. But what he *had* believed, what he had been absolutely certain of, was that if he and Emma were going to break up, *he* would be the one to make the decision. He had simply assumed that whatever doubts Emma might have had, she would never leave him, she would never be the one to end the relationship. He had spent years making himself indispensable to her. She relied on him emotionally and financially. How could she possibly walk out on that? Of course, Seth didn't say this to Emma. Instead, he reminded her of all the history they had together, of how supportive he had been, of how desperately lonely she would be without him.

"We have to break up," Emma said. "It's over, Seth," she said many times that night. And Seth knew there was no talking her out of it. Once Emma had made up her mind, that was it. Seth knew she was stubborn beyond the point of reason. He asked her where she would live. She said she would stay with her mother for a little while, then get a place of her own. He asked how she would make ends meet. She said that between her job at the Miasma showroom and shooting weddings with Simon, she'd get by. She told him that this was going to be their last night together. She would leave in the morning and return in a couple of weeks to collect her stuff. She didn't own very much, anyway. They went to bed. Emma lay with her back to Seth. He put his arms around her. He kissed the nape of her neck. He stroked her face, her breasts, her thighs. She did not push him away; neither did she encourage him. She didn't respond at all. Her entire body was inert. Seth held her even tighter and wept until he fell asleep. When he awoke the next morning, Emma was gone.

Seth got home from work relatively early that night, at ten o'clock, and went upstairs to Trudy's apartment to tell her what had happened. He was still feeling stunned by it all as he sat on his mother's bed. Scarlett sat panting in the corner. "I just want to know, Mom," Seth said haltingly, "why you did what you did."

"Don't blame me because you chose the wrong girl," Trudy Winkler said. She told Seth that his relationship with Emma was doomed from the start.

"Still, Mom," Seth said faintly, "did you have to do what you did?"

A pained expression came over Trudy's face. Seth's mother seemed almost as hurt as he was. "If she just could have picked it up . . . once," Trudy said. "If just once she could have cleaned it up. Would it have killed her? Does she think she's so much better than us? If just once she could have picked it up . . ."

"Here he is, folks," Nick Necropolis growled from the stage of Lone Star Stadium, "the parasite who murdered Tiffany Snopes and Earl Jenkins, Jr.—Jeremiad Hardee!"

As the crowd exploded in boos and screams of fury—Seth couldn't remember ever seeing so many angry people gathered together in one place—the American flag backdrop rose into the rafters of the stage, revealing a large, imposing gallows, with a thick noose hanging from its high beam. Beside the noose stood Jeremiad Hardee, flanked by two uniformed police officers. Hardee, dressed in a pale gray inmate's uniform, hands cuffed behind his back, stared vacantly out at the crowd, his mouth hanging open. Seth was alone among the producers in the New York control room in knowing that Hardee had been injected with tranquilizers to keep him from struggling or crying out on live television. At the foot of the gallows stood a khaki-clad member of the Federal Youth Corps, a drum strapped around his neck.

With the cheering throngs providing a deafening background score, one of the police officers secured the noose around Hardee's neck, then descended the gallows' stairs. The other officer walked to the back of the platform and grasped the lever that would open the gallows' trapdoor. The young FYC member began a drumroll and a hush fell over the huge crowd. For several unbearably long seconds, everyone watching—including Seth—wondered if they were really about to see what they knew they were about to see. The only sound in Lone Star Stadium was the quick-tempo patter of the drum. And then—

"Ah'm human!"

Seth nearly jumped out of his seat. There was a strange, hollow, echolike sound to the voice.

"Ah'm human!" Jeremiad Hardee screamed again, his voice picked up by the nearest microphone on the stage.

"Jesus Christ!" one of the producers in control room number one said.

"Oh my God!" exclaimed another.

"Good Lord!"

"AH'M HUMAAAAAAAAAAN!" Jeremiad Hardee, standing on the gallows, noose around his neck, shrieked.

At that instant, the police officer pulled the lever, the drumroll abruptly ceased, the trapdoor opened, and Hardee's body dropped. A sudden hiss echoed through the stadium, a massive collective inhalation—the sound of sixty thousand people simultaneously gasping. "Hol-eee shit!" someone in the New York control room said. The body seemed to bounce once in midair. Like a bungee jumper at the end of his fall, Seth thought. Then it hung suspended, swinging to and fro. Hardee's feet kicked in the air for three or four seconds, then stopped. His still body swayed back and forth. Everyone watching seemed frozen. Seth had read in high school about suspension of disbelief, and now, whatever everyone all at once seemed to be experiencing was the inversion of that theatrical principle. How many times had Seth seen people hung in movies? A dozen at least. And now he had seen an actual hanging on live TV, and, conditioned by artifice, he couldn't really believe that he had just seen what he knew he had just seen. Suspension of belief. In these few seemingly interminable moments of silence, as Jeremiad Hardee's stiff body dangled at the end of the taut rope, this is what Seth thought he and 50 million other witnesses were feeling.

Nick Necropolis—a professional to the bitter end—broke the collective trance. Leaning into the microphone, he snarled, "Parasite . . . eliminated!"

All of the tension in Lone Star Stadium was released in triumphant applause, orgasmic cries of exultation. The American flag backdrop descended. Hardee's body, the police officers, the FYC drummer, and the gallows were out of sight. Then a large piece of the stage floor, a secret panel, slid away, and a band rose up on another platform, on a stage that had been concealed beneath the stage. A hugely amplified guitar chord thundered through the stadium.

"Ladies and gentlemen," Nick Necropolis roared, "Kyle Trueblood and the Bounty Hunters!"

And there he was, the biggest star in country rock, wearing his trademark black cowboy hat, surrounded by his band, now fully ascended to the stage of Lone Star Stadium. Seth had been expecting it, of course, but the appearance of Kyle Trueblood came as a shock to everyone else in the New York control room. The producers and assistants began whooping and slapping each other high fives. The stadium crowd, meanwhile, which Seth did not think could get any more crazed, seemed to be undergoing paroxysms of ecstasy. The band tore into the theme song from *Justifiable Homicide III*, Kyle Trueblood gripping his microphone and wailing like a savage Elvis:

> *The Bible say an eye for an eye,*
> *You take a life, you gotta die,*
> *Some may call it homicide—*
> *But I call it justice!*
> *I call it justice!*

Though Seth had been wearing his headset throughout the show, he'd stopped paying attention to the constant chatter coming over it. But now he heard Mavis barking orders: "Be ready to cut to me as soon as Kyle is done. I'll do a quick wrap-up. We'll show the slow-mo replay of the hanging. Then I'm going to say, 'I'm human,' Jeremiad Hardee cried, 'I'm human.' If only he had had the compassion to realize that Tiffany Snopes and Earl Jenkins, Jr., were also human. Right after you hear me say that, we cut back to Kyle for the encore. Got it?"

"Got it," Seth heard Sophie Mendel say.

"I call it justiiiiiiiiice!" Kyle Trueblood howled.

Now the crowd was chanting along with him: "J-U-S-T-I-C-E! J-U-S-T-I-C-E! J-U-S-T-I-C-E! I call it justice!"

"Seth? Seth, are you there?" It was Sophie coming over his headset, sounding even more freaked out than before.

"Congratulations, Soph," Seth said. "You hit it outta the park. But you shouldn't be talking to me right now. Stay focused."

"Seth, I'm just—I don't know . . . I mean, did you *see* that?"

"Yeah, yeah, I told you, you did great."

"That's not what I mean." Seth could hear suddenly that Sophie was on the brink of tears. "That was the most horrible thing I've ever seen."

"Kyle's gonna be done with this song in about thirty seconds, Sophie. Don't lose it now."

"Do you know what Robert Oppenheimer said?" Sophie's voice was shaking. "At Los Alamos? After the first explosion of the atomic bomb? He quoted the Bhagavad Gita. He said, 'Now I am become Death, destroyer of worlds.' Seth, what are we doing?"

"Oh for Christ's sake, Sophie, it's just a goddamned TV show!"

< 273 >

O N TELEVISION, TROY MCCRACKEN looked far younger than his age, but up close one could see the fine creases around the apple cheeks, the threads of white in the hair, which was not exactly brown but not quite red, either. From a certain angle, Troy McCracken's face seemed hawkish, cruel. But then he'd smile his radiant smile and his violently blue eyes would go soft, like an angel's in a Renaissance painting. As Melvin Hutchinson sat across from him in the cabin of the presidential helicopter—a huge machine, it seemed nearly as big as Melvin's plane, *Justice One*—a small table between them, the dying sun casting a pinkish light over Troy, the attorney general realized that the President's face could be whatever you wanted it to be: the face of a great statesman or of a bright-eyed Moonie shoving propaganda at you in an airport terminal. On this late-April evening, wearing a shiny blue baseball jacket with "The Prez" stitched in white cursive across the left breast, Troy McCracken looked like a ravaged schoolboy.

"Would you get a load of that view?" Troy said.

Melvin looked down on the Washington Monument, the Lincoln Memorial, the Jefferson Memorial, all of them a dazzling white.

"I like taking a whirl over the town," Troy said contentedly. "It's *our* town now. We own it. Power and popularity—it's an awesome combination. You know what I think about when I look down on this city?"

"No," Melvin replied flatly.

"History. And how we will be judged by history. You know, I sit at Abraham Lincoln's desk. Imagine. The desk of Lincoln. That's what I mean when I talk about history. You know what I love about this job, Hutch?"

"No."

"I'm always learning," Troy said in a voice full of gee-whiz enthusiasm. "This must be one of the greatest learning experiences an American can have."

"That's good, Mr. President. Now, if I may—"

"You've never been up here in the chopper, have you?"

"No, this is my first time."

"I'm sorry about that, Hutch. I should have had you up here before. Though, you know, choppers still remind me of Nam sometimes. You didn't fight in the war, did you, Hutch?"

"No, I was a bit too old for the draft."

"You don't know what you missed. I enlisted, myself. Character-building experience. I mean, horrible and all that, too. War is hell and all that. But it does build character. Anyway, sorry I haven't had you up here before. And I'm sorry we haven't had more meetings, especially one-on-one like this. But, hell, man, you're doing such a bang-up job at Justice there hasn't been much reason to get together and talk."

"Until now," Melvin said sternly. "I suppose you're wondering why I requested a private meeting with you, Mr. President."

"Oh, I know."

"You do?"

"Of course I do. I also realize this whole Vin Ewell business must have you on pins and needles."

"It's not about the vice president."

"Of course it's not. But still, this is a difficult situation, a real pain in the ass, frankly, for all of us. Basically, Muriel's got us over a barrel. Or she has up until now. She doesn't want to pull the plug on the old buzzard and, I must say, I'm touched by her love for Vin. She's still hoping he's gonna wake up and be his old self. Now, I could go ahead and appoint a new veep anyway, but, well, you know, it's a very sensitive situation, PR-wise."

"I understand, Mr. President, but—"

"But it's still hell for you, isn't it, Hutch? Hanging in limbo like this, all the speculation, wondering what I'm thinking, what I'm going to do."

"Yes, but that's not the reason I—"

"I hear ya, Hutch. I read you loud and clear. And I hear the American people. That may sound kinda corny, my using an expression like that in private: *The American people.* But, hell, what's wrong with being a little bit corny? Know what I mean? I haven't been ruined by the cynicism of this town. And neither have you, Hutch. I can tell."

"Thank you." Melvin reached for his briefcase, snapped it open.

"Are you hearing me, Hutch?" Troy asked a bit anxiously. "Am I getting through to you?"

"Oh, yes," Melvin said as he pulled a thick black briefing folder from his case and set it down on the table.

"Vin Ewell's going to be declared brain-dead." Troy stared steadily at Melvin. "Any day now," he said evenly. His face at this moment looked gaunt, haunted. And Melvin thought: Is there anything colder than blue eyes?

"Ewell is a vegetable?" Melvin asked hopefully.

"I said he's going to be *declared* brain-dead." Troy's face broke into a shit-eating grin, instantly transformed from hit man to frat boy. "And the next day, I'm going to name a new vice president. Subject to congressional approval, of course."

Melvin swallowed hard. He glanced down at the fat black briefing book, then back into Troy's frosty eyes. He didn't know how to respond. He wasn't sure the President even wanted him to.

Troy leaned back in his chair and said casually, "That's a pretty serious-looking folder you got there, Hutch."

"Yes, sir." Melvin coughed. "This is what I wanted to speak with you about."

"How do you think you'd be as vice president?" Troy asked, still casual as could be.

"I'm not sure I understand the gist of your question, sir."

"The *gist* is this: Do you think America is ready for a black man as vice president?"

"I think it depends on the black man."

< 276 >

"So, Hutch," Troy said, maintaining his nonchalant tone, turning his head to look out at the pearly twilight, "You still hittin' the sauce pretty hard?"

The matter-of-factness of the question made it all the more stunning. Melvin took a moment to collect himself before answering. "I haven't had a drink in a week."

"Not a very long time on the wagon, is it?" Troy was staring at Melvin again, a deadness in his eyes.

Now Melvin was pissed. "Everything's under control," he said glacially.

"Good to hear," Troy said. " 'Cause, you know, sometimes, when a man drinks, his head gets full of peculiar ideas."

"Well, you needn't worry about that with me, Mr. President."

"That's great, Hutch."

"Though I wanted to meet with you, sir, to inform you of some extremely peculiar goings-on. Do you know anything about Fort Brandriss in New Jersey? It's a drug reeducation center."

"Lemme tell you, Hutch, you have done an exemplary job in administrating the DRCs. Absolutely first-rate."

"Thank you, but—"

"I haven't been vocal enough in my praise. But let me commend you. The DRCs are what this administration is all about."

"Yes, Mr. President, but I have reason to believe that the program at Fort Brandriss has been . . . corrupted."

Troy McCracken cocked his head and squinted at Melvin. "Corrupted? You mean graft? How?"

"No, sir, I mean . . ." Melvin opened his briefing book, began flipping through the pages. "I've pulled files on one hundred former inmates from Brandriss. I've made phone calls; I've talked to these young people and members of their families. Among the young women, in case after case, well, not among all of them, but close to half the young women I spoke with have found it impossible to get pregnant. Many of them, the great majority, in fact, had at least one child already and wanted another. Those who went to see doctors were told they were infertile."

Melvin looked up at the President. Troy stared blankly at him. He shrugged. "So?"

Melvin began flipping through the briefing book again. "I'm talking, sir, about more than twenty women, most of whom had babies when they entered Fort Brandriss and who, once they left the DRC, found they were sterile."

"That's a shame," Troy said expressionlessly.

Melvin took a deep breath. He had lied to Troy when he said he hadn't had a drink in a week. But he'd drastically cut down on his alcohol intake and, on this day, he hadn't swallowed a drop. His head felt as if it weighed a hundred pounds. He cleared his throat before speaking again. "Mr. President . . . I also ran checks on male inmates. I have reason to believe that many of the young men who entered Fort Brandriss HIV-negative left the DRC HIV-positive."

"Really?" Troy said, his voice, his face, remaining utterly neutral. "Is there a lot of homosexual activity at the center?"

"No, Mr. President, there is no sexual activity of any kind at the DRCs."

"Are you sure about that? Not even masturbation?"

"Well, perhaps, masturbation."

"There you go."

"But people don't get AIDS from masturbating, sir."

"Maybe they had AIDS before they entered the DRC. Aren't they tested there?"

"Each inmate is tested during his first week at the fort. But they aren't told the results until after they leave."

"Okay." Troy nodded and stared quizzically at Melvin. "I'm still not sure I'm following you. I mean, these kids are HIV-positive. It's a pity, but . . ."

"But, sir, at least twenty of these young men had no history of homosexual activity—some of them hadn't yet had sex at all; these are fourteen-, fifteen-year-old virgins, several of them—and had never used intravenous drugs."

"So they say."

"Several had been tested *before* they were sent to the DRC and were found to be HIV-negative."

"So they say."

Melvin paused, took another deep breath. "There is, Mr. President, a pattern here."

"A pattern?"

"Roughly seventy percent of the inmates at Fort Brandriss are black. But, of the sterile women and the HIV-positive men I talked to in the last week, one hundred percent of them are black."

"Hutch . . . what are you saying?"

"There's more. Records from Fort Brandriss show that each and every one of these inmates was examined by the surgeon general. Arthur Spooner has been visiting Fort Brandriss at least one day a week for most of the past year."

Troy knitted his brow. "Have you talked to Dr. Spooner about this?"

"I've been calling him for two days. He won't return my messages. Mr. President, I know all this sounds outlandish, horrific, unbelievable. But I am certain that there is a concerted effort going on here —a plan, a program."

"Let me ask you this, Hutch," Troy said slowly, "if such a program existed, do you think it would be such a bad thing?"

"I beg your pardon," Melvin said, not believing that Troy could have said what he just said.

Troy McCracken leaned forward and stroked his chin, his brow furrowed in thought. The President had always struck Melvin as a not very intelligent man who, once he achieved a certain measure of success in life, had decided that he must be pretty bright after all. This sort of ofay was common in the corporate world, and what always annoyed Melvin about the type was that no matter how dumb a white guy was, he always assumed he was smarter than a black guy. "Why do you think I was elected to this office, Hutch?"

"You tell me," Melvin said curtly.

"One: to improve the economy. Two: to deal with crime. And three: to handle America's interests abroad. That's basically it. Do you agree?"

"I suppose so."

"Now, let's forget for a moment reason number three and take a look at reason number two. Crime. Do you know what percentage of crimes in this country are committed by young black males?"

"Not offhand."

"Neither do I. But it's a lot. We both know that. You yourself,

Hutch, have spoken out boldly on this issue many, many times. And, as I said earlier, you have done an exemplary job in fighting crime. That's why you're the most popular member of the cabinet. Damn it, Hutch, that's why you may very well be the next vice president of the United States." Troy flashed his toothsome grin. Melvin did not smile back. Troy turned serious again. "And yet, my man, despite your best efforts, the problem persists. We've tried everything in this country. We've tried namby-pamby criminal rehabilitation programs. We've tried stiffer sentences. More executions. Today, nearly every state in the union has the death penalty. There are more federal offenses punishable by death today than ever before. We keep up-ping the number. And you know what? Crime still increases. It is . . . What is the word I'm thinking of, Hutch?"

"I don't know."

"A conundrum. It's a bloody conundrum is what it is: the problem of crime in general and the fact that most crimes in this country are committed by young black males. And nothing we do seems to help. A goddamned conundrum!" Melvin could hear that Troy loved his big shiny word. "Now, let us move to issue number one: the econ-omy. Hutch, do you know what the single biggest drag on the federal budget is?"

"Social Security."

"Well, Social Security doesn't count. There's nothing we can do about that. Too many old folks vote." Troy chortled. Melvin did not make a sound. Troy put on his severe statesman's face again. "No, Hutch, it's welfare. And you know, of course, who the biggest recipi-ents of welfare are."

"I don't know the statistics."

"Black single mothers. A sad fact. A tragic fact. But a fact. We've tried all kinds of reform. And nothing changes. The numbers just go up. Do you know how much the government spends on single black mothers and their children every year?"

"No."

"Neither do I. But it's a lot. A shitload, man. Billions. Billions upon billions. And the average hardworking U.S. taxpayer just doesn't want to foot the bill anymore."

Melvin felt as if his head were about to split open. He could feel his metal flask pressing against his right breast. Under his left armpit, he could feel the sweaty pressure of Harry's .38 in its new leather holster. This conversation was not going the way he'd wanted it to. Not at all. He wanted to take a drink. Or blow his head off. He couldn't decide which he wanted to do more. "Mr. President," he said slowly, carefully, "I'm really not sure I understand what you're getting at."

"Sure you do, Hutch," Troy said softly. "Have you ever had a conversation with Arthur Spooner?"

"We've talked. Not much."

"By God, he's a brilliant man. A genius, really. I have learned so much from Dr. Spooner these past two years. A talk with him is like a great scholarly tutorial. And you know what Dr. Spooner always says?"

"No."

"Some things are bred in the bone. Bred in the bone. Things like alcoholism, drug abuse, violent criminal tendencies, illegitimacy. These are traits that are handed down generation after generation after generation. That's just human nature. These dangerous, self-destructive traits, they have nothing to do with morality. They have nothing to do with family values. They can't be changed by social engineering. These are genetic dysfunctions."

Melvin could feel beads of sweat forming on his forehead. He worried that he might faint. Only the rage roiling within him kept him alert. "So what's your answer to this *conundrum?*" he said, his voice low and raspy. "Genocide?"

"Goddamn it!" Troy exploded, slapping his palm down on the table. "I hate that word! You are way off base using that word, mister!"

"Then what is it you're talking about?" Melvin asked, struggling to maintain a calm tone.

"I'm talking about eugenics. Do you know that word?"

"Yes, I know that word."

"Do you realize, Hutch, that before World War Two, sterilization of the feebleminded was legal in twenty-seven states? *Twenty-seven states.* The Nazis gave these practices a bad name. Hell, I'm reluctant even to call it eugenics. Arthur Spooner calls it practical, or scientific, genetics."

"A program to infect young men with the AIDS virus. You call that—"

"First of all, Hutch," Troy said firmly, holding up his hand, "the program of which you speak does not exist. Secondly, if it did exist, all it would amount to would be advance executions—slow-motion executions of men who would end up being executed anyway."

"My God," Melvin whispered. "You know all about it."

Troy smirked. "Hutch, there isn't anything that happens at Justice that I don't know about. Henry Beedle gives me a biweekly briefing."

"Beedle?" Melvin said, feeling a pain in his chest.

"I've known him a lot longer than you have, Hutch. And Beedle has let me know that if a program of the kind of which you speak actually existed that you would be adamantly opposed to it."

"Beedle," Melvin said faintly.

"But what's difficult for me to understand is *why* you'd be opposed to such a program—if such a program did indeed exist. Hell, Hutch, I see you on TV. I read transcripts of your speeches, your interviews. Henry Beedle has filled me in on your most intimate conversations. You don't approve of the criminal class any more than I do. In fact, you've done more to raise consciousness about the black criminal class than anyone else in this nation. If the program you're so exercised about actually existed, it would be a way of turning your very rhetoric into action." Troy McCracken leaned closer to Melvin and spoke almost lovingly. "Don't you see, Hutch, it's the only way? We've tried everything else. This is the *only way.* The only way to save America."

Melvin could not meet Troy's azure gaze. He began flipping through the briefing folder, thoughts careening. "You say it isn't genocide. You say it isn't genocide. I have these forms, filled out by doctors at the fort, initialed by Arthur Spooner. Each form has a box marked HANDICAPS. Have you seen these?"

"No, I haven't."

"Under HANDICAPS, sometimes it says 'Illegitimate,' or 'Violent behavior,' or 'History of drug abuse.' Each kid is categorized like this."

"Well, I'd certainly say those are handicaps for getting along as a productive citizen in our society. Wouldn't you, Hutch?"

"But here's a kid . . . his name is Miles Person. And under HANDI-CAPS, one of the things listed is 'Miscegenation.' "

Troy bit his lower lip thoughtfully. "What did you say the name was?"

Melvin hesitated a moment, then said again, "Miles Person."

"Miscegenation," Troy said. "Well, I'd say that's an unusual classification, but I'm not really surprised. This is something else I've discussed with Arthur Spooner. The man is brilliant, like I said. And he's pointed out that race mixing has never been as prevalent in any civilization *ever* as it is in the contemporary United States. This is *not* a strength, you know. It creates confusion, diffusion, all sorts of conflicts. Why do you think mongrelization has always been taboo in societies? There are reasons for this. And Hutch, I know that you are certainly no fan of race mixing. Beedle has told me some of the things you've said on the subject."

Melvin could feel his shirt, clammy, plastered to his chest by sweat. He could hear the dull whirring of the helicopter blades. "Mr. President, whatever my private views—"

"You know another thing Arthur Spooner always says? He says that people always want to accuse doctors like him of tampering with nature. But nature, Dr. Spooner says, can be quite cruel. Why shouldn't we wish to improve on nature's mistakes? I should think, Hutch, that you would agree with that."

Melvin peered out at the inky night. He looked down on all the white monuments, now brightly illuminated. The helicopter was going around in circles. "I can't allow this to go on, Mr. President. I'm going to go public with this. I will tender my resignation tomorrow. Then I will hold a press conference and tell the world what's been happening at Fort Brandriss."

Troy chuckled softly. "Hutch, Hutch . . . Who is the federal official with direct jurisdiction over the drug reeducation centers?"

"I am."

"Yes indeed. Don't you think it's going to be a little suspicious, to say the least, if the attorney general exposes his own secret program? If such a program actually existed."

"I'll explain that I knew nothing about it."

"And who will believe you, Hutch? Even if anyone believed that such a bizarre program could exist, do you think that anyone would buy the idea that such a program could be conducted, under the auspices of the Justice Department, without the attorney general knowing about it?"

"I'll tell the truth. I will tell the truth and take my chances."

"And what if a piece of paper, a directive, say, authorizing this program, with your signature on it, turned up?"

"I never signed any such directive."

"But if one turned up, with your name on it, what could you do?"

"Deny it."

"Tell it to the *New York Times,* Hutch. Tell it to the congressional hearing committee. You're *in charge* of the DRCs, Hutch. There's no running away from it. You don't have a shred of plausible deniability in this case."

Melvin buried his face in his hands. He could feel his whole body trembling. He wanted to cry but fought the impulse. He didn't dare weep before his enemy. "My God," he whispered, "what have I done?"

Troy McCracken removed a microphone, the size and shape of a ballpoint pen, from his pocket and spoke into it. "Let's take the attorney general home, Slick. You know the way." He put the microphone back in his pocket. "I'm not a chess player, Hutch, but I think this is what they call checkmate."

Melvin closed his folder, began fumbling for his briefcase. "Just tell me one thing, Troy. You're the one who authorized this program. From the very start. Right?"

The President stared out the helicopter window, a trancelike emptiness in his eyes. "To die by an assassin's bullet," he said serenely. "It's quite a fate. Think of Jack and Bobby. Think of Dr. King. Of Malcolm X. It's a hell of a way to go. But it's instant immortality. You become a hero to your people. To die by an assassin's bullet."

Melvin could feel the helicopter beginning to descend. He could feel a burning drop of urine at the tip of his penis. "I don't want to be a hero," he said.

"That's good, Hutch," Troy said, still staring out the window. " 'Cause once you're on my team, there's no gettin' off it. Unless I want you cut. And I still think you'd make a pretty good vice president."

Melvin felt as if he had a mouthful of sand. "Thank you, sir," he murmured.

The helicopter touched down. A marine guard appeared in the cabin. Melvin rose from his seat. "You'll be hearing from me," Troy said, still looking out the window. He did not offer his hand for Melvin to shake. The marine escorted the attorney general to the door of the chopper. Melvin stepped out onto the moist grass of his backyard in Elyssia, Virginia. He stood on his lawn, clutching his briefcase, looking up, feeling the whip of the wind generated by the helicopter blades, feeling his necktie flapping behind him, as the President ascended into the murky sky.

(13)

RASHID STARED IN FASCINATION at the photos laid out on his desk at the Norris Center for African-American Arts and Culture. There was something at once enthralling and disturbing about the pictures. In Emma's work, Rashid saw sex at its most raw and fundamental. He also saw a huge talent. But a talent that needed to be shaped, molded, controlled.

"You really like 'em?" Emma asked cautiously as she stood on the other side of Rashid's desk.

"I told you already," Rashid said. "I'm blown away. Blown away. Do you have a title, for the whole group?"

"*Intimacy.*"

"I likes. I likes."

"I can tell that you do." Emma suppressed a laugh of delight. "I don't know, though . . . sometimes, I think, Maybe it *is* just pornography. Maybe I *am* just trying to provoke people."

Rashid looked up and shrugged. "So what?"

"Then, on the other hand, I think, People see more explicit stuff than this on cable every night."

"Yeah, but people can handle sex as entertainment. Sex as art freaks 'em out."

"Aren't you worried about the new obscenity codes? The feds closed down a couple of shows last year, you know."

"Hey, the way I see it, let 'em close us down. We couldn't *buy* better publicity than that."

Rashid showed Emma around the center: the two offices, the bare-walled art gallery, the projection room, the studio, the darkroom (!), the artist's quarters set aside for the first recipient of the newly established Norris Center for African-American Arts and Culture Fellowship. Emma couldn't resist asking Rashid where he had gotten all the money for this, and he was happy to tell her about his inheritance, and about the grants he'd applied for and won to set up this institute. Rashid offered Emma the first NCAAAC fellowship. It wasn't enough money to live on, but it would allow her to quit either her job at the Miasma showroom or her wedding gigs with Simon. And it would give her a place to stay. She had spent the past four nights with Alma in Washington Heights and her mother was already grating on her nerves. The artist's quarters were small but free. "I don't know," Emma said. "Do you think it's safe here?"

"If you feel threatened," Rashid replied, "you can always come and stay at my place on Largent Street. I'm just ten blocks away, and I've got plenty of room."

"Hmmmm. I might feel more threatened in the same house with you than I would staying alone here," Emma said flirtatiously. It had been only four days since the breakup, yet Seth had all but disappeared from her thoughts.

"Life is full of risks," Rashid said. "Are you interested in this fellowship or not?"

➤   ➤   ➤

It amazed Emma that once you made a decision on a major issue—in this case, deciding to leave Seth—all the elements in your life took on a new coherence. She would move to Norris; though she still wasn't sure what sort of relationship she wanted to have with Rashid. She would abort, illegally, pharmaceutically, the child she was carrying. She would quit her job at the Miasma showroom but continue shooting weddings with Simon. On this bright April morning, Emma was rushing to clear out her desk at Miasma. She was already running late for her appointment with Dr. Goldman.

"I can't believe it's all over, just like that," said Tommy Coughlin, the red-haired, freckle-faced salesman who'd always flirted with Emma. "Gone with the wind."

"You'll just have to cherish my memory, Tommy," Emma said, stuffing her handbag with the magazines, random notes scribbled on scraps of paper, postcards, tubes of lipstick, and other insignifica she had collected in her three months sitting in the Miasma window on Park Avenue.

"You probably won't even miss me," Tommy said forlornly.

"Right now, I'm more worried about missing my doctor's appointment.

Tommy stood in front of her desk, hands in his pockets, jangling his keys and loose change. "Well, I hope you'll at least keep in touch."

"I'll drop by sometime."

Emma walked toward the door. Tommy rushed ahead of her. He leaned against the door before she could grasp the handle, flashing his self-conscious grin. "You know something, Emma?" he said. "I've always wanted to fuck you."

Emma gave Tommy a level stare. The morning sun, burning through the glass door, cast a whitish light on the salesman's crimson hair and speckled cheeks. He continued to smile adolescently. Perhaps he thought he was irresistible. Perhaps he thought this was the way a black woman—as opposed to some less exotic type, his pregnant Irish Catholic wife, say—would like being talked to.

"You know something, Tommy?" Emma said. "You never will."

➤   ➤   ➤

Emma sat alone in a corner of the darkened room, contentedly sipping her beer and watching all the gorgeous brown bodies swaying to the sultry music that played on the stereo. Emma had danced with Rashid a couple of times, but she preferred to revert to her typical party mode: sitting in one place and letting whoever desired come up and talk to her. This usually guaranteed that the most boring person at any gathering would end up blathering in her ear. But Emma didn't mind. On this particular night, at this particular party, in the Fort Greene section of Brooklyn, the first exclusively black party Emma had attended in years, she was able to sit, alone and unbothered, for long stretches at a time, just watching other people, taking in the scene, which was precisely what she—the ultimate photographer, an observer to the core—liked to do.

Rashid stood nearby, engaged in an animated conversation with Kilarti Mufoso, critic at large for the *Downtown Clarion,* the woman Rashid had introduced to Emma earlier in the evening as "one of the best friends we're ever gonna have," a Norris, New Jersey, native who, like Rashid, had moved to Manhattan years earlier but had now returned to the old neighborhood to try to revitalize it. Emma felt immediately that Kilarti was projecting a hostile personal ray at her —perhaps she had designs on Rashid?—so she shot one back. Kilarti Mufoso was a middle-aged woman with braids—a hair weave, Emma assumed—running down her back and a deeply lined face with too much makeup on it for Emma's taste. Now Emma tuned out the music that was playing and focused her listening on Rashid as he talked to the critic at large.

"What I'm saying," Rashid exclaimed, "is that we're lookin' at five hundred years of payback comin'. We're just at the start of it, the earliest stages, now. What I'm sayin' is, it is no coincidence that five hundred years after Christopher Columbus quote 'discovered' America unquote, black people went on a rampage against injustice in Los Angeles. What I'm sayin' is, it is no coincidence that this decade has seen the first black mass murderer and that he targeted white folks, Asians, and Uncle Tom Negroes. What I'm sayin' is, this is payback, baby. And this is just the beginning!"

Emma sat listening in a not-unpleasant boozy haze. She thought Rashid was crazy, but she thought that she herself was crazy, too. Just a different kind of crazy. After a while, Rashid brought Kilarti Mufoso over to Emma's corner. "Kilarti's gotta go," Rashid yelled over the music. "She just wanted to say good-bye."

"I'm so glad you're having your debut at the Norris Center," the critic at large said. "We need more artists in our community—more of the right kind of artists. We have to give voice to our culture."

"I don't know," Emma said, barely audibly over the music, "I hear the word *culture* and I reach for my revolver."

Kilarti looked at her curiously. "What?"

"Sorry. It gets late, I have a little too much to drink, and I start quoting Nazis. I was just being glib."

Kilarti smiled thinly. She turned away, kissed Rashid good-bye, and left the party. Rashid sat beside Emma. "She's one of the best friends we're ever gonna have," he said.

"I know. You told me." Emma leaned toward Rashid, kissed him gently on the neck. "Will you be my friend?" she said seductively.

"I thought you'd never ask."

Rashid drove them back to Norris, to his house on Largent Street, where they made sweet and fiery love till dawn. Emma ravished his body. His skin like hers. His hair like hers. His essence. Like hers. And lying beside him, exhausted, as the sun began to peek through the curtains of Rashid's bedroom window, the same two words kept running through Emma's mind: *Welcome home.*

➤   ➤   ➤

It had been years since Melvin had gone on a serious, all-out bender, when instead of drinking copiously throughout the day while performing his duties as lawyer, judge, or attorney general, he said, To hell with the duties, and holed up in his apartment, calling in sick to the office and doing little but boozing and contemplating the state of his life and whether or not he should terminate it. Troy McCracken had deposited Melvin on his lawn in Elyssia, Virginia, on Friday night. Saturday morning, Melvin had *Justice One* fly him to New York. He stopped at his favorite liquor store and bought a case of Jack Daniel's. He entered his apartment on Central Park West at 10:00 A.M. Saturday and commenced drinking. He had not spoken to his wife since Friday morning, when she arrived in San Francisco for a national convention of the Organization for a Child-Friendly Society. On Monday morning, he phoned Henry Beedle—the traitor, that sniveling, bald-headed, brown-toothed motherfucker, how could Melvin ever have trusted him?—in Washington and told him he wouldn't be showing up at the Justice Department today and probably wouldn't show up tomorrow and might very well not show up on

Wednesday. "Tell the press I have the flu," Melvin said, adding pungently, "or some kind of virus."

"As you wish, Judge," Beedle said, giving nothing away in his businesslike drone, though Melvin was certain that by now his deputy had heard all about his airborne conference with the President. "Don't forget you're scheduled to give a speech at Columbus Circle Thursday morning."

"I haven't forgotten," Melvin said. He hung up the phone without saying good-bye. He then peered through the gauzy curtain of his study window, checking out the nondescript gray car twelve flights below, parked directly across the street from the door of his building. Melvin was beginning to discern the pattern. At 9:00 P.M., the nondescript gray car would be replaced by an equally nondescript brown car. The next morning at nine, the gray car would return to take the place of the brown car. Was Melvin merely being watched, or were the men in the cars his prospective assassins?

Melvin spent Monday staggering around his apartment, a glass of Uncle Jack in one hand, his father's Smith & Wesson in the other. They—McCracken, Spooner, Beedle, all those ofays—couldn't let him live now. Could they? Certainly, if he resigned, if he made a move to hold a press conference, he would be killed on the spot. But maybe, even if he did nothing at all, they would have him killed, anyway. Wasn't that what Troy was talking about? "To die by an assassin's bullet." What purpose could it possibly serve them to let Melvin Hutchinson live? Unless . . . unless Troy thought Melvin really was on board, content to let the program proceed. Maybe Melvin was insurance for them. If the truth about what was happening at Fort Brandriss—and maybe at other drug reeducation centers —ever got out, the presence of a black man in charge of the DRCs might help squash the rumors. Or, if real, irrefutable evidence of the secret program emerged, the blame could be laid at Melvin's feet. In either scenario, it would be best to let Melvin live, yes? So, say he kept his mouth shut. Say Melvin didn't reveal what he knew—a revelation that would surely lead to a scandal that would bring down this administration, since no decent American, and Melvin believed that most Americans were still reasonably decent, could tolerate state-sponsored genocide. Would Troy appoint him vice president? Troy had received 20 percent of the black vote in the last election, placing him third among all the candidates. With Melvin on the ticket next time around, Troy could expect to capture 40 percent of the black electorate, maybe more, depending on the competition. Once again, Melvin could represent insurance. But Troy would hold on to his 20 percent no matter who his running mate was. And, hell, the son of a bitch already had stratospheric poll ratings. What did he need Melvin for? Maybe—now—to keep him quiet? But the best way to do that was to kill him. Before he could kill himself. They would blame the assassination on narco-terrorists and Melvin would go down in history as a martyr of the drug war.

But assassination was always a messy business. Better to keep Melvin alive, no? As long as he kept his mouth shut. And why wouldn't he keep his mouth shut? Why, when you got right down to it, should he even oppose what was happening at Fort Brandriss (and perhaps at other DRCs)? The people who were being sterilized and contaminated were precisely the people who were dragging down the race. Melvin thought of all those ignorant, gum-cracking faces in the auditorium at Samuel Adams High School. Weren't they all future convicts and unwed mothers? Most of them, anyway. Many of them would probably wind up in DRCs. Why not move to eliminate them once they got there? What was it Troy had said? That this was the only way to save America? Why couldn't Melvin simply remain silent? Why couldn't he get with the goddamned program?

One reason, and one reason only: because his son had been subjected to the program. If anyone else's mother had come to him and told him what she believed to be happening at Brandriss, would Melvin have believed her? And if he believed her, would he have cared? He would never know for sure. But he had a pretty good idea. Blood was thicker than conviction.

So, Melvin thought as he blundered about his apartment that Monday afternoon, if he was to die, whether by an assassin's bullet or by his own (or, perhaps more precisely, one of Harry's), it would all be because of Willow and Miles. His one error, his one lapse of judgment in a lifetime of propriety, had already cost him his daughter. Or so he believed. But, now, he thought, perhaps the true mistake was not his roll in the sand with Willow but his failure to acknowledge the result of his action, to acknowledge his child. And the failure to acknowledge his second child was what had cost him his first child. And now, before he had ever known him, he was going to lose his second child, his only son. "The wages of sin," his mother would have said.

Staring out his study window at the nondescript gray car early Monday evening, Melvin wondered about love. Not a subject he'd ever given much thought to. But now, now that he believed his life was about to end, he wondered whether he had ever really been in love. He knew he wasn't in love with Dorothy. And that was okay. Being in love had never been an issue with them. What they had was a partnership, a successful merger. Dorothy had been an ideal wife, a perfect mother. She was the best partner a man like himself could have hoped for. He certainly hadn't been in love with Willow. Their encounter had been fueled by drugged, drunken lust, nothing more. When Melvin thought of the passion, the fervor, the devotion that he associated with the term *in love,* he knew that he had had this feeling for only two people: his mother, Athena, and his daughter, Abigail.

The telephone rang, with such jolting unexpectedness that Melvin spilled some of his Jack Daniel's. "Hello."

"Hi, honey."

It was Dorothy. His partner. She sounded as if she was phoning from a crowded room; Melvin could hear the chatter of women's voices in the background. Dorothy was speaking in her public voice. She told Melvin how well the conference was going, how insightful everyone's speeches were, how much concrete progress had been made. He knew he would have to wait until she returned to New York or Virginia to hear the low-down truth of what had happened in San Francisco.

"Everybody here is talking about Troy and this Vin Ewell business," Dorothy said. "It's getting a bit ridiculous, don't you think?"

"Oh, yeah," Melvin said.

"I mean, how long can they drag this out? It's incredibly irresponsible. Have you heard anything new?"

"Not really."

"Oh, honey, I just want this waiting game to be over."

"Me, too, Dottie. Listen, sweetheart . . . I want you to know that whatever happens, you have meant the world to me."

"Oh, Mellie, I love you, too."

"Yes, yes, I know, but, well, you never know what might happen."

Dorothy made a funny little sound, an exhalation of anxiety. "Melvin . . . why are you talking this way?"

"Well, honey." Melvin paused. "I just want you to know how much you mean to me. There're a lot of things we just don't talk about." Dorothy was silent on the other end of the line. Melvin could hear the busy chattering in the background. "I think we both have a lot of very powerful feelings inside us. And, well, honey, I feel that on a very deep level, we really understand each other. But we don't talk about our feelings very much. You could say we don't have to. That that's how deep our understanding of each other goes. But still, there's just so much I need to say to you. I mean, we never really talked about what happened to Abby. We lost our daughter. And we never really dealt with it—together. And I don't know what's gonna happen in the next few days. Maybe something good. But maybe something terrible. And I just want you to know, Dorothy, that . . . well, I guess I have sort of a confession to make." Melvin paused again. The chatter on the other end of the line had grown louder. "Dorothy? Dorothy! Are you there? Dottie!"

"Hi, honey," Dorothy said breathlessly. "Sorry, I had to step away from the phone for a minute. Things are really crazy here. Still, I think we've made a lot of progress. Now, what were we talking about?"

"I . . . I . . ."

"Oh, I remember. You were telling me how much I mean to you. And, Melvin, honey, you mean the world to me, too."

"Thank you, Dorothy."

"Now don't be so gloomy. I'm sure Troy is going to make a decision soon." Dorothy lowered her voice. "And we will be Mr. and Mrs. Vice President!"

"Yeah, well, maybe . . ."

"I gotta go now, Mel. I'll be back in New York Friday night. Keep the faith, baby."

"Okay." As soon as Melvin hung up the phone, the downstairs buzzer sounded. "Yes," Melvin said into the intercom.

"Ms. Cushing here to see you, sir," Winston, the doorman, said in that voice of his, laced with a lilting contempt. "And she has a young chap with her."

>   >   >

Up close, in the light of Melvin's living room, the resemblance was even more uncanny than it had been at Fort Brandriss. Despite the pale skin and the hazel eyes, it was Melvin's own face he was looking at—much, much younger, of course, but even the worry lines that creased Melvin's forehead were slowly developing, just barely discernibly, on Miles's face. "Do you remember Mr. Hutchinson?" Willow asked as the three of them stood in the center of the living room. "You met him on your last day at Fort Brandriss."

Miles stared at Melvin. "I think so," he said quietly. "I think I remember."

Melvin was unsettled by the lethargy in Miles's voice. Then he remembered that Willow told him that Miles's post-Brandriss examination had revealed traces of Thorazine in his body. It wasn't enough to inject him with a fatal virus. Spooner and those monsters had to drug the kid out of his mind, as well. "Nice to see you again, Miles," Melvin said gently.

"I need to speak privately with Mr. Hutchinson, Miles," Willow said. She looked at Melvin beseechingly.

"Sure," Melvin said. "We can go into the study. Miles, why don't you stay here in the living room." He picked up the remote control from the coffee table and handed it to Miles. "You can check out the Knicks game. Do you like basketball?"

"Yes."

"Great. We'll be right back. Make yourself comfortable."

Alone with Willow in the study, Melvin peered out the window. It was nine o'clock. The brown car pulled up behind the gray car. The gray car drove off and the brown car took its parking space. "We're under surveillance here," Melvin said. "You shouldn't stay very long. What's going on?"

"Rodney's missing," Willow said. "He hasn't been home since Saturday night."

"Is that unusual?"

"Yes. If he hadn't come home on a Saturday night, it would be unusual. For him to not show up on a Sunday night is bizarre. It's Monday night now and he hasn't even called. I just got scared, Melvin. I know I should have called before coming over, but—"

"No. No, it was smart not to call. I'm sure my phone is being tapped."

"Have you talked to somebody about Miles? About Brandriss?"

"Yes, but the less you know about it, the better."

"Jesus Christ. What are we gonna do?"

Melvin wanted to curse himself. Why had he given Troy Miles's name? What the hell had he been thinking about? "You should go home. Leave Miles here. I'll find a safe place for him to stay. I'll get back in touch with you, let you know where he is and what's going on."

Willow went home and Melvin was left standing in his living room while Miles stared at the baseketball game on TV.

"So you like hoops?" he said, unable to think of anything else to say.

"Yes," Miles replied robotically.

"Do you play at all?"

"I'm not very good."

Melvin smiled and sat down beside Miles on the couch. "I was never very good at it, either. I wasn't bad on defense. I blocked a lot of shots. And I was a pretty good rebounder. I could always jump high. But I had no shot at all . . . none. Poor eye-hand coordination. Bad aim. I love watching the game, though."

"Me, too," Miles said, adding, in the same monotone, "Are you going to help us find my father?"

"If I can."

"I don't understand why I'm here. Are we in danger?"

"Possibly. What has your mother told you about what's going on?"

"Nothing. Just that Dad is missing."

"That's good." Melvin's thoughts were scattered. He knew he had to get Miles out of here. But how could he without being seen? Surely, the stakeout boys had seen Willow and Miles enter the building together. And seen Willow leave alone. What the fuck had happened to Rodney? What could they possibly want with him? He glanced at his watch: 9:20. What the hell was he going to do with Miles? Then he remembered: Didn't Winston's shift at the front desk end at ten o'clock? On several occasions, he'd seen Winston, out of his doorman's uniform, wearing a trench coat and a floppy, battered plaid hat, pulling out of the building's garage in a decrepit Oldsmobile, headed for home, wherever home was. "Excuse me," Melvin said to Miles. He walked over to the intercom and buzzed downstairs.

"Yesssss?" Winston asked snidely.

"Winston, it's Melvin Hutchinson. I need to ask a favor of you."

One hour later, Hector Ramirez had replaced Winston at the front desk; Winston sat in Melvin's living room, watching the Knicks game, sipping a glass of Jack Daniel's, fondling the crisp one-hundred-dollar bill Melvin had given him, and awaiting the attorney general's return. And Melvin, dressed in Winston's trench coat and floppy plaid hat, behind the wheel of Winston's Oldsmobile, pulling out of the underground garage of his building, said to Miles, who was curled up on the floor of the backseat of the car, "Just stay cool, son. And stay *down*. Till I tell you otherwise."

>   >   >

On evenings alone in her apartment, Alma Person frequently engaged in vociferous and conveniently one-sided arguments with people from her turbulent past who, in addition to not being present in her home, were often dead. "What the hell do you know about him, Mama?" she barked at Athena Hutchinson. "If I want to marry him, I'll marry him," she'd say, lashing out at her angry giant of a mother in a way she'd never dared while Athena was alive. "And ain't a goddamned thing you can do about it!" Alma would pace up and down the long corridor of her Riverside Drive apartment. Suddenly, she'd whirl around and confront the specter of her good-for-nothing ex-husband. "Go ahead and marry the white bitch!" she'd yell with a vehemence she'd rarely displayed before the flesh-and-blood Rodney Person. "Let her trample all over you! See if I care, you bastard!" In this way, Alma refought battles lost long ago, settled old scores that had remained lopsided for years. Emma had recently put a crimp in her routine. With her daughter coming and going at all hours lately, Alma could never be sure when she might have to end one of her tirades abruptly. She knew Emma already thought she was a nut. She didn't want her only child to think she'd become completely unhinged. But it had been three days since Alma had heard Emma's key in the lock of her front door. She assumed her daughter was spending all her time in Norris, preparing her show. Now and then, she'd worry about Emma, about how she was dealing with her breakup with Seth, how she was handling her career, what she was doing with this Afro-American Arts Center, or whatever it was called, in Norris, New Jersey, of all places. But Alma's concerns were fleeting. Emma had always been able to take care of herself.

"You damn right!" Alma yelled, sitting now at her kitchen table, thrusting a finger at an invisible antagonist, in this case, an official from the board of education who, years earlier, had tried to deny her full disability benefits. "I'm gonna get every penny that's comin' to me! Every red cent!" The doorbell rang, giving Alma a start. What was Emma doing ringing the doorbell? Had she forgotten her keys? That wasn't like her. Alma went to the door and looked through the peephole. She saw some disheveled man in a weird raggedy hat. Was this some homeless bum wandering around the building? Why didn't the no-good landlord hire a security guard? "Who is it?" Alma said.

"It's me, Alma. It's Melvin. Your brother." Alma was taken aback by this surprise visit. When was the last time her famous brother, Mistra Big Shot, had actually dropped by her home? She couldn't even remember. Years and years. She undid the chain and flung open the door, then froze when she saw the pale young man standing shyly beside Melvin. She recognized him immediately.

"Please let us in, Alma," Melvin said, watching his sister glare at Miles. "Please, Alma. He's your kin."

>   >   >

At the opening of Emma Person's photography exhibition, *Intimacy*, on a Tuesday night in late April, the guests—most of them important

< 298 >

civic figures in Norris, New Jersey, or Rashid's friends from New York—milled listlessly about the gallery, glasses of wine in hand, looking abashedly at the blown-up black-and-white pictures of headless, contorted, copulating bodies, then quickly looking away and whispering in puzzled tones about what it was they were seeing. Emma stood in a corner of the gallery, near the bar, downing glass after glass of wine, rattled by having so many people in one place at one time scrutinizing her work, but feeling neither pleased nor disappointed by their reactions—most guests came up to her and, shaking her hand gingerly, said they found her photos "interesting" or "very interesting." She knew that Rashid had given Kilarti Mufoso her own private look at the show the day before—Emma, wishing to be absent from the preview, had stayed in Rashid's house on Largent Street—and that Kilarti's review would appear in the *Downtown Clarion* tomorrow. But there was only one person whose response Emma was really concerned about. Alma Person stood among the other guests, many of whom she had known from her years living in Norris, black beret tilted carefully atop her head, cigarette held between skeletal reddish brown fingers, staring intently at one photograph before moving slowly to another, then staring hard and long again. Alma was, of course, the only guest who knew what had inspired Emma to take these photos, and Emma was worried about what emotions the work might provoke in her always-unpredictable mother. That—along with the fact that she was rushing to get all the photos properly framed and hung, and that she loved sleeping with Rashid—was one reason why Emma had stayed away from Alma's apartment the past several days and nights.

After examining each photo, Alma walked toward Emma, a serene expression in her eyes. "They're beautiful," Alma said softly. "They're just beautiful. They have . . . integrity. I'm really proud of you, sugar." Emma threw her arms around her mother and they held each other in a long embrace.

Rashid, meanwhile, seemed frazzled as he worked the room that evening. Emma, watching from a distance, couldn't always make out what he was saying to the guests, but he seemed to be fishing for compliments, exuding anxiety. That night, back at Rashid's house, after the show, Emma asked him if he was happy with the opening.

He shrugged."Let's see what kind of reviews we get." Hardly a ringing endorsement, Emma thought. But she didn't care. Her mother had loved her work. And Alma's approval had been more important to Emma than she'd ever recognized before. Emma slept peacefully that night.

>   >   >

Emma felt an odd sensation as soon as she opened the front door to Alma's apartment on Wednesday afternoon. Some instinct conveyed to her that there was somebody else—someone other than her mother—in her mother's home. Emma walked into the kitchen. It was empty. She poked her head into the living room. Nobody there. She walked down the long corridor of the apartment she'd grown up in. The master bedroom was deserted, but the door to the bathroom was closed. She assumed Alma was in there. But she felt—she *knew* —someone else was present in the apartment. The door to Emma's childhood bedroom, the room where she'd spent several nights recently after her breakup with Seth, was shut tight. She slowly turned the knob and cracked open the door. She saw the back of a head resting on her pillow. At that moment, a hand touched Emma's shoulder. She turned around with a gasp. Alma stood in front of her, in the shadowy corridor, that strange look of serenity—the expression Emma had seen the night before at her opening—in her eyes. Alma raised a bony index finger to her lips.

"Shhhh. He's sleeping." Alma placed her hand on Emma's shoulder again and, as gently as possible, pushed her daughter away from the bedroom. She carefully shut the door. "He's tired," Alma whispered. "He's not feeling very well. He's been sleeping all day."

"Who is it?" Emma asked, trying not to sound as alarmed as she felt.

"It's Miles."

Half an hour later, Emma sat across from Alma at the kitchen table, under the harsh fluorescent light, an untouched cup of coffee growing cold in front of her. "Now let me get this straight. Dad and Willow had a fight. Dad is missing. And you're taking care of Miles as a favor to both of them."

"That's right," Alma said, that dreamy, almost beatific look still in her eyes.

"Mom, that makes no sense."

"Why not?"

"Because you've always hated all of them! Willow, Dad, Miles! I couldn't even mention their names in this house for years!"

"Keep your voice down, sugar. I told you, Miles isn't feeling well. He needs his rest."

An ugly feeling was welling up inside Emma, an emotion she hadn't experienced in years: that sense of jealousy, a blind contempt for the little interloper. When was the last time she had seen Miles? Seven years, eight? She couldn't remember. When was the last time she'd even thought of the little bastard? But she recognized all too well this mindless rage, this sense of rivalry that burned anew. Miles had already stolen her father from her. Now, here he was, after all these years, stealing the affection of her mother.

"This is just too weird, Mom. I don't know if I can handle this."

"He'll only be here a little while."

"So I can't stay in my own room?"

"I thought you were staying in Norris."

"I am. But if I needed to, I couldn't stay here. Because of Miles. Is that what you're telling me?"

"Oh, I'm sure we could work something out," Alma said airily.

"Mom, this is really bizarre. I don't understand it."

"Miles needs our help. He's your kin, Emma."

"Okay. Fine. I just came to pick up my tripod, anyway."

"It's in the bedroom. Wait here. I'll go get it. I don't want you to wake him." Alma hurried down the corridor.

"Thanks, Mom." Emma sat at the table, waiting, smoldering.

>   >   >

Emma was still in a sour mood two hours later as she carried her tripod along Jefferson Avenue and saw, from a distance of three blocks, the small band of people carrying signs, marching in a circle, and chanting in front of the Norris Center for African-American Arts and Culture. As she drew closer to the picket line, she could make out the words of their anthem: "One, two, three, fo'—porno trash has gotta go! One, two three, fo'—porno trash has gotta go!" It took a moment for the instinctive sense of denial to slip away and for Emma to realize, with a sickening sensation, that these people were demonstrating against *her*. She was only a few yards away from the center now. She guessed there were about twenty people in the chanting circle. The protesters were young and old, some clean-cut and respectable-looking, others decked out in fashionable street garb. But they all seemed extremely agitated. A crowd was gathering to watch the demonstration. "One, two, three, fo'—porno trash has gotta go!"

Emma slipped unnoticed past the picketers. She grasped the handle of the door to the NCAAAC. The door was locked. "There she is!" somebody yelled. Emma turned and saw the demonstrators converging upon her. "You ought to be ashamed of yourself!" a woman shrieked.

"You're a disgrace to the community!"

"We don't need this shit here! Black people have enough problems already!"

"What's wrong with you, bitch? Keep your freaky shit to yourself!"

"Pervert!"

Emma struggled with the doorknob. She dropped her tripod, began fumbling for her keys. She felt that at any moment the crowd was going to start tearing at her. The furious voices melded together: "Bitch! Pervert! Ashamed! Disgrace! Community!" She was pressed against the door, which was still jammed shut. She considered simply running into the crowd, but she feared for her safety. "Fucked-up wanna-bes like you! We don't need this shit! It ain't *art!* Ought to kick your skinny little ass!" Finally, Emma felt the door give way. A firm hand gripped her by the arm, pulled her inside. The door slammed shut again. She stood in the vestibule, facing Rashid.

"Come upstairs," Rashid said, sounding panicked. "I think we'll be safe up there."

Once inside the director's office, Rashid thrust a copy of the *Downtown Clarion* at Emma. She quickly scanned the review by

Kilarti Mufoso. While she didn't read the entire screed, certain phrases jumped out at her like the cries of the protesters:

> As a proud native and resident of Norris, New Jersey, I applauded the opening of the Center for . . . a bitter disappointment. An affront to black people everywhere . . . Not a celebration of our vibrant culture but a rejection of it . . . an artist running away from her blackness . . . Nothing connoting black authenticity . . . her own sexual perversions . . . indulging in the worst excesses of neurotic white artists . . . Illusions of "universality" . . . Demeaning to our people and our community . . . Instead of producing art that might inspire those of us who are seriously engaged in the black struggle . . . her own perverted fantasies . . . nothing feminist or womanist about it, either . . . Why must we see these nude white bodies in our proudly black community? . . . Most offensive of all are the photographs of African and Caucasian bodies entwined in pornographic . . . A black man humping a white woman . . . A black woman subjugated by a white male . . . The last thing our community needs . . . Does the artist herself wish to be white? Is that why she insults her own people so? . . . inauthentic . . . a traitor . . . It is up to the people within the community to protest against trash like this. . . . I would urge all concerned African-Americans in Norris . . . a demonstration . . . a boycott . . . send 'em a message . . . Of course, I oppose censorship in all its forms, but . . . Emma Person is part of a retrograde movement led by white-worshiping bourgeois Negroes. . . . Why doesn't she spend her time and whatever talent she may possess making art that uplifts the race, that celebrates black culture, that gives authentic voice to our struggle? . . . An organized protest is in order. . . . No porno trash in our community! . . .

Emma set down the newspaper and laughed. "Well, looks like I pushed some buttons."

"You think this is funny?" Rashid exclaimed. He was pacing the floor of the small office. The chanting of the crowd on the street below was so loud, it sounded as if the protesters were in the same room with Emma and Rashid. "This is some serious shit here, Emma!"

"Well, maybe it's like you said: We couldn't *buy* better publicity than this."

"No! I said we couldn't buy better publicity than having the white right-wing government shut us down. Having our own people protesting against us—this is a disaster! This is a fucking disaster!"

Emma was unfazed. In fact, she felt strangely proud, almost tickled. "I'm sure it will all blow over in a couple of days."

"We have to issue an apology," Rashid said, his voice trembling. "I'll write it up, but you have to sign it. We have to tell the community that we made a mistake."

"Forget it. I'm not apologizing to anybody. I *like* my work. And until last night, I thought you did, too, Rashid. That's what you told me, anyway."

"I *do* like it. I guess I do. But this isn't about art, baby. This is about politics. You have to understand my position in this community."

The telephone rang. Rashid lunged for the receiver, but Emma picked it up before he could. "Hello."

"Hello, may I please speak with Emma Person?"

"Speaking."

"Oh, hey, I'm surprised you're there."

"And who are you?"

"This is LaPhonso Nicholson from the *Downtown Clarion*. I'm just a few blocks from the center. I tried to get in, but I couldn't get past the demonstrators."

"No shit."

"I wonder if I could ask you just a few questions? And, I'm required to tell you that I'm recording our conversation."

"All right."

"The reaction to your work here in Norris is obviously overwhelmingly negative," the reporter said. "What is your response to your critics?"

"What is my response to my critics?" Emma repeated the question. She looked up and saw Rashid staring at her, his eyes wide with fear. "I have just one thing to say to my critics." She paused. "Are you sure your tape recorder is working, LaPhonso?"

"Yes."

" 'Cause I want to make sure you quote me accurately."

"I will."

"This is my response to my critics."

"Yes?"

"They can kiss my black ass."

> > >

Once the sun went down, the protesters went home and Rashid and Emma felt safe enough to leave the NCAAAC. But even in his home on Largent Street, Rashid continued to pace the floor, stealing peeks at the street, worried that demonstrators might show up on his doorstep. He had spent hours trying to talk sense to Emma, trying to get her to see the necessity of a public apology, but she just sat there in Lorena's old armchair, the picture of obstinacy.

"Why should I apologize when I'm not sorry?" Emma said.

"You don't even see what you've done," Rashid fumed. "You're such a self-absorbed, irresponsible artist, you can't see how you've offended your community."

"I have no control over people's reactions. What's mystifying to me is how you could praise my work one day, then hate it the next."

"Maybe I didn't see it for what it is."

"So Kilarti Mufoso and the Norris *community* have to tell you what to think?"

"Maybe there's some truth in what she had to say about you," Rashid said coldly.

It was the first thing Rashid had said to Emma that really hurt her. "What do you mean?"

Seeing Emma's pain, Rashid sharpened his tone. "Maybe you *do* want to be white."

Emma threw back her head and sighed in exasperation. "Rashid, that is such bullshit. The whole concept is such a crock of shit: If some black person doesn't follow some vague code of blackness, then they must want to be white. Don't you see how stupid that idea is?

Don't you see how *you* or anyone who buys into that idea is buying into the notion of white supremacy?"

"I don't know how you figure that."

"Because you, Rashid, are assuming that whiteness is something one would wish to aspire to. By assuming that all black people who aren't like you want to be white, you're placing whiteness above blackness. I'm just being myself, damn it. I'm not *trying* to be, or secretly *wanting* to be, anything or anyone else. But because Kilarti doesn't like my work and can't deal with it on any complicated level, she just attacks me for somehow not being black enough. I am who I am and I don't see white people or any fucking body as being better than I am."

"Well, you've only gone out with white boys the last few years."

"So what?"

"You let that Jewish bitch shit on your doorstep for two months."

"I thought it was a dog."

"Why don't you just admit it?" Rashid said quietly, almost compassionately.

"Admit what?"

"That you don't really know who you are. That on some level you wish you were white."

"I'm just not buying into this madness, Rashid. 'Cause that's what we've got in this country. This racial madness. It's like a form of insanity, a disease of the mind. And you've been poisoned by it."

"*I've* been poisoned?" Rashid snorted. "I *know* who I am."

"As do I."

"No. Because in your heart of hearts, you want to escape your blackness. You want to be white."

All at once, Emma felt the full emotional weight of the pressures of the past few weeks: her pregnancy, her breakup with Seth, the abortion, uprooting her life and deciding to move to Norris, the negative reaction to her work, Miles showing up at her mother's apartment. . . . There was just too much going on, too many strange and painful things to absorb. Now here was Rashid, this man she had known for just a little more than two weeks, this man she thought would save her, who seemed to understand, to appreciate her art, this brother who had given her shelter from the storm, turning on her, attacking her. This was all too much. All of it was too much. She fought the urge to cry. "Why are you saying this to me?"

Rashid knelt beside the armchair. He placed a hand on Emma's thigh and stared into her eyes. "I can help you," he said calmly. "But first you have to face the truth. Just admit it. You want to be white."

Emma felt tears sting her eyes. "Why are you doing this?"

"I want to help you," Rashid said soothingly. "Just say it. You want to be white."

The only thing Emma wanted to be at that moment was left alone. She felt so wounded, so wrung out, she was ready to say anything just to get Rashid to leave her alone. "I . . ." she said faintly. "I . . ."

The doorbell rang. Rashid rose warily, peered through the window curtains. He turned to Emma, the fear back in his eyes. "It's the cops." Emma quickly wiped away her tears and tried to compose herself. Rashid leaned into the front door. "Who is it?" he said gruffly.

"Justice Department," a voice answered.

Rashid opened the door. Emma, still sitting in the armchair, saw a bald, bespectacled white man in a dark suit, flanked by another white man in a dark suit and a uniformed white police officer, standing on Rashid's porch. In the distance, out on Largent Street, she could see a silent red siren atop a police car. "Good evening," the bald man said. "We're here to see Emma Person."

Emma could see Rashid's body turn rigid, not with fear now, but with resistance. "Y'all got a lotta nerve," Rashid said, his voice stronger than usual, deeper, blacker. "If y'all wanna close down our show, you can come by the Norris Center for African-American Arts and Culture tomorrow morning. It's at Sixty-six Jefferson Avenue. We'll be waitin' for you."

"We've already been there," the man said politely, "but—"

"But don't be showin' up at *my* door, at my *home*, at this hour a the night to harass us."

Emma rose from the armchair and walked to the door. The bald man flashed a sickly little smile at her. His teeth were tinted brown. "Are you Emma Person?"

"Yes, I am," Emma said, feeling strong again, emboldened by Rashid's aggressive attitude. Now that she, too, was standing in the doorway, she could see two police cars and a sleek black limousine parked in front of the house.

"My name is Henry Beedle. I work for the Justice Department. I wonder if you would be so kind as to step into my car here? I need to talk with you. Privately."

"You got a warrant, man?" Rashid asked.

Beedle cocked his head in a quick birdlike motion and stared at Rashid. "Whatever for?"

"I'll talk to you," Emma said, a touch of grandiosity creeping into her voice. "But I can tell you right now, I stand by my art."

Beedle smiled, showing his tiny, rusty teeth. "Nobody cares about your *art*. I need to speak with you about something important."

>   >   >

Emma sat beside Beedle in the backseat of the limo. One police car drove in front of them; the other cop car tailed them. "Where are you taking me?" Emma asked.

"Oh, we're just driving," Beedle said. "No place in particular. We'll drop you off back at home soon enough. Sorry to have surprised you like this, Ms. Person, but we believe you can help us. I'm deputy attorney general and I work very closely with your uncle, Melvin Hutchinson."

Emma felt almost woozy with a sense of unreality. Uncle Melvin? What did *he* have to do with anything? What the hell was she doing in this car, with this peculiar man, driving around Norris, New Jersey, late at night? "All right," she said.

"Your uncle is being blackmailed. This afternoon we arrested Willow Cushing."

"Willow!"

"Your stepmother."

"You arrested her?"

"On charges of extortion," Beedle said in a measured, lawyerly voice. "Willow Cushing has accused the attorney general of being the father of her child."

"What?"

"Miles Person. Your half brother, yes?"

"Yes."

"Well, this Willow Cushing, your stepmother, is claiming that she had a liaison with Melvin Hutchinson. That he, and not Rodney Person, is the true father of Miles. Willow attempted to extort money from your uncle in return for her silence. Are you getting all this, Ms. Person?"

"I'm getting it, but . . . but . . . it's unbelievable."

"Believe it. Are you aware of the fact that your father has been missing for several days?"

Emma said nothing. She wondered if anything this Beedle was telling her was true. How did it jibe with Alma putting up Miles? Alma had told her that Rodney and Willow had had a fight. She'd also told her Rodney was missing. But Emma's mother had said nothing about Melvin, or about blackmail. What the hell was going on here? Emma raised her hand to her forehead. She closed her eyes and rubbed her brow. "I don't, uh . . . I . . . ."

"Well, your father has been missing for several days," Beedle said curtly. "I hate to be abrupt, Ms. Person, but we desperately need your help, and time is of the essence."

"All right, but wait a minute. . . . Why are you the one telling me all this? Why haven't I heard from my uncle?"

"Events have been unfolding very rapidly. Your uncle, as we speak, is working to find your father, following every lead to track him down. We *think* Rodney Person may have had something to do with this, but right now we're assuming he's innocent. In any event, Hutch is trying to find him."

"Okay. So what do you want from me?"

"Miles Person has also disappeared. No one is sure if he's at all aware of his mother's scheme. She refuses to tell us where he is and we're afraid that some harm may have come to him. Do you have any idea where Miles might be?"

Emma looked at Beedle. She couldn't make out all of his features in the shadows. The light from streetlamps the limo sped past bounced off the thick lenses of his glasses. "If you're suggesting that I have something to do with this blackmail, I can tell you I don't know a damn thing about it."

"And I can tell you that you're not a suspect. At this time."

That last line irked Emma. "Look, mister—what did you say your name was?"

"Beedle. Henry—"

"Look, Beedle, I don't know you, and I don't know what the hell you're talking about. I don't know where my father is. And if I knew where Miles was, I wouldn't tell you. And, in fact, I'm not saying another damn thing to you. If you really do work for my uncle, tell him to call me himself." The words were tumbling out of Emma now, beyond her control. "But frankly, I think my uncle is a right-wing nut, and if you work for him, then you must be a right-wing nut, too. Now take me home."

Beedle was silent for a long moment. When he spoke again, his voice was as cool and measured as before. "You may not be aware of this, Ms. Person, but you just revealed to me that you do indeed know where Miles is. I think it would be in your best interest to give me the exact location."

"Am I under arrest? If I am, then read me my rights and get me to a phone so I can call my lawyer. Otherwise, take me home. Now."

"As I said before, Ms. Person, events have been unfolding very rapidly over the past few days. And your name has come up in another, different investigation. I believe you know a Dr. Marcia Goldman."

Emma's throat went dry. "Who?" she murmured.

"Dr. Marcia Goldman was arrested yesterday on charges of illegally distributing the abortion pill. Chances are she'll plead guilty and could be looking at ten years in prison. A list of her patients was seized in the arrest. Anyone who accepted the pill from her is liable to be sent to a drug reeducation center for six months. We know you had an abortion last week, Emma. Have you ever been to a DRC?"

"No," Emma croaked.

"Nasty places. Miles can tell you so." Beedle paused. "I don't know what you think of your stepmother or your father or your half brother. And I don't care what you think of your uncle or of me. But thanks to Dr. Goldman, we have enough evidence to put you in a DRC for six long months. And just think of the detrimental effect that could have on your *art*."

"Fuck you."

Beedle ignored the remark. "Time is of the essence, Emma. One way or another, we're going to find Miles. If you tell us where he is, we'll forget you ever popped an abortion pill. If you don't wish to cooperate, well . . ." Beedle's voice trailed off ominously. The limousine came to a halt in front of Rashid's house. Emma looked out the window. She saw Rashid's silhouette in the open doorway. "Looks like you're home, Emma," Beedle said. "Shall we call it a night?"

Emma felt even more dizzy, as if she couldn't think straight. She had thought that everything Beedle was telling her might be bullshit —until he'd mentioned Dr. Goldman. They must really have her in custody. How else could Beedle have known about the abortion? And since he was right about that, maybe he was right about everything else. So was it true, this business about the extortion? If so, what the hell was Miles doing at her mother's place? Was *Alma* in on this plot? No way. Impossible. Emma wanted to call her mother, to ask her what, if anything, she knew about all this. But Emma knew she didn't have time to make the call. She had to tell Beedle what she knew now or remain silent and invite an almost-certain sentence to a DRC. Alma had to be innocent of the blackmail. And Miles was innocent, too. They were both being manipulated by Willow. So what harm would it do to Alma or to Miles if Emma told Beedle what she knew? None. Willow was the culprit here. And maybe Rodney? No. Couldn't be. Her father wasn't conniving enough, or venal enough, to attempt something like that. But Willow . . . Willow . . . What the fuck was she trying to pull? If Emma didn't tell Beedle what she knew, whom, ultimately, would she be protecting? Willow! Was Emma willing to do six months in a DRC to protect that white bitch?

Henry Beedle cleared his throat. "Well, Ms. Person, if you have nothing more to say, I bid you good night. We'll be rounding up Dr. Goldman's patients in the next few days, so perhaps I'll see you again soon. In the meantime—"

"Wait a minute," Emma said. "Wait."

>   >   >

The rally was for AMAP—Armed Manhattanites Against Parasites. It took place under a warm sun on a gorgeous penultimate day of

April in Columbus Circle. On a large stage set up near the statue, which stood atop a tall pillar, of the Italian who, in search of a different place altogether, blundered into the New World, one speaker after another told tales of heroism by ordinary New York vigilantes who had, in self-defense or on citizen's patrol, bravely murdered would-be muggers and vandals. Melvin Hutchinson sat on the stage, in a backbreaking wooden folding chair, Henry Beedle seated beside him. It was the first time they'd seen each other since Melvin's meeting with the President. They had both been reticent, wary, that Thursday morning. Melvin was quite drunk already and when he was called to the podium, he took care to measure his steps. He gripped the edges of the lectern to steady himself and stared out at the subtly swimming mass of faces, most of them white, though there were a few African-Americans in the crowd. He opened his mouth to speak, but no sound emerged. He had thought he would launch into one of his four or five standard speeches, but he suddenly could not remember any of them. Melvin looked at all the faces staring expectantly at him and said the first thing that came to his mind.

"I used to believe in the future." Melvin paused, clutched the lectern a little tighter. "I mean, the idea of a *better* future. . . . I used to believe in progress. Maybe sometimes two steps forward and one step back. But general forward movement. Not a stagnant catastrophe. But that's where we're at now, isn't it? Maybe we just took it all too far. Everything. I . . . I thought I was fighting for something worthwhile. Freedom. Justice. Whatever the hell they are. Integration? Well, maybe nobody ever really wanted it that much, anyway. I look around today and I realize that all we've achieved is a condition of static violence. Or maybe it's a slow-motion civil war. A war without objectives. A war without end. With no possibility of victory. Not even a war of principle. It's just rage. It's just . . . lashing out. Static violence. A stagnant catastrophe." Melvin turned and looked at Henry Beedle. The expression on his deputy's face was one of utter panic. What was Beedle so afraid of? Did he think Melvin would expose the Brandriss program right here, right now? Melvin didn't even know himself, didn't know what he would say next. He turned back to the crowd. "I never thought I had . . . all the answers," he said haltingly. *"Most* of them, yes." The crowd tittered nervously. "I thought I had most of the answers. But now . . . I don't know. What's the answer? We've come to this impasse. This . . . condition. And, seriously, people . . . I'm asking you. What's the answer?"

"Hang 'em high!" a voice in the crowd yelled.

"Hang 'em high, Hutch!" somebody else screamed.

Within seconds, the chant rose up. "HANG 'EM HIGH, HUTCH! HANG 'EM HIGH, HUTCH! HANG 'EM HIGH, HUTCH! HANG 'EM HIGH, HUTCH!"

Melvin turned and saw Beedle scuttle across the stage and grasp the arm of the rally's chief organizer, the head of AMAP. The chief organizer rose from his seat and gestured to the leader of the marching band that was gathered at the foot of the stage. While the crowd continued chanting, the band broke into a manic rendition of "The Battle Hymn of the Republic." Suddenly, Christian Emerson, Melvin's main bodyguard, appeared at the attorney general's left shoulder. Beedle came up to him on his right. "What do you say we go down and greet the folks, eh, Judge?" Beedle yelled over the chanting and the brass. Next thing Melvin knew, he was down on the street, surrounded by bodyguards—Christian Emerson's hand resting like a lover's on his right hip, slowly pushing him through the swarm of admirers—stretching out his arm, reaching past his cordon of protecters to touch the citizens who lunged forward, straining to make some fleeting physical contact with him. And Melvin smiled. He beamed. He did relish this hurly-burly, the singular, warming sense of love he got from a frenzied crowd of people chanting his name. His right hand grasped one hand after another, countless hands—and then came the shock. Melvin had rubbed palms, had literally pressed the flesh, on a regular basis for more than two years. He knew the textures of all sorts of hands, could perceive the normal temperature, the general level of warmth of a human hand on a seventy-degree April morning in New York City. But the hand that Melvin suddenly grasped in his own was rigid cold, deathly absent of warmth, of the flow of blood. The feel of it was hideous, otherworldly. Melvin looked into the face of the woman whose hand clutched his in a rigor mortis grip and it was—how could it be?—with its powerful cheekbones, its iron stare, the face of his mother. This woman, this ghost of Athena Hutchinson, tilted her head at an unnatural angle and said, "How do?" Melvin felt as if he was about to scream in horror, but, before he could, Christian Emerson had pulled him away from the icy hand and he was trudging forward through the crowd again.

Melvin could see, beyond the shoulders of his bodyguards, a clearing, an area defined by police barricades, isolated from the groping mob. In the center of the clearing was Melvin's limousine. Police officers milled around the car and—oh no!—there was Wendy Hoffman of POL, microphone in hand, camera crew in tow. How the hell had she weaseled her way into the protected area? Melvin and his security detail pushed their way through the police barricades. Wendy Hoffman, with her fatty face and bottle-blond curls, moved toward Melvin with the mike. Melvin felt Christian Emerson's hand leave his side. All of his bodyguards seemed to step away from him at once. He felt suddenly exposed. Wendy Hoffman was upon him. "Judge Hutchinson!" she squealed. "Judge Hutchinson!" Melvin did not even hear the first shot. He only saw Wendy Hoffman's head explode in a shower of blood. He was momentarily blinded, with the reporter's blood in his eyes. When he could see again, Wendy Hoffman's half-headless corpse lay at his feet, its chubby right hand still clutching the microphone. Screams rang in Melvin's ears. Then he heard the second shot. He didn't know where that bullet landed. Hands were all over him now. He was shoved down and into the limo. He remembered the scene at Sam Adams High almost four weeks earlier. Only now, after he tumbled into the backseat of his Lincoln and sat up to collect himself, he had to wipe blood and brains off his face. Christian Emerson was sitting across from him again, gun drawn. Henry Beedle was beside him. Sirens screamed. Melvin stared at his palm, smeared in red, with bits of Wendy Hoffman's brain, like tiny pieces of raw hamburger, clinging to his fingers. Through the tinted bulletproof glass of his car window, Melvin saw people scattering in every direction. The limo lurched forward. They were speeding up Central Park West. Henry Beedle had lost his cool. He was slumped in his seat, holding a hand to his chest, hyperventilating. But Melvin, even with all that blood still on his face, felt perfectly calm. "Henry," he said, "I want to see the President. Today."

>   >   >

Emma slept till noon on Thursday. The night before, after Henry Beedle returned her to Rashid's house, Emma told Rashid that Beedle had questioned her only about Dr. Goldman and her abortion. Rashid still did not know that Emma was related to Melvin Hutchinson and she wanted to keep it that way—for as long as possible. Rashid cursed the government, though Emma wasn't sure what upset him more: that Beedle would wish to grill and harass her about her abortion, or that he had not come to close down her photography exhibition. Rashid did not badger Emma any more that night about her show or her authenticity as a black person. But, as they slipped into bed, he mentioned something about having to do "damage control" the next morning. By the time Emma woke up, Rashid was gone. She was pleased to see that he had left the keys to his Dodge for her. He had promised to lend her the car days earlier, but, in the wake of the *Intimacy* controversy, Emma wasn't sure he'd live up to his word. Emma did not turn on the TV or the radio in Rashid's house that afternoon, and when his phone rang, she let the answering machine respond, but kept the volume on the device down to an inaudible level so she wouldn't have to hear who was calling. The radio in Rashid's car had been stolen long ago, so as Emma drove to Blissfield, New York, to the two-family home Trudy Winkler owned, to pick up her books and a few other possessions, she had heard nothing about the shooting that had followed Melvin Hutchinson's speech that morning.

Pulling into Trudy's driveway, Emma felt as if it had been two years, rather than two weeks, since she'd last seen this house. As she entered the vestibule, she heard Scarlett barking crazily in the upstairs apartment. The Doberman appeared at the top of the staircase. In the gray five o'clock light, Emma could see Scarlett only in silhouette: the pointy ears, the head cocked at an angle of intimidating alertness, the outline of the powerful muscles. Scarlett bounded down the steps and Emma feared that the Doberman might rip her to pieces. But once Scarlett reached the floor of the vestibule, she began sniffing Emma affectionately and licking her hands. Emma knelt down and nuzzled the dog. "You're all right, aren't you, honey?" she said. "You're not so bad after all. You're pretty happy to see me, aren't you?" Scarlett replied with a pleasant grunt.

Acting on impulse, Emma climbed the stairs to Trudy Winkler's apartment. She had no idea what she would say to Seth's mother or why she felt the sudden desire to see her. She rapped on Trudy's open door. "Hello?" No response. She entered Trudy's apartment and walked toward her bedroom, Scarlett trotting amiably at her side. The door to the bedroom was open; Emma could hear the television. "Trudy?" She walked into the room. Trudy was sprawled on the bed, snoring slightly. On the nightstand, Emma saw a full glass and an empty bottle of wine. The TV was tuned to the Preview channel, an endless loop of listings, informing viewers of what they could see on their hundreds of channels, plus trailers of the films available on Pay-Per-View. "All your favorite stars," a jolly voice announced, "your favorite movies. Available at your fingertips. Coming up, a look at today's special feature!" The terrified face of a young black man filled the screen. He seemed to be crouching in an alley. "Please," he begged, "don't kill me! Please don't kill me!" Nick Necropolis, standing over the cowering young black man, appeared on screen. A voice-over growled, "In this neighborhood, *somebody* has to dispose of the trash." Necropolis inserted the barrel of his gun into the young man's mouth. "You fought the law, homeboy," Necropolis rasped, "and the law won." The screen went black as the gunshot sounded. The title of the movie appeared in bloodred letters: *Justifiable Homicide II*. "This time," the voice-over snarled, "it's ideological."

Emma returned downstairs to the apartment she'd shared with Seth for six months. She went to the storage closet, pulled out some empty packing boxes they'd brought with them from Vymar, and began scanning the bookshelves. It was a strange, dispiriting feeling, separating her books from Seth's. For so many years, their possessions had been intertwined. Now she was wrenching them apart. After loading the first box, Emma paused. She needed to hear some music. The CD player and 95 percent of the compact discs in the apartment belonged to Seth. Emma pulled her eleven CDs from the rack: one Billie Holiday record, one John Coltrane, one Ray Charles, one Sarah Vaughan, one Thelonious Monk, one Aretha Franklin, two Miles Davis, two Rodney Person, one Franz Schubert. She popped the Schubert CD into the machine. She loaded two more boxes of books, leaving all these peculiar empty spaces on the shelves, and listened, over and over again, to the slow, mournful, almost unbearably sad piece, the Piano Trio in E-flat. Emma could imagine what Rashid would say when he saw the one anomaly in her CD collection: "Schubert! What the fuck are you doing listening to this white music?" Emma laughed bitterly. It occurred to her that there were no people left in the United States of America; only your own people. Only races, genders, ethnicities, sexual orientations, cultures. What you believed and how you acted on those beliefs mattered far less than what you looked like and whom you slept with. Conviction, an individual consciousness, meant nothing when blood and skin were all. Maybe Rashid was right. Maybe this was the way it had always been. Maybe this was "reality." What was the point of fighting it? Emma pressed the STOP button on the CD player. She removed the Schubert record, placed it back in its case, and chucked it in the wastebasket.

Emma carried the four boxes of books and the ten CDs outside and stuffed them in Rashid's car. She returned to the apartment. There were still several pieces of furniture that belonged to her. She'd have to come back another day to collect them. She walked into the bedroom she'd shared with Seth and lay down on the bed. She could smell the smell of Seth on his pillow. She buried her face in the pillow and curled her body into the fetal position and, just as she felt she was about to cry, Emma fell asleep.

➤   ➤   ➤

Emma awoke to the sound of a distant siren. The bedroom was dark. Only the red digits on the clock radio pierced the shadows: 9:02. Emma quickly rose from the bed and went out to Rashid's car. She wanted to be away from Blissfield before Seth got home. Standing in the driveway, she could see smoke billowing in the sky. It seemed to be coming from a house down the road, maybe half a mile away from Trudy's. Emma pulled out of Trudy's driveway, drove two blocks, then turned on to Mohican Road, a long strip of grand houses and tidy lawns, heading toward the highway.

Mohican Road was a violent phantasmagoria. There were people everywhere, some running, most yelling, all of them hysterical. Emma saw two young white men in suits and ties screaming and pointing at each other over a white picket fence. Suddenly, one of the men jumped over the fence and began pummeling the head of the other man. There were so many people on the street, all of them white, most of them seemingly in their thirties and forties, darting about in random directions, that Emma could only drive at ten miles per hour, honking her horn to clear a path. She heard cries and crashes everywhere. All at once, a house on the left side of the street burst into flames. She saw more well-dressed young white men tumbling out onto the road, tearing at each other. She heard what could only have been a gunshot, then another, and another. She pressed down hard on the car horn, but with all the noise around her, nobody seemed to notice. A middle-aged man wearing a pale blue shirt and plaid pants fell with an awful thud on the hood of Rashid's car—had someone hurled him?—then rolled onto the street. More gunshots rang out. Another home burst into seemingly spontaneous combustion.

Emma turned on to Pieter Bliss Avenue, the main drag of Bliss-field. Pieter Bliss Avenue was even more out of control than Mohican Road. There were bodies twirling, tumbling, lunging, fighting, running everywhere. The sound of shattering glass filled the night air. The quaint old band shell in the center of Pieter Bliss Avenue was ablaze, an enormous bonfire illuminating the pandemonium. Emma saw an Asian man emerge from a food shop with a pistol in his hand. He began firing wildly. The rioters on Pieter Bliss Avenue were younger than those on Mohican Road. And the rioting seemed more focused. Gangs of young white men were tackling Japanese, Koreans, Indians, anyone who looked different from them, and beating, pounding, kicking their victims. A shower of glass cascaded on the hood of the Dodge. "Get her!" Emma heard somebody yell. She looked to her left and saw a group of five or more young white men, a couple with crew cuts, a couple more with long hair and goatees, charging toward her. "Get the nigger bitch!" one of the suburban thugs cried. Emma pushed her foot down on the gas pedal and tore through the crowd, speeding down Pieter Bliss Avenue. She didn't care whom she hurt, whom she ran over, whom she killed. She only knew she had to get out of Blissfield. She had to live.

In her rearview mirror, Emma saw more fires breaking out, more people spilling into the street. But she was away from the epicenter of the riot. She turned onto the highway. She didn't even know where she was driving. She was just driving. Fleeing. Then she looked at the odometer. She was almost out of gas. She saw a sign on the highway: HALLISBURY, EXIT 21. Hallisbury. Why did she remember that name? Oh, yes. The "black" suburb. Emma turned off on Exit 21. She found herself on Douglass Street, which, so far as she could tell, was the main artery of Hallisbury. There were lots of people milling about, all of them African-American. But there was no violence, no chaos. People spoke in subdued tones. Emma pulled up alongside an old man wearing a straw hat, a white T-shirt, and khakis; he was sitting on a sidewalk bench. He was alone, and he seemed to be surveying the scene on Douglass Street with a sadness in his eyes.

"Excuse me, sir?" Emma said. "What's going on?"

The old man looked at Emma oddly. "Ain't you heard?" he said. "The President done been shot. He's dead."

(14)

URIEL EWELL PATTED HER silver hairdo and took a moment to compose her face into a look of mournful resignation, then stepped through the front door of the vice president's residence for what she knew would be one of her final walks from the house to the limousine, past the gauntlet of cameras and blazing lights and microphone-wielding reporters who wondered what she was thinking and whether her husband would live another day. Twenty-four hours earlier, her agent had closed deals with a major New York publisher *and* a major Hollywood producer. Details were to be kept secret, but Muriel didn't know for how long. She had to move fast. Arthur Spooner had been applying subtle pressure for two weeks, but Muriel was worried that if she pulled the plug on Vin, it might adversely affect her book and movie negotiations. Now that the contracts were being drawn up, she could hardly wait to get to Bethesda Naval Hospital. Dr. Spooner was waiting for her in the limo. He put on his most reassuring Marcus Welby half smile. "How are you, Mrs. Ewell?"

"I've been better," Muriel said wearily. "I hardly slept a wink last night." This was the truth, though Muriel's insomnia was due to the millions she stood to reap from her lucrative deals and the fact that she couldn't stop pacing about her bedroom, planning what she would do with all that money.

"Still," the surgeon general said compassionately, "your mind is made up?"

"Oh, yes. I'm sure this is the right thing to do. I've thought about everything you've said. You've been wonderful at explaining my options. But I did have to consult one more source." Spooner stared uncertainly at Muriel. "I prayed a great deal last night," she explained. "And now I feel confident that this is the best solution. What's more, I think that Vin would want it this way."

➤   ➤   ➤

Lincoln, Kennedy, Garfield, McKinley: Troy McCracken had decorated the Oval Office with portraits of his favorite Presidents. Melvin took in the pictures of the dead white men while the current commander in chief jabbered on the phone, ignoring his attorney general. Finally, Troy finished his call. He sighed. "Well, Hutch, you don't look too much worse for wear, given the day you've had."

Melvin had, of course, showered and changed clothes since this morning's shooting. "Thank you," he said evenly.

Troy sat behind his desk—Lincoln's desk—in his shirtsleeves. His shirt was an immaculate white, with a button-down collar; his tie was blue with red stripes. "I can imagine what must be going through your mind right now."

"Can you?" Melvin said.

"The sniper hasn't been caught yet. But we'll catch him. By midnight, I'm sure they'll have the bastard. I suspect it's some mafioso. Or some spick from one of the drug cartels. But shit, Hutch, you are one lucky son of a bitch. You must know that."

"I guess I am."

"You're a goddamned hero now, Hutch. Not that you weren't before. But Jesus Christ, survive an assassination attempt and you are a fucking god in the eyes of the American people. Look at Reagan! I hope you appreciate this, Hutch. In any event, I just want to say congratulations. I'm glad you're still with us."

"I have a question, Mr. President. Did you mean to kill me or just scare me?"

Troy smiled slyly. "Hutch, this government had nothing to do with what happened this morning. If we wanted to kill you, you'd be dead already."

"So you just wanted to scare me?"

"Aw, Hutch." Troy sighed. "You're asking all the wrong questions."

Melvin said nothing. He sat perfectly still in his chair, staring at the President.

"Hutch," Troy said. "Do you know what is happening . . . right now . . . at Bethesda Naval Hospital . . . as we speak?"

Melvin remained silent.

"Muriel Ewell is pulling the plug on Vin. It's probably already happened. I should be getting the call confirming it in just a few minutes. Vin's gone, Hutch. He's outta here. History. In about one hour, I'm going to go out to the pressroom and make an announcement. I've got a speechwriter putting the finishing touches on my statement. As we speak. Then, Hutch, tomorrow afternoon, I'm going to hold a press conference in the Rose Garden. And standing at my side will be my choice for the man to serve as the new vice president. And I'll level with you, Hutch. I haven't made up my mind yet. It's you or Brad Blythe. I really don't know who I'm gonna go with. But you've got the inside track, my man. I just need to know: Are you on board?"

"On board?"

"You know what I mean."

Yes, Melvin knew what he meant. He sat in his chair, feeling utterly at peace because, though he did not know whether he was making the right or wrong decision—or what its implications would be—he knew precisely what he had to do.

>   >   >

Flanked by Secret Service agents, Muriel Ewell and Arthur Spooner walked down the gleaming white corridor toward Vin Ewell's suite. "I know it's hard to say anything reassuring at a moment like this," Dr. Spooner said. "But you should rest assured, Mrs. Ewell, that your husband had the best care available. The best care in the world. Dr. Cassidy is the leading expert in the field."

"Oh, I know," Muriel said. "And it *is* reassuring. You have been terrifically reassuring, Dr. Spooner. I only hope that, once this ordeal is over, you and I can keep in touch."

"Of course."

One of the Secret Service agents opened the door to the vice president's room.

In the movies, when a woman faints, she does so gracefully. She closes her eyes and drops to the floor in a balletic swoon. This was not the case for Muriel Ewell, who unleashed a bloodcurdling shriek, whose eyes remained open as her body went rigid and fell backward in a dead drop, her head hitting the linoleum floor with a horrid *crack* after she saw Vin Ewell sitting up in bed, Dr. Cassidy, a look of astonishment on his face, standing at the bedside, and Ewell, oxygen tube removed from his mouth, managing a weak but evil little smile as he looked at his wife and croaked, "Hello, darlin'."

➤   ➤   ➤

The phone on Troy McCracken's desk beeped. "Here's the call we've all been waiting for," he said, lifting the receiver.

Sitting across from the President, Melvin could not remember when he'd ever felt so preternaturally rational. Certainly not since Abby had died. There was no sword of justice in his mind's eye. No questions of morality plaguing him. No doubt in his heart. He did not worry about what the long-term consequences of his action would be. He had a pretty good idea, however, of the immediate consequences. He did not feel happiness or anxiety or sorrow. Only a raw determination. His mind was made up.

"Alive!" Troy yelled. "Are you shittin' me?"

Melvin heard the President's words but did not take the time to try to understand them. He rose from his chair. How would history judge him? Who gave a shit?

"That's unbelievable," Troy mumbled. "What a day. What a fucking day."

Melvin reached beneath his suit jacket and pulled his father's .38 from its leather holster. He held his arms slack at his sides. He felt the pistol, in his right hand, touching his thigh, through the cotton of his pant leg. He wondered briefly if what he was about to do would actually solve the problem. He could only hope that if one cut off the head of the snake, the body, too, would die.

"No, I won't do anything. Call me when you know more." Troy hung up the phone. He looked at Melvin and shook his head. He laughed lightly. "Well, Hutch, you're not gonna believe this, but—"

Melvin raised his arm, pointed the gun at Troy McCracken's left breast. "And remember," his father had said long ago, "don't pull the trigger. Squeeze it."

Troy looked completely baffled. "What the fuck are you doing?"

Melvin heard the bang. The gun kicked back in his hand. The foul smoke filled his nostrils. He looked at Troy. The President stared back at him, his face, even now, full of incomprehension, his blue eyes wide with puzzlement. There was a little burst of red now, dead center in the left breast pocket of his snowy shirt. The little circle of blood began to expand. Troy opened his mouth but said nothing. He looked like an idiot. Melvin heard the doors behind him burst open. He turned around, holding the gun to his temple, ready to fire into his brain. He saw two Secret Service agents—familiar faces, though he didn't know their names—pointing their pistols at him. He saw light explode from their guns. He could actually see the two bullets sailing toward him across the Oval Office. He watched them floating in the air, more intrigued than frightened, and felt them both, hot blows to the chest, on impact. He was propelled backward; his body sprawled across Abraham Lincoln's desk.

(15)

O NE YEAR HAS PASSED since the assassination of President Troy McCracken. And the events of that terrible night are etched in the minds of all Americans. We saw many of this nation's finest communities go up in flames. Such was the grief of the good and decent Americans who loved Troy. We all watched the trial of the real culprit behind the murder of our beloved President and all good and decent Americans cheered the verdict. Forty-eight hours from now, we will see justice done. And I say to you, my fellow Americans, that it is time to turn the page. Time to close this painful chapter in our history and to move on, buoyed by the faith in God and country that sustained Troy McCracken and continues to inspire all good and decent Americans today."

Seth Winkler hit the PAUSE button. Seth, sitting in the living room of his town house on the Upper East Side of Manhattan, liked watching four televisions at once. Connected to each of his four TVs was a VCR. He had not been able to catch President Vin Ewell's Oval Office address earlier that evening—he'd been working late at the office (though, in his new role as executive producer of the *Mavis!* show, he didn't work quite as long or as arduously as he had when he was a mere assistant or associate producer)—but, of course, he had Consuelo, the maid, tape it. Now he had four different tapes cued to four different points in four different VCRs, casting four different images on four different televisions. Seth sat on the couch, dressed only in a *Mavis!* T-shirt and his underpants, his hair down, eight different remote controls—one for each TV and one for each VCR—plus an array of newspapers, tabloid clippings, and the transcript from the trial spread out before him on the coffee table. He stared at the image frozen on TV number one: Vin Ewell, gaunt, white-haired, still managing to look distinguished even though the left side of his face—what with that almost-imperceptible downturn of the mouth and the subtle sag of his eye—showed the traces of his near-fatal stroke. He fast-forwarded the tape in VCR number one and watched the President's droopy mouth flap up and down with surreal rapidity. He hit the PAUSE button again, then PLAY. This was the second time in the past hour he'd watched the Ewell speech, and he could remember which sections he wanted to focus on.

"Willow Cushing is the worst breed of left-wing radical: ruthless, violent, willing to do anything to overthrow the government of the United States. I understand that many Americans today question the character of Melvin Hutchinson. But I knew Melvin Hutchinson. I served in the McCracken administration with him. Melvin Hutchinson was a friend of mine. Melvin Hutchinson was no radical. Melvin Hutchinson loved this country. And he loved Troy McCracken—like a brother. But Hutch was, if you will, brainwashed by Willow Cushing. She threatened him with blackmail. She accused him of being the father of her child—an allegation that no one has been able to prove. Nevertheless, Hutch was deeply disturbed by this accusation. He knew that it would be embarrassing to his family, potentially devastating to his career, and possibly damaging to the McCracken administration."

Seth hit the PAUSE button. The past year had been so crazy, so full of shock and weirdness, that he hadn't ever sat down to try to piece everything together, to make sense of it all. Tonight, he would begin to try. While Vin Ewell, slack-jawed and slope-eyed, remained frozen on TV one, Seth hit the FAST FORWARD button on VCR two and the image on TV two, Willow Cushing, short-haired, clad in a white blouse and demure pink jacket, sitting in the witness chair, jerked and jumped in hypermotion. Seth picked up one of the newspapers that lay before him on the coffee table and scanned the obituary column. RODNEY PERSON, COMPOSER OF "RADIANCE," FOUND DEAD IN EAST RIVER, a headline read. The dateline was two days after Troy McCracken's assassination. Rodney Person, the story said, had not known how to swim. Traces of alcohol and marijuana had been found in his body. Wandering, stoned and drunk, the newspaper deduced, along FDR Drive, Rodney had tumbled into the water and drowned. Seth hit PAUSE, then PLAY on the remote control for VCR two.

"I loved Rodney," said Willow Cushing, sitting in the dock. "I suppose you're going to accuse me of murdering him, too."

"No, only of psychologically torturing him," said the voice of the offscreen prosecutor, "the same way you psychologically tortured Melvin Hutchinson!"

Willow Cushing raised a hand to her forehead and looked as if she was about to cry. "Oh, God. If you want to kill me, why don't you just go ahead and kill me? I just can't take any more of this."

Seth hit the PAUSE button. He punched PLAY on VCR one and Vin Ewell continued his Oval Office address. Meanwhile, he fast-forwarded the Willow Cushing trial tape in VCR two. "Moreover," Vin Ewell drawled, "she convinced Hutch that the U.S. government was systematically exterminating African-Americans. And she led him to believe that Troy McCracken was behind this scheme."

Seth paused Vin Ewell and played Willow Cushing. "I only *suspected* what was going on at Fort Brandriss. Melvin confirmed it," Willow said, her voice shrill and panicky.

"Do you really expect us to believe," the prosecutor intoned, "that this government is systematically exterminating its citizens?"

"Not exterminating!" Willow cried. "Infecting, sterilizing! It *is* happening! Melvin knew!"

Seth paused, then fast-forwarded Willow and hit PLAY on Vin Ewell. "Please understand, my friends," the President said, slightly slurring that final *s*, "that the former attorney general was a patriot. A true patriot. But he was also a man. A very vulnerable man. He was, as his widow, Dorothy Hutchinson, has said, still haunted by the untimely death of his daughter. He was a man who took his responsibility as the nation's foremost law-enforcement official extremely seriously. Evidently, the combination of Willow Cushing's extortion and her outlandish *conspiracy theory*"—Ewell put a special stress on the two words—"pushed a vulnerable, sensitive man into a psychological abyss. Part of Melvin Hutchinson believed Willow Cushing's bizarre tale. But the better angels of his nature told him that what she said was a slimy lie! Hutch resisted her attempt at blackmail, refused to buy into her slimy lie of genocide. And then came the fateful morning of that fateful day, one year ago. Willow Cushing, an accomplished markswoman, gained access to an abandoned office just off Columbus Circle in New York City and, with a high-powered rifle, fired two shots at Melvin Hutchinson. Willow Cushing was obsessed with Hutch. And obsessed with overthrowing the McCracken administration. When Hutch refused to believe her slimy lies about the U.S. government, she tried to assassinate him. But her aim was slightly off. Instead of killing the attorney general, she murdered Wendy Hoffman, special correspondent for the Politics channel."

"Yes," Willow, now in PLAY mode on VCR two, said, "I learned how to shoot when I was a girl, at camp, but—"

"And after trying to shoot Melvin Hutchinson but inadvertently shooting Wendy Hoffman, you fled the building, leaving your rifle behind!" the off-camera prosecutor bellowed.

"I haven't fired a gun since I was sixteen!"

"And yet you signed the papers for the very rifle used to kill Wendy Hoffman, did you not?"

"It's a forgery! I've never bought a gun in my life! Never!"

Pause. Back to Vin Ewell on TV one.

"Convinced that it was the U.S. government that had tried to murder him, Melvin Hutchinson, his mind clouded by fear, threats of blackmail, and outrageous conspiracy theories, took the life of his dear friend Troy McCracken."

Pause, then fast-forward on Ewell. Back to Willow Cushing.

"Oh, God, you don't see what's happening. You don't *want* to see what's happening." Seth hit the STOP button, turned off TV two. He hit PLAY on the Vin Ewell tape.

"The jury convicted Willow Cushing on charges of murder and extortion and she was subsequently sentenced to death. You can watch the live broadcast of Willow Cushing's execution Thursday night on Pay-Per-View cable TV. Check your local listings for times in your area."

Seth carefully scrutinized Vin Ewell for signs of brain damage. It was rumored that the President was not all there. Some people said that if Ewell was reading a TelePrompTer, he was okay, but that he couldn't carry on a normal conversation without lapsing into incoherence. That was why he had given only scripted speeches and had not held a single press conference in the year since he'd emerged from his coma. It was even whispered that Ewell only lip-synched his speeches, that the texts were actually delivered off-camera by a professional impersonator.

"All good and decent Americans deeply mourned the death of Troy McCracken. We witnessed a sometimes-violent outpouring of grief in suburban communities all over America."

Seth hit PAUSE on Vin Ewell and turned his attention to the still image on TV three: Mohican Road in Blissfield, New York, on the night of Troy McCracken's assassination. There were people everywhere, frozen in the midst of gestures of fear and violence. An overturned car, on fire, dominated the foreground of the image. In the background, a large house was aflame. Fire provided the only light in the scary nightscape. Seth leaned forward and squinted at the picture. He hit PLAY on VCR three. A woman lurched out of the background. She was wearing only a nightgown, drenched in blood. In her right hand, she carried a bloody butcher knife. She seemed to be shrieking, crying out in some primordial blood lust, though with all the noise on Mohican Road, one could not clearly make out the sound of her voice. And, in the firelight, one could not really discern all the features of her face. But even still . . . Seth hit PAUSE. . . . He stared at the woman's face for perhaps the twentieth time . . . and this time, he was all but certain . . . it was his mother.

Seth punched the STOP button on VCR three and the image disappeared. He returned to Vin Ewell.

"And so I say to you again, my fellow Americans, it is time to turn the page. Troy McCracken would have wanted it that way. There remains important work to be done. We must move on. We must continue to fulfill Troy's great legacy. Dawn McCracken has asked me to thank you all again for the love and support you have provided her and Justin and little Ashley in this difficult time. And my lovely wife, Muriel, and I would also like to thank you, from the bottom of our hearts, for your love and support as I have worked to overcome my misfortune of last year. Together with Vice President Brad Blythe and every last person in this administration, I will continue to strive to make Troy McCracken's grand vision of America a reality. God bless you and God bless the United States of America."

Willow Cushing had never stood a chance. No one had come forward to corroborate her story about Fort Brandriss. The defense had decided not to call on either Alma Person or Miles Person to testify, since Melvin, evidently, had not told his sister anything about the alleged eugenics program and since Miles could barely remember what he had eaten for breakfast this morning, let alone what evil deeds may have been done to him at the drug reeducation center. Yet—and here was, to Seth's mind, one of the most peculiar twists in this whole weird saga—Willow had named Alma Miles's legal guardian. The two of them lived together in Alma's crumbling cavern of an apartment in Washington Heights. Seth tried phoning Alma, but her number had been changed and was now unlisted. He knew he could get the number if he really wanted to—but he didn't really want to.

And Emma Person, the great love of Seth's life, had seemingly dropped off the face of the earth. No one, not even Emma's best friend, Naima, could tell Seth her whereabouts. Emma had disappeared without a trace.

"Yo!" Mavis Temple's voice boomed over the living room's intercom. "Turn off the damn TVs already and come to bed!"

Seth leaned toward the speaker phone that rested on a stand near the couch. "I'll be up soon, honey," he said to Mavis, who awaited him in the master bedroom on the third floor of the town house they shared (but *she* owned). "I just want to watch a little bit of our interview."

"Well hurry up!" Mavis commanded.

What Seth really wanted was to watch more of Willow's trial. He wanted to review again the tapes of Vin Ewell's speech and the Blissfield riot. He wanted to continue to try to put this all together, to figure out what had really happened with Melvin and Willow and Troy and Miles and Emma. But he could do that some other time. He turned off TVs one, two and three, turned off VCRs one, two, and three, and turned his attention to TV four and the tape in the VCR connected to it, a feature on Mavis Temple broadcast the night before on a new celebrity interview show called *Reality*. The segment began with a montage of tabloid covers showing Mavis and Seth, smiling, locked in a warm embrace. MAVIS GETS HER MAN! one of the headlines announced. Seth, sitting alone in the living room, sighed happily. Seeing his image on the TV screen, he felt as if he was sinking into a luxurious hot bath. There he was, pictured with his fiancée, one of the most famous people on the planet. Soon, he would be almost as famous as she. This was only the beginning!

"I just feel so lucky," Mavis said to the TV interviewer. (Seth couldn't even remember his name. And, really, who cared? *He* would never be as famous as Seth was about to be!) "So blessed. To find love, true love, at this point in my life. It's like a miracle, a gift from God. Now I know that God really does believe in Mavis Temple."

Seth fast-forwarded to the part of the interview featuring him, Mavis, and Trudy sitting in this very living room. "Mavis and I are best friends," Seth said. "That's the most important thing." Watching himself on TV, Seth couldn't help but feel proud. He'd come up with a good line and he'd delivered it well. He was, in fact, great on TV. A goddamned natural! Trudy Winkler, on the other hand, looked a bit awkward sitting beside Seth and Mavis on the couch. She was going to have to work on her telegenics.

"So what about children?" the little nobody interviewer asked.

"Oh, we'll adopt," Mavis said. "There are so many little black children out there, sad little orphans who need love. I lost both my parents at a young age, so I know what it's like to be a little black child alone in the world."

"And Mavis," Seth interjected, "can give these kids so much. I hope I can, too."

"And what about you, Mrs. Winkler?" the interviewer asked. "Are you looking forward to being a grandma?"

"Oh yes!" Trudy enthused. "Very much so!"

Both Seths, the one on camera and the one alone watching himself on TV, grinned. From their very first meeting, Mavis and Trudy had gotten along wonderfully. The two of them were, in a weird way, very much alike.

"But she'll be more than a grandmother to our children," Mavis said.

"What will she be?" the interviewer asked.

"The mammy!"

All of them—Mavis, Seth, Trudy, and the interviewer—burst into laughter. And no one laughed as hard as Trudy. "The mammy!" she repeated. "Oh, Mavis, you're just *too* much! I'll be the mammy!"

"Yo!" Mavis called over the intercom. "When are you comin' to bed? I neeeeed you."

Seth knew what that meant. Mavis would have to be served. "I'll be right up, sweetie pie," he said into the speaker phone. He clicked off TV four and VCR four. He began the long trudge up the stairs to the master bedroom. He knew he had a good life. He knew he should be happy all the time. His wedding was going to be the media event of the summer. But Seth couldn't escape a shadow of melancholy. He hoped he'd be able to get it up for Mavis. Sometimes, lying atop all that undulating flesh, he felt as if he were bodysurfing. What the hell. He would just close his eyes and, as usual, think of Emma. As he mounted the final flight of steps, he thought about the children he and Mavis would adopt someday. Would Mavis really insist that they adopt only black children? Couldn't they have at least one white kid? But then it occurred to Seth that, as the children of Mavis Temple, they wouldn't really be black *or* white or any race at all. They would be something so much better, so much more transcendent than that. They would be famous.

       ➤   ➤   ➤

Oh My People, Oh My Soul was the title—suggested by Rashid Scuggs—of Kilarti Mufoso's first photography exhibition at the Norris Center for African-American Arts and Culture. The NCAAAC had become quite popular in the year since its first exhibition, Emma Person's *Intimacy*. The shows that followed that initial debacle had all been the sort that satisfied the tastes of the community. And Kilarti's photo series—pictures of black people who lived in Norris, New Jersey—followed the pattern. The show consisted of solemn portraits: dignified black women standing and singing at Norris's

First Baptist Church; little inner-city children staring bleakly into the camera, their eyes revealing nothing but pathos; gang members, arms folded across their chests, glaring fiercely; sad-eyed old men sitting in Benny D.'s barbershop. The guests at the opening, most of them important civic figures in Norris or Rashid and Kilarti's friends from New York, gathered around the photos, nodding and murmuring their approval. When they came up to Kilarti, the guests didn't simply tell her they liked her work or found it interesting. They *thanked* her for making the pictures. They seemed, more than anything, grateful. Because they were seeing themselves as they wanted to be seen.

"Well, you know," Kilarti said to one of the well-wishers, "when I saw the type of work that was out there, I thought, I can do better than that! And Rashid has been so encouraging." Kilarti turned and looked around the gallery. "Where is that husband of mine, anyway?"

She spotted Rashid in a far corner of the room, holding court before five or six guests. Rashid was talking—as most people in America were probably talking—about the hanging that was scheduled to take place the following evening. "You *know* I'll be watchin'," Rashid said. "The race problems in this country were bad enough before that crazy white bitch came along. Like my mama used to say, 'You stir up old shit, it'll stink.' "

"So you don't believe Willow Cushing's story?" Eugene Little, standing beside Rashid and wearing his black leather cap, asked.

"Fuck no!" Rashid replied. "Black people—we're destroyin' ourselves fast enough already! Why the fuck would the government go through the trouble of destroyin' us? It's not worth their time."

"A lot of black folks believe her, though," Eugene said.

"Sure they do. Folks see what's happening to our communities and they want to believe there's some larger force at work. I don't blame 'em. But tell you what: Had a *sister* come out and said what Flower or Blossom or whatever the fuck her name is said on the stand, I'da believed it. But this aging hippie white chick, she was just obsessed with destroying black men. That's all. She destroyed Melvin Hutchinson. She destroyed Rodney Person. I don't know why she couldn't just leave our men alone. Her little zebra child got AIDS and she had to find a way to rationalize it. I think she just made this shit up."

"And what about Melvin Hutchinson?" Eugene asked.

"Hutch was a troubled brother," Rashid said pensively. "What else can I say? I didn't like him. Didn't like his politics. I'm glad he killed that fucking McCracker. I'm glad about that. But Hutch, I think, was just a fucked-up brother who got involved with too many white folks."

Kilarti tapped Rashid on the shoulder. He turned and smiled at his wife. She tilted her head toward the center of the gallery. "There's someone here to see you," she said coldly.

In an instant, Rashid saw whom Kilarti was referring to. It was easy to pick her out of the crowd as she stood, arms folded across her chest, staring at a portrait of a little black girl sitting on a stoop and looking pitiful. Morgan Bradstreet was, after all, the only white person in the room.

Rashid excused himself to the group and walked over to Morgan. She had phoned him a week earlier, saying she would be in New York for a short while visiting her parents. Two days before Kilarti's opening, Rashid and Morgan met in New York, at Carbunkle's, for a drink. She looked good, Rashid had to admit, healthy. But what cheered him when he saw Morgan was that he felt absolutely nothing for her. He had forgotten that she even existed. Like Emma Person. Even with all the shit in the press about her family, Rashid had managed to expunge Emma from his thoughts. Emma had entered and exited his life so quickly, it was easy to imagine he'd never met her at all. Morgan, at Carbunkle's, told Rashid she was working for a publishing house in London, that she was off heroin, off any sort of medication, feeling pretty good, starting to write again. Rashid bragged to her about the success of the NCAAAC and his impressive new bride. They spent less than an hour together. Rashid had mentioned Kilarti's exhibition in Norris, but the last thing he expected was that Morgan would actually show up.

"So what do you think?" Rashid said, coming up on Morgan's shoulder as she regarded one of the portraits of a furious gang-banger.

"I think it's dead," Morgan said quietly.

Rashid was stunned. "What do you mean?"

"I mean, look at these pictures. They're all clichés. These people

—she's embalmed them." Morgan's voice was calm, analytical, and a bit sad.

"I don't know what the fuck you're talkin' about. No. *You* don't know what the fuck you're talkin' about."

"I'm sorry, Rashid, I'm not trying to be rude. I just think these photos are totally lifeless."

"You wouldn't understand them, anyway. It's not a world someone like you could ever relate to."

"Well, I have eyes, Rashid, and I just don't think this is good art."

"Yeah, but it ain't about *aesthetics,* Morgan. It's about something more than that."

"And something less, too, I'd say."

Rashid could feel a fit of hysteria coming on. He had to be careful. He didn't want to cause a scene. He noticed that guests were turning and staring, wondering, no doubt, who this woman was and what she was doing here. "Well," he said curtly, "I think you better be on your way. A girl like you doesn't want to get caught in a neighborhood like this after dark, know what I'm sayin'?"

Morgan gazed at Rashid, a sorrow in her eyes. "Yeah," she said softly, "I know what you're sayin'." She turned and walked out of the gallery.

Eugene Little came up to Rashid. "Who was that?" he asked.

"One of my old students," Rashid said.

"Nice girl?"

"Naw. Just a silly white bitch."

➤   ➤   ➤

Henry Beedle had had a recurring nightmare for several months now. In this dream, he was lying in his bed, unable to sleep because he knew that men—men in uniforms—were coming for him. He didn't know what they would do to him exactly—incarceration, torture, summary execution, something along those lines—but he knew, in this dream, that at any minute the men in uniform would kick down his door and take him, as he screamed and squirmed and struggled in his pajamas, barely able to see without his spectacles, to the place of his doom. Beedle tried to dismiss these dreams as part of a silly and unnecessary sense of guilt. But that only led him to wonder: Was it really guilt he felt? It was more a clammy sense of complicity. He didn't feel as if he had really *done* anything. But he felt as if he had been a party to a sinful deed—as if he was an accomplice. God, he missed Troy. And Hutch. Who would ever have imagined the McCracken era would end the way it had? With everything that had happened, Beedle rationalized, it was only normal that he'd feel a bit paranoid these days; that he would suspect his phone was being tapped; maybe worry, now and then, that he was being followed, or staked out. These were natural fears, something he would just have to get over. Besides, if he *was* under surveillance, he would have to know about it. He was, after all, the goddamned attorney general of the United States, and, paranoid though he might be, he wasn't ready to start spying on himself.

Henry Beedle also wondered if perhaps his anxiety came from a sense that somehow something would crack, that the story the American people had so thoroughly bought might unravel. But there were no signs of that happening. If the original program had been flawed, the cover-up had been perfect. It was so much easier—so much more digestible—for people to believe that a single crazed ex-hippie was to blame for the derangement of America's premier crimefighter and the assassination of a President than to believe that what Willow Cushing said was happening at Fort Brandriss actually had been happening. To think the latter was to buy into a conspiracy theory—and most Americans were extremely reluctant to believe in conspiracies. Sometimes, Beedle thought that reluctance was due to semantics more than anything else. That spooky word: *conspiracy*. In fact, conspiracies took place *all the time*. It was only natural for people with common interests to join together to thwart the opposing interests of other people. This was the essence of human nature. It happened in business, in politics, and, first and foremost, in families. Conspiracy happened every day. People just didn't call it that. People believed only what they wished to believe. And, when it came to conspiracies, they believed only what they could see. They wanted the smoking gun, the transcript of tapes, the video of the plotters hatching their scheme. The American imagination was a puny thing.

And so the most successful conspiracies had to exceed that which could be easily imagined. No average person would think to gun down a President, publicly, in an open car, in broad daylight; or to urge terrorists to keep hostages in captivity—in order to discredit a rival politician—until after an election; or to eliminate inconvenient people in an orderly, systematic, but surreptitious way. No ordinary person could imagine such a thing. That was why extraordinary people were able to get away with it.

Still, Henry Beedle fretted. Throughout Willow Cushing's trial, he had kept waiting for the defense to turn up some of the people Melvin Hutchinson had contacted, those former Fort Brandriss inmates and their families who suspected the truth. But no such witnesses emerged. Beedle had, of course, shredded all the files pertaining to inmates who had undergone Dr. Arthur Spooner's treatment. And still he worried. What if some industrious reporter found a credible source somewhere? But the press was no more interested in Willow Cushing's conspiracy theory than the public was. The straightforward tale of a pathological woman bent on destroying the government she despised and the man who had spurned her was so much easier to grasp—so much sexier. Then Beedle worried about all the people who might come to Willow Cushing's defense, in the same way that people had come to the defense of Sacco and Vanzetti or the Rosenbergs. But the ground never swelled. A few radical feminists squawked about Willow's victimization, but Troy McCracken had a popularity rating of 80 percent at the time of his death and all those Americans who loved him wanted to see some culprit—someone other than Melvin Hutchinson, whose popularity stood at 70 percent the week he died—punished for the President's death. And even still, Henry Beedle was anxious. What if the killing of a white President by a black cabinet member provoked an all-out race war? To Beedle's relief, it didn't happen. The violence that broke out in suburbs all over America after Troy's assassination had been, for the most part, white-on-white violence: Thirty-three whites were murdered by other whites that night. Here and there, minorities were attacked and, in twelve cases, killed. But the fatalities were Asian, not African-American. And, instead of a racial cataclysm, Troy McCracken's death at the hands of Melvin Hutchinson only widened the canyon of distrust and discomfort between blacks and whites. Troy McCracken had become a God. Troy McCracken avenues, schools, highways, civic centers, and shopping malls were popping up all over the country. Melvin Hutchinson, meanwhile, had become an oddity. Not a villain, but a freak. Nobody really knew what to make of him, and thus few people discussed him at all. The rage that Troy McCracken's worshipers felt was directed at one frail, pale, middle-aged woman.

➢   ➢   ➢

"So are you going to the hanging tomorrow night?" Arthur Spooner asked Henry Beedle as the two of them sat alone in the Eagle Room on Wednesday evening.

"I haven't decided yet," Beedle said. "Dean Rockport is flying up on *Justice One*. I might join him."

Beedle and Spooner had met to discuss a very specific matter, but, in the customary way, they talked about it very unspecifically. They talked, generally, about the presidential campaign. The Ewell-Blythe ticket had won every American party primary so far, but people were concerned about how Vin and Brad would fare against the competition in November. Vin Ewell, after all, had made very few campaign appearances; and when he did, he stuck to basic stump speeches and avoided the rough-and-tumble of campaigning. Brad Blythe had been the man out front, and crowds, as well as the media, obviously loved the guy. It was Blythe, not Ewell, who seemed the true heir to the McCracken legacy. To Henry Beedle's mind, it was Blythe, not Ewell, who was pulling in the votes. When it came to the general election, Vin Ewell might actually prove to be a liability.

"So how is the President's health?" Beedle finally asked, tired of beating around the bush.

Spooner took a thoughtful sip of cognac. "I've been monitoring the President's condition very carefully, and I would say that another stroke is imminent. In fact, I would guarantee a massive stroke."

"A fatal one?"

"Yes."

"When?"

"Two weeks. Maybe three. But certainly before the convention."

Beedle had gotten the information he wanted. And it was very good news indeed. He almost thanked the surgeon general but then, fearing that perhaps the Eagle Room was bugged, thought the better of it. So Beedle simply nodded and said, "Hmmmm."

Clarence, the butler, entered and, removing Beedle's dirty ashtray, replaced it with a clean one. "Thank you, Clarence," Beedle said. Clarence grunted in response and, without a smile or another word, left the room. Was it only Beedle's imagination or had the once-congenial servant turned hostile in the past year? Well, Beedle supposed, perhaps you couldn't blame him, given what had happened to Hutch. But, hell, he was being paid, and damn well, for service with a smile. Beyond that, though, Clarence's surliness gave Beedle the creeps. On some level, it provoked his fears of a large-scale black rebellion.

"Did you happen to see the poll in the *Post* this morning?" Spooner asked.

"Glancingly," Beedle said.

"Oh, you should take another look at it. The subjects were asked whether they believed the story about eugenics at Fort Brandriss. Something like ninety percent said they did not."

"Hardly surprising."

"I agree. But there was another, more interesting question. I can't remember the exact phrasing but it was something like, 'Would you approve of a program to sterilize and/or eliminate worst-case social parasites at America's drug reeducation centers?' Did you happen to see those results?"

"No, I didn't."

"Forty-five percent of respondents said yes! Another ten percent had no opinion, which, as far as I'm concerned, is as good as a yes. And I'd bet my bottom dollar that at least a quarter of the people who said no really, in their hearts, thought yes but were too timid to admit their true feelings to a pollster. So kick in another ten percent in favor. Which means that *sixty-five percent* of Americans approve of what we were doing at Brandriss!" Arthur Spooner grinned, the crow's feet at the corners of his eyes crinkling cheerily. "Sixty-five percent, Henry. We've had to put the program on hold for now. But once we get Brad Blythe elected, I say we should redouble our efforts!" Spooner paused. He looked at Beedle uncertainly. "Are you with me, Henry?"

Beedle tapped his pipe against the side of the ashtray. "I've got to run. Let's talk again soon."

➤   ➤   ➤

Entering Troy McCracken Stadium with Dean Rockport and a substantial security detail, Henry Beedle noticed a small group of protesters surrounded by a couple of TV news camera crews. He worried for a moment that support for Willow Cushing may have been larger than he knew, but then he heard the leader of the protesters, an earnest white woman who looked to be in her fifties, talking at a reporter with a microphone: "We, too, are happy to see justice done to anyone who would have plotted against President McCracken. We all loved Troy. The only thing we're objecting to is the method of elimination. We're environmentalists and we don't think the air should be polluted in this way."

The next thing Beedle knew, he was sitting in his front-row seat, watching as the American flag backdrop rose into the rafters of the stage. He saw the criminal—the parasite!—clad in a drab gray prison uniform, strapped atop a forty-foot-high pole. Her head slumped forward and Beedle wondered if she was even conscious. As the crowd cheered, Nick Necropolis emerged from stage left, holding high a torch. With the eighty thousand people in Troy McCracken Stadium clapping rhythmically, egging him on, Necropolis walked around the stage once, shaking his torch, then, with dramatic deliberateness, touched the flame to the pole. A stream of fire shot up the stake and, in a sudden *whoosh,* Willow Cushing's entire body was aflame. Everyone in the stadium, except Beedle, was on their feet, screaming. Beedle watched the plume of smoke unfurl from Willow Cushing's burning body into the dark night sky. He heard the throngs around him unleash the fearsome chant: "You-*ess*-AAY! You-*ess*-AAY! You-*ess*-AAY! You-*ess*-AAY! You-*ess*-AAY!" Suddenly, Beedle was on his feet, too, and he could feel his body jerking violently, beyond his control, his hands reaching up into the air as he gyrated with near-psychotic abandon, feeling the blood of his ancestors roiling in his veins—and, as he came, and the warm, gooey semen filled his pajama bottoms, Beedle bolted upright in his bed and heard, as if still in a dream, the cry burst from his mouth: "WIIIIIIIIIIIITCH!"

➤   ➤   ➤

"So tell again about America."

"What do you wanna know?"

"I want to know why you feel the way you feel."

Emma and Martin sat in white plastic chairs, sipping cheap beers in a pleasant café on the Old Town Square, in this ancient city of black statues and Gothic spires, flyers advertising classical-music concerts littering the cobblestones at their feet. It was Thursday afternoon. Emma had known Martin for only a couple of weeks. It had been more than a year since she'd had a man and she was growing accustomed to being alone. For the first time in her adult life, she'd been content to be alone. But Martin was gradually taking her out of her aloneness. She loved his smooth dark features, loved the way he walked with his head literally held high. He was like a perfect African sculpture. Martin was a musician, a saxophone player, of all things. And his love of his work inspired Emma. Though she had brought most of her camera equipment with her, she had not taken a single photograph since she'd arrived in this city. But the urge was slowly coming back. In any event, Emma was safe here. She made good money teaching English. And she'd grown extremely fond of this city. She even loved the sound of its name, the way the word felt in her mouth: *Prague.*

"It's not such a good place for black people," Emma said.

"You are joking," Martin said. "All Africans want to go to America."

"And many black Americans want to go to Africa."

"Maybe they should. I love Africa, but there is nothing for me there anymore."

"I could say the same thing about America."

"But in America, you have the rap, the jazz."

"Yes, that is America."

"There is freedom."

"For some. If you want it. Then again, I think of something some-one once said: 'What the slave wants is not freedom, but a slave of his own.' "

Martin laughed. "Emma, you are—how do you say . . . hard on America's case?"

"You forget, Martin, I'm a fugitive from justice."

Martin stared inquisitively at Emma and she hoped he wouldn't ask her to elaborate. She had told him when they first met that she was in trouble with the law in America. That was all. Emma was still too stunned by what had happened in the States to talk about it. She had fled the country the day after Troy McCracken and Melvin Hutchinson were killed, the day before her father's body was discov-ered. For many months, she had worried that Henry Beedle and his minions would try to track her down. Finally, she decided she wasn't important to them. Emma and Alma had managed to exchange mes-sages through a network of European contacts. And Emma read about her family's travails in the American newspapers. Yet she al-ways had a strange dreamy feeling when she learned new details about what was happening. Emma, like Alma, believed Willow Cush-ing's story. She had grieved for Rodney, for Melvin, for Miles. She knew that her stepmother was going to be hung that night in America. And, though she felt sorry for Willow, it was in the abstract way that one pitied a poor stranger. There had been times when Emma felt she should go back home and take on the powers that be, fight the good fight. But she was not much of a fighter. After a year in Prague, Emma Person was certain of only one thing: She would never return to the United States.

"Well, I think I go and see America on my own," Martin said.

"Maybe you should."

They were silent for a long time.

"What do you think of, Emma?"

"I was thinking I'd like to take a photo of you."

"It's true?"

"Yes. I think it would make a lovely picture."

➤   ➤   ➤

It was almost ten o'clock by the time Alma Person returned to her block on Riverside Drive. She had been working evenings for the past several months, teaching functionally illiterate adults how to read and write. As she walked toward her building, Alma spotted the brown car parked across the street, could see the outlines of the two male heads in the car. "Aren't y'all gettin' sick a this already!" Alma yelled across the street. She stopped in front of the entrance to her building. She could see the heads, in silhouette, turn toward her. "Of course I know you're there!" Alma shouted. "Keep watchin'! Y'all ain't gonna see shit!" The shadows in the car moved about uncomfortably. "Good night, boys!" Alma called before walking into her building.

Miles was sitting at the dining room table, eating a sandwich and looking over a homework assignment, when Alma entered the apartment.

"Hi, sugar,"Alma said.

"Hi, Alma."

Alma sat across from him at the table. "Working hard?"

"Yes, ma'am. I have a test tomorrow. But you know what?"

"What?"

"My memory is getting better. I remember a lot more than I used to."

"That's good, Miles."

They were quiet for a while.

"I've been hearing a lot of stuff about the family lately," Miles said tonelessly.

"What have you heard?"

"They're going to kill my mother tonight, aren't they? Or maybe they've already done it."

"They've probably already done it."

"It makes me sad," Miles said, though his voice sounded neutral.

"Me, too." Alma stared at Miles. How she had grown to love him over the past year. Now, together, they would have to wait for a better epoch. And maybe for a cure. "I have to ask you something, Miles."

"All right."

"You know what you are, don't you?" Alma said. "What you can be—no, *must* be—no matter how much others may dread and despise, try to kill it before it *can* be, because they cannot deal with it because they know what it is, not consciously, but in their viscera, in their pores, so you must know it, too, but not just in your blood and skin, since, like the man said, blood and skin do not *think*, you must *know* it, recognize it, so you can see, *see*, why they are threatened by you and will try to crush and destroy and exterminate you—so I ask you, sugar, you know what you are, don't you?"

Miles stared at Alma, unblinking, not quite comprehending, but absorbing, and asked tentatively but without fear, "What am I?"

"The future."